GUN PLAY

WITHDRAWN

GUN PLAY

WITHDRAWN

First in the *Shooting Shrink* Series

Hollidaysburg Area Public Library

by
Michael Thompkins

Pittsburgh, PA

ISBN 1-56315-339-4

Trade Paperback
© Copyright 2006 Michael Thompkins
All rights reserved
First Printing—2006
Library of Congress #2006922177

Request for information should be addressed to:
SterlingHouse Publisher, Inc.
7436 Washington Avenue
Pittsburgh, PA 15218
www.sterlinghousepublisher.com

Pemberton Mysteries
is an imprint of SterlingHouse Publisher, Inc.

SterlingHouse Publisher, Inc. is a company
of the CyntoMedia Corporation

Cover Design: Jamie Linder
Interior Design: N. J. McBeth

All rights reserved. No part of this publication may be reproduced, stored in a retrieval system, or transmitted in any form or by any means—electronic, mechanical, photocopy, recording or any other, except for brief quotations in printed reviews—without prior permission of the publisher.

This is a work of fiction. Names, characters, incidents, and places, are the product of the author's imagination or are used fictitiously. Any resemblance to actual events or persons, living or dead is entirely coincidental.

Printed in the United States of America

To Judith, always first.

Then Chris Vogler, mentor at large, and Lisa Ann Martin, my agent.

Finally, a certain travel agent, all my editors, and the citizens of the Coachella Valley.

WITNESSES

It was the shooter's favorite time of day in the desert. The dawn was cool for early March in Palm Springs. Across from the eighteenth tee at Tahquitz Creek County Club where he knelt, he could make out details that by noon would not be discernible. By midday, the sun would shoot off like a flashbulb, blind the eye to detail, and make the hit harder. He could see his target, a middle-aged male, teeing off the seventeenth tee.

Target. Alone. Good. Almost an impossible shot. One hundred and fifty yards with a silenced Glock .40. Only a hundred people in the world would try. Nobody as good.

Suddenly, a lone cyclist riding a rust-streaked twenty-year-old Schwinn came round the bend on the Coachella Valley Bike Trail that ran through the otherwise silent arroyo. The chain on the old bike made a solitary sound as it passed through the rear wheel. The cyclist was a bearded kid in his early twenties with a guitar case on his back. He looked homeless and shaggy, like a 60's hippie.

The Schwinn would pass by the shooter in ten seconds, thirty yards from his position. From that distance, the kid would be able to see him and could easily be hit. The Glock was tucked in the small of his back. The kid smiled at him. He smiled back, reached behind his back and put his hand on the pistol. He loved the feel of the weapon in his hand. He wondered if the kid could identify him.

The shooter stood down; he could deal with the kid later. He watched the cyclist retreat and approach the turn onto Golf Course Drive, where the bike trail and the street merged for a mile. A peace sign adorned the kid's guitar case.

The contract required the shooter to stick around Palm Springs for a week in case the buyer needed more of his services. He didn't like sticking around after a hit but it would give him time to see if the kid could identify him. If he could, he would eliminate him. He never left witnesses.

Hell with the kid. Pop him later if need be. Get the mission done. Buyer wants the job done today without fail.

The kid was the only passerby on the bike trail in the twenty minutes the shooter had been waiting. A few joggers would start to venture out soon but he would be gone by then. The last three mornings he had reconned the area and observed the target at exactly the same time. The target predictably played alone, before regular tee times.

BMNT. Becoming Morning Nautical Twilight.

It was night into day. Dark pools of shadow were slowly giving way to small pockets of gray ground fog. It had sucked every bit of moisture from the night air but wouldn't last long when the sun was fully up. Nothing would outlast this sun. The little patches of fog provided cover from a distance. The arroyo was part of a flood viaduct system that ran miles in either direction. The shooter leaned against an electrical tower that rose fifty feet and was part of a high power line intersecting the arroyo. He watched his target move down the fairway in a golf cart, park the cart, and approach the green.

The shooter moved away from the tower, took a comfortable shooting stance, drew the Glock and aimed at the red pin flag on the green. The target was preparing to chip. The shooter returned the weapon to the small of his back and was ready. There was a round in the pipe. A weapon should always be ready — not like on TV. He was being paid well to make this shot. He wouldn't miss.

The rabbits were having a field day all around him in the sagebrush-strewn arroyo. There were a dozen of them jumping all over the place. They popped out of their warrens and sniffed out the day. He liked wild things. They had nobility to them. They were killed to feed something else further up the chain. The shooter wondered about coyotes, and the bobcats and foxes that hunted them. Counting coyote tracks to keep from boredom while he waited, he noticed two had moved through earlier. For a moment, he pondered what would hunt him and kill him eventually. He was not naïve. Maybe different, maybe brutal, but not naïve. The animal images left his mind.

Target! Accountant's putting out and heading up to the next tee. Earn the money. Best at this. Best in the world.

When the target reached the tee box, in one smooth movement that took less than three seconds, he cleared the weapon from the small of his back, placed the sights between the target's shoulder blades, squeezed the trigger twice, and shot him.

Target down.

The target fell in a way that confirmed a kill. Having seen many targets fall all over the world, he knew a kill shot.

Tossing the pistol and his gloves in some nearby brush, and keeping the binoculars, he hoped they would find the Glock and know how good this shot really was. He wanted to be sure they knew it was a pistol. The Palm Springs cops might miss that. At a hundred and fifty yards with a handgun — this was one for the books.

Leaving the gulch immediately, the shooter knew he had not been seen except by the hippie kid — the rabbits witnessed everything.

DOC AND THE COPS

I was dying for my coffee.

"Doctor Reynolds, I keep waking up with the same nightmare," Officer Pete Navarez said during the last ten minutes of our early morning counseling session. "I shoot the same perp all over again but different witnesses keep appearing on different nights. Sometimes I can recognize the other people; sometimes I can't make them out. They're all citizen bystanders. You've heard this ten times already. When's the goddamn thing going to leave me alone?"

"Pete, you know I have my own nightmare about the fire-base in 'Nam. I can't offer you anymore than eventually the frequency of the nightmare will decrease. The depression will go away; the insomnia will go away. I can't make promises about the dream except the frequency will decrease. Sooner or later."

Thing is I didn't know when his nightmares would decrease. I had asked his family doc to put him on an anti-depressant, a costly and effective one that boosted both serotonin and dopamine levels. Simple enough because Pete's family doc was my wife, Dr. Nancy Reynolds. Psychologist and physician: between the two us, if it was human and broken, we could try to fix it.

I had Pete working out religiously every morning before his patrol shift. Much to my professional chagrin, though, I could neither dictate nor even predict when the trauma that accompanied his shooting a perp six months ago would leave him in some kind of peace.

My psych eval on Pete ended in a diagnosis of Post Trauma Stress Disorder, PTSD, with Depression. I was the Palm Springs police psychologist, and I was supposed to help him. Be easier if I had my coffee.

"It was him or me. I had to put him down," Pete said, his forearms tensed in frustration. "The guy was on dust. He just killed his girlfriend. We've gone over this twenty times. The shooting board cleared me six months ago. I'll never forget the day — day before Thanksgiving 1996. I'm fine when I keep busy. I know that I would do the same thing again. The public paints me a hero or a villain depending on their politics; I can deal with all that. So why won't the dream leave me alone?"

I partly knew how to help him as we sat together in my office in downtown Palm Springs. Part I knew was that Pete had to accept being a competent police officer and let the other side of his feelings surface. I suspected anger, sorrow, and fear were waiting to meet him in his dream, and they weren't just the feelings related to the shooting. Not only did I have to help Pete clear out his emotions about the clean shoot, but also, any others that rode out with them.

Part I didn't know was whether in the same situation, I could have been as competent and as courageous as he had been. Could I help Pete carry this? My own nightmare wouldn't completely leave me alone, either; it visited once or twice a month. I never had depression or insomnia, just the nightmare. I lived with the same nightmare for twenty years like an old friend visiting in the dark. The rest of the month it took up residence in my trick back.

Sometimes I found myself softly shaking inside when I counseled Pete. I'd been a soldier once and never fired a shot. We were two sides of the same coin, one side with the action, and the other side with the feelings. I recognized this part of being a psychologist; it sucked. Look at a patient, see yourself – it's all done with mirrors.

"Pete, I don't know that I could've done what you did. I don't know if I have the courage in me that you demonstrated two months ago." If I didn't disclose my own fear, how could Pete talk to me about his? "But I do know about feelings. They have to have their day or they won't go away. They just hang around like uninvited family guests. Push them away and they make life miserable. Get to know them, make a little room for them somewhere, and you can figure out a way to get them to move along. Sometimes they even have messages to deliver."

"What do you mean, Doc? My wife keeps asking for the same thing. How do I feel?" Pete shifted his gun belt, which had about twenty pounds of equipment on it. I could see a black Glock automatic, a radio, handcuffs, mace, and extra magazines for the Glock.

"I mean, the next time the nightmare wakes you up, get up and pour yourself a drink. Go out on the deck and try to remember every detail of the dream — what color shirt the bad guy was wearing, who else was in the dream, where was it taking place, and most importantly, what you were feeling. Write it all down and bring it to me next week."

"Is that what you do with your nightmare?" Pete asked.

"Pretty much. I see different faces in my dream, too. I've told you about the Marines that got shot after they extracted me because I was 'too valuable an intelligence asset.'"

Michael Thompkins

"Whatever you say, Doc. After that article in the *NY Times* about top shrinks, everyone on the job knows you're the best in the state — maybe the country. We're lucky to have you consult for what the department pays you."

I nodded. They paid me squat. It didn't matter.

"I know you're not doing it for the money; you're doing it 'cause Lt. Wade's your buddy. I'll try anything you say. You got me this far."

I didn't really know how far either of us had come. I was treating Pete by the book but sometimes the book wasn't enough. My mind was sliding sideways. Part of me was no longer in the room with Pete. Part of me was back in 'Nam.

I'd been sent from Honolulu to Saigon to follow up on some intelligence I'd uncovered and debrief a wounded Marine officer who was in Honolulu on his way home with his leg badly shot up. He was more concerned about enemy troop concentrations than his own pain. Based on his intel, command cleared me out of Hickham Airfield to Saigon by transport then on to a forward firebase by helo. I arrived at the small village at 10 a.m., and it was already a hundred degrees.

The Huey pilot said, "Sir." I was a first lieutenant and he was a warrant officer. "Possible incoming. Be ready to leave on my call."

"I just got here."

"And we're going to leave when I say so," he said. "Sir, I lose your ass, I lose my bird."

A kid with an M-16, who clearly had lied about his age to enlist, showed up and escorted me from the Huey to the headquarters tent. The CO, the exec and a bunch of Marines were sitting around a folding table. Twenty minutes into the debriefing —long enough to confirm the intel — the mortar attack began.

"Get his ass to the bird," the CO ordered.

"I'd rather hang. There's gotta be something I can do."

"Lieutenant, the intel is worth more than you," he said. "You damn well know that."

He nodded at two of the grunts. They dragged me to the chopper and threw me inside. Command extracted just me because I was too 'valuable an intelligence asset to risk falling into enemy hands.' As the helo lifted off, I felt shame like I had never experienced in my life — six marines died doing what they were trained to do — I was flown out like a candy-ass civilian.

GUN PLAY

I couldn't look the pilot in the eyes. We flew for two hours side by side and never spoke a word to each other. It was a year before I spoke to anyone who didn't speak to me first. I was promoted to major during my three-year tour for "being an exceptional intelligence officer and a credit to the Army." It never made up for the men who died at the firebase.

"Doc, you okay?" Pete pulled me back to the present.

"How's sex going?" I came back speed-shifting therapy gears, remembering that for the two months following the shooting incident Pete had withdrawn from physical intimacy.

"Coming back with a vengeance," he replied with a smile, crooking his little finger in sexual innuendo.

"Good sign. See you in a week. I think things are beginning to lift for you."

Pete stood up adjusting his gun belt and his point of reference. He looked at me hard, not missing for a minute where I'd spun out. "Don't worry about it, Doc. I'd go through a door with you anytime. You'll make out just fine."

Pete got me as well as I got him. Therapeutic transparency was supposed to be a good thing. Some patients helped heal the doctor. Used to feel guilty about that.

"Only other thing that will help is the thing we haven't figured out yet."

"What's that?" Pete asked.

"We haven't figured it out yet."

Pete thought a minute and said, "We will."

"Yes, I believe we will."

Pete reached the door and assumed his officer-on-duty posture. I walked him out the office door and locked it behind us. We walked together to his patrol unit. There were only two cars parked in the lot on Belardo: my red '94 Land Cruiser and Pete's beige patrol unit with a yellow stripe down the side. It bore the inscription "Palm Springs Police." Our session had started at 6 a.m., first light. I didn't usually start this early, but I'd pretty much do whatever it took to help a cop.

"Starbucks?" Pete asked.

"Want to join us?"

I was meeting my best friend Brett Wade, also Palm Springs PD, around the corner and one block up on North Palm Canyon Drive. Brett and I met nearly every morning at Starbucks; the time varied depending on his duties and my counseling sessions.

"Gotta roll. Thanks though. Lieutenant Wade is the best brass I've ever served under. He's one of us. Nothing he asks for that he couldn't and wouldn't do himself."

"Next week."

"Thanks for helping me, Doc." Pete opened the door of his unit.

"Don't know who's helping who." I turned to walk away then turned back.

"Sure you do," he said.

Pete closed the door and turned on his unit's radio. It started squawking incessant chatter between the dispatcher and the twelve units patrolling the three zones of Palm Springs. For cops, everything had a number — every unit, every shield, every weapon, every perp and every incident. The numbers helped them insulate from the rude reality of police work. Psych evals on cops always included compulsion. They would assign a number to every tree and bush if they could — survival on the street was dependent on the residue of this compulsion.

Pete rolled his window down, hung up the handset and said, "It cracks me up. Doc, either way we both got screwed."

"What do you mean?"

"I shot the bad guy 'cause I was doing my job," he said. "You didn't shoot anybody because the brass extracted you; you were doing your job."

"And."

"We both end up with nightmares. We both get screwed." Pete put the unit in gear and backed away.

I turned the corner onto Tahquitz and headed up the block to Starbucks on North Palm Canyon. It felt cold for an early March morning in Palm Springs, sunny and in the low forties. The wind was blowing a sensory sampler of sand, fertilizer, engine exhaust and freshly brewed coffee.

Brett was waiting to slip in line when I walked in the front door. He acknowledged my presence with a "Hey" and ordered for both of us. "Double-tall bone-dry cappuccino and a single-tall Americano."

"Morning Lieutenant, Doc. Can I get you gentlemen anything to eat?" the barista asked.

Palm Springs was a small town. Like any small town, the coffee crew knew everyone.

"We'll stick with coffee," Brett said, adding water to his Americano.

Our coffee in hand, we went out to the patio and snagged a table with a perfect view of Palm Canyon. I took a sip of my double tall bone-dry cappuccino and felt contentment for the first time since my alarm went off. If I were in a coma for five years and woke up seeing only the camel-humped palm trees and hearing only the thumpity-thump of the brick lined intersection of Tahquitz and Palm Canyon, I'd know I was home.

"How's Pete Navarez?" Brett must have seen Pete's unit.

"He's going to be okay. It'll be a while longer but he's getting better. You know I shouldn't even be telling you that."

"Excellent. Good work Doctor," he said. "Hard to shoot people." His jaw pulled back into his neck slightly and his eyes went somewhere else far way. "Coffee's strong." He quickly changed the subject.

"Still miss 7-11 coffee?"

He sat down in his chair with an economy of movement that reminded me of a shaven-head black Jackie Chan. "I'll give you that the scenery is a whole lot better here but I really got used to watered-down coffee in the military. Besides, all the cops I know hangout in up-scale shops now. Donuts are dead. We got low-fat, grease-free cops."

Brett was the first Afro-American lieutenant in the Palm Springs Police Department. He actually had two jobs: the training of all officers, and troubleshooting for the chief. He'd spent five years before that with Riverside Sheriffs as a detective sergeant. Having gone through sniper school in the Special Forces and routinely turning down offers for mercenary consulting, he was also the Palm Springs PD weapons expert.

We had been friends since the fall of '74 at Officer Candidate School, Ft. Benning, Georgia. Both UC Berkeley grads, class of '74, we'd never met until OCS. One black and one white, but two mostly green candidates for the right to put officer bars on your helmet as a target, we struggled together to complete the six-month training, survive Southern racism, and become officers. He — a poster boy for integration in the army. Me— a whitebread Berkeley liberal. The Army not caring what color you were — their favorite color being puke green — as long as you could fire an M-16. We were commissioned officers together and were still working on the gentlemen part twenty years later.

Brett went on to IOBC (Infantry Officer Basic Course), a Ranger Company, SOTIC (sniper school), Special Forces Selection and made it to his team in time to help cover the retreat from the fall of Saigon — "I was coming and they were run-

Michael Thompkins

ning." Once, while drinking — Okay drunk — Brett told me that he was this century's equivalent of a gladiator.

I went on to the Intelligence Officer Course, an oxymoron, and was assigned to Honolulu debriefing Vietnam returnees in 1975. We lost the war, and the brass wanted answers. I found some, but they weren't interested – political deceit and command cover-your-ass-'cause-it's-a-cluster-fuck won the day. I managed to keep in touch with Brett's location during the war but we lost each other afterwards. We hooked up again ten years ago.

"Check him out." I signaled Brett to look at a kid with a guitar case dressed in retro-sixties clothes just getting off an ancient bike.

The kid was wearing a tie-dyed tee shirt with Nirvana stenciled on it, a down vest, dirty bell-bottom jeans, and sandals. He sported a short brown beard and shoulder-length light brown hair. The guitar case had a peace sign on it. He was six feet, 180 pounds, had two inches on Brett and me, and was a street kid, but without the drug vibe.

"Already done that," he said. "Street kid but special, though. His name is Chris. We've talked a dozen times in the last few months. I like him."

"Special kid?" I had never heard him talk this way before — he usually played straight tough guy, and got good reviews for the part.

"Peace sign on his guitar case?" I asked.

"Uh-uh," he said.

"I haven't seen a peace sign for fifteen years."

"Me, neither. Want to meet him?" Brett stood up.

"Sure," I said.

Brett glanced at Chris and waved him over. Brett wasn't in uniform, but he might as well have been. Chris obviously knew him, smiled and headed over as if someone of higher rank had ordered him — it's called command presence. "Hey, Lieutenant Wade. What's going on?" Chris asked.

"Coffee, want to join us? And remember I told you to call me Brett," he said, smiling at Chris.

"What's your gig, man? You a cop too?" Chris swung his long legs over the back of the chair, straddled the seat, and then sat down with his guitar on his lap, gangly energy spilling out of the chair.

"He's a head doctor, name's Tom Reynolds, but everyone calls him Doc." Brett answered for me.

"Doc, cool. I'm Chris."

A big bus went by on North Palm Canyon and I had to wait ten seconds before I could be heard above the engine rumble. "What kind of music you into?"

"Alternative rock. Used to play grunge in high school. Love Kurt Cobain and Nirvana, that kind of stuff – he's my man. Sometimes I go way back and play John Lennon. I really dig good lyrics. Lennon and Cobain are my two favorite songwriters."

"Cobain popped himself, didn't he?" Brett asked.

"Yeah. Bummer. I was in my junior year. Saw him at the Arena and the Croc in Seattle in January, and he was dead in April. Grunge died with him." Chris echoed the same feeling for Cobain that I had carried for years after John Lennon's murder in 1980.

"Write any lyrics?" Brett asked.

"All the time. I write some lines, forget to jot them down, and then sometimes later remember them."

"Get a notebook; write it all down." Brett said. "I got a sixties music collection to die for, Dylan, Lennon… We overlap on Lennon."

"Rad."

"You live in a group house?" I asked.

"Nah. I live outside. Rest of the guys in my band live together. We practice in the garage at their house. I could move in with them, but right now I like the fresh air. I take as many showers as I can there but I don't want to crash their scene."

"You sleeping out on the bike trail near Tahquitz Creek?" Brett left out the cop tone but he knew exactly where Chris was sleeping.

"Yeah, I just hop on my old clunker and ride in the trail along Highway 111 pretty much this time every day. There are some old warehouses right off the trail just beyond the golf course where the trail turns in along the trailer parks. The sheds keep the wind out at night, and I got a zero-degree sleeping bag."

Chris reminded me of Brett and myself, when we were exploring the world, wanderings that took us to remote jungles and strange cities in and out of uniform. Places where we had a difficult time figuring out whom the enemy was, and witnessed the seemingly limitless human capacity to screw others or turn them into global market share.

"You get women to sleep with you?" Brett asked.

"Sometimes, man. That why I need the showers."

"Christ, Doc, kid's homeless and he's doing better than me."

"You looked as hip as Chris, you'd be doing better," I said.

"How can a cop look hip?" he shrugged.

Sleeping outside was a long time ago for me. Palm Springs had its locals and its snowbirds that flew down from up north and wintered here. You could divide the snowbirds and the locals into the rich and the rest. The rich had their second homes out by Palm Desert and Indian Wells, and the rest lived in trailer parks, condos and cheaper digs. Some, like Chris, lived outside.

"The shower thing is the tough part," Chris said.

"You don't smell bad," Brett observed bluntly.

Chris's complexion had the glow you see on snowboarders at Squaw Valley.

"Good, I just wish I could shower everyday. That would be awesome."

"Do you know what a bivy sack is?" Brett asked Chris, changing the subject.

"Nah."

"Basically it's a tube made out of Gore-Tex and looks like those tunnel things made out of plastic that little kids play in," Brett said. "It measures six feet by two feet and keeps the rain off. I used them in the army. Got two in my garage. Surplus. Want one? Keeps you dry."

"Yeah, man. Thanks, I can dig that. I've got a good bag but when the dew gets it wet, it sure can get cold. If it gets soaked, it's useless."

"Where did you grow up?" I said.

"Spokane, Washington."

"Do your parents know you're here in Palm Springs?" I asked.

"They know where I am. They're complete phonies. My dad's like a fundamentalist. He and I are not good together; all he has are his judgments and his way. He's got a case of spiritual Amway. If you're not buying his rich and reborn brand of soap, he doesn't listen to you. Everyone else is a troublemaker according to him. My mother is more open, but she'll never stand up to him. She's afraid of him. I don't trust my dad." He looked directly at Brett. "And the only black people he knows clean the church."

Brett nodded, not reacting.

"Hey, Doc. Dig this dream I had last night and tell me if I'm crazy," Chris said.

People were always looking for me to comment on their dreams, their relationships, and most importantly, their sanity. I held honorary memberships with Brett's Special Forces A-team and his current cop friends simply by providing free curbside consultation about their mental state. Fear of losing your mind is a basic symptom of the neuroses we all share. I tell them that people who go crazy don't ever worry about it. They just pass go, forget to collect their $200, and keep right on going past Boardwalk and Park Place — continuing on to Crazy.

"Let's hear it." Maybe I could help Chris in the same way.

"I'm in my home and it's really high up on Mt. San Jacinto and almost everybody else's home is below mine. Like, I've been meditating a lot and I'm really feeling together. It's not an expensive home, just up really high on a mountain. Everybody knows I'm together. Everybody's jealous of my home because it's so high. The people down below have more stuff than I do but they're still jealous of my home and my songs. The birds aren't jealous though. They fly by and visit but don't bother me. Then a big hawk comes sailing by, and, get this, the hawk's head is Bill Gates' head. And he is the first bird to want my house, 'cause it's higher than his. So what do you think of my dream, Doc?"

"I think you're not going to go to work for Microsoft," I said.

"Absolutely not, man."

"Could shoot the hawk," Brett said deadpan.

"If you aren't going to work for Microsoft, what do you want to do?" I asked Chris.

"My music, man. John Lennon. I wanna be the next John Lennon. Whattaya think of that? You think I'm crazy?"

"Do you think you are John Lennon?" I asked, doing the reality check he had asked for.

"No way man, but I want to be like him, to write music about hypocrisy, lies and... possibilities."

"Not crazy," Brett said.

"Absolutely not," I confirmed the assessment.

"Rad."

Chris turned his attention to a young woman standing inside Starbucks and said, "Gotta say hello to Suze. Can you watch my guitar a minute?"

"Sure, we'll be here awhile," I said.

Chris smiled and headed inside from the patio where we could see him chatting with a very attractive young blond woman who looked like she might be a local college student. Suze wore sandals, a simple yellow sundress and sunglasses. She and Chris touched pelvises together briefly.

"I wonder if Suze's daddy knows about this?" Brett said.

"Probably not. How do you know about Chris's music? Kurt Cobain and Nirvana? Alternative music?" I asked.

Michael Thompkins

"I like rock music and nobody should've missed Kurt Cobain and Nirvana," Brett replied. "What were you doing? They helped make MTV, 1991-1994. No group has had a bigger effect on rock in just three years. Cobain defined grunge music. Alternative music is what's happening now; Smashing Pumpkins are on top. Totally unique sound. Then there's Bush, Pearl Jam and Beck."

"I heard Nirvana a lot. The kids had MTV on all the time but I just never paid attention. Mostly I listen to classical and sixties stuff, and tune out the new sounds. You know I'm oblivious."

"You're as old as the music you listen to," Brett said.

Quiet for a minute, we sipped our coffee and watched a large group of pale yet-to-be-sun-toasted tourists cross North Palm, heading for the Desert Museum. The day was beginning to warm and we would see eighty-plus degrees by afternoon.

Brett looked lost in thought.

"Something about Chris?"

"Yup," he said.

"Like looking in a mirror twenty years ago?"

"That too," he said.

"What else? The homeless part?"

"Nah. Be black — be homeless. Been homeless in lots of places. Berkeley, 'Nam, South American jungles." Remembering distant places, his eyes became remote.

"What else then?"

"Remember what happened to Lennon?" he asked, looking intensely at me.

"How can I forget?" John Lennon was a god to me the year he died.

"Why is it that the John Lennons die young?" I asked

"Don't know, but maybe we can do something about the next one," Brett said.

"Worth trying. Does Chris have any talent or does he just have a homeless dream? Does he really have a chance to be a rock star? A John Lennon?"

"Does it make a difference?" he asked.

I shook my head. "Start with the bivy sack."

"See where it goes from there," he said.

"Keep having coffee with him."

"Absolutely," he said.

From where we were sitting, I could see Chris inside standing in the order line with Suze, flirting his brains out — he was homeless but not clueless.

Brett's conversation had moved on and he was in the middle of his usual diatribe against the press and the politicians whom the police department had to go to for money and approval.

"Goddamn press is too liberal. They worry more about the perp than Pete Navarez. You know Navarez is married to an Agua Caliente?" he asked.

"No," I said, filing a mental note under Patients-cops-Navarez-PTSD-married to an Agua Caliente Indian.

"She's only one quarter Indian but she still gets some money every month from the tribe," he explained. "They're saving it for college education. Her uncle is on the Tribal Council. But Navarez won't live on the reservation. If he did, he'd get beaucoup bucks."

"Why not?" I asked.

"Says that 'he won't live on bluecoat land.'"

The Agua Caliente band of the Cahuilla Indians were the original settlers of Palm Springs. They now owned close to half of Palm Springs due to the Checkerboard Land Settlement during the 1877 Hayes administration.

"Navarez is a good man," I said. "I don't know who is helping whom. Back to the press. From where I sit, I'm not sure it's because the press is too liberal or too conservative as much as they're a bunch of sharks. They follow the blood in the water. Anything for a story."

I noticed Chris wave goodbye to Suze and start back to us. He walked through the door to the outside patio toward our table. He playfully squashed the remains of the paper cup from his iced tea, turned it into a pretend basketball and attempted a fall away jump shot at the trashcan parked near the door. The paper cup arched gracefully through the warming morning air and looked for a moment like it would swish. At the last second it fell short, hit the rim of the trashcan and landed in the lap of an Armani suit worn by a man in his thirties.

"Sorry, man. I missed. The cup was empty. Did any spill on you?"

"You fucking little misfit!" Armani lost it.

"I'm sorry, man. Really. It was an accident."

"They shouldn't let your type in a public place like this," Armani sneered.

"Hey, just a minute here. I'm really sorry. I was just fooling around. I didn't mean to hit you with the cup. No need to..."

"Stay on the street where you belong," Armani spat.

"Enough! You apologize to someone and they don't accept your apology then it's their problem." I spoke loud enough for the whole patio to hear.

"I thought I was the one who needed to learn to keep my mouth shut," Brett said.

"Takes one to know one," I said. "Your idea to help him."

"Haven't even given him the bivy sack yet," Brett said.

Armani was on his feet towering over Chris and heading for me. He sneered, "You like these dirty street kids?"

"I like this one."

"Me too," Brett added.

Chris stepped up to Armani in a conciliatory fashion, "He's a cop. He's cool. Relax, man."

Armani looked at Brett and demanded, "You're a cop and you let this sort of street scum in here? Do something. You work for me. Kick his ass the hell out of here. He probably doesn't even have a home. Probably sleeps on the street."

"Kick his ass the hell out of here?" Brett repeated. He looked at Armani, and coiled into his frame. I could see his — *tempt this guy into taking a swing, show him whose ass gets kicked the hell out* — thoughts.

Brett's beeper went off. We were saved by the cell.

If Brett didn't have time for further hassle, neither did Armani who rudely waved us off and walked away. Chris and I were left listening to Brett talk on his cell phone that had materialized out of his fanny pack, where it lived with his off-duty Sig Sauer .40.

"Yes, Sir. Chief, I'm with the shrink. He'll have to drive me. I don't have my rig," Brett said perfunctorily into the phone. He had walked to Starbucks from police headquarters, after an early morning training session with a uniform.

"Tahquitz Creek. Got it. I'm rolling, Copy that, sir," Brett said to the chief. And then to me, "Armani left?"

I nodded, glad to see the jerk leave.

Brett smiled and began to uncoil. "Body at the Tahquitz Creek Golf Course. Gotta go. Can you drive me?" Not really a question.

I wasn't seeing clients until the afternoon so I had both time and curiosity. "Let's go."

Shrinks need curiosity by the caseful.

Chris chimed in, "Tahquitz Creek. I sleep out there. Ride in this time every morning."

I tossed Brett my car keys. If we're going to speed, he needs to drive.

"I know. See you later," Brett started toward my Land Cruiser.

"Cool. Nice to meet you, Doc," Chris said. "Thanks for the talk. Good to know I'm not crazy. Sorry about him. I didn't mean…"

"Screw him. He's trouble." Brett said.

"I know. He's just like my dad," Chris said.

Brett started walking. I shook Chris's hand then jogged after Brett, already halfway to my truck.

When I got to the Land Cruiser, he was already behind the wheel. I rode shotgun.

As we pulled onto Belardo, he asked, "Armani just took off?"

"Yeah… he didn't want to have to hurt you."

PISTOL TO PIN

The horn hurt my ears.

Two minutes after the call, Brett was using it relentlessly to clear a car full of tourists in downtown dawdle out of our way. The chief called him out to Tahquitz Golf Course because the on-call detective had the flu, and Brett was the department's utility infielder. Although it wasn't his current assignment, he was a trained investigator with an excellent case-clearance record.

"It'll be a zoo when we get there," Brett said. "Stay close to me and no one will question you. Don't touch anything."

"Yes, sir."

We moved fast through traffic out North Palm Canyon, swung left on Ramon, ran the rig up to eighty for a couple of miles, and then slowed to take a right on Crossley. At the intersection, I could see the golf course laid out along a flood aqueduct that used to be Tahquitz Creek in some earlier geologic time — it would take a twenty-year flood to make it qualify as a real creek again.

"Chief's going to make me the lead investigator, and partner me with Joan Fleming when she gets back from Riverside," he complained.

"Problem with that?"

"I like to work alone. That's why I took the training officer slot," he replied.

"Opportunity to learn politics."

"Yeah," he said frowning.

"How's Joan to work with? I've met her twice, I think, at department seminars."

"I see her in group training situations but I've never actually worked with her," he said.

"What do you know about her?"

"She's in her mid-thirties, and an ex-elite marathoner that almost made the Olympic team in college," he said. "She clears her cases well, and came here from someplace up North, maybe Oregon. Spectacular body. Nice tan. We had a drink."

"You had a drink?"

"Yeah, we had a drink but it didn't go anywhere. She really turned me on. I could tell she was interested too, but she sort of shut down right in the middle of the initial dance. I don't know what she thought about me; there was no opportunity for me to find out. She shook my hand after the drink. I never got to first base with her. I thought she was shy, a little uptight, and perhaps a perfectionist."

"I remember the spectacular part. What kind of drinks you have?"

"She had a Napa Valley Chardonnay."

"What did you have?"

"I had a scotch. Wasn't what I really wanted to have."

"Yes?" I waited.

"Wanted to have a Black and Tan," he said, smiling.

We rolled past the golf course entrance. A Cathedral City uniform recognized Brett, and waved us to continue on Golf Club Drive. Tahquitz Country Club was an extremely popular tourist course owned by the City of Palm Springs and managed by Arnold Palmer's company. We came around a corner into flashing police lights, Christmas in March. Just as we pulled to the curb, I imagined Chris riding a bike from out near here, seven miles to the downtown Starbucks.

I stepped out of the Land Cruiser and nodded to the Palm Springs police chief, who was typically managing his department in the middle of the action rather than from a desk. He nodded back to me but was looking for Brett. The two of them ended up in a huddle near the ball washer. We parked near the green of the 17th hole, a long par 4 that I had played many times. All the activity was centered about thirty yards away up a little rise on the next tee. There were a dozen uniforms, techs, and EMTs working the scene. The air smelled of eucalyptus, freshly mown grass, and death.

Brett came over, and motioned for me to follow him up the little rise on the course to the 18th tee. I could see a golf cart and the victim. I'd seen dead bodies before in the military and doing critical incident debriefs for the department. I always managed to forget the rush and the sick feeling in my gut that accompanied the realization that someday I'd look like this, too. You can train your body not to overreact, but you can't completely remove the response— dead bodies repulse the living.

The victim was lying on his face with an entry wound right between his shoulder blades. The EMTs had just finished trying to resuscitate him. Cops have to wait for the medics to try to resurrect the victim even when it's obviously and finally hopeless. The EMTs have to do what the law requires — they dictate death.

The victim had played his last hole. There was a golf club on the ground, a three wood. He had been preparing to tee off. His golf ball sat on a tee in the ground an inch from his outstretched right arm.

Brett gathered everyone around him, and told them what they already knew: he was the lead. They looked up, accepted that he was in charge without comment, and returned to their specific tasks.

"Low velocity entry wounds," Brett said.

"Pistol rounds?" I asked, vaguely remembering basic ballistics.

"Yeah. Probably not a Nine though."

A uniform stared at me and asked, "What's Doc doing here?"

"My ride," Brett answered him. Crime scenes were sacred ground, consecrated by the victim's death. I didn't belong there without a purpose.

On that cue, I backed up off the edge of the tee with my hands up in the classic gesture of submission to police authority, and took a look around. About 100 feet behind the 18th tee was a 50-foot high hedge of California Bay Laurel that screened it from a development of townhouses. The 17th green had two sand traps, one on either side. A stand of eucalyptus framed the side of the green that bordered the road. In the same fashion, a stand of date large palms framed the 18th tee — the crime scene minus the body was postcard pretty.

Across Golf Club Drive from the 17th was another flash flood viaduct area about 500 yards wide dotted with chaparral, sagebrush, tumbleweed and windblown trash. The Coachella Valley Bike Trail ran through the southern border. The viaduct was part of the larger flood control system that meandered through the valley. In some places it had been transformed into Bermuda grass golf holes, in others, left wild — it was always ready to do its job.

I looked up and in the distance I could see snowcapped Mt. San Jacinto where Tahquitz Creek began as a wet creek. The Palm Springs Aerial Tramway started at the Valley Station near my home and climbed a mile nearly to the summit of the mountain. Its signature silhouette was on all the Palm Springs logos; it was the highest ride in town notwithstanding the jackpots at the Indian casinos.

Brett walked over to where I was standing. "I can get a lift back when we're done here."

"How long you going to be?"

"Rest of the day probably."

"What do you think?"

He knew I could keep my mouth shut — what happens on deployment, stays on deployment.

"Professional hit," he said.

"How can you tell?"

"Just guessing so far," he said. "I don't like that the shooter might have used a pistol."

"Where does Chris sleep?" I asked, changing the subject.

Thoughts of Chris had hung in the back of my mind since Starbucks. Curiosity about where he was sleeping got the better of me. Curiosity was the curse of shrinks. I had a little time to kill, and the dead body made my skin crawl. Walking might help.

"Down the bike trail about a mile, where it turns back along Highway 111," he said. "Look for the first abandoned commercial building."

I didn't even ask how he knew exactly where Chris spent his nights.

"Later," I said.

I walked down off the tee and passed two uniforms rolling out the unnatural-yellow crime scene tape. They were taping off the entire tee box area; no more golf today. It was starting to get warm. I unzipped my fleece vest, and felt the early heat of the desert on my back. It felt life-giving and replaced the skin-crawling sensation of proximity to death. My quirky-since-'Nam back liked warmth and hated cold; every few months, it put me in a brace for a day or two.

Coachella Valley warmth attracted millions of snowbirds from all over North America seeking some respite from harsh winter further north. It made the Palm Springs climate appear healing and totally benign. It was easy to forget that the desert can be deadly. Summer arrives, and the thermometer sometimes climbs over 120 degrees in July and August. Without water and cover, heat can kill as sure as bullets.

I waited for a patrol unit to pull out and head south down Golf Club Drive, which would be closed most of the day for the scene investigation. I walked across the road and onto the bike trail. Glancing ahead, I saw a jackrabbit clear the trail in one jump. Following him with my eyes out into the viaduct area, I lost him about sixty yards away as he went behind a little rise covered with tumbleweed. His arroyo air smelled strongly of sage.

I covered a mile in the next fifteen minutes. The bike trail left the viaduct, and meandered by a trailer park on the right and the boundary of yet another golf course on the left, Cathedral Canyon Country Club. I could hear golf carts, birds,

Michael Thompkins

trucks from Highway 111, and, always, the mechanical sounds of water being moved. Deserts were full of the sounds of water pumps — the artificial hearts of modern desert civilization on life support.

The bike trail was not well maintained. Wild grasses, succulents, and California poppies made their best attempts to overgrow the trail encouraged by every leaked or spilt drop of water or the occasional rain.

Then I was at the place where Chris slept. It was an old dilapidated tin-roofed building fifty yards off the bike trail in a small industrial area called Bankside, not far from Brett's home. Crawling under a fence and through a pile of cardboard boxes, I peered into the building.

I smelled him before I saw him — he stank.

The smell came from an old wino who acted as some sort of sentry for the encampment. Wondering if I was friend or foe, he decided and waved me over. He didn't have access to a shower either but with radically different results than Chris. He was wearing tattered jeans and a torn, stained, white tee-shirt with a Palm Springs Police Mounted Enforcement Unit logo probably given to him by one of Brett's officers.

"I just want to see where Chris lives," I said by way of explanation.

"You a friend of his?" he asked intently.

"Yes, although I only met him this morning." I didn't sound convincing when I said it, but he had already decided to let me pass for who knows what reason.

"His stuff is inside," he said, pointing inside the building.

"You guard the place?"

"Yeah," he said. "Chris helped me with the paperwork for my disability."

Young Vagabond Prince Chris helps the wino onto welfare.

"Here's some money." I handed him a ten knowing it would be used for cheap jug wine. Long ago surviving and outgrowing the early blush of being a psychologist – the trying-to-understand-and-change-everyone syndrome, I now passed whole days, not giving a shit what strangers were thinking or feeling.

"Thanks," he said, almost falling down when he grabbed the cash. He put a hand on my shoulder to steady himself.

I stared at his hand. He removed it with a smile.

"Be nice if you wouldn't mention to Chris I was here. Can I go inside? I just want to see where Chris is staying."

"No problem. He's only visiting for a while, anyway. Nice young fella." He was eager to desert his post to spend his windfall on wine

I waved goodbye to the wino; he walked off happily. Walking inside the concrete warehouse, I spotted Chris's stuff immediately. He was living in a corner of the building nearest the entrance. Cardboard lay on the ground, covered with a closed cell foam pad and a bright orange sleeping bag. A red, plastic shopping hand-basket, full of sheet music, was parked right next to the bag. A barrel sawed in half was being used for a fireplace. I remembered some of my encampments all over Europe and the U.S. twenty years ago; they looked pretty much the same. Suddenly I felt like the intruder I was, and left.

I walked the mile back to the scene. As I rounded the last turn, I looked for my rabbit friend. Instead, I saw Brett behind the little rise that the hare had disappeared into. It was now ten-thirty, seventy-five degrees heading for north of eighty and I was sweating. I walked up to him; he held a long-barreled automatic and a pair of latex gloves in his right hand.

"Found it under a bush over there. Gloves were six feet away from the piece." He lifted it toward me holding it by the end of the barrel. He was wearing latex gloves. "Glock .40. Excellent and expensive weapon."

"It's going to piss off the tech people when they see you found it."

"Nothing I can do about it," he said. "They couldn't imagine a pistol shot coming from this far away. Out of their experience. Gloves mean the shot came from here."

"Neither can I. A hundred and fifty yards with a handgun. Out of my league." I looked at the pin on the green 150 yards away.

"Professional, elite, world class," he said. "Pistol to pin, 150 yards. Be a seven iron, right?"

I smiled, "Yeah, but with a seven iron, the target is a thirty-yard-by-thirty-yard green, not a two-inch center mass for a kill-shot."

"This shooter didn't even have to wonder about it," he said.

"Geez, that's good."

"It's goddamn good," he said.

"You figured it wouldn't be a Nine. Why a .40? Isn't it heavier to carry than a Nine?"

"It's heavier but necessary at this distance," he said. "I shot a guy once with a Glock Nine at 120 yards."

"And?"

"Didn't kill him, just paralyzed him," he said. "Nine didn't have enough impact velocity to get through his spine."

Michael Thompkins

I thought about that a few moments then went ahead and asked him. "Did he deserve to be shot in the back?"

"Maybe," he said. "He tried to shoot me first. He was going to keep at it."

I nodded, and changed the subject. "I saw Chris's place."

"Find what you were looking for?" he asked.

"Not yet."

He nodded. "Something else to think about...."

"What's that?"

"Chris rides through here every morning," he said.

"Chris? A witness?"

"Maybe he saw the shooter or his car," he said.

Then we both noticed my rabbit friend again, clearing ten feet in one spring. We watched him for several long moments as he covered fifty yards in four hops.

"Maybe him too," Brett said.

NICE DEPLOYMENT

The shooter walked the Lykken Trail. It ran behind downtown Palm Springs at the 1400-foot elevation of Mt. San Jacinto, pretty much paralleling Palm Canyon Drive. Palm Canyon was a main artery for human traffic. The Lykken trail was a main path for rabbits, fox, coyote, feral cats and dogs, deer, snakes, and rodents. Their droppings were everywhere.

If you believed the myth, the occasional mountain lion wandered down from higher elevations to hunt coyote or feral dogs. Lions will sometimes strike a human. As a rule, they're not afraid of them. Hitting at fifty miles an hour, they like to snap the neck. However, a big cat would have smelled the shooter and never approached him. He would have turned tail instinctively and headed to higher elevation— sensibly scared for his life, and never knowing why.

It was high noon the same day the shooter had displayed world-record pistol skills at the eighteenth hole at Tahquitz. He was memorizing escape routes and placing bags in caches on different trails. If he had to deploy for a week, he was determined to be ready. Tomorrow he would locate the kid and stakeout the firm where the accountant he'd popped worked. See which cops were assigned to the case. The cops would be the rest of the day at the shooting scene. As long as he was waiting on the buyer's instructions, he might as well do some recon. Good intel is everything.

The sun was directly over his head, and he was drenched in his own perspiration. He loved sweat and fatigue. They meant he was home. He'd spent more time in his life living outside under adverse conditions than inside in comfortable human habitation.

He had spent earlier years in the Army Rangers, and then moved on to becoming a hit man. Becoming a professional shooter had been attractive primarily because it allowed him to continue to live, more often than not, outside the circle of people. He was an outlaw.

Hunting humans provided tactical and tactile excitement. It came with its own smells, sounds and feel. Weapons turned him on more than women. However, it was becoming increasingly difficult for him to sustain the high. He had been getting a little bored lately with his work.

Michael Thompkins

Hundred and fifty yards with a handgun. World class. What next? Problem with popping people for a living: nobody shoots back. Not like the Army. Not like 'Nam. Gotta figure out a way to keep the game alive. Gotta find the next challenge. Need something new.

He arrived at the third area he wanted to place a cache, directly over the Palm Springs Desert Museum at the intersection of the North and South Lykken Trails and the Desert Museum Trail. There was a natural little cave that had been sculpted under three large boulders by a winter flood creek. He took out one of the waterproof dry bags and taking items from his backpack began to load it.

Glock .40, spare magazines, morphine syringe kit, IV kit with Lactated Ringers, hand warmers for the drip bag, Clif bars, two water bottles, Kerlix bandage, Quik Clot and a space blanket. Roll the top of the bag, clip the seal, and bury the bag. Hate to use the morphine and the drip. Have to inject them. They suck. Can't be ready enough.

He was partly finished with his chores and found a large boulder to sit on. He still had to hike six miles further up to hide another dry bag and a rope at the top of a cliff. He'd brought a frozen bottle of beer in his pack, and there was still some coolness in the bottle when he took it out. Opening the bottle, he savored the moisture on his lips. From his perch, he could see twenty miles down the Coachella Valley. He loved heights, and had graduated number-one in his class at Army Jump School and Mountain School — heights helped his head.

Kick-ass view. Starbucks. Indian Canyons. Palm Canyon Drive. Tahquitz Canyon Drive out to the airport, police headquarters, cops, new challenge.

Air's dry. Beer's wet. Sierra Pale Ale. Good stuff. Nice deployment. Excellent.

Need to pee.

The shooter reflected on his favorite movie outlaws, Butch and Sundance. Having seen their movie a hundred times, he toasted his favorite hero, shouting out, knowing no one could hear him.

"I'm the man, Butch. I'm the man."

THE KID

The shooter waited patiently — the kid belonged to him now. Since 5 a.m. the day after shooting the accountant and caching supplies, he'd hidden across from the abandoned warehouse where the kid slept. After walking a mile or so from the arroyo across from the sixteenth at Tahquitz, he'd easily found the kid's bike outside the abandoned building.

When the kid came out and mounted his bike, the shooter would step out from the trees and cross his path. Again. If he saw recognition in the kid's eyes, the kid was a gone. It was just before dawn and the stars were receding. The workers were beginning to show up at nearby Bankside businesses — a rental yard with a big crane, a car dealership, and a machine shop bordered the kid's flop. He flashed on the kid being on the road. Maybe twenty percent of his own sleep had been in beds; the rest were outside. He smelled first pots of coffee being brewed and fish fertilizer from the golf course. The trees in which he was hiding were on the 6th hole of Cathedral Canyon.

Target!
Kid's getting on the bike.
Damn it. Some old wino stopping the kid. Talking to him.

The shooter used the few moments that the wino and the kid talked to check his weapon, a Glock Nine. It was plenty enough weapon for the distance. He made sure there was a round in the chamber and the hammer was cocked. Bringing the Glock up to a two-handed firing position, he placed the fixed sights on the kid's chest. He tracked the kid as he walked out to the bike trail — the Nine never left center mass.

Ready.
Both of them moving toward the trail while they talk.
Could do them both.
Go away, old man.

He thought about leaving cover and walking past both the kid and the wino. It would require killing them both, and be too big a mess. The cops would spend too much time investigating.

The wino and the kid walked past the shooter's position.

Michael Thompkins

Situation's a no-go.
Stand-down.
Abort.
Do the kid later if need be.
Get some coffee.
Stake out the accounting firm.
Stand-down.

A TIGER AND A TEAM

The morning after we rolled out to Tahquitz, I met Brett for coffee at the same time. Coffee was a regular thing. We spent hours, drinking coffee, arguing our perspectives, and working the woman-watch. It pretty much comprised our religion — beyond the Bible as a benchmark.

"Joan is meeting me here," Brett said, taking the first sip of his watered-down Americano.

"Am I going to be in the way?"

"You're always in the way, but no more than usual," he said. "Last night, I was thinking about Chris again and the fact that he rides through the crime scene every morning about the same time. The shooter probably went there at least a few times to line up the shot; I would have. I want you to help me ask Chris what he remembers seeing. He likes us both and you might be able to help him jog his memory. The chief trusts you and said you can consult on an active investigation. He wants you in on this."

"Chief's a poor judge of character." I wondered about consulting on an ongoing. What were Brett and the chief up to?

"He likes me too. Proves he's a poor judge," he said.

"If the shooter did go there to reconnoiter, what says he came at the same time as Chris rode by on his bike?" I got the feeling that Brett was leaving something out.

"Just a hunch," he said. "If I'd made that shot I would have reconned the area on several mornings, and checked every angle thoroughly. It should take Chris a little over an hour to ride in here. He says he gets here around the same time every day. That puts him at the scene at first light. Pretty much the T.O.D."

"Who was the victim?"

"Martin Jonas, CPA, white, 5'10", 180 pounds, 52-year-old partner in an accounting firm right here in the Valley," he replied. "Joan and I have a 10:30 a.m. appointment with one of the partners. Guy's name is Bergman, Peter Bergman. Maybe we'll learn something."

"A professional hit on an accountant? Why? I don't get it."

"Professional murder is equal opportunity, and my money's already on the wildcard," he said. "Remember the rules of homicide? Follow the drugs, the sex, and the money. People are usually murdered for drugs, sex, money, or spousal control. Which goes with accountants?"

"Okay, money, I get it. The accountant was dirty or discovered something by accident."

"By the way, I'm going to put Chris up at my place for awhile."

"Say what?"

"You heard me," he said. "I'm going to put Chris up at my place for a while. It's not like I have a woman or anything. I got an extra bedroom, and he could use a break. I want to keep pursuing what he might have seen out there."

"And you call me a bleeding-heart liberal," I said. Our friendship had endured him calling me a white-bread pontificating liberal snob and me calling him a conservative Uncle Tom.

"Look, whether Chris saw something or not, the minute I start questioning him, he's at risk," he said.

"Why?"

"Because, if I had done this hit, I might just stick around for a while, make sure no one saw me, find out whom the police were questioning, and take out anyone who could make me," he said. "And what if I had been ordered to stick around?"

"You're giving this guy a lot of credit. I think he's long gone."

"You're probably right," he said.

"You're also making Chris a target," I said. "Whether Chris saw the shooter or not, this works for you. Either way you're using Chris to set the guy up. You think the shooter might stick around to see if anyone can identify him. So if the shooter's seen Chris out by Tahquitz, if he sees him with you, and if he makes you as a cop, then you're using Chris as a target."

"That's a lot of ifs. With the life Chris lives, doesn't he already have a target painted on his ass? And I am going to take him in," he said.

"So you're a generous bastard."

"Look. I have to question him about what he might have seen," he said. "I'd like to give him a place to live. The other possibility is not likely, but I'm not going to ignore it."

"Point taken." The possibility of Chris being a target was remote.

"Besides, I need this one," he confessed.

"Not enough to just save lives any more? Not enough to just give Chris the bivy sack?"

"Something like that. Things change," he said, his eyes softening.

He'd told me about his plan a few years ago — save some lives to make up for the ones that he had taken.

"Worth more points this way?"

"Maybe," he said. "I've seen too many damn kids die."

I looked up as Chris pulled up on his bike. When he parked his bike against the fence that separated Starbucks' outdoor patio from the sidewalk, the wrought-iron scroll shook.

"Hey, dudes," Chris pointed inside, went in, and collected his iced tea. Sitting down with us, he took the Martin out of its case and began softly strumming some Beatles' melodies. "You guys hang here every morning?"

"Pretty much," I replied.

"I prefer 7-11 but they don't give you a place to sit, and the scenery is never as good," Brett said.

"The iced tea is way better here," Chris said. "Every few months, I play my guitar in the evening right here," he pointed to a spot near the door. "The manager pays me with credit on a Starbucks card."

"There's something we need to talk about." Brett got right to the point, changing the subject.

"Cool. Shoot."

"You remember when we ran off yesterday morning?" Brett asked.

"Yeah. You dudes flew out of here to Tahquitz. I heard some guy got shot out there. When I rode home last night, there was yellow tape all over the place."

"Well, there's a slight chance you might have seen the shooter or maybe his car or something that might help us. It depends on your schedule and some blind luck." Brett's tone serious now.

"What did he look like?" Chris asked.

"Hey, if we knew that, we wouldn't need you," Brett said. "What's your usual schedule, riding through that area? How come you ride in so early?"

"I don't know. I just like mornings. I wake up; I want to move and get my iced tea. My dad used to wake me early just 'cause he thought I was lazy. Asshole. But I got used to the early morning and now I dig it."

"I guess you showed your dad," I said.

"Man, nobody shows him nothing. Never could win an argument with him, but he was right about mornings. Give the devil his due. What time is it now?"

"7:16," Brett said, glancing at his watch.

"Then I guess I rode through there sometime around 6 o'clock every morning for the last month or so."

"When did you say the time of death was?" I asked.

"The coroner estimated T.O.D. at approximately 6 a.m.," Brett replied.

"I don't get where I fit in," Chris said.

"Do you remember seeing anyone on your trips through there in the last month?" Brett asked.

"Saw the same sweet lady running a bunch."

"What did she look like?" Brett kept the questions coming.

"A fox," Chris purred.

Men can always bond around the way women look. Secure the perimeter, check out the foxes and then the cortex can finally fire — the fundamental truth about men, Psychologist Handbook, page 97.

"How tall was she, what color was her hair?" Brett continued the questions.

"Normal height, brown hair, blue eyes, nice smile, small tits, tight abs and a nice butt."

"Photographic memory for women?" I asked.

"Every sweet detail," Chris said.

"Lucky bastard. Age?" Brett asked.

"Twenties."

"Talk to her at all?" Brett asked.

"No," Chris paused. "She smiled at me, though."

"Being on the street sure doesn't cramp your style," I said, remembering Suze.

"I do okay, man. Still like to have more showers though."

"Women do like you to smell good," I said.

"Like I move around a lot and I could shower twice a day. I sweat when I even think about music," Chris said.

"Or women?" I asked.

"Women and music, I drip sweat."

"Got an idea about that." Brett replied, opening the door to his plan.

"You remember anyone else besides her?" I asked Chris.

"There was an old guy on the porch of one of the townhouses. He had gray hair, and was watering something on his deck. He was older than you dudes."

"He must have been goddamn ancient. See anyone else?" Brett asked.

"Guy with binoculars, once."

Brett and I looked at each other, binoculars — bingo!

"What did he look like? What was he watching with the optics?" Brett asked with practiced casualness.

"I didn't really pay attention 'cause I was still waking up," Chris said. "He was thirty yards across the aqueduct from the trail and was wearing a golf cap. I thought he was bird watching."

"Are there birds to watch out there?" Brett asked.

"Absolutely," I said. "This whole valley is a bus station on the Pacific Migratory Flyway that goes from South America to Alaska."

"Doc's right. Lots of birds. Lots of birdwatchers," Chris said.

"How many times have you seen this o-r-n-i-t-h-o-l-o-g-i-s-t with the optics?" Green Beret with a master's degree in English literature, Brett liked to spell hard words.

"Once, man. Yesterday," Chris answered.

Brett and I looked at each other.

"Can you remember seeing a car nearby on Golf Club Drive?" Brett asked.

"Nah, I don't think about cars except to stay out of their way on my bike."

"How far away was he from you when you saw him?" Brett continued.

Chris paused a moment in thought, then said, "Well, the dude was kneeling on a little mound in the middle of the aqueduct."

"If we went out there, could you show me?" Brett asked.

"Sure. Do you, like, think I saw the killer?" Chris started shaking his legs with a nervous energy.

"Probably just an birdwatcher," Brett replied.

"Gentlemen," a woman's voice called out to us.

Women-watching was our most important activity so the three of us came to attention in our reptilian brains—the deep part under the cortex.

Detective Joan Fleming walked up to us. She was 5' 6", brown hair, and blue eyes. She wore no makeup or jewelry.

"Joan, you know Doc, and this is Chris." Brett's greeting was clipped.

Joan reached across the table and shook my hand.

"Chris, this is Detective Fleming," Brett said.

"Hi, Detective Fleming," Chris beamed a smile at her.

"You can call me Joan. This is Palm Springs and we don't need formality like they do in L.A." Joan shook Chris's hand, and then looked at Brett. "I got back from court in Riverside last night, looked over the scene photos, studied the initial reports and bagged evidence. I'm glad to be working with you. I'll learn a lot, and I'll try not to cramp your style — totally my privilege."

Brett started briefing her. "All right, Joan. One, Doc is going to be helping us on this one with the chief's blessing. Two, Chris has been riding through the crime scene every morning and yesterday he remembers seeing a guy with optics. Three, we have a 10:30 meeting with one of the victim's partners."

She repeated the one word, "optics."

"Yup," Brett said.

"Victim have a spouse?" Joan asked.

"No, he was single," Brett replied.

"Any more on cause of death?" she continued.

"Bullet penetrated his heart," Brett said.

"Hell of a shot," she said.

"About 150 yards with a Glock .40," Brett said. "I'm not sure I could make that shot myself." He was looking at Joan's breasts. She didn't miss it. They were worthy of the look. They weren't 150 yards away.

"This isn't good," Joan said. "The idea of a killer at large with that kind of skill scares me. Why take the shot with a pistol instead of a rifle? And an expensive pistol that he throws away. I don't get it."

"Concealment." He kept his eyes on her face and off her body. "Less chance of being observed with a handgun. We're both carrying at least one handgun right now and no one can see them. It gives him the advantage of working under any condition. A long gun can't be hidden from view."

"Could mean something else," I suggested.

"What's that, Doc?" Joan asked.

"That he's really a professional and challenging himself," I said. "Make it a little harder each time so he doesn't get bored. Anything you do long enough, you get bored."

"Doc, that's pretty good," Joan said. "I heard you know your shit. I read the paper."

Chris had been sitting, practicing chords and listening. Making ready to move along with his day, he stood up to head out, and encased the Martin. He made a strumming motion on the cover. "Excuse me. Gotta take off, hookup with my band and practice."

"You wanna be the next John Lennon, you gotta practice, eh?" Brett said.

Chris gave him a thumbs-up.

"Before you take off, there's something I want to talk to you about. I live over by Cathedral Canyon Drive in Cathedral City. In fact, it's near where you're sleeping now. I have an extra room, and I can let you stay there for a while if you like. It would make it easier for you to help us. I'll meet you there at 4 o'clock." Brett pulled out pen and paper, and wrote down directions, not even waiting for Chris to respond.

"Cool, you have a shower?" Chris asked.

"Two of them. After a deployment, that's what my team used to care about first. Get your stuff and meet me at my house at four o'clock. Can you find the place?" Brett gave the directions to Chris.

"Thanks, man. No problem," Chris said excitedly. "I'll be there at four. I guess I won't need that bivy sack."

"Look, if you two are going to live together, let me cook your first dinner to celebrate.

My house, anytime after 5:30. You too, Joan." I loved to cook — any excuse to open wine and sautee herbs.

"See you all tonight. Naw, wait a minute, I'll meet you at the house at 4:00 p.m." Chris looked at Brett, waved goodbye, and headed out.

"Thanks for the invite. I'll be there for dinner," Joan said. "Can Doc cook?"

"Seen him shoot, seen him cook," Brett said.

"And?" she asked.

"Come to dinner. If he picks up a weapon, take cover," Brett said, smiling at me.

"Sweet of you to give Chris a place to stay," she said. "His music? Does he have any talent? Does he have a chance?"

"We'll find out," Brett said with an optimistic tone.

"I never thought of you as a father," I said to Brett.

"Don't start on me with the psychology. Okay, let's get a few things organized." Brett shifted gears.

"What about the guy with the optics?" Joan asked. "What does Chris remember about this guy?"

"He doesn't remember any more than a golf cap and the binoculars," I said.

Michael Thompkins

"I'd like to have Doc hypnotize Chris. See if we can get more detail if he's willing," Brett suggested.

"So that's what you told the chief in order to get his approval of my involvement?"

"I told him that I wanted you to hypnotize Chris to see if he remembered anything or anybody from the scene," Brett replied. "I think the chief has his own plans for you, though. There are no other psychologists in town with forensic training, you're ex-Army Intel, and you could make the department look good. I think the Chief plans to on-the-job-train your ass. Move you to investigations. He knows your reputation, and he may even pay you more."

"Sure, we're all in this for the money. You know hypnosis isn't admissible in court," I reminded him.

"I don't care about court, but I do care about getting a possible ID on the shooter," Brett said.

I was already on billable hours, at a deeply discounted rate, with the department because the city was always in a budget crunch. Palm Springs was a small town on its way to a bigger city, and people often wore more than one hat. I'd done a fellowship in forensic psychology but had gone into clinical consulting. Drag out the books. Did I really want to be involved with active investigations? It was a big leap. How would Nancy feel about it?

"Joan, do you have any problem with my involvement in this case?" I didn't want to step on her toes and half-wished for an excuse to back out.

"Let me see," Joan said. "One, I get extra help on a case from our famous department psychologist, two, learn about hypnosis, and, three, get a free meal at your house tonight. I'll also be the first woman in the department, not in training, assigned to work with 'Lieutenant Special Forces.' It beats being in that Riverside courtroom with no air. I'm think I'm in heaven. We'll make a great team."

Team? Brett and I looked at each other. *Team?*

"All right, so everybody's in." He didn't sound certain of it at all. "Let's go interview the partners. You coming?" looking at me.

"Why not? No patients 'til after lunch."

"You two want to be there when I hypnotize Chris?"

"Wouldn't miss it," Joan said.

"Me, too. I'm in," Brett said.

"I'll plan for tomorrow morning in my office if Chris is willing."

"One more thing bothers me." Joan changed the subject.

"What's that?" I asked.

"I get the shooter carried a handgun for concealment but why'd he drop it?" she asked.

"Maybe he didn't want to risk being caught with it," Brett said.

Time to start proving my value. "The shooter might be showing off by leaving an expensive weapon for you to find. It's an extrapolation of basic marking behavior."

"Doc, what the hell does that mean?" Joan asked.

"Christ. Extrapolation of basic marking behavior? In English, please," Brett said.

"Like I said, shooter's maybe a little bored and looking for ways to make what he does more exciting. Do anything long enough, it's boring. So he makes the impossible shot with a pistol instead of a rifle. Simple enough so far, but that's still not enough recognition. So he gives us the pistol, then fantasizes us sitting around talking about what a great shot it was and how he has the stones to drop the piece. Which we're doing, aren't we? Bingo. He has his recognition. It's like a cat marking its territory. The shooter's weapon is now his marking. It tells us he thinks he's the best and he's here. He could have a reputation for this type of drop already."

"Geez, that's good, Doc," Joan said. "He's like a cat marking his territory. I can see that."

"Good stuff, Tom. Like this is what's really the basis for a killer's signature, right?" Brett asked.

"Yes, the deepest part."

"Like a cat marking his territory. Never thought of that," Brett said.

"Actually, he'd be more like a tiger marking his territory," I said.

"That's what we used to call snipers for either side that spent too long in the jungle," Brett said.

"Tigers?" Joan asked.

Brett just nodded.

"Shit," Joan said.

"No, pee," I said. "Tigers mark with urine."

"Just like he peed on us," Brett finished it.

ARMANI REDUX

"You doing okay back there?" Brett asked.

"Hell no, but if I sit sideways I can still feel my butt," I said from the back seat of Brett's car, a '68 Mustang Shelby Fastback, white with a blue racing stripe — arguably the fastest ride belonging to a Palm Springs cop. Forever working on it, he happily announced last month that the car was finally all Ford original factory parts. I didn't find it very comfortable, though, stuffed into the tiny rear bench seat. The interior of the car smelled of Armor All.

"Good," he said without an ounce of sympathy.

She and Brett talked about the various transmission and engine modifications available for the '65-'69 Mustang, the signature car of the sixties. I sat silently sideways making sure blood got to vital organs.

We turned off Highway 111 that ran from Palm Springs out to where the real money lived in Palm Desert, and took a right onto El Paseo Drive. When the developers built Palm Desert, they needed a gimmick to tempt the rich and famous to buy a second home here in the middle of the California desert, so they laid out a street to mimic Rodeo Drive in Beverly Hills. It was complete with expensive jewelry stores, designer clothing shops, a Ferragamo shoe store, and incredibly expensive places to eat, and drink espresso for four bucks a cup.

They succeeded. Folks came in droves to have their sixty-to-ninety-year-old skin surgically shifted to Palm Desert plastic-pseudo-youth, follow their portfolio up and down, sit by the pool, obsess about golf and shop El Paseo.

Pulling into the parking lot of a three-story office building, Brett parked as far away from other cars as he possibly could to protect his thousand-dollar clear-coat paint job. We walked around to the front of the building and into the lobby. Checking the building directory, he read off the engraved plate trimmed in gold, "Jonas and Associates, PS, Certified Public Accountants, Suite 245."

We rode the elevator up to the second floor. Jonas and Associates was located on the same floor as a brokerage firm and a wholesale jeweler. Joan badged the receptionist, and announced us. She left us to cool our heels a few minutes while waiting for Mr. Peter Bergman.

"Mr. Bergman will see you now," she announced and pointed to a door behind us.

On cue, the door opened, and Chris's Armani antagonist from Starbucks stepped out into the reception area. He took one look at the three of us, failed to suppress a startle of recognition and beckoned, "Officers, please come into my office."

When Bergman turned to lead us into his office, Brett looked at me and mouthed "asshole."

We followed Bergman back into his spacious, corner office, and took seats across from his designer desk. He was wearing another Armani suit today, which looked a little too slick on him to fit my image of a certified public accountant. His office was furnished out of the Sharper Image catalog, complete with enough electronics to open his own franchise. The place smelled of electronics and leather.

"Officers, Martin's death has brought the shortness of life home to all of us here," he said. "I will miss his guidance immensely. He was the senior partner and I'm the most junior. My other two partners are in New York at a training seminar. I'm in charge. We're all shocked that he was murdered and I want to do everything in my power to help catch his killer, but I don't understand why some officers came here yesterday and sealed Martin's office with yellow tape. Was there a crime committed here?" For now, Bergman was simply going to ignore our first encounter at Starbucks.

Joan took the lead. "There's probable cause that evidence exists in the victim's office connected to his murder. It's routine to obtain a search warrant and seal the office until we can close the crime scene investigation and move to more peripheral areas. We're following normal police procedure. The court order allows us access to all financial, personnel, and client records of this firm," she cranked it up. "We'll do everything in our power not to interfere with the day-to-day business of your firm, but our duty is to the victim."

"Of course, Detective, we all feel the same way," Bergman said. "It's just that some of that information is privileged and if it leaked out, our clients would be very unhappy indeed."

"You can be assured that we'll protect the privacy of any client information unless it becomes pertinent to our investigation," she replied. "Even under those circumstances, that evidence would only be made public at the time of a trial. The police, as a matter of routine, do not adopt a cozy relationship with the press."

"Why are three detectives assigned to this case?" Bergman asked. He was sweating in his air-conditioned office, and trying to get some reach on Joan.

"The lieutenant and I are the detectives assigned to the case, and Dr. Reynolds is the department's psychologist,' she said. "He's assisting us."

Bergman looked at me in a way I'd seen many times in my career — as if to say "you may be a shrink, but you ain't finding out shit about me."

"How would you characterize your relationship with Martin Jonas?" she asked Bergman, taking out her notebook and flipping to a blank page.

"Well, I am the youngest partner here and I've brought a lot of business to this firm.

Our largest client, Global Energy Trading, is my account. Martin was appreciative of my accomplishments and he convinced the other partners to reward me with my partnership in less time than anyone had ever received it. I am incredibly grateful for that and the mentoring he gave me. He and I sometimes played golf together. This is not a big firm, although large national firms have voiced interest in acquiring us, owing to our local connections. Local firms choose us because we go way back in Palm Springs."

Bergman loved to say "I."

"Do you know of any problems Mr. Jonas was having? Gambling? Alcohol? Drugs? Sex?" she continued.

"Martin's character was impeccable. Certainly not," Bergman protested

"Do you know of anyone who might have threatened Mr. Jonas?" she asked.

"No."

"Do you have any idea why someone would want to kill him?" she added.

"Martin was a powerful man and he has held on to the firm for the last twenty years resisting numerous take-over attempts," Bergman said. "Sure, he's had people angry with him, because he was a perfectionist and a scrupulous accountant. He was a bachelor and lived alone in a condo in downtown Palm Springs near mine. He was obsessed with his work and this firm; he called us his family. The idea of someone murdering him is absurd, and I cannot even accept that his death is real; never mind imagine someone who would have reason to…"

Brett who had been quiet until now interrupted, "Who are the largest clients of this firm?"

"Global Energy, the City of Palm Desert, the City of Palm Springs, the Agua Caliente Indian Tribe, Imperial Valley Association, and most of the golf course owners all retain us," Bergman bragged. "Our client list is extensive. We work to grow our client base daily." He frowned at Brett's interruption.

"What do Global and Imperial Valley do?" Brett asked.

"Global buys and sells electricity, the cities and the Indians you know, and Imperial Valley is a middle man to golf courses," Bergman replied.

"Do you have any idea what Martin might have come across that would be worth killing him for? Cooked books? Tax evasion?" Brett asked, apparently seeing little advantage to hiding his wildcard theory.

"I'm not aware that he discovered anything at all," Bergman warned. "That is just the kind of speculation that might cost us clients. I will not tolerate any embarrassment to my clients. I remind you that you've promised discretion, Lieutenant. If any of our clients are bothered unduly, I will have to seek remedy."

"We be only askin' you, sir." Brett used the black street dialect he carried with him from the Hunter's Point projects of San Francisco.

A vein on Bergman's face flushed red, protruded, and twitched.

"Mr. Bergman, can you remember anything suspicious occurring at the firm in the last three months?" Joan interrupted.

"We had a break-in three weeks ago that we reported to the Palm Desert Sheriffs. Nothing was taken," Bergman said. "I don't see how that event could be related to Martin's murder."

"Mr. Bergman, we'll decide what's relevant to our investigation. Nothing was taken?" she asked.

"We discovered that someone hacked into our computer system," Bergman said. "They looked through our records, but I've no idea what they were looking for, because they didn't take anything."

"How did they gain access to the offices?" she continued.

Bergman shifted positions in his chair several times. "The officer who took the report said that someone must have left a door unlocked."

"What computer was used to access your system?" she asked.

"Following the break in, we hired a computer consultant. He believed it was the computer in Martin's office," Bergman scratched the back of his head.

"Was he certain it was Martin Jonas's computer?" she persisted.

"Yes, I believe so," Bergman said.

"Well, we thank you for your time, Mr. Bergman," Joan said, wrapping up the interview. "As we said, we'll have technicians in Mr. Jonas's office who'll be collecting information and at some point, we'll release the office. Until then, no one is permitted to enter it. Also, we'll need a complete list of the firm's clients. We'll need to talk to the computer consultant. We may need to talk to you again, interview the

Michael Thompkins

rest of the partners and all of the employees, at least briefly. We're grateful for your help this morning. If anything comes to mind, please call us immediately."

"I want to do everything in my power to help the police find Martin's killer." Bergman paused, "And I regret getting upset over that unfortunate young man."

Brett turned and tightened. He looked hard at Bergman. Then in a light, offhand tone, he said, "Oh. You mean my friend Chris."

Bergman came up short for words, flushed, rose, came around the desk and led us silently out the door.

In the parking lot we walked by a vacant, light-brown Chevy Suburban with "Tribal Ranger, Agua Caliente Band of Cahuilla Indians" stenciled on the side.

Brett said, "Indians. Wonder what they're doing here? We'll let it go for now, and find out later. Maybe ask Pete Navarez."

We walked back to the Mustang, climbed in and headed for El Paseo. Brett turned the corner. As we passed a large building with a modern sculpture in front, Joan pointed out Global Energy Traders.

"Global. We'll be back to visit them," she said.

On the way back downtown, Joan smiled, "I would give a week's salary to have a picture of Bergman when you said Chris was your friend. Bergman was gone. He had no frame of reference for you and Chris."

"He's a self-centered ass," Brett said. "Question is, is he involved in his partner's murder?"

"Here's my psych eval on Bergman," I said. "He's a textbook narcissist, in love with his own ego. People like him drive me nuts. Conceit like his starts with normal teenage self- centeredness, hits the Ugly American in the middle, and goes all the way to crime. We're becoming a goddamn nation of narcissists — the label fits Bergman like his Armani suit. I'm afraid we're all going to turn out like him."

"You're pontificating again," Brett said.

"Hell, he gets to you more than me," I said.

"Yup. Thinks he's better than me," Brett said. "Screw him."

"Bergman thinks he's better than everyone," I said.

"I don't care about everyone. That's for liberals like you," Brett said.

"Settle down, boys," Joan said. "We need to find out everything about Peter Bergman. Find out if he had a motive; we got jack without a motive. And we need to follow up on this break-in. And Lieutenant, it might not be such a good idea to let Bergman know you don't like him."

We settled down.

"I think we should move ahead on the assumption that Martin Jonas was shot because he discovered some cooked books," she said. "We need to look at every client of this firm. The computer geeks can look for the cooked numbers and we can feel out the clients for a vibe. The break-in supports Brett's wildcard theory. Jonas's computer gets searched and then he gets killed; that's some coincidence."

"Whoever broke in could have been looking for what Martin Jonas had discovered," Brett said. Then he changed the subject. "I'd like Doc to hypnotize Chris tomorrow morning if Chris is willing. Maybe we'll get lucky and come up with a better description of the guy with the optics. I'm getting a bad feeling about this shooter."

"I don't think that I'm going to want to hear this," she said.

"Anyone who assumed they could make a shot like that has to be ex-elite," Brett continued.

"Elite?" I asked.

"Army Special Forces and Rangers, Marine Force Recon, Navy Seals ...."

"I knew I didn't want to hear this," Joan said.

"Didn't want to consider it, myself," he said. "Elites are supposed to be the good guys. Maybe even a SOTIC graduate, like me."

"SOTIC?" she asked.

"Special Operations Target Interdiction Course, the Sniper Course," Brett replied.

"Where do they come up with stuff like SOTIC?" She added.

"Army's got people who lie awake coming up with stuff like 'army of one,' 'be all you can be,' 'win hearts and minds'..." Brett said.

"And?" I fed him the line.

"Army still be about killing people." He didn't say it like it was always bad work.

She gave him an appraising look and said, "Who, really, are you?"

"I just be a poor dark boy born in the 'get-tow.'"

She just shook her head, smiled at him patiently, and changed the subject. "So we got a shooter who could have been trained by the same Uncle Sam you were, one dead partner, and another partner who may or may not be involved. We've got no motive. Doc's right, we got jack."

"We've got something," Brett said.

"What?" she asked.

Michael Thompkins

"Guy with optics near the crime scene at the approximate time of the murder," he reminded us as he turned off Belardo and into my office parking lot.

Joan jumped out to facilitate my crawling from the back of the Mustang. I said my good-byes and got caught briefly in the current between the two of them. This was going to be fun to watch for me and even more for Nancy. She wouldn't rest until Brett was happily ensconced with a woman that she approved of. For her, romance was a sport complete with rules — "quality girls for quality boys," being rule number one.

"You in for dinner tonight?" I asked Joan.

"Yeah, I want to meet Nancy," she replied. "I hope she likes me."

"You're bound to hit it off with her," Brett said.

"Why do you say that?" She asked looking genuinely puzzled.

"Two smartest women I know," Brett said.

"You know more than two women?" she asked him smiling.

"Barely."

BOCCA

The shooter's name was Bocca. Later on the same morning he had to abort doing the kid, he was watching the building that belonged to the accountant. The contract required him sticking around Palm Springs for a week or more to make sure additional cleanup wasn't necessary. It was okay with him; he liked Palm Springs. He liked the wilderness around it, and he liked being in a strange place. Palm Springs suited his style of operating better than any other city he had ever deployed in.

The Army Rangers had given Bocca the tools invaluable in his current career: the skill to kill from a great distance, survive in the wilderness for as long as necessary, and conceal and surveil for extended periods of time. Tools he honed daily. His experiences in the Army had given him the motivation for his work.

Bocca's parents were gone and he had no siblings. He didn't allow himself friends, just women for a night or two. Aside from the hunt itself, the only real pleasures he had were learning about unfamiliar places, reading military history, whiskey and occasional women.

Mastering new terrain was a joy to him. An expert in maps, compasses and GPS systems, by the time he left Palm Springs he would know the area better than most of its inhabitants. At his home base in England, he kept an extensive collection of U.S. military histories; he enjoyed reading about the Vietnam War in particular.

Targets. Two cops. One black guy in his mid-forties. Looks like a pro. Stunning tan bitch cop in her thirties. Getting out of a Shelby Mustang a hundred yards away. Cops' shields flashing. Another guy in his mid-forties. Definitely not a cop. Who the hell's he? Stick around and find out. Cops investigating the hit? Who's the third guy?

Seen the black cop before somewhere. Pro. Never forget a face. He's a pro for sure. Tell he's a pro by the way he carries himself. Always ready.

Can't be seen by the black cop. Who the hell is he? Know him.

They went into the building. Bocca didn't follow them. He walked down to the shopping area, bought a coffee, a local morning paper and returned to his rental car. Glancing through the headlines, he drank his coffee, and wondered where he'd seen the black cop before. He knew it was somewhere in the Army. It would come

Michael Thompkins

to him or he'd call one of his intelligence sources and get a background check on the guy. That would cost him money but he wasn't about to let this one go.

Bocca sat there for thirty minutes before they came out.

He was ready.

He placed all three of them in the center of the optics.

He shot all three of them.

He used a Zeiss 170mm telephoto.

He would take the film to Costco, then fax it to his intel guy.

It was hot and he was hungry.

Ice cream. Two cops, chocolate and coffee — black cop, tan bitch cop. Second guy — definitely vanilla. Second guy could use some sun. Things the mind can come up with. Occupational hazard. Too much time alone and the mind roams.

Stang's moving. Can see it from a quarter mile away.

Bocca followed them back to downtown Palm Springs on 111, where the cops dropped off the other guy in a parking lot behind North Palm Canyon on Belardo. Bocca decided to stay with the guy and find out who the hell he was that he had ridden tag-along with the two cops.

He parked his car a couple of blocks away on South Palm Canyon, walked through a passageway to Belardo, and then to the building the third guy had entered. He noticed the sidewalk star tile for Debbie Reynolds and stepped on her. Palm Springs copies Hollywood — cute like Cannes. He wasn't worried about the second guy stumbling into him. Guy wouldn't know him from Adam. When he walked up to the office, he read the sign on the door.

Tom Reynolds, Ph.D., Consulting Psychologist.

Damn it. Police shrink.

Goddamn shrinks screw everything up. Screwed up Special Forces Selection.

Follow the shrink. Lead to the kid.

AUDIENCE

I was turning into a Frenchman — either planning or preparing my next meal. Home alone, I was enjoying every minute. I put Bullet with Butterfly Wings by Smashing Pumpkins in the CD player and strained to understand the lyrics.

In the kitchen preparing herbs from our little garden out back, I chopped garlic, rosemary, marjoram, and basil for the base of my puttanesca sauce. I sauteed the herbs in olive oil, then added fresh Italian red and yellow plum tomatoes. Finally, I added some chopped Kalamata olives, and turned the heat down under the pot to let the sauce simmer. I had iced two French whites and a red sat on the counter uncorked and breathing. I especially enjoyed French whites because they carried the names of the little villages where they were produced. I liked to find the village on the map of France.

I glanced at the clock. Nancy wouldn't finish with patients until 5:30 p.m. I had finished typing up a consultation on an admission to a local psych hospital at 4. Brett, Joan and Chris were due at 6.

While prepping the sauce, I sipped a glass of Saint-Romain white and reflected on all that had happened since Tuesday morning when Brett and I had rushed out to Tahquitz Creek. Meeting Chris, learning of Martin Jonas's homicide, visiting Chris's encampment, riding out to the dead accountant's firm; it all occurred in just two days.

My back definitely liked things slower. It tensed as I remembered yesterday and today, a familiar grabbing, no sharp pain. Exercise helped. If I pushed my limits, I would get short stabbing pains like a cable was loose on the Eiffel Tower, and it was time to wear the brace for a few days. Damn thing began after the helo extraction in 'Nam.

The orthopedic specialist, that Nancy had insisted I consult, called it idiopathic-functional back pain. Translates to "we don't know what causes it, we don't know what cures it, we know it won't kill you, and don't forget your co-pay." I turned to alternative medicine, a booming billion-dollar industry in California. My chiropractor said I had subluxations and adjusted my spine. My massage therapist worked at loosening my too-tight connective tissue; he wanted me more compact, and closer to the ground. My acupuncturist said I had "weak kidney chi."

Michael Thompkins

As usual, I was cooking way too much food, and I hoped my guests would bring their appetites. If my metabolism ever slowed down, I was in trouble. I covered the saucepot, sliced the salad, and buttered the garlic bread. I laid out some Papillion Roquefort, duck liver pate and olives for appetizers. Then took my wine out to the back deck. The sage was in full yellow bloom, elderly cactus men with spiny arms were staring at trailing bougainvillea, and the sand changed colors as dusk covered it like a blanket.

Our house was in the north end of town and backed right up against the Mt. San Jacinto foothills, same as my office. There were no homes behind us, just a rugged slope up the mountain with a few fire trails winding their way up the slope. I sat on a bench and had the uncanny feeling of being watched. A coyote about a hundred yards up the slope from the house cruised among some big boulders maybe looking for his supper. A perfectly wild thing, heading about his business, watching me, he meant me no harm. I intended him none.

As I walked back into the kitchen to stir the sauce and assemble the salad, Brett and Chris walked in the front door. Brett was family and had a no-knock warrant for our house. On their heels, Nancy and Joan arrived two minutes later.

"Hey Doctor, how was your day?" Brett asked Nancy. The affection between Nancy and Brett ran deep. He gave Nancy a hug that lifted her off the ground before introducing her to Joan. The two women started a serious conversation.

Nancy said, "I had a crappy day with a bad outcome, a stillborn. I can't ever seem to get over babies being born dead. It's utterly devastating to the parents."

Joan moved over next to Nancy to listen intently; Brett and Chris were more interested in food.

"Smells great. What are we eating?" Brett asked me.

"I'm starving," Chris echoed.

"My Pasta Puttanesca with garlic bread and salad. But first, lots of appetizers," I said, leading them out to the rear deck where I opened a Saint-Romain red. It was a light burgundy from the Cote d'Or that was especially nice in the heat; the French sometimes even iced it. We ate our way through the Papillion Roquefort and pate.

"Do you guys have an Internet hookup?" Chris asked.

"Sure," Nancy replied as she and Joan walked out to the deck to join us.

"Would it be all right if I did some e-mailing before supper? I have friends in Spokane and Maui, I haven't connected with in weeks."

"Absolutely," I said. Computer's in the den. Just turn it on and it's set up to automatically log on to Internet Explorer. It's cable so the screens are pretty fast." I pointed in the general direction of the den.

Chris headed back into the house, and we sat in a small semicircle on the deck, sipping our drinks.

"Guys. I know you want to talk cop business," Nancy said. "I find this all an interesting diversion from a bad day. Brett, anything about Chris, I want in on."

If I was lucky, this might help in the inevitable "contract renegotiations" with her about my new job. If she liked helping Chris, it might be easier for her to accept me working on the investigation.

"Me, too. I want to help," Joan added. "I can't believe what you are doing for Chris and I know you don't want to make a big deal out of it, but if you need anything, let me know, okay?"

"Thank you both," Brett said. "Let's talk about where we are in this investigation. Let's hope we can get a better description of the birdwatcher with binoculars when Doc hypnotizes Chris tomorrow."

"We can try," I said.

Joan changed the subject. "The forensic accountants arrive tomorrow to completely go over the accounting firm's books, so we need to start on the list of clients and interview them all. It's going to be a long process with the shortage of manpower we have to deal with. I also want to go over the reports from the break-in more closely."

"I found something in the accountant's golf bag that really interests me. Get this. He had a separate appointment book for his golf and tennis times. He was an obsessive. All of the entries in the appointment book are for tennis and golf, except one. Look at what he scribbled: Global, Palo Verde; Imperial Valley Golf/Palm Springs, 2/13, 2:22p.m."

"What's Global?" I asked.

"Our first clue," Brett said.

"Global Energy Trading in Palm Desert," Joan said. "Remember Bergman bragged that they're the firm's biggest client and his account. We drove by the building, remember?"

"Yes, I remember now," I said. "What do they trade?"

"They trade electricity and gas," Joan explained. "Didn't you read all that stuff in the papers about deregulating electricity and gas last year? It's a big deal now. They trade electricity like stocks and bonds."

Michael Thompkins

"Palo Verde, Imperial Valley and the rest of the note, what does it mean?" I asked.

"Don't know but I'm going to find out," Joan said.

"Why do you think he had that note in his golf and tennis appointment book?" Brett asked.

"I'm guessing that he put it there to hide it or he forgot it was there," Joan said.

"All right. More later," I said. "I'm going inside, to cook the pasta and then we eat."

While I tossed the pasta and a little salt into the bubbling water, Nancy and Joan collected Chris. I put the garlic bread in the hot oven. Ten minutes later, we sat down on the deck and ate.

"This sauce is to die for," Joan said.

"Don't feed his ego. It's too big already," Nancy cautioned.

"Big red sauce made by man with big ego," I said. "We can bottle it and sell it. We'll call it Big Ego Red Sauce."

"Might pay more than being a cop," Brett suggested.

"Or being a shrink," I said.

"The way the HMO thing is going, it would pay more than medicine, too," Nancy said.

"Dudes. Cut your whining and eat," Chris said.

"Hey, Joan, where'd you go to school?" Chris asked. "Why'd you become a cop?

"I went to the University of Oregon in Eugene and majored in criminal science and psychology. I thought I wanted to be a forensic psychologist, but after I got my degree, I went to work for the University of Oregon PD. I worked there for five years, got my gold shield, and never looked back at school. I liked being a cop too much."

"You were a marathoner?" Brett asked.

"I made first alternate on the Olympic Team in my junior year, but nobody dropped out. I didn't get to go."

"Pity the perp trying to outrun you," Brett said.

"You don't run those kind of miles now, do you?" I asked.

"No, I want to have a little body fat in some places," Joan said, smiling.

Brett and I stared at each other so we wouldn't investigate Joan's efforts. She and Nancy laughed at us.

"You know, women look too," Joan said.

"Say what?" Brett said.

"Nancy, why do men think that they're the only ones that look at bodies?" Joan asked.

"Well, in all honesty, most women either don't know they're doing it or won't admit it," Nancy replied.

"Right on, sister," I said.

Finishing dinner, we settled back into the deck chairs. The sun had fallen behind the mountain and there was just a little bit of ambient light left. It was starting to cool down and would be in the forties by the middle of the night. Brett was explaining to Chris that he and Joan would be watching over him a bit until we knew more about the birdwatcher with binoculars.

"Some of the major bands like Bush have their own bodyguards. This'll be cool," Chris said.

"Maybe it's cool to you but it's work to us, and eventually you'll get tired of hanging out with adults," Joan said. "I'm sorry that you're in this position."

"Ditto," Brett said.

"Yeah, but I get a new roommate and place to shower," Chris smiled with satisfaction. "And bodyguards."

"Maybe we can even find the band a gig," Brett suggested.

"A what?" Chris asked, astonished.

"Well, there's no free lunch," Brett said. "You can't be jobless forever."

"What are you up to?" Nancy asked Brett.

He just shrugged.

The dishes had been cleared and night had fallen. The only illumination remaining was from the moon, the bright glow of the quartz-halogen patio light and a little light escaping through the kitchen's French doors. I contemplated going in to get a sweater if we stayed outside on the deck any longer. Chris was perched between Brett and Joan; Nancy and I sat directly opposite them. We were sitting on the deck in a loose semicircle. Looking up I could see the red lights on the signal towers at the top of Mt. San Jacinto and a few surrounding stars — points of light pulsing at the pinnacle.

Suddenly, a little circle of red light appeared on Chris's chest. The crimson spot flickered and moved to his right thigh.

Brett cleared his Nine, shot out the porch light, and yelled, "Get out of the killzone!" He pushed Chris out of his chair onto the floor of the deck.

The double French doors to the kitchen exploded into shattered glass.

Michael Thompkins

How? Where is this coming from? My cortex kicked in— someone was shooting at us. Ears ringing, rolling across Nancy, I took us both to the floor.

Joan, snaking through the French doors, killed the kitchen light. We followed on all fours into the kitchen. Glass marbles rolled around the kitchen floor from the shattered door.

Miraculously, no one was hit. Bitter cordite replaced the smell of sage. It was pitch black.

"Joan, stay here with Chris and Nancy. Tom, come with me. Stay low and as close to me as you can," Brett said.

Joan didn't question a word Brett said.

I did. "Call for backup?"

"Shooter would be long gone by the time they got here," he answered me. "Better chance on our own to catch up to him. We wait for uniforms and he's gone." He started moving through the kitchen entry toward the living room.

"Doc, hold on a minute," Joan said to me.

"What is it?"

"You're going to need a gun."

My hands were shaking, and my back burned.

Brett pulled up his right pant leg, unholstered a small automatic, and held the grip out to me. It was his backup gun. Giving it to me could get him in trouble.

I took the pistol from his hand.

Nancy looked at the gun, frowning.

"There's a round ready to fire. You remember which end the bullet comes out?" he asked.

I nodded.

He showed me the safety.

I thumbed it off.

"Let's go," he commanded.

I followed him through the living room and out the front door. We lived at the end of a cul-de-sac, and neighbors were coming to their front doors upset by the gunfire. I ignored them. I stayed as close behind Brett as possible. It took all the energy I could summon to stay with him as we went straight up the damn slope.

I had never seen anyone move as fast as Brett in the dark. I could barely see my feet; I trusted that if I followed him closely, he wouldn't lead me over a cliff. How the hell could he see where he was going? With the night vision of a cat, at two hundred yards or so up the sandy, rock-strewn slope, he held up his arm in the standard op signal to halt-hold-be-ready. Our ascent of the hill had been swift and direct.

"How'd you know where to go?" I asked.

"Heading to where I'd take that shot from," Brett said.

"What's to stop him from shooting us as we come at him?"

"He can't see any more than we can unless he has night-vision optics. The field of vision is so narrow with those that as long as we keep moving or take cover, he can't locate us. He'll be worried I'll call a helo and light up this whole hillside."

"Why don't you?" A helo and backup seemed safer than wandering around in the dark.

"Call for the helo, and I get the cavalry," Brett said. "Don't need the cavalry yet. Don't want this guy shooting a helo down. It would have a seriously restricted hover pattern this close to the mountain and running lights would make it a target. I've seen too many birds blown away by small arms or rocket-propelled grenades. I wish I had a radio, though, to let Joan know we're okay. I totally screwed up here. I should have anticipated this. I blew it. We shouldn't be chasing him up this hill but I'm pissed. I didn't take Chris off the street so he could be shot at."

We were moving again. The first part of the hillside had been open terrain. We were about four hundred yards from the house, nearing the crest of the first ridge. I had hiked up here before. I remembered there was a fire road behind this ridge that went on up the mountain. The road was used by utility people to maintain power lines and by occasional hikers. It had a locked gate at the entrance about a half-mile from my house.

Near the crest of the first ridge, we came to a field of giant boulders. The combination of the night, the boulders, the moonlight, and the desert sand reminded me of pictures of the surface of the moon. The small pistol in my hand felt strange, yet comforting. Brett's presence had always been like having my own personal bodyguard, but out here in the dark at the top of the ridge, I needed more than a bodyguard, I needed a gun. Brett was at home here. He had known instinctively that shooting the porch light out was the only tactical response that might help us, and whether the shooter could see us up here.

"Shooter's gone," he said, searching the ground near where we stood. Following his lead, I looked for casings.

"Wasn't for the moon...."

"Couldn't see shit," he said.

Fifty yards from us something shuffled in the brush. We covered the sound and studied the movement.

"It's an animal," he said.

"What kind?" I could see a bit of movement but not the shape of the creature.

"Coyote? Feral dog? It's about that size. Could be a bobcat. There's a rumor that a few mountain lions still live on the mountain, but not this low. "

The creature turned away before we could quite make it out.

Combing the clearing, we couldn't find a shell casing. Ten minutes later, we gave it up, and Brett motioned us down the road. It would be easier going down the road, although we would end up a half a mile from my house. The shooter gone, it was time to relieve Joan from the duty of protecting everybody in the house. From the clearing, my house was black and only vaguely outlined by the driveway light.

It took us ten minutes to get back to my driveway. We'd been gone for twenty-five minutes, which must have seemed an eternity to Joan and the others. We walked around the house to the back patio.

Brett announced loudly, "We're back. All clear."

Joan rose from prone near some cacti growing at the edge of yard and holstered her weapon. Brett knew exactly where to find her.

"Good play," Brett said, nodding to Joan.

It slowly dawned on my too-long-out-of-the-military-mind that he was praising the tactical position she had taken to protect the others in the house. I would have stayed huddled in the cover of the house with the others and flunked the test.

"Thanks, boss," Joan said, stepping on the deck.

Chris and Nancy, overhearing our conversation, came out the French doors, glass marbles crunching under their feet.

"Are you both all right?" Nancy embraced me.

She was shaking, glaring at the gun I was carrying.

"No problem," Brett replied. "How about you two? Chris, you okay?"

"Just a little shaky. First time I've ever been shot at." He looked a little pale.

"First time is always the hardest," Brett said. "It takes a while to get it out of your mind."

"I saw the red dot on my leg and that's all I can think of now. I'm going to have nightmares about red dots. "

"It's okay to be scared," Brett said. "People who don't get scared are dangerous. Fear needs to be titrated, not ignored. "

"Then I guess I'm not dangerous, because I'm definitely scared."

While the rest of us talked, Nancy started to walk back into the house.

Her shaking grew.

Her gait became wobbly.

Suddenly, she slipped on pellets of safety glass. She dropped to the deck and landed hard on her butt, and began to cry softly.

Picking up a small handful of glass marbles, she let them cascade through her fingers.

"It's broken," she whispered hoarsely.

I sat down next to her on the deck, and held her. I knew better than to speak. Finally her sobbing subsided, and we stood up together.

Inside Brett got on the phone, reported to the chief, and then went outside to call off the patrol unit that responded to my neighbors' calls. I could deal with them later.

I held Nancy. She finally stopped shaking.

Brett came back inside. "I should have seen this coming. I wasn't ready tonight. This guy's incredibly lucky and I screwed up. I'm sorry."

"How did he locate us here?" I asked.

"He must have staked out the accounting firm this morning, followed us to your office, waited, and followed you home."

"Good guess," Joan agreed.

"He's been way ahead of us," I said. "Way ahead. I didn't see anyone following me."

"I can't believe this guy," Joan said. "He thinks he's so good that he can just shoot Chris in the leg to let us know what a goddamned pro he is. He pisses me off."

"He can't be that good. He missed," Chris said.

Missed? I looked at Brett, Brett looked at Joan, and Joan looked at me.

"Wait a minute, you three. What's going on here?" Nancy said.

Joan answered, "The shooter, who has to be our birdwatcher, lit up Chris's leg after he lit up his chest. For some reason, he changed his mind. He chose not to try to kill him — just to wound him."

Nancy asked "He was going to shoot Chris in the leg?"

"Yes," Brett said.

Silent for a minute, we absorbed the shooter's intention.

Chris broke the silence, "Why would he do that? I get it that he thinks I can identify him and place him out at the Tahquitz, but why is he playing with me? What's that all about? Doc, you called him a tiger. Tigers play with their prey, don't they?"

"Yes, tigers do. All cats do," I said. "I don't know why he's toying with us. Chris, you might be able to place the shooter near the crime scene. Wanting you dead makes sense, but this playing with you just doesn't add up." Then I remembered something. "All sociopaths are social failures. Being a hit man means being a loser. Being the best hit man would compensate, in part, for his failure as a human being. That would leave him with needing enough people know how good he is. That's where we come in."

"That's good, Doc," Joan said. "I can see all that based on him leaving the gun. But changing his aim? I'm not sure that works for me."

Something was still stuck somewhere. My theory didn't quite cut it. I looked at Brett.

"Doesn't quite cover it," he said.

"I know. There's something we're missing," I said.

"It'll come," Brett said.

"He's really good. You got that part right," Joan added. She studied me. "Doc, you really want to know what makes him tick, don't you?"

I nodded.

"I don't give a shit. I just want to bag him," Brett said.

Then it hit me in the head. "He's after Chris, all right, but for some reason — I can't see all of it yet — it's personal for him. There's no other explanation for him toying with us. It's a message. He's after Chris and one of us. He recognizes one of us."

"I buy that," Brett said, excitement in his voice.

"Me too." Joan said.

"It's not just about Chris anymore," Brett said

"Chris's got company," I said.

"I'm the most likely candidate," Brett said, the excitement in his voice turning to a measured deliberation.

"He could have three agendas — the contract, showing off, and something personal," I said.

"Showing off? Like the shooter thinks that being a hit man is all he is?" Chris asked. "Like if I thought being a musician was all I am?"

"Yes," I said.

"If this is all he has, then he has to have someone to prove he's the best to," Joan said.

"Like my band needs an audience," Chris said.

"Exactly, we're his audience," I said.

"Like I know about wanting a bigger audience," Chris said.

"Yeah, but your audience are fans," Brett said.

"This shooter's audience is his victims," Joan said.

HUNT BEGINS

Bocca sat on the downslope side of the clearing, looking through the optics he carried in his MacPac, his favorite backpack. He leaned against a giant boulder in front of him. It formed a perfect blind. With an unobstructed view of the shrink's deck, all he had to do was drop his head for the boulder to shield him. He had years of practice crawling to within a hundred yards of a target and staying concealed for hours. Hunters have used blinds to hide themselves from a target since before history began. Somewhere along the line, humans became targets for a fee.

Bocca followed the shrink home from his office about an hour ago. It took him half an hour to park the car where he could get to it quickly and walk up to the clearing using an old fire road. His plan was to see who came and went at the shrink's house.

His present position was two hundred yards from the back of the shrink's house. At one point, while the shrink was bringing wine bottles out to the deck, he had actually looked up at Bocca's position. Had he sensed him? Simply dropping a few inches behind the boulder, Bocca was invisible. There was a coyote looking for food a hundred yards below him, and the shrink had probably been watching the animal.

Study the target. God, gotta love the feeling. Stalking the target. Planning and implementation. Hunting's better than sex. Sometimes sex leaves you feeling disconnected and tight. Hunting always leaves you feeling whole, connected, and powerful. Take what you can get away with.

Most people avoided this world like the plague. They wanted nothing to do with the heat, cold, dirt, sweat, animals and killing. They wanted butchers, cops and soldiers to deal with it so they could be safe in their cocoons. By default, Bocca took whatever he wanted and worked for people who took whatever they wanted. He knew that the buyer who hired him needed to win at any cost, just like him.

Simpatico. Way the damn world works. Not an outlaw world yet but getting there — still a few freaking heroes out there to contend with. Survival of the fittest. Strength rules. Nothing new here. In synch, 'cept for the nightmare.

GUN PLAY

Sometimes Bocca wondered about seeing a shrink to help him with his nightmare. Shrinks were supposed to be like doctors and medics. They're all non-combatants and pacifists, and supposed to support soldiers like him. The Army is trying to change them to soldier-medics. "Shoot and suture" is supposed to replace unarmed "docs." In Bocca's mind this will never happen. Medics and shrinks may carry a gun but they'll never be able to use it; they're not made of the same stuff.

Once a medic had treated a superficial wound for him and he had appreciated his help at the time. The shrink that kept him out of Special Forces wasn't anything like that medic. He hated the Special Forces shrink and couldn't ask for help with the nightmare because of him.

Targets. Whole flock of targets. Probably the shrink's wife, lady cop, black cop and the kid. Christ. Sometimes you lie in a blind all day and get nothing; sometimes you get the whole herd. Kid showing up is good luck.

Bocca watched them as they drank wine and ate hors d'oeuvres. Then the kid went inside the house for a while. They drank, ate and talked as Bocca lay perfectly secreted and silent. He had carried the Nine up to the blind in his pack by mistake. The idea hit him.

Pop the kid. Make up for this morning's stand-down. Shoot the kid. Just get it over with. Eliminate him. No worrying that way. Excellent. Crawl to within a hundred yards of the deck. Slow. Easy. Don't get spotted. Easy.

They looked like actors on a stage, completely back lit by the porch light and the lights from the house. They were talking but he couldn't quite make out their words. It was just like a silent play; he liked plays. The director had total power over the actors and the audience; Bocca imagined that he was the director and they were his actors.

Rest the Nine on a rock. Light up the kid's center mass. Start the squeeze. Trigger's got a ten-pound pull. Seven...eight... nine. Damn, the kid moved. Reacquire the target.

Red light.

Know the black cop from the Army. Where?

Green light. Reacquire the target. Put the red dot on the kid's chest.

Red light.

Know the black cop. May need the kid to figure out who the black cop is. Not enough intel, yet. Wait to see if the kid is useful. Pull down. Just wound him. Shake them all up. Put the red dot on the kid's thigh. Wound him. Play with them.

Green light. Go.

Michael Thompkins

Bocca did something he had never done before: he let the whole situation get really personal. Recognizing the black cop fired something deep; something he didn't really understand. Some strange force grabbed him.

Bocca squeezed the trigger at the same second the patio light failed. Without the light, a dark curtain fell across his eyes. For a fraction of a second he was blind, and his shot went high into the French doors. He missed — an improbable thing in itself. The cop had shot out the light; Bocca was up against another professional this time. He was up against really good competition this time. Someone he knew from somewhere.

Cop screwed up the shot. Spotted the laser. Shot out the light.

Now, go! Back to the clearing.

Cop and the shrink in front of a streetlight moving straight up the mountain. Safe to run to the car.

Shrink sensed him.

Cop's fast.

Who the hell is he?

The hunt begins.

PANNING THE UNCONSCIOUS

"Tick." The little wand in a box clicked every time it moved to the right or the left.

"Listen to the metronome and focus on the sound of my voice," I instructed Chris.

I started Chris's hypnotic induction complete with an audience. Brett, Joan, Chris, and I were all crowded into my office the morning after the attack at my house. Brett and Joan were seated on my office couch, and Chris was relaxed in my leather chair. Getting to work on a possible ID for our shooter seemed the best response to the events of the night before.

My office window opened on the backside of downtown, which rapidly ran out of space where the Desert Museum abutted the base of Mt. San Jacinto. It got steep quickly at the Museum, and this boundary helped create a relaxing and focusing effect.

"You're going to feel drowsy, and your body will feel heavy like you're falling asleep." I continued Chris's induction, being careful to stay awake myself.

No coffee yet, but I could smell Starbucks through the partially open window.

I instructed Brett and Joan to remain quiet, and reminded them that anything Chris said that didn't relate specifically to the investigation was confidential.

Most people think hypnosis is like voodoo but it's more like daydreaming. Freud, currently maligned for misogynous mistakes, was the first to prove that we all have an unconscious mind. Daydreams, night dreams, and meditation all access the unconscious, but hypnosis provides the psychologist the simplest, most effective route to the deepest part of our mind. Sure we know where the brain is but the mind's still a mystery— doesn't stop us from practicing, though. Psychology's bible, the Diagnostic and Statistical Manual, is thicker than a phone book — a guide to something invisible and unknown.

"Listen to the metronome. I'm going to count to ten backwards. When I reach three, you'll be in a trance. Your body will feel heavy and your eyes will be closed.

Michael Thompkins

You'll still hear the sound of my voice, and be able answer my questions. Brett and Joan are here in the room." I monitored Chris for signs that he was accepting the induction.

"Ten, nine, eight, seven, six, five… your eyes are closing. Your body's heavy …four, three…." I glanced over to make sure I had one subject not two or three. Sometimes, observers can be inadvertently induced along with the subject — usually the ones who swear they can't be hypnotized.

"What's your name and where are you from?"

"Chris Parks, I'm from Spokane." I knew he was safely entranced by the slow, sleepy tone of his voice.

"Chris, what do you like to do the most?"

"I like to write and play my music, travel, and learn about new places."

"What's your favorite music?" I was trying to establish an easy conversational tone to my questions. Chris's street slang was missing; his speech was well enunciated and grammatically correct.

"My absolute favorite is grunge music. I love Nirvana. I like sixties music too, especially John Lennon songs. My band plays alternative."

"How long have you been into music?"

"Since I was a little kid. My parents wanted me to be a classical musician; my dad made me take lessons."

"When did you decide to stop the lessons?" I wasn't trying to get anywhere yet; I just wanted to establish a rhythm with my questions and his answers.

"When I got into grunge, my dad said he wouldn't have any part of my music lessons anymore. I was only supposed to play 'clean' music. Nirvana was the work of the devil, according to him."

"How long did you live in Spokane before you moved here to Palm Springs?" I asked, thinking I had picked a safe and innocuous subject.

"I lived in Spokane for too long. All my childhood, until…"

"Until what?" I prompted him blindly.

"Until I left home the week after graduation." Chris's body stiffened and he winced.

"Why so quickly and without plans?" Didn't make any sense. Most kids don't leave so quickly.

No answer. Chris's right leg started slowly shaking.

I asked again. "Why so quickly after graduation?"

"I made my father stop hitting my mother."

His answer jammed everybody's breathing. I let it hang there for a full minute.
"Then what happened?" I prompted.
"I hit the road. I began the trip that brought me here to Palm Springs."
"How long had your father been hitting your mother before you left?" I didn't really want to pursue this subject and scrambled for a graceful way to move along.
"He hit her all through high school," Chris said. "He lost his job and drank. My mom was responsible, in his mind, for everything that went wrong with his life. Never should have married her according to him."
"He blamed her for his problems?" I asked.
"Only one thing worse than women for my father."
"Yes?"
"'Goddamn liberals.'"
"Did you like high school?" I tried to find a path back to the present.
"I liked my music and my friends. I had a 3.5 GPA."
"Where else have your travels taken you besides to Palm Springs?"
"I've traveled to England, France, Maui and then here," Chris said.
Move to the present.
"You've been living in an old warehouse just off the bike trail. Right?" I shifted to the investigation, and shelved my feelings about Chris's past. Get on with the purpose of the session — think like a cop, not a shrink.
"Yes, but I like it a lot better at Brett's place. I have my own shower and he treats me like family," he said.
Joan gave Brett an appreciative look.
"Chris, I want you to focus on the times you rode your bike from where you slept out on the bike trail into downtown Palm Springs. I want you to remember those times, and tell me if you saw a man with binoculars near Tahquitz Golf Course."
Brett and Joan leaned closer to make sure they heard Chris's answer.
"I saw a man with binoculars once. I saw him on the trail near where it turns to run along Highway 111 near the golf course."
"Describe him in detail."
"He was about Brett's height, built the same wiry way," he said. "White, not black like Brett. The binoculars were around his neck. He was harder and meaner-looking than Brett. His mouth was really ugly. He was wearing a golf cap."
"Color of his hair?"

"Black."

"What did you think he was doing with the binoculars?"

"Watching birds," he said.

"What made you think he was bird-watching?" I asked.

"Well, he seemed at home in the brush, and there were birds around. I guess I just assumed he was watching the birds. I'm a birdwatcher, too. I especially like raptors, red-tailed hawks and bald eagles."

"Did he have any scars or other marks on him that you noticed?"

"I didn't see any. He looked like an athlete."

"What made you think he looked like an athlete?"

"He was real lean and had nothing but hardness about him like he was used to physical work. He was average looking but his mouth was mean, real mean." Chris didn't ponder his answers, recalling details with ease.

"Anything else that would distinguish him?"

He was silent for a minute. If someone walked in on us at this moment, they wouldn't be able to tell Chris was in a trance. They would assume he was napping.

He interrupted my thoughts; "He had a beard."

When he said, "beard," Brett and Joan exchanged frustrated looks.

"The birdwatcher had black hair and a black beard?"

"Yup."

"Think carefully now, was there anything else about the man with the binoculars that was unique? That could help us identify him?"

"He was dressed in khaki shorts and a polo shirt," he said.

"How old do you think he was?"

"Early forties. He might have been a little younger than Brett but I can't be certain."

"If you see this guy again will you recognize him?"

"Absolutely. He scares me, though. I don't want him to hurt my mother." Not everything reported from a trance state makes literal sense.

We were at the end of Chris's memory of the man with the beard and optics, so I looked at Brett for direction. He nodded, 'we're done.' I kept silent for a few minutes in case Chris added something spontaneously.

"Chris, I'm going to count backwards from five, and you're going to wake up. You will remember nothing from this and you will feel as relaxed as from a nice nap. Five, four, three, two, one…"

Chris opened his eyes and began stretching out like a cat awakening from an afternoon nap. He smiled at Brett, Joan, and then me.

Joan smiled at Chris reassuringly. Brett seemed a thousand miles away.

"Did it work?"

Oh yeah, it goddamned worked.

I just nodded reassuringly.

Hypnosis is a bit like panning for gold — the unconscious is the river, the questions are the sieve, and sometimes the gold hurts.

PARTNERS?

Joan and I walked over to Starbucks from my office. Brett had to run out to headquarters to sign something. Chris rode with him. They would meet us in ten minutes. Silence ruled following the session; Chris's induction needed a bit of digestion.

It was already seventy degrees and climbing into the Palm Springs desert furnace. Joan seemed to be warming herself up to share something with me. We sat at a table for four, protected from the sidewalk by a wrought iron fence. I waited for her to start. She was fidgeting, and for the first time I sensed the edge in her that Brett had mentioned.

A few doors down a produce truck pulled up in front of California Pizza Kitchen. The driver began to off-load crates of tomatoes and seasonal vegetables. An empty tour bus pulled up, parked on North Palm, and waited for the tourists that would soon arrive to buy tickets for the tour of the expensive, empty second homes of the Hollywood crowd, the owners likely working on movie sets somewhere.

More trucks began parking on North Palm Canyon for the Street Fair, the high point of Palm Springs' activities tonight and every Thursday night. In a few hours the refrigerated trucks would start arriving from the Bakersfield growers and the San Diego fishing boats. We'd be able to buy arts, crafts, strawberries from Mexico, scallops from San Diego and potatoes from Bakersfield. My favorites were the apricots from Modesto that wouldn't be in season for several months. By noon, North Palm Canyon would be closed to through traffic — pedestrians would prevail.

"Doc, I need your advice about Brett and me," Joan said. "Did he tell you about our 'drink'?"

"I know you guys both showed up at police seminar a while ago and ended up going out for a drink. Besides telling me that, he was vague."

"Vague. That's exactly what it was," she said, playing with her keys. "Now it's even more ambiguous because I work with him, and this case has us tied together pretty closely. I still have feelings for him; they never disappeared. Back then, I didn't read things right. I was a little lonely and I don't do this stuff well. In fact, I suck at it. I'm a perfectionist, and that doesn't work with dating. I have a hard time letting go. So I go warm then I go cold, and I send mixed messages. I'm better at running 26 miles than flirting. Now I wonder what he's feeling. Is he still interested in me? I don't know how to begin this stuff. I'm sorry to put you in the middle, but it would help if I knew."

"Christ, Joan, the whole romance thing is an asshole process for everyone except the folks who shouldn't be hooking up anyway," I said. "No real person survives the dating game without appearing a complete fool and baring his butt. And what man wouldn't be interested in you?"

"That's sweet," she said. "You're easier for me to read than him but you're taken. Give me some advice."

"How do you run 26.2 miles?"

"Never thought about it, Doc. You train..." she replied.

"And?"

"You train more," she said.

"And?"

"You train some more." Her face projected the tension. She continued fidgeting with her keys.

"Where's the point where you let go? In the run, right?"

She looked at me and slowly shook her head. "Exactly. I don't know how to let go."

Brett and Chris pulled up in the Mustang, and parked behind the tour bus. Brett got out of the driver's side of the car, and his eyes swept the street and the top of nearby buildings. He motioned Chris to get out of the car. Brett positioned himself close to Chris and scanned the rooftops with his eyes. As they walked across North Palm, Joan noticed them and came to full ready alert in less than a second. Her keys were silent; the questions about Brett were gone. She was on-duty.

"I'm not done," she said.

"I know. More later."

Brett and Chris were discussing music when they walked up. Chris had a just-showered sheen to his brown shoulder-length hair, and had trimmed his beard. Brett's eyes never settled in one place while they were talking; Chris was clearly covered.

"I totally like Smashing Pumpkins. They just got six Grammy nods. They sometimes sound like Metallica ... a lot of techno sound. I love 'Tonight, Tonight'."

"That's from 'Mellon Collie and the Infinite Sadness,' isn't it?" Brett asked.

"Dude, you really keep up on rock."

"I try," Brett said.

We went inside, stood in the coffee line, and ordered our drinks. When they were ready, we went back outside and found our table still vacant. Joan fussed and went back to fix her drink twice.

"You going to drink that or sell it?" Brett asked, sipping his watered-down.

"I like my things a certain way," she said.

Brett let that one ride.

"We need to talk about the case," Joan said.

"Chief wants to meet with us at noon at the airport fountain," Brett said.

"Why the fountain?" Joan asked.

"He wants this investigation done on back channels and on land lines."

"Why?" I asked.

"Our shooter is a tourist nightmare, and the city is a client of the victim's firm," Brett said. "He doesn't want this to hit the media, and wants to keep it from the Feds as long as he can."

Chris seemed to be humming a tune and oblivious to our discussion. I was wrong.

"Like, maybe it's none of my business, but do you two go out?" He quit his humming, and looked alternately at Brett then Joan.

"He's my boss," Joan protested.

"I told you I'm not your boss," Brett said, his face screwed tight.

"Wow, I didn't mean to get anybody hot," Chris apologized quickly.

"I think we're all a little uncertain of our roles here. I know I am until I've met with the chief." I tried to tone things down a little.

"Doc's right." Chris saw the escape hatch and changed the subject. "Brett's set me and the band up to audition for a gig."

"Where?" I asked, wondering if it was a good idea to expose Chris in public like that. What was Brett thinking?

"Brett set up a meeting this morning with Jay, one of the owners of the Saloon. He needs a band to do warm up. The Saloon showcases rock, country and some alternative rock."

"When's the audition?" I asked.

"This afternoon. If Jay likes us, we start soon. We're also playing in the parking lot next to the Saloon tonight. It's part of free music at the Street Fair. You guys all have to come."

"Sure," Brett answered for all of us.

GUN PLAY

"An audition this afternoon? Is the band ready?" I asked.

"Absolutely, we've been practicing for two months."

Chris looked at Brett's watch and stood up to leave. "I should boogie," he said.

"Jay is going to watch Chris until after the audition this afternoon," Brett explained. "He's ex-Marine and has a permit to carry because of the nightclub. Our shooter seems to prefer early morning and night so I think we're safe during the day. I've gone over the details with the chief and he gave me the okay to put Jay in the loop. If Jay needs to leave Chris, he'll call a uniform."

"Chris, let me walk you over to the Saloon," Joan said.

"Cool. Thanks."

Chris took a few steps away from us, and prepared to make his now signature, fall-away jump shot with his empty cup. The trash can hoop was eight feet away. I scanned for Armani suits.

"Here we go again," Brett warned.

This time Chris scored: the empty cup arched gracefully into the trash. There were two young women sitting near the trash so his risk-reward curve was better this time. He knew it, and got smiles.

"Joan, come back here, and we'll go out to Global," Brett said. "I called out there and the owner comes in at 5 a.m. I want to hear what she has to say about the note you found in the accountant's golf bag. Her name's Conto."

"Okay. Last night I did a little research on Global on the Net, and I'll fill you in on the way. Back in five," Joan said over her shoulder. She followed Chris closely.

Chris waved goodbye.

We watched them cross North Palm against the light as Joan motioned oncoming traffic to stop in a manner that identified her as plainclothes police with a single gesture — a palms-up-freeze-your-ass-until-I-release-it. When they were crossing the street, Joan stayed close to Chris, ready to put herself between Chris and any danger. I wondered if I was capable of that kind of courage. Would I be able to put my body between a shooter and an assignment? Sure, I could for Nancy and my kids, but for someone I had known for two days?

If they were being watched, the shooter would not have expected her move. I had a lot to learn. I agreed with Brett that there was little chance of a daytime attack; the shooter's escape strategies would be less effective in the daylight.

"Joan's a good cop," I said. "She moves well."

"T.I.C." Brett said.

"Say what?"

"Tits-in-command," he said.

It cracked me up. "Military? I don't remember that one."

"Naw, I made it up." He was smiling with pride.

"She does move well."

"Don't start on me," he said.

"Well, Chris, and anyone else who wants to, can notice that there's something between the two of you."

"Yeah, well, I don't know what the fuck to do about it," Brett said. Whenever he used the "f" word, the universal military modifier, he was talking close to the bone.

"I can't tell if she is interested or not," Brett frowned.

"Oh, she's interested. I can testify to that in court."

"Then, I don't get it," he said. "I'm her superior officer, but she knows we're just two detectives working this case. If she likes me then why does she call me Boss? Even as a joke, it just muddies the water."

"Well, for one thing, women in this situation try to please everybody else first and themselves last. You've seen it. Invite five men and a woman to a meeting that you're in charge of and show up late yourself after a flat tire. The woman has made the coffee and introduced everybody. Invite six guys without a woman, and there's no coffee and no one knows anyone. It's cultural training; it's not in the DNA. From the time they're little girls, they are bombarded with messages about pleasing men and other women. When Joan thinks about romantic involvement with you, she first wants to please you and represses the possible professional harm to herself. It comes out as 'boss.'"

"Jeez, Tom, how do you come up with this shit?" he asked. "I never think about that kind of stuff. I just thought she was riding me."

"It's not voluntarily thinking anymore than you had to think about shooting the porch light out. It's automatic for me after all these years. Sometimes it drives me crazy. Sometimes I don't care why people do what they do, and still my mind won't quit."

"I get it. I always sit so I can cover the door at a party," he said. "I can't shut the tactical thinking off. It drives me crazy too. We'll make a good team. With our skills we'll clear the entire homicide board pretty damn quickly."

"You're changing the subject." I didn't know how I felt about his newfound appreciation of my figuring-people-out skills. I was really only in this for Chris so far, and would deal with future investigations after this case was over.

"So. Let me change it again. Doctor, help me out with your psychological skills," he said.

"How come I had such a strong instinct to give Chris a place to stay then I find out that his father hit his mother just like mine did? Coincidence? Help me out here, I don't get it."

Brett had told me about his folks years ago in a couple of clipped sentences. "He hit her for years. I got big enough. I stopped it." We hadn't discussed it since. His mom divorced his dad after Brett left home.

"I don't know. Could be coincidence, could be synchronicity."

"Synchronicity?" Brett asked, shaking his head in confusion.

"The tendency for various aspects of the collective unconscious to manifest themselves in the events of peoples lives, including various attractions and repulsions, appearances and departures."

"I remember the word — something from psychology — but how does it explain me and Chris?" he asked.

"Well, synchronicity would suggest that your unconscious mind and Chris's unconscious minds are both connected to the great collective unconscious. Your both having had some experience with family violence would then connect you in a mysterious way."

"And who is responsible for this brilliant idea?" he asked.

"Carl Jung, one of Freud's students."

"Interesting idea," Brett said. "Star Trek-ish. It still could be just a coincidence though."

"Some coincidence."

"Don't you have dreams with this Jung fellow in them? You consult with him even though he's dead? " Brett shook his head slightly, as if to say, "nobody's weirder than a shrink."

I nodded. The daydreams and night dreams with Jung started twenty years ago after I left the military.

"Let's talk about the case," he changed the subject again.

"Yes, let's talk about working together. Tell me more about why you want me on active investigations?" I asked, wanting to be crystal clear with Brett before talking with the chief at the noon meeting.

Michael Thompkins

"I think you'll be great," he said. "You already consult with the department. The Chief likes you. We could even start you on California Peace Officer Training and put you out on the street for a year, but that would be a waste of your time and the department's money. What we really want is what you have already: insight into the human mind. I don't know where you come up with half the stuff you come up with, but most of it passes my 60/40 substance-to-bullshit-ratio test. Let's get one thing clear...."

"Yes?"

"It's not like you're the head and I'm the body, okay? Partners. Copy that?" he asked.

"Partners. Got it."

His mind was already made up. "Partners."

I was already deeply involved, and my rear deck and French doors were the visible evidence. "I don't want to be a cop. But working with you and helping you take bad guys off the street sounds attractive in some perverse way."

"We'll have to clear it with the chief but I already know what he wants," he said.

"What about Joan?"

"You, I know I can put up with. We'll see about Joan," he said.

"You'd like to see about Joan?"

"We'll see. It's way too complicated while we're working together. You'll have to talk to Nancy about all this."

"Already did. We talked all night. We didn't get any sleep. We're just going to have to survive this case and see what happens after that. Knowing our shooter is out there, and that he knows where I work and live, shatters both of our carefully constructed lifestyles. But there's something in it for me. What's in it for Nancy? You know that one of Nancy's medical school friends was killed by her boyfriend. Every time she sees a gun, she relives that. She was open enough about her own feelings last night. She said she already knew what I was going to do and why. It was my decision, she'd try to live with it, but she reserved the right to lose it again. Also, she loved you too much to deny you my help."

"Some sister," he said.

"She was right about me deciding already. When you put the gun in my hand and we went chasing off up the hill, I knew. I won't sit by and let Chris get killed. Don't know how much help I'll be, though."

"We'll get you a permit to carry," he said.

"I think Nancy was referring to my helping with my brains."

"You need the gun to protect your brains."

"Without being a real cop?" I could imagine carrying a handgun, but not going to cop school in my forties.

"There's plenty of precedent for it. Crime scene techies and private investigators carry. You'll have to do the background check like everybody else. Christ, Tom, everybody has a handgun these days. Some states don't even require a permit. I'm not saying I like that. If I had my way, everybody with a handgun permit would go through a psych eval and I'm a conservative."

"I haven't spent any time with a handgun in a while. We've pretty much stuck to rifles."

"We can go out to the police range and get you up to speed. Remember the rule for handguns. Put three rounds to center mass. Forget about wounding or disarming anyone. There's only one reason to fire on someone, and that is to take them down."

"What happens if I screw up and shoot someone when I shouldn't have?"

"They'll go easier on you than they would on me because you're just a civilian and all you have to do is act like a 'prudent man' according to the law," he said. "They'll crucify the department, but we're used to that. We'll talk to the chief about a gun permit this afternoon and get his blessing on your help with the investigation. I think he's been planning this all along. We need to know what makes this shooter tick. I've been racking my brain, trying to remember somebody that might have this kind of grudge against me. I need you to help me figure this guy out fast and I won't have you unarmed."

"I want to keep Chris alive, and I want to stay alive too. I'm in for Chris, but the rest isn't in focus yet." It scared me. "When I get stuck in the doorway, do me a favor?"

"Okay?"

"Push me out and pull the ripcord."

"I've done that a few times," he said.

"I'll bet you have."

CORRUPTION IN THE COACHELLA

When Joan returned, we rode together the twelve miles out to Palm Desert in Brett's car with me curled up in the back seat. Again.

"All right, give us the Idiot's Guide to Energy Trading," Brett said. "I need to understand what I'm seeing when I get there."

"Me, too. I don't understand any of this," I said. "When did you research this, the middle of the night?"

"I had a little trouble sleeping after the shooting. I figured we needed to understand Global."

She took out her notes and started explaining that Global trades in electricity and natural gas markets. The two apparently go together because gas is sometimes used to generate the electricity. California, with an economy bigger than France's, is the largest market in the United States for both. Using oil or nuclear energy to produce electricity is dirtier and more dangerous so they're out of the picture for now. Almost all the natural gas in Southern California comes from West Texas via two parallel pipelines that cross New Mexico and Arizona and enter California at Barstow. At Barstow, the lines start to split up. Some go to Northern California by way of the Central Valley; the balance comes to us, and then over the Grapevine into L.A. The rest of the natural gas comes from Canada.

Joan went on that it was pretty much the same deal for electricity. Monster 500 megavolt lines come from Hoover Dam through Las Vegas and also enter California near Barstow. From the north, monster lines bring electricity from Canada, Washington and Oregon. In the business, Canada, Washington, Oregon and West Texas are referred to as "supply" and the California Southland is called "the great big sucking sound."

She finished the research. Global Energy Trading has been in business for two years. They resell electricity from their suppliers to Edison, the City of Palm Springs and smaller outfits like Imperial Valley Golf. Electricity can only be stored for a day or two at the most, so some of the deals made today are for power that is going to be used next week or later. They call this 'trading in futures.' Martin Jonas's firm has been their accountants since the beginning.

"Wow. You're all over this stuff," Brett exclaimed.

"Hey, I'm not just another pretty face," Joan said, pretending to pout.

"You're a pretty face, all right. Seriously, I'm impressed," I said.

"Me, too. I appreciate your doing the homework," Brett was quick to add.

"Thanks, guys. I love to be apppreciated for my mind."

We drove by the Palm Desert Historical Society on our way into town. They had their work cut out for them. Palm Desert was an infant city and the Historical Society had its home in the city's first fire station, circa 1952. History began in Palm Desert around the year I was born — neither of us qualified as old yet in my mind.

We turned onto El Paseo, parked in a lot near the intersection of Monterey, and walked several blocks up a side street to Global Energy Traders. In front of the building, an ugly big box-like faded-bronze statue complete with conduits and a tower pretended to be the power transformer of the future. We climbed the steps to an enormous glass doorway. Just inside, a security guard met us.

"Hi, Doc, how are you?" The guard acknowledged Joan and Brett with a nod.

How'd he know me? It took me at least ten seconds of search through my mental RAM to locate the file in which the guard's name was located. Patient? Finally, I grabbed it. "Jason, it's been awhile. I'm doing well, how about you?"

I remember the circumstances that brought Jason to me with a consulting request from a family court and his family doc. At the time, Jason had had adolescent adjustment disorder stemming from his parents' divorce. He had suffered from anxiety, insomnia and poor grades. I had badly wanted to help him; kids and cops both got to me. Jason's parents were divorcing and arguing over his custody.

"Things are a lot better than when I last saw you, Doc," Jason continued, grinning.

"Fantastic. Jason, this is Lieutenant Wade and Detective Fleming. Guys, this is Jason White, an old friend."

"Are you working for the cops, now, Doc?" Jason said, with a look of surprise on his face.

"I'm thinking about it," I said.

"Cool. I meant to call you back then to thank you for helping me, but I just never got around to it. You helped me, you know. I did pretty well in high school and now I'm taking criminal science at the College of the Desert, and doing security work here and at the Desert Museum."

Michael Thompkins

I remembered the circumstances surrounding the few brief sessions we completed over six years ago, and how much I had liked Jason. My therapeutic strategy was to get him focused on academics as a way to a future, as well as a way of separating from his parents and their anger at each other. I guess I'd been successful.

"Yeah, I got two more years of college and then I'm going try to get on the Palm Springs P.D." He was eager to update me with his life.

"You want to sign up for long hours, poor pay, and the public expectation that cops do everything perfect?" Brett asked him.

"Yes sir, I do. I know that being a cop has a downside but I'm still interested."

"Jason, don't let the lieutenant scare you off. He likes being a police officer in spite of the hassles." Joan gave Brett a dirty look.

"Come and see me when you're a senior and I'll see what I can do to help," Brett finally offered. "We're here to see Ms. Conto. She indicated the security guard would meet us. I guess that would be you, huh?"

"Affirmative, Lieutenant. Ms. Conto briefed me earlier this morning. Follow me," Jason said, leading us into an interior courtyard open to the sky.

The offices were laid out on two floors around the walls of the courtyard. In the middle was another enormous sculpture that looked like a Chihuly, one of those futuristic and very expensive glass pieces by a Northwest artist that always caught Nancy's eye. Everything was opulent and overstated for clients. The air smelled like freshly minted money.

The building directory was also made out of glass and tilted on a big pedestal so that it was easy to read. Each Global Energy listing had a little glowing electric utility pole next to it. Global took up the whole second floor.

Jason led the way to an escalator that took us up to the second floor. A dozen or so pretty pricey-looking Southwestern oil originals hung on the lower level walls. When we reached the top, we turned a corner and went to the front-corner office, the one that would own the best view.

"Here we are." Jason opened the door to Conto's office. "Ms. Conto will be here momentarily. She instructed me to make you comfortable and to tell you that Mr. Bergman will be joining her at your meeting. They're finishing some work in another area. Would any of you like a drink? I can make drip coffee here or I can have espresso delivered from El Paseo."

"No, thanks," Joan said.

Brett shook his head no.

"Not for me, Jason," I replied.

"Well, I'll get back to my work. Ms. Conto said to have seats and enjoy the view."

"Take care of yourself, Jason. It's great to see you doing so well. Call my office sometime and we'll meet for coffee. We can catch up." I shook his hand.

"I'll do that, Doc. I will definitely call you."

"Call me when you're ready to get on the job," Brett added.

"Thanks Lieutenant. I will," Jason said with a grin, closing the door behind him.

"Bergman's here? This gets better every minute," Joan said.

"It could just be coincidence. He does work for them," I wondered out loud.

Conto's windows were wide, with spectacular views to the west of Mt. San Jacinto and Palm Springs, to the south of the Santa Rosa mountains, and to the north of Rancho Mirage, Cathedral City, and the other cities of the Coachella Valley. Palm Springs was surrounded on two sides, east and west, by wilderness.

Without warning, the door opened, and Bergman and Conto walked into the room.

"Good morning, Officers, what can I do for you?" Conto asked. "Peter tells me that you've already met him. He also advised me that you are interested in my company because I'm a client of his firm and somehow, you mistakenly think we need to be included in the investigation of Martin Jonas's death."

Conto wasn't happy with our presence — murder being when even the rich get to meet the law.

"We'll decide where the mistakes are, Ms. Conto," Joan said, stepping up quickly to engage Conto and show her shield.

"I'm well aware that there are questions surrounding Mr. Jonas's death," Conto said. " I just don't like to think about the murder of someone I know professionally or personally. It just doesn't happen in my world." Conto chose words carefully. She was more closely held than Bergman was; the psych eval on her would definitely take longer.

Joan laid down the law. "We're here to conduct a murder investigation, and you asked what you could do for us. Provide us with full access to your firm and your dealings with Mr. Bergman's. We can go to court and accomplish the same result. Perhaps, you would prefer a court order?"

"Please," Conto said holding her hand up. "You will have my full cooperation without any court order. It is just so unsettling to be involved in a police investigation."

Michael Thompkins

    Up to this point, we hadn't heard a word out of Bergman. . In the few minutes since his entrance, he hadn't said a damn thing. For a guy like him, that had to mean something. His conceit was like a rock on a roof — sooner or later, it was going to roll down on you.

    "Hey people, there's no need to be heavy handed with Ms. Conto," he said. "Let's all get off to a good start. Ms. Conto, what do you say to a tour of the trading floor for the officers and the doctor? They might find something interesting. Give them some insight into how benign your business is and how it couldn't possibly be connected to Martin's murder."

    Bergman said "Ms. Conto" like he wasn't used to using the formality. He pronounced the word murder like it was a $200 shirt purchased at a store on El Paseo that he took home and discovered was defective. He lived at "'have more" height, and looked down at the rest of us from there — one of the retarded rich, missing the gene of 'noblesse oblige'.

    We were on our feet and off to the trading room on Conto's heels. The trading floor was twenty by fifty feet with three elliptically shaped walnut desks arranged symmetrically. One wall had several picture windows, and the entrance wall had a built-in six-foot-high by ten-foot-wide illuminated electronic display showing a contour map of the western United States. There were close to twenty traders and support staff in the room. The volume of conversation made it almost impossible to hear each other. Everyone in the room glanced our way, recognized a tour, flashed busy-little-beaver smiles, and went back to ignoring us.

    I took a closer look at the wall display map and recognized exactly what Joan had so accurately reported earlier. The big display covered gas and electricity in the entire western United States but only the lines dealing with California were illuminated. The remainder of the West Coast's web was marked out but not lit-up.

    Conto and Bergman stood quietly like good tour guides and gave us time to let the trading room sink in. A thick carpet cushioned the floor, dark teak paneled the walls, and three enormous desks were strategically positioned to provide perches for three large monitors at each desk displaying Reuters, Bloomburg and Telerate trading media. Everyone in the room was wearing a star-set, the latest handless telephone headsets.

    She began the audio portion of our tour. "Welcome to our trading room; every trading day we buy and sell natural gas and electricity. We start early at 5 a.m. because of time zone differences. 5:00 a.m. here is 8:00 a.m. in New York. Normally, there are from eight to fifteen people in this room performing various tasks."

GUN PLAY

I could barely make out what she was saying over the din of dollars being made.

"Global Energy Traders is one of the real success stories in our valley," Bergman chimed in.

"Who do you buy from and sell to?" I asked.

"Well, we buy natural gas mostly from Texas and some from up north in Canada. We buy electricity mostly from independents in Nevada and from the Hoover dam grid, and again, some from up north. Our big buyers are primarily Southern California Edison and Southern California Gas. We also have smaller independent buyers like our own Imperial Valley Golf Association, the Coachella Valley cities, and of course, the Indians."

"I thought all this was handled by government agencies." I said.

"Most people think that because until last year it was. Deregulation allowed power to be sold without state-controlled prices. The end-user will profit with lower rates."

I thought to myself, *lower rates*?

Brett repressed a smirk. "How do you buy and sell electricity?" he asked. "I mean natural gas can be measured by volume so I can visualize that being stored. I don't understand how electricity is stored."

"That's a good question, Lieutenant. Electricity can't be stored for very long because it degrades over distance. That's why you see booster transformers on residential power lines. Electricity can be stored for only a day or so, but it can be measured discretely as it moves around on the big transmission lines. That's where we come in. Users like Edison can't always predict how much power they will need everyday. We get a cool overcast day in the valley during the summer and air conditioning gets turned down a bit. Edison thinks it needs to buy only so much power. Then, surprise, the sun comes out or we have two thousand more tourists in the valley than expected; suddenly Edison needs more. We provide the original power and the extra power. We also sell contracts to deliver power for periods of time at the lowest possible rate."

"So why do you need an accounting firm like Mr. Bergman's?" Brett asked. "What was your relationship with the victim?"

The "victim" attracted the attention of everyone in the room. They all looked at us.

Conto motioned us to step back out into the hallway so she could keep the new topic of conversation from the employees — Brett turned the tour tougher for her.

"Our quarterly and annual reports are prepared by Mr. Bergman's firm because the law requires they be done by independent C.P.A's. They also do our taxes." She pronounced "taxes" in Southland fashion, as if they were something smelly on your shoe.

"Can you imagine any reason for Mr. Bergman's boss to have been murdered?" Joan confronted Conto. So much for the tour... back to work.

"Peter and I have been discussing this and neither of us can see how Global could be connected in any way to the person who did this awful thing."

"Ms. Conto, I found a note in Martin Jonas's golf bag," Joan said. "It read 'Global, Palo Verde; Imperial Valley Golf/Palm Springs; 2/13, 2:32pm.' Do you know what that note might mean?"

"I have absolutely no idea," Conto responded very carefully. "Global could mean our firm and Palo Verde is an electrical interchange in Arizona. You know already that Imperial Valley Golf and Palm Springs are clients of ours. I suppose that Martin might have written himself a note to check on something."

"Do you have any idea what the date and time might mean?" Joan continued.

"That is totally confusing to me. I don't see how that could refer to anything," Conto said.

The interview wasn't getting us anywhere.

Joan gave it up but not without a penetrating stare at Conto. "Thank you for the tour, Ms. Conto. We will call you when we need to come back. Good day, Mr. Bergman." She abruptly drew the interview to a halt.

"You'll need to return?" Conto asked.

"I'd love to come back and look at your maps some more," Joan said, smiling with sarcasm.

While heading down the escalator, Brett echoed in a barely audible voice, "Love to come back and look at your maps?"

Joan smiled. "She was lying about the note."

"Maybe," Brett said. "But weren't you the one who told us maybe it wasn't a good idea to let Bergman know we didn't like him? Good for the goose, good for the gander, eh?"

"All right. You got me on that one but I just don't like her. What do you think, Doc?" She asked.

"Maybe she was telling the truth about the note," I said. "Maybe not. I don't have a read on her yet."

Joan frowned. "Do you two like her?"

"What's not to like? Looks. Money." Brett said, pushing Joan's buttons. "Okay, let's go talk to the City of Palm Springs financial officer next," he suggested as we walked the couple of blocks and piled back into the Mustang.

"Is he in?" I wondered out loud.

"If he is, good. If he isn't, we help ourselves," Joan replied.

"Then we meet the chief?" I asked.

"Yup. What happened to your patients today?" Brett asked.

"Cancelled them," I replied.

"Hope they survive," Brett said.

"I hope I survive," I said, remembering the shattered door at my house.

"Conto's definitely pretty cool and calculated, but she was lying about the note," Joan brought it up again.

"You really didn't like her," Brett said.

"And, you did?" Joan said.

"Like I said, she's good looking and rich; what more could a man ask for?" Brett asked. "Besides, I still like Bergman for hiring the hit man. Conto could be dirty in some way though; plenty of dirt to go around."

"Sand," I corrected.

"What?" Brett asked.

"Sand. We're in a desert. Plenty of sand to go around," I repeated.

They smiled patiently at me.

"Bergman's dirty. I can feel it," Brett said.

"That bitch too. I'm feeling that," Joan said.

"Settle down, you two," I said.

A second patient set of smiles.

"The thing I noticed is that Bergman behaved entirely different than when we saw him at Starbucks and at his own office. There may be something between those two," I said.

"Conto and Bergman?" Brett asked.

"Yeah, I just got a hunch about them," I answered. "Something about the way he called her Ms. Conto. He's used to calling her something else."

"She called him Peter. You think he's screwing her?" Brett asked.

I shrugged.

"I like it. Bergman's boffing his biggest client and covering up her dirty doings," Brett said, eager to put Bergman in a cell. "His boss catches him so he has his boss whacked. I really like it; that Armani bastard sucks."

Michael Thompkins

"So, you don't like Bergman and that makes him guilty of contracting Martin Jonas's murder? I know I'm the new doc on the block, but don't you guys need evidence or something like that?"

They both ignored me as we pulled out into traffic. Joan played some music on the way that I didn't recognize.

"Who?" I asked.

"Smashing Pumpkins: heavy metal meets techno," Brett answered.

I remembered Smashing Pumpkins was one of the alternative groups Chris mentioned the other night, and I had listened to them at home. The music was a body rush but I still had trouble understanding the lyrics.

"The world is vampire, sent to drain, secret destroyers hold you up to the flames," Joan, knowing the lyrics, sang along with a sweet voice. "Despite all my rage I am still a rat in a cage, now I am naked, nothing but an animal."

The song finished. "'Bullet with Butterfly Wings,'" she announced the title.

"Bullets don't come with 'butterfly wings,'" I said, remembering last night.

"Come with goddamn red dots," Brett said.

ENTERTAIN THE CHIEF

We pulled into the City Hall parking lot and located the offices of the city's chief financial officer, Kirk Belgrade. He was in, no surprise to Brett. What didn't he know about Palm Springs?

"Afternoon, Officers," Belgrade said. "The mayor and the chief both called me and told me to give you anything that you might need. I'm at your service." He was a shade too eager.

A thin man of medium build, about my age, with furrowed brow and stiff bent shoulders, he looked like he could be scared to death by a "boo." His office, civil servant Spartan, was located at other end of the accounting world from Global. It smelled of printer ink, copy machine fluid and sweated-into-polyester. The sounds of airplanes taking off slipped in through partially open windows.

"What's the city's involvement with Martin Jonas's firm?" Joan asked, getting directly to the point.

She and Brett were developing a killer interrogation technique. Joan took point. Brett pretended she was his bodyguard or something, and hid his lethal ability — it was Broadway to watch.

"Martin Jonas's firm provides the city with oversight accounting, consulting, quarter-end and year-end reports. This is all a matter of public record and disclosure." Belgrade was all business. "We have some perfectly awful office coffee if you would like."

"We're coffee-ed out, but thanks," Joan said. "We'll need to bring a couple of techs down here to go over the city's relationship with Jonas and Associates during the last two years. Can you assign one of your people to assist them? It shouldn't take more than an afternoon initially."

"Certainly. What are you looking for?" Belgrade asked.

"A motive for Martin Jonas's murder," she replied.

"I assure you that you're not going to find that here, Officer."

"Nonetheless, we'll need to look," she insisted.

"I'll comply fully as the mayor has instructed me."

"Whom do you deal with at the accounting firm?" she asked.

"Mr. Bergman and his assistants."

"What do you think of him?"

"Off the record?" Belgrade said.

"Sure, if you want," she said.

"Well, he's a good accountant," he explained. "I always get what I need for assistance, but he's too rich for my blood, with my city salary and all. Those really expensive clothes and fast cars are out of my league. It's hard for my people to relate to him."

Joan nodded and changed the subject. "Exactly what did the mayor say when he told you to cooperate with this investigation?"

"'Give them whatever they want.'"

"He didn't suggest that you keep anything from us?" Joan asked.

"I don't know what you mean, Officer," Belgrade said, hesitatingly.

Joan didn't lean on him even though she must have seen the little bead of sweat forming on his upper lip.

"Never mind, we'll get to that later," Joan finished. "Thank you for your help. We'll be back."

Belgrade's stiff posture uncranked a notch as we left.

Outside the city offices, Brett motioned for us to follow him across the street to Fountain Plaza. We sat down on the concrete wall that circled the fountain facing the city hall and police headquarters. It was twenty yards in diameter and the cascading water was a pleasant white- sound break from jet engines, car horns and engine noise. The fountain had been built in 1968 with a single rock transported from central Mexico. It was a perfect place to meet if you didn't want to be overheard. A plane took off, and I could barely hear when Brett started talking to the chief on his cell phone.

"Chief, we're all here. Copy that." Brett pushed the kill switch and said to us, "Five minutes."

"What'd you think of Belgrade?" Joan asked.

"Hiding something," Brett replied.

"He did seem scared," I added.

"Wonder what of?" Brett mused.

"We'll find out," Joan said as if nothing would ever elude her investigative scalpel for long. "I want to check with the chief before I lean on him."

"Wouldn't want to try and keep a secret from you," Brett said.

"You wouldn't stand a chance, Lieutenant," Joan smiled at him.

"Not a chance," Brett said. Deadpan.

"There's something else I've been wondering about." Joan changed the direction of her comments at the same time a 727 changed its flight path to avoid Mt. San Jacinto.

"What's that?" Brett asked.

"Shouldn't one of us sit down with Chris? Tell him what he told us about his father and mother during hypnosis?"

"At the right time," I said.

"I'm not sure it's our business," Brett said.

"Let me get this straight, Mr. Take-in-the-Homeless and Doctor Cop. We're trying to keep Chris alive and neither one of you knows if hearing him report that his father hit his mother is any of our business." She, questioning Brett and me in the same way women have been shaking men out of trees about relationships since civilization began. We, falling from the trees, and instinctively hiding in our caves.

"I'll talk with him," Brett said reluctantly.

"I'll leave it alone unless Chris brings it up," I said. "I don't want to be the meddling shrink; better it comes from Brett."

They both looked at me with surprise.

"Some help from a shrink," Brett said.

Across the street, I saw the chief step out the back door of headquarters and cross the small parking lot next to the Police Boxing League building. He passed in front of the Riverside County Courthouse, and crossed the street towards us. A man of medium build and complexion, he had a farm-raised quality to his carriage; hard work didn't look like it would scare him. I'd had many dealings with the chief. I liked him.

"Chief." Brett stood up when the chief arrived.

"Lieutenant, Detective, Doc." The chief greeted us and got started quickly. "First order of business is each of you report directly to me on this case using back channels. I don't want to read anything about this in the paper unless I personally put it there. Until we clear the city of any possible involvement, I promised the mayor to keep this investigation out of the papers."

"Second order. Doc, I will have the paperwork processed for you to be consulting on this investigation and to carry a concealed weapon. Lieutenant Wade will be your liaison.

Michael Thompkins

"Third. Lieutenant, it'll be your black ass if the Doc gets hurt."

It was one of those moments when a white man jokes to an Afro-American about color and pulls it off. Just the chief and Brett, wearing the same insignia and taking the same risks every day. I first saw it in 'Nam — it's been stunningly scarce since.

"Finally. Doc, we'll take this one step at a time and see how it works out. Also, I know that you're king in your practice, and I know your reputation. But understand that I'm king of the police department. It's not a democracy. Understood?"

The chief got three quick nods of agreement.

I also wanted to take it one step at a time. One investigation might be enough for me. Nancy didn't like events so far; how would she feel about me doing this all the time? Still, a shrink's got to do what a shrink's got to do.

"Now, how do we catch this guy?" the chief asked. "I can't have people being killed on Arnold-Palmer-managed golf courses. Tourists come here to spend lots of money, gamble, play golf, ride the tramway, soak up the sun, have great sex, eat great meals, drink margaritas, and go home with souvenirs. Shootings get in the way. Tell me what you three have so far."

"We have a dead accountant, the senior partner of a local accounting group," Brett started. "Firm has a large list of clients, including the city of Palm Springs. We know it was a professional hit, and we have a possible witness. Then our shooter tried to shoot our witness last night at Doc's house. I managed to screw up his shot when I spotted the laser on the witness' chest, then leg. We're now protecting him 24/7, and working the firm's client list. I'll let Joan speak to that."

"That amounts to a lot of possible, Lieutenant," the chief said. "You've got zip. Leg? Why did he try to shoot your witness in the leg?"

"Yeah, we got zip," Brett explained, not sounding defensive. "We think the shooter has something personal going with one of us, and that's why he only tried to hit the witness in the leg. It was intended to be a very personal message to one of us. Maybe me."

"What do you mean that the shooter has something personal going with one of you?" The chief had concern in his voice.

"Just a hunch. It explains why he didn't shoot to kill," Brett said.

The chief still looked puzzled. "Run it by me again why the shooter sticks around?"

"Good assassins sometimes check for witnesses," Brett explained. "And if the shooter's contract is for more than one hit, then he sticks around anyway. It could have been in his contract. All I had to do was bring Chris in for questioning and the shooter needed to know if Chris could identify him. I think he made a run at Chris last night because he crossed paths with Chris out at the scene. Chris saw a man with optics at the scene he can identify. Doc hypnotized him this morning, and we got a fairly good description. We know the guy had a beard."

"And to think that I have a lieutenant who knows how assassins work," the chief said, shaking his head.

"Trained by Uncle Sam," Brett said.

"Okay. I can see it's probably not just about the kid anymore. If it were, he would have shot to kill. That's a message," the chief said. "And I stand corrected. You got more than zip; you got trouble. This guy is definitely over my head, but my choices are limited. I can call in the Feds, and have them take over. They'll come, screw up my town, and cause exactly what the mayor wants to avoid. Or, I can trust the three of you to get this done for me. If you handle this, I'll be in your debt. If you screw it up, we'll all pay the price. We have a clock running on this. I can't stall the Feds forever. I don't know why you have taken this kid in but that's your business. It's against departmental policy for you to shelter a witness in your home but I'll let that slide." The chief spoke sharply, but with a soft edge. "Joan, what do you have on the accountant's clients? I want to know who hired this shooter."

"We know that seventy-five percent of the accounting firm's income came from just three accounts: the city of Palm Desert, the city of Palm Springs and Global Energy Trading. We just came from Global and then Belgrade," Joan said.

"I don't want to hear this." The chief shook his head in dismay. "I want you three all over Global. Doc, I want you to figure out a way to outsmart this guy. There has to be a way to use his thinking against him. That's why I want you on board."

I nodded, wondering if I could give him what he asked. "I'm guessing the shooter's next attempt will be at night, at Brett's house. The shooter must have shown up at my house because I was easy to follow and he may have already tailed me to Brett's house. Chris and one of us are his targets. So I would expect him to go there next as soon as he figures out Chris is staying there."

Brett picked up on my idea. "So we set a trap for him at my house. I'll ask one of the guys that I'm training to help us if that's okay with you, chief?"

"Affirmative. Do you want Riverside SWAT in reserve?"

"No, too many uniforms and he'll smell us." Brett was more confident than I was at this point. I would take a battalion of SWAT.

"When?" the chief asked.

"I'll let you know," Brett answered.

"All right. What frequency will you use for communication? In case I need to reach out."

"Sir, I don't think you want to know that," Brett said. "I'll keep my cell on vibrate."

"Okay. I don't know about it, then. You think this guy is Einstein or something?" the chief asked.

"Not Einstein, just well trained by Uncle Sam," Brett replied. "He could have our frequencies with equipment from Radio Shack within ten minutes. I have some tactical radios I borrowed from my friends in the Army."

"Borrowed?" the chief asked.

"Friend of mine is a commo officer."

"Is there anybody who isn't a friend of yours?"

"I know at least one," Brett reminded the chief.

Chief nodded.

"Doc, tell me, why is this guy getting so personal?" the chief asked.

"I don't know that yet, sir. I do know that he's a sociopath."

"And what does a sociopath do?"

"He is without conscience," I said. "Win at all cost, and sell yourself to the highest bidder. He's on a personal philosophical mission: he wins when he can prove the rest of the world is just like him."

"And?" the chief asked with a wry smile.

"I know," I said. "Some days it looks like he's right."

"Doc, you're amazing," the chief said. "We just try to stop these assholes. You actually try and understand them. You three have about a week or less to net this clown. After that, it's out of my hands and the mayor's as well. I can only keep the Feds out of this for so long. This morning I got an inquiry from Interpol routed through the FBI that may be about our guy. Our report on the Tahquitz shooting triggered it. Seems this MO fits a guy that's been operating in Europe for the last ten years. Interpol thinks he launches from London and his name is John Bocca. Rumor is he always meets with the buyer before agreeing to the contract. When they get my response, one thing will lead to another and eventually this case will be taken away from us."

"Had to happen. We know our guy is good," Brett said.

"What about the buyer who hired this guy?" the chief asked.

"I like Bergman for it," Brett said. "He stands to succeed the victim and Doc thinks he might have something going with the most important client of his firm, Ms. Conto. She runs Global out in Palm Desert, a big new energy-trading firm making lots of bucks."

"One more thing we got, Chief," Joan said.

"What's that?"

"I found a note in the victim's golfing appointment book. The note was about Global. It reads 'Global, Palo Verde, Imperial Valley Golf/ Palm Springs. 2/13, 2:32p.m.'"

"The victim had a separate appointment book for his golf times?" The chief looked amazed.

"Yes, sir," Joan said.

"Know what the note means?" the chief asked.

"Not yet," Joan replied.

"Dig; find out."

"Yes, sir."

"What about the city's involvement in this?" The chief brought up a topic that was obviously uncomfortable for him but he dealt directly with it.

"Chief financial officer is hiding something," Joan answered the chief.

"Aren't they all?" The chief was again shaking his head.

"Chief?" Joan asked.

"Suits and politicians. Go slow with the city if you can," the chief said with a sardonic smile.

"Got it. What else did Interpol say about this guy? Military background?" Brett asked.

"You're not going to want to hear this," the chief warned.

"Chief?" Joan asked again.

"He's the best shot they've ever seen. They confirm five hits in five years, all done from approximately a hundred yards away with a handgun. They suspect he launches from south of London and is ex-U.S. Army. 'One of your misfits,' the limey called him."

"This part dovetails with maybe him knowing me," Brett said.

"They have no prints on the guy," the chief went on nodding his agreement with Brett. "They've got a list of possible ex-military but it's too long. He's invisible and gets top dollar. The rumor is that he always meets the buyer. They got the intelligence from other assassins in prison."

"He always meets the buyer?" Brett seemed to find this odd.

"Weird, huh? Most assassins don't even want to know the buyer." The chief seemed to be on the same wavelength.

"This could fit our shooter's personality," I said. "He likes to have an audience and that's why he meets the buyer. He's a control freak."

"It's him." Brett said. "I'll wager my finally taking the captain's exam against some Charger tickets. "

"I'll take that bet," the chief said. "No real evidence it's him yet. You know I got season tickets anyway. And if you had captain bars, you could take my place at some of the asshole administrative conferences. Let me see if I got your plan right. Let the bastard keep coming at you, and one of these times he'll screw up. It's bound to happen. Do I have it right?"

"We're cops, we can't just go hide," Brett said.

"Son, that's not a plan," the chief said.

"It's a cluster fuck," Joan said, shaking her head.

We eyed her appreciatively.

"Something else," the chief added.

"Chief?" Joan asked.

"You three be careful out there," the chief warned. "I don't want to lose my entertainment."

"Entertainment?" Joan asked.

"Yeah." The chief smiled smugly. "You three are the most entertaining thing that's happened to me since I took this job. I got the three musketeers here. A black ex-Green Beret who takes in a homeless white kid — reverse underground railway. A police psychologist who I just okayed a gun permit for — Christ, the lefties in the media gonna love this. And, my best woman detective; bit of a perfectionist, in the middle."

"Protect and serve and ...." Brett fed me the line.

"And entertain the chief," I said.

STREET FAIR

Nancy and I were walking from our house to Crazy Shirts to join Brett, Joan and Chris at the Street Fair. It was a warm evening for early March. The walk downtown was only a mile and a half. I figured we could get a lift home later.

Nancy had spent most of the day delivering two babies at the hospital and running back and forth to the office. She was sharing the two birth stories with me; they were her favorite part of medicine.

I knew well the patterns of our life together for more than twenty years. Our son was in his junior year in computer engineer and our daughter had just started pre-med at UC Davis. We had just finished the "long climb" to an empty nest. Two decades and Nancy still smelled unbelievably good to me. She always smelled like coconut oil, plumeria or hibiscus; she knew the smells that nailed me. She was 5'7", brunette, who in her mid-forties passed for thirty-something; she had the lean body of a runner. Ever since I had known her, she had logged fifteen miles a week. She had the high cheekbones and the classic features that most women coveted.

We met while she was rotating through a pathology clerkship and I was stationed in Honolulu. Life was simpler then, before raising two kids, and we were trying to get back to simple again. Walking was part of the plan. Heading south on North Palm Canyon toward the Street Fair, we walked slow enough to hold hands.

She was wearing a red Tommy Bahama sundress with white tropical flowers on it and black Ferragamo sandals; she might not have a lot of free time to shop but her clothes were always knockouts. "Can we stop at Lev's?" she asked.

"Sure, he always loves to see you."

Halfway into town, we ducked into Lev's Mini-mart. It had the helter-skelter mess of the small middle-eastern groceries in London. Cans of food, bottles of liquor and fresh produce were arranged on rickety shelves in a puzzle that provided a solution at a premium price point to tourists staying in the downtown hotels. Lev was a Ukrainian refugee who opened his mini-mart five years ago and thrived off the tourists; he was also Nancy's patient.

"Doctor Nancy, you're so beautiful and smart," Lev complimented her as we walked through the door. We were always running into Nancy's patients and fel-

Michael Thompkins

low docs and, predictably, most of the males were enchanted with her — a lot of men lined up waiting for me to die.

"We just dropped in for quick hellos. We're meeting friends at the Street Fair. How are you?" Nancy took his hand.

"Well, I am happy but I have cold for a week and my chest hurts," Lev said. "I need to make appointment to come see you."

I knew what was going to happen next; she was going to treat Lev right there in the store. For him to take time to close the store and come to the clinic where Nancy practiced with four other family docs would be a hardship for him and his customers.

Out came her stethoscope, which she kept stashed in her purse, and Lev was an instant patient. She had him sit on the counter and listened to his chest. The door opened, and a customer entered. With an appreciative nod from Lev, I promoted myself from shrink to clerk. I sold a bottle of Chivas for the first time in my life, $23.50 for the fifth. I wrapped it in a narrow brown bag and felt a new sense of satisfaction. Doctor or liquor clerk? I was meant more for the clerk job. Why? Standing there in her Tommy Bahama dress, with a stethoscope in her ears, Nancy was one hot doc, and those are the kind of impure thoughts that liquor clerks have. I was horny, what's new? Try listening to patients' sex problems all week and see what happens.

"Green goop when you cough?" the doctor asked the patient.

"Yes," he replied.

My fantasy ended with the details of the diagnosis.

"Okay. I'm going to write you a script for erythromycin. You'll be better in a week. If not, then you have to come in to the office. Got it? Are you allergic to anything? I don't have your chart with me." She took a pad from her purse.

"I am no allergic. Thank you so much for taking care of me. You are the most beautiful and smartest doctor in the world. No offense to you, Doctor Husband," he nodded my way.

"None taken," I smiled at him. "And I liked selling the Chivas."

"You come and learn more anytime," he offered. "I will mail a check for visit to clinic tomorrow."

Nancy took out her prescription pad and wrote Lev his script. While they chatted about his wife and children, also Nancy's patients, I reflected on his repeated exclamation of Nancy's beauty. Truth is I liked to stop at Lev's so that I could be reminded of how beautiful she was. We tossed out our goodbyes and promises to return soon and were back on North Palm Canyon near Amado.

The number of people on the sidewalk had picked up as some folks parked out by Lev's, and walked down to the fair. Thursday night Street Fair was the weekly central social event of 'the historic village of Palm Springs.' There were fancier, more exclusive events in the city, but they weren't weekly and they weren't egalitarian — the heralded and the homeless were both welcome at the Street Fair. As we walked, I slipped my hand onto her cute Bahama'd butt.

"Watching me playing doctor does it for you?" she asked.

"Every time," I said.

I told her about my day with Brett and Joan: the hypnosis, Conto and Global, Belgrade and the meeting with the chief.

At the mention of Joan's name, Nancy jumped in. "Tell me all about what Joan was wearing? How'd Brett treat her? Tell me everything."

"She was working. What do you think she was wearing?" I said.

She looked at me like, "you didn't pay attention." I imagined a large bow and quiver of arrows on her shoulder when we talked about Brett and Joan working together. I filled her in on every detail that I could remember about Joan and Brett. I finished by telling her about the electricity that I felt between them when I left the car. Psychologist Handbook, page thirty-six: learn to gossip with the best. Page thirty-eight: spill all to your wife.

"So how is Brett going to deal with last night?" Nancy changed subjects.

She had a way of going at stuff like a guided missile. We could see the Street Fair in the distance and I could make out the lines of the big Moonwalk tent where kids jumped around in pretend-weightlessness.

"We think that the shooter will hit next at Brett's house trying to get to Chris and Brett. Brett is the most likely candidate for the shooter's second target, but Joan and I need to be extra alert, too. We may want to stay at the hospital or my office tonight. We have the beginning of a plan in place." I sounded more confident than I was.

"Do you think that protection is the only reason Brett's giving Chris a place to live?" Nancy said. Her radar was relentless, uncovering everything in its path.

"I think that there's some new part of Brett coming out here. He would probably help Chris whether he's a witness or not."

"He's adopting Chris," she said. "It's exactly what he needs, to learn to nurture something."

"Silly me. I thought I was the psychologist."

"No one can figure their own best friend out, especially men."

"I know what happened last night upsets you, and that you don't want me carrying a gun, but I have to help Chris," I said, playing the Chris card.

Her raised eyebrows and questioning look would eventually lead to "contract re-negotiations" between us. Street Fair was interrupting their beginning. The street was mobbed now and it was difficult to walk and talk; I was off the hook, temporarily.

We were walking side by side down the street. The middle of the street was occupied by vendor stands for six blocks; there were stalls for artsy-craftsy frou-frou, fruit, veggies, and prepared food.

It was almost seven o'clock and it had been dark for a while, but the fair was as bright as day. There was candlepower from the mercury streetlights added to the vendors' lights and an occasional string of colorful Christmas lights. Fried onions, sausages, falafels, and Philly-steak sandwich smells filled the air. We hadn't eaten yet, and I wanted to taste some of everything just like a little kid. Before I could order a snack, I spotted Brett and Joan standing in front of Crazy Shirts.

Nancy and Joan greeted each other with hugs and picked up their conversation where they'd left off last night, as if twenty hours never happened.

"Joan," I greeted her with a smile.

"You guys eat?" Joan asked, and my stomach growled.

"No, but the poor boy is starving," Nancy wrapped her arms around my waist.

My stomach insisted on letting me know I hadn't eaten since breakfast. I had walked past the salty-sweet smell of Kettle Korn and had just gotten my gut settled when my hunger flared up again over chocolate fudge: nothing better than a dinner made up of snacks.

"Later," Brett dismissed my hunger. "Let's go watch Chris. He's playing out back. They've already started. I left him alone, but there's so many people, he's safe."

"Good plan." Nancy gave me her "you'll get to eat, just be patient" look.

We walked through the Crazy Shirts store, and out their back door to avoid the walk around the end of the block. Brett knew the manager from a time when she had called the police about a shoplifter, and she was more than willing to let him use the back door.

We stepped out the door into a couple of hundred people listening to Chris playing his Martin along with another guitarist, a bass player, and a drummer. For a recently assembled band, they were obviously comfortable playing together. I didn't recognize the song, but I appreciated the band and Chris had a decent voice.

Brett mouthed the words "Nirvana." This time I remembered Kurt Cobain and grunge.

The crowd was the eclectic mix you would expect at a free concert; high schoolers, tourists, college kids from the College of the Desert, retired folks, and bikers. The parking lot being used by Chris's band was wedged between a restaurant serving the freshest fish trucked in from the coast, and the Saloon, where Chris had auditioned for the owner. The crowd pretty much filled up the empty space in the parking lots not occupied by cars, the community discovering that openness and tolerance actually promoted business. The restaurant and bar owners had willingly given up part of their parking to allow this impromptu music.

It did create a bit of a backup on Indian Canyon, so one of Palm Spring's finest was directing traffic; Brett waved to him. Chris's group finished their song and announced a break. A couple of other groups were hanging around in the midst of their performance preparations.

Chris walked over to us. "What'd you think?" Obviously in his element, he wore a look of pure pleasure. "Jay wants the band to open for Country Chix tomorrow night."

"That's wonderful, Chris," Nancy said.

"Excellent," I said.

"Nice sound," Brett said. "You'll go over big."

Joan then proceeded to make me feel all of the ten years I had on her, by discussing in detail what Chris and his friends had done to the Nirvana cut. "I liked the way you guys made the music feel more hopeful than the original."

"Well, Cobain could get into a downer and I like to lift the guitar a little."

"Downer. Deadly downer," I said. "He blew his brains with a twelve gauge."

"I miss him every day," Chris said.

"Him and John Lennon. Hard to get a Martin to sound too depressed," Brett added, referring to the very expensive and sweet-sounding acoustic guitar that Chris had managed to keep in his possession all the way from Spokane to the streets of Palm Springs.

"That too," Chris added.

"Chris, what's alternative music?" Nancy asked. "What's grunge? You were talking about it earlier."

"Alternative's been around for a long time but really got popular after grunge died in '95; Nirvana was grunge. After Cobain popped himself, grunge died a year later. We were mostly playing grunge and alternative tonight."

"How long have you been playing?" Nancy said.

"I've been playing since I was five years old. I had ten years of classical lessons but it wasn't any fun for me until I hit high school, and started writing my own music. My folks insisted I learn classical music but they couldn't dig it at all when I started a band in high school. Like, I was always supposed to be a student, and never a musician."

"Well, you're that now. And a good one," Nancy added with her usual enthusiasm.

"Thanks," Chris said.

The crowd chatter in the parking lot was loud.

"I need to whiz before I play again. I'm gonna head over to the bar," Chris said.

"I'm buying at the Fish Place when Chris is done. Everybody in?" I asked.

"Yes," Nancy said.

"Yeah," Brett said.

"Absolutely," Joan said.

"Rad."

After stopping to chat with some fans, I could see Chris head south across the lot and into the Saloon. Then, in a too-short-to-take-a-leak time span, he flew out the door and ran toward us. Brett, with his be-tuned-into-what-is-going-on-around-you military mindset, was all over it. Joan watched her partner come to attention, and followed his eyes to Chris. She moved her hand towards the weapon under her windbreaker. Joan was ready too; cops were always ready.

"I think I saw him!" Chris reached us, panting.

"Who?" Nancy was quick to ask. Docs are always ready, too.

Shrinks are rarely ready.

"The guy with the binoculars, the birdwatcher," Chris said, looking scared.

"Did he recognize you?" Brett asked Chris.

"He smiled at me; don't know whether he recognized me or not."

"Where exactly did you see him?" Brett continued.

"He was going into the men's room when I was coming out."

"And?" Brett's eyes shifted to the Saloon door.

"Dude just smiled at me. That's all. Didn't say a freakin' word."

Brett was dressed in typical off-duty uniform: military-type shorts, running shoes, a tee shirt with some exotic hunting destination on it and a vest. From his usual fanny pack, his Sig-Sauer Nine appeared in his hand, reflexively pointed at the sky in a safe-carry position and without changing his gaze, he announced, "Let's go have a look."

We crossed the parking lot and entered the Saloon in two groups with Brett and Joan in the lead. We didn't know if we were looking for a witness or the shooter yet, but Brett and Joan were taking point to protect us. We stood just inside the door of the packed bar. The jukebox was playing a tune I recognized by the Spice Girls.

The owner, Jay, who had been removing empty glasses from the top of a piano, came up to us with a concerned look on his face. The five of us filled the free space of the entrance. At the other end of the bar, I could see a corridor with restroom signs overhead and doors to the men's and ladies' rooms.

"We got a little situation here, Jay," Brett said.

"Whatever you need, Lieutenant."

"You three stay here," Brett said as he motioned to us.

Brett signaled Joan to follow him down the corridor.

"Let's take a look," he said to her.

I watched them enter the men's room, and seconds later they were both out with a young "cowboy" following on their heels. The cowboy was shaking his head in disapproval at Joan visiting the men's room, even though she was obviously an armed police officer. He took one good look at Brett and ran.

"Clear," Brett said as they returned to us.

Joan and Brett huddled as Brett gave directions, "Okay, we look for him without uniforms. I want a shot at Chris spotting him in the crowd without his sensing the cavalry coming. We all stick together and if we spot him, Joan and I will approach him."

"I'm sorry, Chris, but we need you to help us spot this guy if you can," Joan said.

"I've gotta run out and tell my friends that I'll be going with you guys. They can watch my stuff," Chris said.

"I'll go with you," Joan said.

"First, I need a description of this guy and what he's wearing," Brett said.

"A white shirt and a golf hat. He walked by me so fast that's all I remember."

"And you think he was the same guy that you saw with the optics?" Brett asked.

"Yeah."

"Let's go over to North Palm Canyon and cover the Street Fair once through," Brett said.

The five of us left the bar with Jay extending an invitation on the way out, "Y'all come back and try one of my mint juleps."

"Copy that, Jay. Introductions later. We need to tag someone," Brett told him.

"Roger that, Lieutenant. I'm gonna have the kid open tomorrow night."

Brett, Nancy and I stood and watched Joan and Chris walk over and speak to the band. When they returned, we all walked over to North Palm Canyon through an alley south of the bar. Chris, Joan and Brett were in the lead; Nancy and I pulled up the rear. When we got to North Palm, we turned north and walked through the vendor stalls. Occasionally, I could see through the crowd across to the other side.

"White polo and a golf hat," Nancy reminded herself.

We were trying to spot this guy in a crowd of probably 5,000 people packed into a six-block area; it was going to be hard to hunt our birdwatcher.

At one point as Nancy and I were passing a stall that sold hand-blown Indian glass sculptures, Chris must have thought he saw something because our whole party moved into a trot and didn't stop until we came to the north end of the fair. The end was marked with orange police stanchions, and Brett waved us all into a circle just beyond the last stalls.

"What did you see, Chris?" Brett asked.

"A flash of a white shirt up ahead, and then it was gone."

"Anybody else see anything?" Brett asked.

Everybody shook their heads. The crowd was so heavy that you could lose your own mother ten feet away. For the next twenty minutes, we searched for any signs of our birdwatcher. Staying together, we walked the fair, up one side and down the other. We ended up where we started and Brett led us back to the parking lot where Chris's band had played. Most of the audience had moved along, probably to saunter through the fair stalls. The band that jumped in and performed after Chris's band had already finished and the musicians were putting away their instruments.

"Let's go eat at the Fish Place and do some thinking," Brett suggested.

"Let me grab my stuff." Chris headed toward his things.

Chris walked a few feet, thanked his friends for keeping an eye on his stuff, and picked up his guitar case. He hadn't used the Martin tonight opting for an electric, but he and the guitar seemed inseparable. A small round object fell off the case and rolled quietly six feet across the asphalt. Brett snatched it up, took one look at it and pocketed it. Everyone figured he was a quarter richer, but the hardened look on his face said it was not a windfall.

"What've you got?" I asked him.

"Later."

Within five minutes, Brett, Chris, and I were enjoying Sierra Pale Ale, while Nancy and Joan were splitting a bottle of Monterey County Chablis. We had all ordered our entrees at the cafeteria-style kitchen. Tommy, the maitre d', had seated us at one of his best patio tables arranged among potted palms. We were warming up on raw oysters and shrimp cocktail. I was finally eating and had gone to food heaven.

Nancy patted me on the stomach and said, mockingly, "Poor boy was starving."

"Not anymore," I said as I wolfed down a raw oyster on-the-half-shell appetizer and sipped my beer. Life was good, birdwatcher or not.

"Nancy," Brett said. "Chris had to help us look for this guy tonight and Doc has carte blanche from the chief to be involved, but I could get in trouble for bringing you along to look for this guy."

"I was never there. I already figured it out," Nancy replied.

"Thanks," Brett said. "He was watching us the whole time. He wanted to see if Chris recognized him."

"Say what?" I asked.

"Who?" Nancy asked.

"The guy with the optics. The birdwatcher," Brett said with certainty.

"I don't understand." Joan was watching Brett intently.

Brett emptied one of his vest pockets and tossed the coin he'd picked up in the parking lot onto the table, the one that had rolled off Chris's guitar case. The one I had asked about.

"What is it?" Chris said, speaking for all of us.

"Ranger coin. When you finish Army Ranger training, your friends give you one. If you ever get caught drinking with Rangers and not carrying it, you buy. There's only one reason this coin was on Chris's guitar."

"I don't get it," Joan said.

"Me either," Nancy said.

I couldn't see how it all fit together. "This guy is an ex-Ranger like you, and he must know you are, too. I can see that, but how did he find out? Does the shooter know you?"

"Damned if I know," Brett said. "Probably paid for intel on us."

"I don't like this," Nancy said with a frown.

"But I thought you were Special Forces? That isn't the Rangers, is it?" Chris asked.

"No, but Special Forces are usually Rangers first. It's part of the training sequence," Brett explained.

"Chris's birdwatcher is our shooter," I said.

"Yup, and he's challenging me in some way," Brett said.

I looked at the Ranger coin on the table. The inscription on the coin read, "Rangers lead the way."

"He was checking Chris out to see if Chris recognized him?" Nancy asked.

We all stared at the coin. The probability that the birdwatcher-shooter followed us slowly sank in.

"And Chris did recognize him," Brett said. "The shooter knows that now."

"Doc, I get the shooter challenging himself with a world-class pistol shot, and then leaving the gun as his marking," Joan said. "I get him trying to wound Chris, at your house. I also get the part where he checks to see if Chris recognized him, and the part where he makes us as cops. But I don't get this last part. Why does he deliberately leave the Ranger coin? That's over the edge. Who does this guy think he is? Why leave the coin?"

"The shooter has to have something real personal with the Rangers or with Brett," I said again. "It has something to do with why he just wanted to shoot Chris in the leg,"

"Is he crazy?" Joan asked. "He must think we can't catch him no matter what he does. Some kind of agenda about the Rangers and Brett? What kind of perp is this guy? Is he crazy, Doc?"

"He's not crazy. Like I said, there's only one kind of person behaves like this: a sociopath — a person who has been living alone a long time, without any regard for rules. He makes up his own rules. Leaving the gun was showing off. Aiming for Chris's leg and leaving the coin are personal. Now, we know his other target is Brett. We don't know why yet. But we do know this makes him more dangerous. Sociopaths are special types of criminals. They need to show us that the social contract we live by is meaningless. If this tonight is really our hit man, then he has thrown out all the rules. He's even thrown out hit man rules."

"Doc, you sure about all this?" Joan asked.

"No, it could be worse. He could be flat-out crazy."

"We have to assume the shooter and the Tahquitz birdwatcher are the same person," Joan said. "He knows Chris can identify him, and who Brett and I are. He's after Brett too."

"Got to be," Brett said.

"I think this guy's an animal," Nancy said simply.

Everybody was quiet for a minute or so thinking about what Nancy had said.

"He is. Most people want to make crime about good and evil in some fundamentalist sense — we haven't outgrown Puritanism — painting everything good and evil," I said. "It's usually more about the animal in all of us. If a cat maims a bird and plays with it, we smile. Our shooter plays with wounding Chris and we're surprised. Most of us control the animal inside, but sociopaths don't."

"He's like some predatory animal. Following us, watching us, baiting us with the coin…." Joan said.

"If he's like an animal…" I said.

"Yes?" Joan asked.

"He's a tiger in a tea room."

RANGER COIN

Bocca followed the kid into the Saloon to see if the kid recognized him. He smiled at him, and the kid smiled back just as if they were strangers — they weren't. The kid's eyes stayed fixed on Bocca for just a second too long. He let the kid leave.

Just a few minutes earlier, Bocca had been watching the kid performing Nirvana. The kid touched the electric guitar like it was a living thing. Bocca's own taste in music went to the classics or the Beatles because they relaxed him. Something about the way the kid held the electric made him think that he might play classical guitar as well as grunge. It was blind luck spotting the kid and his band. He had come to the fair just to relax. Then he had seen the kid talking to the two cops, the shrink and the shrink's woman.

Somehow the kid got hooked up with the cop. He couldn't see how, but when he came out of the Saloon he knew that the kid made him from the bike trail. When he saw the kid running to tell the cop, he was double certain.

The black cop was good; Special Forces training and all. His name was Lieutenant Wade. The tan cop's name was Fleming, a detective. Bocca had called one of his intel sources and paid $3000 to get the information. It was expensive but the first rule is to know your enemy. The shrink's name had been on his office door: Dr. Tom Reynolds, Ph.D., Psychologist. There was no military background available on the shrink.

The lieutenant's smart. Figured out the kid might have witnessed something even before he had shot at them at the shrink's house. Give him that. Then the lieutenant used the kid as bait. Trolling.

Met the lieutenant somewhere before. Army? Where? Memory stuck somewhere.

Bocca pulled back his observation post to where he could see the cops but was still concealed in the crowd of music lovers. He watched the whole group head over to the bar, undoubtedly looking for him. They'd be out in a minute, and would start a search for him. If they called for uniforms, he would have to disappear. Enough cops, even he was at risk. If the lieutenant didn't call for uniforms and he was betting he wouldn't, it would be interesting to watch them while they searched.

Toss the golf hat. They're out looking, not waiting for more help. Stay behind them. Heading over to the Street Fair. Move in front of them. Watch them. Keep backing up. Front tail them.

Bocca was not carrying; he avoided carrying a weapon in public unless he anticipated using it. He thought of himself as the best in the world at what he did. He liked the feeling of surviving on his cunning alone with just his mind and his body as weapons.

Best feeling in the world — don't need anyone, can do anything, make the rules, totally invulnerable.

The fair reminded him of carnivals when he was a kid. It always struck him as odd that in tense situations like this one or even in critical situations like when his Ranger unit was under attack, he would enjoy the odd smell, sight or taste. Once, his unit had been pinned down and a couple of guys had been shot up while someone was cooking on a hill nearby. He remembered feeling hungry in the middle of that firefight.

Horny now.

Bitches are spectacular. Shrink's woman's ten years older but just as stunning. Younger one, the cop, looks tough enough to be a soldier. Same height and build, both brunettes. Killer ass. Haven't had a woman in awhile. Watch the distance, they're getting too close. Kid might have seen him. They're running. Okay, it's cool. Kid's confused. He doesn't know what he's seen. They're walking slowly again. Enough of this. Outta here.

Bocca gave up his surveillance and headed back down the alley that led to the parking lot outside the bar, where the kid's band had played. The lot was packed and a different group was playing; they were doing Beatles' stuff with an absolute lack of talent. They were murdering "Strawberry Fields." His favorite music being butchered in his presence set him off.

He was angry at the band for brutalizing the Beatles. Angry that he stopped having fun at the fair. Angry that the kid could make him and the cops had stumbled onto the kid. Angry at the lieutenant for being Special Forces.

He understood those angry feelings, but what he couldn't figure out, was an even deeper rage at the lieutenant. Bocca was shaking a little; he never shook. He looked at his chest and he was definitely trembling a little. Then it hit him.

It's him!

Lieutenant was on the Special Forces selection committee.

Bocca remembered the lieutenant. Now, he was entitled to some personal satisfaction for once. Some revenge. He hated Special Forces; they'd kicked him out.

He'd wanted somebody to pay for that mistake for a long time now. Now he understood the force that made him want to shoot the kid.

Somebody has to pay. Lieutenant has to pay.

After graduating Ranger School, he'd applied for Special Forces. He'd aced Jump and Sniper Schools. He did a tour in 'Nam but then, after all that, he didn't make it through the S.F. Selection. They told him that his psychological profile was not what they wanted; they said he was not good enough.

Goddamn shrinks; whoever let them in this man's army should be dragged out and shot. Not good enough, my ass. Special Forces' shrink sucked.

Bocca was not balanced psychologically, the shrink had said. He hated him for his report. He knew he was good enough to have been selected. He despised the committee that kicked him out. They never should have listened to the shrink. But the guy was just being a shrink. The lieutenant was a soldier and should have known Bocca was qualified and overrode the doctor. Bocca left the army behind after that, started his new career and hadn't looked back, until now. Hell, they'd even trained him for it. He would show them, right here and now, and have fun doing it.

He strolled over to where the band was playing, and took the coin out of his pocket. It was so loud and so dark that he knew no one would notice him. The band was playing the last bars of "Strawberry Fields."

Quickly. Where to leave the coin? Got it. Put the coin on the kid's guitar case. No way he'll miss it there. Let the lieutenant know he's been made. Look. No one noticing. Place it on the case. Done. Outta here. Still shaking.

Later, sitting in his room at the Palm Springs Marriott, Bocca thought about crossing the line. The rule was never make a contract personal. He knew that when he placed the coin on the kid's guitar case, he'd lost it.

Uncork the Balvenie Doublewood single malt. Pour a couple of inches. Burns going in and burns going down. Body still too tight. Christ, those bitches were hot. Could use their kind of release. Could do the two women right now. There it is. There's the loosening. Slide a little; slide into the whiskey. Shaking stopped.

He was usually wired tight as a drum before a kill, taking beta-blockers to make certain his body reacted the way he willed it to react. Then the hit was over and release began. Sex, alcohol, or both, and he could feel the hardness soften and something let go.

Just this one deployment, he was going to show off, let somebody know that he was the best, and pay the lieutenant back. One of the things missing in his job was that there was no one to show off to. Just this one time. He was good enough to get away with it. He was tired of operating every time in a vacuum, without any fun.

Doesn't get any better than this. Not a chance in hell they'd catch him. Two cars, two condos and ten escape routes in the area. Let'em try. No way. Army of one.

Bocca had spent a pleasant week setting up in Palm Springs, arranging his condos and his escape routes, and climbing the mountain trails that came right down to the city streets. He loved height; it gave him power over people. He remembered scouting the area from the trail up over the museum, and thinking that he owned this town; anybody with his skills could. It would be fun, just this once, to mess with the cops. He'd show them how vulnerable they were to an elite soldier like himself. *Eat this town alive.*

As he sipped the single malt, Bocca was flooded with images of Horley, England, where he kept his other life. He kept a nice flat near Gatwick Airport where he could launch from for any assignment; London was so easy to take off from. He enjoyed thinking of himself as an American expatriate.

He had been working with a Swiss broker as an agent. He had his rules and made them clear to the Swiss. Bocca stuck to them. He always met the buyer. No one with a young family, no high-profile people, and no cops. Well, he had his rules, until this time.

The alcohol relaxed him and he thought about Ye Five Bells, his favorite pub in Horley. The best thing about his other life was the village and the pub. It was so near Gatwick that lots of airline personnel, travelling business people and even former military like himself lived there and worked globally. It was a life, his R&R.

Any night of the week he could go drinking at Ye Five Bells, meet a traveling woman and find some companionship. The women were fun for a fling and were always impressed with his sexual powers. They complained that most of their "suits" didn't satisfy them. The Asians had taught him how to pull all his heat into his core — "to ride the snake in the spine." Bocca's potency fascinated his women. They were just as hungry as men; he knew that truth well. Whenever they looked for anything more than casual sex from him, he would feign a new assignment and move along. Women made a man soft; they were just beautiful baggage.

Bocca knew that he couldn't leave Palm Springs for a week; that was in the contract. The buyer might need to add on to the original hit. Buyers were suits without Glocks; they wanted to have the benefits of dirty but couldn't do dirty. They paid him excellent money to do it for them.

Can't leave until the kid and the lieutenant are dead. The lieutenant had to pay.

The Balvenie put him into a light sleep while still sitting in the chair. Twenty minutes later, he was in the middle of the nightmare he had been having since he left the

Michael Thompkins

Army, sometimes once a month. Sometimes it would go away for six months and then come back all over again with a stronger grip on him. Always the same sense of powerlessness he had when the Special Forces bastards decided he wasn't good enough.

The dream always took place where it really happened, Fort Bragg and Special Forces Selection. In the dream he relived the day when the shrink, the colonel, and the rest of the committee told him he was not selected. It truly knocked the wind out of him because he had passed all of the physical requirements for selection, all of the weapons requirements, and all of the tactical training. One morning he was called from his barracks to see the colonel. He knocked on the door, went in and stood at attention in his cammies in front of the colonel and the shrink. The committee had just met and decided Bocca's fate.

"Son, I regret to inform you that your psychological profile doesn't allow us to select you," the colonel had said. "You're a good soldier but our primary mission is to win hearts and minds. You're just too much of a loner."

Hearts and minds. He was so pissed that he didn't say squat. He just shook his head when they asked him if he had any questions. "Dismissed." About face and out the door. He walked out into the Carolina midday heat, as hot as Palm Springs, but more humid.

Hot. Cold. Wet. Sweat. What? Where? The nightmare again.

Bocca woke up with his heart racing. He was drenched in sweat and had a pounding headache. This time, the lieutenant was in the dream. The dream confirmed what he already remembered earlier at the fair.

Lieutenant was one of the selection officers. Same face.

In the dream, the lieutenant had been wearing fatigues with a Vietnam Combat Patch. He didn't miss the patch because Bocca, too, had served in 'Nam. The Lieutenant had been sitting outside the colonel's office reading some papers. He hadn't even introduced himself to Bocca, just ignored him. He just rode into Fort Bragg, rostered up on a selection committee, and screwed up Bocca's life. The lieutenant had blackballed him.

Bocca felt an ancient agenda spool in his spine.

Kill the kid. Kill the lieutenant.

Twenty years ago and the lieutenant still had to pay.

Lieutenant took something — take something from the lieutenant.

Ride into his town. Take some time. Enjoy it. Make him pay. Take something from him. Then kill the bastard.

THE SALOON

My patients had told me about The Saloon many times over the last two years: how it'd started out a simple biker bar and grown into something bigger. It was now a watering hole where the desert rats that drove Harleys coexisted with the rich desert-rat wannabe's who rode over on the same model bikes from Beverly Hills. Everyone was welcome. Straight, gay, or bi, all got along or got tossed out by the two new owners who were ex-Marines, friends of Brett, and gay.

The night after Brett found the Ranger coin, Brett, Joan, Nancy, and I walked through the front door of the Saloon into the noise of fifty conversations and the beer-sex-sweat smell of a pub. The jukebox was playing Elton John. We'd all agreed to meet here and enjoy Chris's first performance. I had spent the day catching up on clients; Joan and Brett had gone over the data from the accounting firm, looking for leads. Brett and Chris were sleeping at police headquarters until we set up to trap the shooter at Brett's place.

Jay and Bob, the Saloon owners, were both over two hundred muscular pounds, six feet-two, and spoke with soft long-voweled Southern accents. They hailed from New Orleans. They wore shorts, polo shirts, and fanny packs like Brett, which contained concealed weapons. Fanny packs were the warm-weather 90s sartorial equivalent of the custom-tailored shoulder holster that James Bond wore; Palm Springs was warm so shorts and polos replaced the Saville Row suit — with considerable loss of panache.

"Hi, Doc, Brett has told us all about you. If you ever need anyone killed, we're your boys," Jay said. We were in such a hurry last night there had been no time for intros.

When I shook Jay's hand, *my mind drifted back in time to a flag-draped casket in a Piedmont, California cemetery.*

In the casket, a black barely-shaving short-timer from 'Nam who, with thirty duty days left in-country, had run out of wake-ups and was being buried with a

Michael Thompkins

bronze star. Mortar attack had wiped out half his platoon. He had saved the rest of his men and almost saved himself until a sniper took him out.

Me? Grave detail. I had flown into Alameda Air Station from Honolulu on a C-140 with the body bag, delivered it to the funeral home, met the band and the rest of the detail at the cemetery the next day, and commanded the detail.

A Criminal Investigation Division sergeant was questioning the mother of the corporal —actually only pieces of him left — when I showed up. I asked the sergeant what the hell was going on? He was an ambitious shit – read the personnel file on all returnees to Oakland — alive or dead. Grave robber. File said the corporal was gay. Asshole sergeant figured he'd screw the family out of the death insurance, save the government some money and ride it to another stripe. Just 'cause the kid was gay.

I talked to him alone next to some grave markers. I called him a necrophiliac, and asked him if he was ready to ship to 'Nam tomorrow. He'd never been. I told him I could arrange it. He ran.

The mother came up to me and wanted to know if she'd still get her son's insurance — needed it to feed the family.

I asked her, why shouldn't she?

She kissed me. Her lips were sweaty with fear and June California heat.

I made a vow to myself I'd carry to the grave.

It's called a flashback. Everyone I ever met, who was in the military, had some.

"Doc? Doc? You all right?" Jay asked.

I recovered my mind. "Sorry, you reminded me of another time," I said.

Jay looked at me like he knew it was about 'Nam.

Brett looked at me as if to say, "wake-up."

I refocused on my manners, "My pleasure. This is my wife, Nancy, and you've met Joan." I shook Jay's muscular, outstretched hand adorned with a huge ring, a sunflower-yellow sapphire set in a cluster of diamonds — a jewelry store on a finger.

Jay and Bob were paradigms of southern gentility in the California Southland, both executing small gentleman's bows to the ladies. Almost identical in appearance, Jay had blond hair in contrast to Bob's brown. Jay also had a scar on his right ear.

GUN PLAY

"Doctors, Lieutenant, Detective, if there is anything we can do to make you welcome at the Saloon, please let us know," Bob said.

"It's always fabulous to meet Brett's friends," Jay said.

"How's the kid doing?" Brett was anxious to check on how the day with Chris had gone.

"He's backstage in the band room," Jay said. "They're warming up and adjusting their amps. We'll be ready to open the doors in about ten minutes. One of us has been all over him since Joan dropped him off this morning. I wasn't really worried, though; a shooter would have to be nuts to try anything in downtown daylight. Chris is a good kid and big-time talented; who would want to kill him?"

"I think it's the same guy who did the golfer out at Tahquitz," Brett told him.

"I heard about that, hundred yards or better with a handgun. Impossible shot," Jay said.

"Come on. Let's get you folks some good seats before we let the mob in." Bob motioned for us to follow him through the bar and into the band room. He chose the centermost table. It was right in front of the stage and a line of speakers that seemed to hold more potential energy than a row of transformers in the Southern California power grid. I hoped I wouldn't go deaf tonight. Brett and Joan arranged their seats so that they could see the stage and cover the entire room. Chris came out on stage, waved to us and started tuning an electric guitar.

Brett nodded thanks to Jay and Bob, and they were off to spread their Southern charms on the two hundred customers in line out front. The doors from the main bar opened behind us. The room took less than five minutes to fill up. Conversation became difficult, so I went on woman-watch. Despite the average age in the room being twenty-something, Nancy and Joan were two of the most beautiful women in the room. Why do women continue to grow more beautiful with age and men don't seem to hold up quite as well?

The band room was the size of a basketball court and windowless. The floor was concrete slab, and the tables were retro-'50s with aluminum legs and Formica tops. On the walls were framed posters of groups that had played the room. The ceiling was a collector's item. Although it was ten feet high, past patrons stood on tables at the end of an evening to sign the ceiling with the same sense of celebration with which stars adorn our Palm Spring sidewalks.

The air conditioning was barely managing to cool the surge in temperature caused by that many people in close quarters; I was sweating. The band had stopped tuning. Everyone was waiting.

Michael Thompkins

Jay jumped up on the stage that ran the length of the long exterior wall. "Ladies and gentlemen, welcome to the Saloon. It's show time! We have two bands for you tonight. A local band, for the first time on a Palm Springs stage: the Chris Parks Band. Later, one of our favorites, the Country Chix. Put your hands together and give a large Saloon welcome to Chris Parks and his band!"

The crowd was clearly used to hearing an eclectic mix at the Saloon. I hadn't imagined it possible that the same crowd that would be interested in country music would like the music that Chris's band began to play. More than the lyrics, I was amazed at the drive of the music itself. I was a veteran of the rock concerts of the sixties like Santana, the Stones, and Janis. Chris's alternative music was very much an offshoot.

"I'm never alone, I'm alone all the time.
Are you at one or do you lie?
We live in a wheel, where everyone steals.
But when we rise, it is like Strawberry Fields."

Brett leaned over and identified the band, "Bush."

The music had a palpable driving rhythm that made my head sweat and my spine tingle. It was powerful enough to penetrate even religious reserve — a primitive bass undercurrent moved electrically through the audience.

I looked over at Nancy; she hadn't missed the Strawberry Fields line. Brett and Joan kept stealing glances at each other. Where were they going? I was sure Nancy had her theories. She tried to help Cupid, sometimes with some success, frequently with failure. My experience at helping Cupid was dismal and I'd given it up a long time ago.

The next song announced by the bass guitarist as being written by Chris himself, was titled, "My House is Way Up High." It had the same driving bass beat as the last song, and I could barely make out only two repetitive lines of the melody,

"My house is way up high. I feel like I can fly."

Chris's song was a musical translation of the dream he had shared with Brett and me on the day I had met him. Brett nodded acknowledgment of the source of Chris's song. I would have liked to hear the rest of the lyrics to the song, but all I could make out were the two lines. My hearing was being slowly numbed by proximity to the speakers. I'd already lost some of my hearing range temporarily.

Chris announced a number, "We'd like to play 'Cupid de Locke' by Smashing Pumpkins."

"Cupid hath pulled back his sweetheart's bow, to cast divine arrows into her soul.

To grab her attention swift and quick..."

This one was a ballad, so one of the guitarists switched to an electronic keyboard. The smiles on Brett and Joan's faces showed they took the insider meaning built into Chris's selection for the good-natured tease it was. The band finished the song and the set. Suddenly the sound was gone replaced by applause that lasted a long time. Conversations began.

Chris jumped down off the stage, and ambled over ten feet to our table; he shook outstretched hands on the way. He was pumped. The remaining band members left the stage and joined other tables. There would be an intermission before the second band joined the evening.

"What did you think?" Chris asked.

"I loved your song, 'My house is way up high,' " Nancy said enthusiastically.

"Me, too," Joan said.

"I'd love to hear you guys play more of your original songs like the one you just did," I said.

"Cool," Chris said. "Brett? What did you think?"

"We need to get you playing more of your own music. How many songs have you written?" Brett replied with as much run-on excitement as I had ever seen him muster.

"Wow. You really think? I've written six songs of my own so far." Chris looked surprised at everyone's enthusiastic take on his songwriting.

"I think there's a lot of work ahead but you need to have the band start playing your songbook as much as other groups," I said, agreeing with Brett.

"Yeah, the audience seemed way more turned on by your song than the rest of the set," Joan said.

The next band had come out, and Jay was back up on the stage again. He picked up the mike, still in his shorts, polo and fanny pack. He was not a small man; he loomed over the room. I liked him in his roles as manager, host, bouncer, bodyguard, and emcee. He exuded an aura of calm competency, and was obviously really good with people. I was warming to him quickly. Not all of Brett's ex-military friends were initially as pleasant— a few of them I'd met had been cooled by their careers, paying a price for their professional proximity to death.

The conversation in the room lowered, and then stopped.

Michael Thompkins

"Ladies and gentlemen, please welcome Country Chix," Jay announced with voice projection that didn't really require a mike.

The Country Chix were good. I enjoyed listening to them run through a review of female country and western singers from Dolly Parton to EmmyLou Harris. The good news was that I could hear all their lyrics because the amps were not turned up as high. My hearing was gradually returning. Bad news was that Country Chix were clearly a let down after Chris's band. They were a band that earned their living in bars like the Saloon, playing other groups' songs. They were instrumentally and vocally good, but they were not original and never would be. The audience, on the other hand, somehow knew when they were listening to Chris's band that they were witnessing the birth of a new talent.

The audience's reception of Country Chix was polite and restrained without much intensity. They finished their set and the band room was again taken over by conversation. The music had lasted an hour and a half and the room was emptying fast. As the doors opened and the audience cleared out, we sat and watched both bands pack up and carry their instruments off. We were still talking at our table five minutes later when Jay showed up and offered to bring celebratory drinks. The room was empty except for us. It was time to savor Chris' success and forget last night's shooting.

"What can I get you for drinks? I make an outstanding mint julep. Best in California."

"Why not?" Brett accepted. "We aren't on duty and it's been a long day. I'll have a mint julep, just one. We still need to keep an eye on Chris."

Nancy and I signed up for the mint juleps. Chris, barely twenty-one, asked for a beer.

"I'll take a virgin mint julep if you can make it. One drink and I can't shoot straight." Joan seemed to make no judgment about Brett's having a drink. It wouldn't have stopped him if she did. Dead drunk, he was more lethal than any of us.

"No such thing as a virgin mint julep, but I think I know what you want," Jay said. "I'll make something Southern that's fruity without the booze."

Brett pulled a chair over from a neighboring table, signaling Jay to sit with us.

"Let me supervise the mint juleps and then I'll join you," Jay said.

"Chris, what are you thinking?" Joan asked.

Chris seemed to have a pensive look. "Like, a week ago, I was living out of my sleeping bag. And that's cool. I had no complaints. Now I have a place to stay, new friends and the band had its first gig here."

"And...?" Joan went on.

"I like this better. This is awesome."

The celebratory mood surrounding the bands first successful gig took over. Nancy and Joan chatted with Chris about his songs. Jay and a bartender appeared with our drinks complete with sprigs of fresh mint. The juleps were stunning and we all toasted Chris. On a warm night, they were better than perfect. We were having a good time, and it was about to get better.

"Last time I had one of these was on Frenchman Street in the Quarter," I said.

"Some of my tribe lives near there on the other side of Elysian Fields Ave.," Jay smiled back.

"Boundary of The French Quarter and a couple of blocks from Frenchman Street? Right?"

"Good memory, Doc," Jay said.

"He never forgets anything," Nancy said.

"Chris, Bob and I would like to have you get your original songs together and play here for a while," Jay said, changing the subject. "You'll be the house band. It would give you a chance to have a large practice room, play to a small house, and organize your songs. It would help us out, too. Next Thursday can be your opening night as the main attraction. Until then, you open for Country Chix."

"Cool. I have to talk to the rest of the band but I know they're not going to say no."

"One more thing," Jay added.

"What?" Chris asked.

"You have to come up with a better name for your band than 'The Chris Parks Band.'"

The rest of the band had left with friends, after collecting their instruments and waving goodbye from the other side of the room.

"Bring them all in tomorrow at lunch time and we'll draw up a contract," Jay said.

"Thank you, sir." Chris used the "sir" word for the first time since I had met him.

"Don't call me sir," Jay said. "It makes me feel old and we queens worry about our age."

Nancy looked at her watch and said, "Don't mean to be a party killer, but I have early hospital rounds."

Michael Thompkins

    I took my cue and sucked up the sweet sugary-minty syrup at the bottom of my julep, the best part. Chris got up to get something from the stage, and everyone agreed to meet at the front door in two minutes.
    "Thanks for helping Chris out. Jay, I owe you one," Brett spoke softly to Jay.
    "Lieutenant, you don't owe me nothing," Jay said. "I'm short a band, they're on the cutting edge of pop, and this really helps us out. I already have the bikers, the queers, and the cowboys coming here. If I can start to draw some of the alternative music crowd, Bob and I will be eating well."
    "You and Bob already are living well," Brett said, meaning more than food.
    "Thanks," Jay said, beaming.
    "Okay, party's over. I'm turning into a pumpkin." Nancy was standing to leave. We all headed out of the band room and into the main bar area. We waited there a few minutes for Chris to catch up.
    "As of tonight, the Saloon is officially my favorite pub," I said.
    "We're honored," Jay said, smiling.
    I had a julep in me. I'd enjoyed the music, the Saloon atmosphere, and the company. I felt like my new job might just possibly work out. I was full of myself, as Nancy would say. She was looking real good to me. I held the door for everyone with a little smirk on my face — complacency combined with a little lust and mint julep.
    We all stood in a little circle on the sidewalk in front of the club savoring the band's success and the company. The parking lot was empty. Brett, a few steps ahead of us, scanned the parking lot.
    I looked at my watch 10 p.m. The cool desert night had come to Palm Springs. Life was good.
    My complacency was turned on its ass by the goddamn little laser dot.
    Again.

BODY BAG

This time it appeared on Brett's chest.

Jay was closest to Brett, reacted first, and pushed Brett onto his knees.

The red dot moved to Jay's shoulder.

Jay spun away from Brett in a violent pirouette as if he had been kicked in the chest by a horse.

"Pop. Pop."

A second red dot appeared on Jay's left shoulder. A more vivid red color that spread quickly across the front of his polo — blood spurted from the dot.

Brett rolled to his knees and pushed Chris to the ground, sprawling on top of him. As if they had rehearsed it, Brett rolled off Chris, and Joan began dragging him behind a car out of the kill zone.

Instantly, Brett had his weapon in hand and began running towards the rooftop of the building at the far end of the parking lot, seventy yards away. I don't know how he located the shooter in the dark. The building fronted on North Palm Canyon and housed Muriels, a popular nightclub. Halfway to the building, when he could insure his field of fire, Brett opened up.

Thirty seconds passed and the stench of cordite from Brett's Glock filled the air.

I dragged Jay behind the parked car where Nancy had crawled to relative safety. Despite her obvious terror, Nancy immediately put all her attention on Jay's shoulder, which was now heavily stained with blood.

There were no more shots fired from the rooftop. Brett's quick return fire must have come close enough to the shooter to suppress his sniping. Joan, carrying a roamer, a hand-held radio, called the shooting in and ran after Brett. I could hear at least three sirens sounding from three separate directions. I prayed one was the medic unit.

Nancy seemed to be effectively stemming Jay's bleeding, but transport time was critical in a gunshot wound. No more gunfire meant Brett and Joan had not engaged the shooter again.

"Shit, that burns." Jay spoke for the first time since he went down.

I was relieved to hear him talk.

"The medics are close. Stay still, so I don't lose this pressure," Nancy instructed her patient.

Bob came flying out the front door of the Saloon, and headed for the huddle around his partner. He saw the blood and immediately fear was written all over his face. A Heckler and Koch Nine hung by his side.

"It was meant for Brett; the red dot was on his chest first. Jay saved his life," Chris said, as if Brett or he was responsible for Jay's injury.

Bob didn't respond to Chris with words. He just put a reassuring hand on his arm and then looked at Nancy and asked, "You've stopped the bleeding?"

"Pretty much," Nancy said not taking her eyes off Jay.

"It burns," Jay said to Bob.

The medic unit rolled up and stopped, its stentorian siren suddenly silenced. I stood up from the cover of the vehicle and waved them toward us. The exact instant the medic unit arrived, I glanced up and saw the first black and white turn the corner on Arenas, coming the wrong way on Indian Canyon. The medics jumped out of the truck carrying their bags and came over to where Nancy had her fingers in Jay's shoulder. They glanced nervously around, concern that they might be in a kill zone written all over their faces.

"I'm Dr. Reynolds. We need to transport the victim A.S.A.P. to Desert Memorial. I don't want to take my fingers out of this wound, and I want to talk to the Triage Nurse in route. God knows they'll be busy enough on Friday night."

"Okay, Doc, we'll bring the stretcher. I'm going to start a Lactated Ringers drip." The senior medic spoke as the younger one went back to the rig to get a stretcher.

As they transferred Jay to the stretcher with Nancy attached to his left shoulder and Bob to his right, the first uniforms pulled in beside the medic unit.

I pointed at the building the shots came from. "Lieutenant Wade and his partner headed for that roof. There were no more shots fired at us after the one that hit Jay. The lieutenant returned fire and gave chase. Detective Fleming's with him."

Fortunately, the uniforms recognized me from somewhere, most likely sitting at Starbucks with Brett, and took my report at face value. The officer spoke into his shoulder mike; the response he got was to secure the parking lot at the rear of the building. Brett was taking tactical command from the rooftop. He and Joan were still in one piece for the moment. The two officers started running towards the far end of the parking lot.

"See you later at the hospital," Nancy yelled to me, as she squeezed into the medic unit alongside Jay, who was still conscious.

Although Jay looked like he might be going into shock, he was still talking to the medics. "Tell the lieutenant that...." he started to say, flinched in pain, and didn't finish.

I walked over and sat down on the pavement next to Chris, whose color wasn't much better than Jay's. We sat listening to the police radio in the parked unit and the still approaching sirens. It sounded like four units had responded to the call, roughly a third of the night watch from all three sectors.

"Your wife's amazing," Chris finally said. "One minute she's in the Saloon chilling out and having a drink. Next she has her hand in Jay's shoulder so that he doesn't bleed to death. Then she's in the medic unit taking charge. She doesn't seem upset or excited. How does she do it?"

"She's a professional. After a while, you become objective and unemotional, or you can't keep doing it."

"It's my fault," Chris whispered.

"What's your fault?"

"That Jay got hurt; it's all because I can identify this guy," Chris said with his street slang missing.

"Only one person's at fault, and that's the guy doing the shooting. Jay did what he did because of the same professional training that Nancy showed." I put my hand on his shoulder.

"I understand, I do. But I still feel like it's my fault." He was near tears.

"Welcome to adulthood. It means that there's more stuff to feel guilty about than when you were a kid," I said.

Officer Pete Navarez walked toward us. I remembered the last time that I'd seen him, the morning the case began.

"Hey Doc, Lieutenant Wade wants me to bring you and the kid to him on the rooftop. The area is secure, and the dogs are about to begin a search for the shooter. How's Jay doing?"

"Nancy was controlling his bleeding, and he was talking when the medics took him. He was shot in the upper left shoulder." I gave Pete the little I knew.

Pete looked at Chris and said, "With Doc's wife on the case, he'll be okay. If I were shot, she'd be the one I'd want taking care of me. She's a really good doc; she's mine."

Nancy was everyone's doctor. She had so many patients that she forgot their names. We had a secret code with which she would signal me when she couldn't retrieve a name from her overloaded memory banks. I was supposed to stick out my hand, introduce myself, and then the patient would be forced to introduce himself to me. She would be saved the embarrassment of being caught forgetting their names. She could recall minute details of their medical histories, but sometimes their names were buried underneath it all.

"Doc, I'm glad you're working with Lieutenant Wade," Pete said.

"Thanks. A lot has happened since our session," I said.

Pete led us from our hiding spot behind the car. "I can see that."

"I thought you were doing the morning shifts. How come you're on duty now?"

"Somebody called in sick so I'm pulling an extra shift. I thought maybe volunteering would be good for my attitude," Pete grinned. "You know, kill off the nightmare with a little extra attitude."

I knew what he meant. I was trying some of the same. The three of us walked across the parking lot and up the back stairs of the building where the shot had come from.

The tables were turned; I could feel Pete watching me to see how I was handling myself. I was his shrink but this time the bullets had come my way.

"You two all right?"

"I'll be fine when the shaking stops," I said.

"If it stops," Chris added quietly.

When we reached the second floor landing, we continued up an iron fire stairway to the roof. At the top, we were on a perfectly flat composition roof. The music from Muriels vibrated under my feet.

Brett and Joan were huddled with two uniformed Riverside County deputy sheriffs who responded to the call for assistance even though the city of Palm Springs wasn't their turf. The smaller towns of the nearby area used Riverside County Sheriffs under subcontract rather than maintain separate police departments. For cops there are three kinds of people: fellow cops, citizens, and perps. Cops will do everything in their power to keep citizens from being vics, and are generally indifferent to the plight of perps — fellow cops get their instant-undivided attention.

Brett waved us over and asked Pete to take Chris to my house. We needed to continue to search for the shooter. Brett instructed Pete to get out his riot shotgun and sit in my living room with Chris until somebody relieved him.

"Doc staying here with you?" he asked Brett.

"Yeah, he's getting on-the-job training," Brett said. "Chris, I'll relieve Officer Navarez when we're done here. Get some rest; I'm sorry this happened. Let's just hope Jay is going to be okay. He has Nancy with him, that's a plus."

"He just pushed you down and saved your life," Chris said.

Brett nodded and signaled Navarez to get Chris moving to my house "Pete, see if you can find out why there was a Tribal Ranger Suburban outside the Tahquitz vic's accounting firm on Thursday. Find out what they were up to," Brett said.

"Sure, lieutenant. I get to do a little investigating."

As Chris and Pete climbed over the edge of the roof, Brett and the two sheriffs were busy talking and left me to the view from the top of the building. I tried to stop my shaking.

I was perched six feet above the streetlights. Looking north two miles up North Palm Canyon toward Los Palmas, I saw the area where my home was tucked into the foot of Tachevah Canyon. Looking south down South Palm, I could see the vague outlines of the Indian Canyons several miles away. East, out Tahquitz, at about a mile and a half, I could see a kaleidoscope of lights from the airport. West from the roof top, there were three blocks of streetlights near my office, then Tahquitz Canyon at the foot of Mt. San Jacinto. The mountain rose 10,400 feet from base of the canyon to summit. I was standing dead center in a picture full of manmade light on three sides — the fourth side nothing but a big-black-wild hole.

I woke up from my trance as a Palm Springs officer came over the roof on the fire escape with a huge gray German shepherd K-9 cop behind him. The officer immediately pointed to the area on the roof from where our shooter had most likely taken aim. The shepherd began smelling the area thoroughly.

"How do you think Chris is holding up?" Brett finished talking with the sheriffs and coming over to where I was standing.

"You notice that he lost the street dialect?"

"He must be scared," Brett said.

"How many times were you in a firefight at his age?" I snapped at him.

He didn't answer, just shook his head at me, like, "Remember…"

Michael Thompkins

I couldn't believe I'd even asked the question. He probably couldn't remember how many times an enemy had tried to kill him when he was Chris's age. Feeling protective of Chris, defending his right to be scared as well as my own, I'd jumped on Brett. The absurdity of what I said slowly sunk in. "Sorry."

"Chris has a right to be scared, and you have a right to be testy. You're just being protective," he said. "One important thing to remember about fear…"

I nodded my attention to what he was saying.

"Never an excuse to do something stupid." He changed the subject. "Dog's ready, let's go."

"Which way?" I asked, already knowing in my gut it would be into the black hole.

"Follow the dog, he'll show us," Brett said, already moving.

We climbed down the fire escape into the middle of Palm Canyon and followed the German shepherd. He led us down Palm Canyon, before turning on Tahquitz towards the Desert Museum. By the time we arrived at the parking lot at the rear of the Palm Springs Desert Museum, we were a posse.

The first dog immediately found a body in the middle of the lot, and went berserk with barking.

Brett got on the radio and limited the response. Whatever happened here, we had enough uniforms. We formed two circles around the body in the shadowy lot illuminated only by a few overhead lights. Standing in the outer circle, I couldn't make out the victim.

Joan took one look at the body, and quickly turned toward me. "Doc, it's the security guard from Global Trading. He's… gone. What was his name?"

I could smell grass clippings from the nearby golf course and taste salt from my own sweat. I was still gasping for breath from the trot with the dogs, and had trouble seeing clearly. My back had tightened up; it felt like there was ground glass in some of the joints. I finally got my vision back, took a step closer to the body, and looked straight into the unfocused eyes of my former patient-turned-security-guard… "Jason…Jason White," I said barely audibly. Part of me thought I could still talk to him so I asked him in a whisper, "*What happened?*"

He didn't answer me.

I turned my eyes away, and focused on Brett.

"Shit bad luck," he said. "He must have ran into our shooter and challenged him. He must have thought the shooter was going to boost a car or something."

I finally worked up the nerve to look at Jason again. He'd been shot in the chest and just below the throat. My eyes watered.

"How?" I listened to myself ask the stupid question.

"Shot him in the chest and throat, in case he was wearing Kevlar," Brett said.

We were standing in a rough circle around Jason's body. The dogs continued to bark, still nuts. They ran up the museum trail a hundred yards and returned three times until their partners motioned them to sit. The dogs looked disgusted with us for not following them.

Brett radioed for a coroner and techs.

"Hey, Lieutenant," one of the K-9 officers spoke impatiently. "I'm ready to do what they pay me for. Why are we hanging back?"

The trail ran for a mile from a corner of the parking lot straight up the mountain. I had climbed it once, and remembered how steep it was. At 1400 feet of elevation in a mile, the Museum Trail hooked up with the Lykken Trail, which ran nine miles perfectly parallel with downtown Palm Springs. The trail junction, steep and rocky, looked straight down on our present position. Somewhere up there in the black hole over our heads, the shooter was perched prepared to use us as targets.

"I'm calling off this response," Brett announced.

"What? I don't get it, sir," the officer replied, confused, pissed.

"Our shooter is not a regular perp. He is an ex-ranger and the best I have ever run into. Your dog goes up there after him, and he will gas them with tear gas or shoot them with a silencer. If he were a regular perp, we'd be all over him in five minutes. But his present position, up there in the dark, is the perfect tactical position. First he'd kill your dog, then he'd shoot each one of us while we sweated our way up after him." Brett pointed up the Museum Trail into the black hole.

"Yes, sir," the K-9 handler acknowledged his superior, but didn't believe Brett's assessment of the situation for one minute. He was clearly unaccustomed to standing down; he was used to supplying tactical solutions, not quitting the chase.

"They don't think I made the right call," Brett said quietly.

"And if one of them or a dog was shot?" I asked.

"Then they wouldn't question my call as much. We would have at least tried; it bothers them because I won't do anything. Just the way it is with cops."

The K-9 handlers simultaneously nodded their compliance and shrugged their confusion. They gathered up their dogs and started the walk back to their vehicles.

Other police and EMT vehicles, and a Crime Scene Unit pulled into the parking lot. The EMTs checked Jason's pulse and proceeded with the empty ritual of resuscitation. The techs started stringing yellow tape. Between this scene and the top of the roof from where the shooter had fired on us earlier, the techs were going to have a busy night. The chief arrived, got out of his car and walked over to where we were standing.

"Well, things certainly got out of control here, Lieutenant," the chief said, clearly unhappy to have had his evening interrupted by our disaster.

"Yes sir," Brett replied. "No way we could've anticipated this outcome. Security guard came out of nowhere. If our shooter had run into any other citizen, he wouldn't have even paid attention to him. Jason must have tried to arrest him, probably got scared, drew his weapon and didn't have any idea who he was messing with. If he'd ignored the shooter, he'd still be alive. Just goddamn bad luck."

The EMTs gave up on Jason, stopped the resuscitation, and removed the airway bag.

"This is a screw up, and it's going to be bad press." The chief nodded in the direction of the media vans pulling up on North Museum. "Three people are shot in four days and two are dead. This shooter's eating us alive. How's the owner of the Saloon doing?"

"Shot in the shoulder," Brett said. "He's at the hospital with Doc's wife glued to his side."

The EMTs laid a body bag out next to Jason. I've hated those things from the moment I first saw them in Honolulu. Jason was just a kid who was supposed to have the rest of his life ahead of him, one that I'd played a part in. His only future now was a vinyl bag, zipper sealing his fate.

"He was just a kid," I said.

Brett saw me looking at the bag. "I told you that it could get worse."

"You did; I just didn't believe it. Whatever this costs me with Nancy, I can't quit until it's over. I owe that much to Jason. I didn't shrink his head so the shooter could shoot him in the goddamn neck."

"Good," Brett said.

"I'm supposed to figure this guy out. I'm getting nowhere. So far, three rounds go to the shooter. Round one, the accountant. Round two, my house. Round three, tonight. I'm not figuring this guy out fast enough. I'd be better as a TV shrink."

"Aren't you shrinks supposed to be easier on yourself than this?" the chief asked.

"What do you mean?" I asked.

"I'm not the tactician that the lieutenant is," he said, "but it seems to me that our shooter couldn't have known about the kid's gig tonight at the Saloon until they put out signs. Odds of him hitting in public were zero. Nobody could have seen this coming. No one could have anticipated him shooting in a congested downtown area like this. And now he's missed twice, once at Doc's and once tonight."

"He's going to think about and plan his next move a little more carefully," Brett said. "He knows we'll be ready next time. He knows he's used up his free passes. I buy Doc's idea about where he hits us next."

"You three need to be ready for him before he tries next," the chief said.

"We will," Brett promised. "Chief, he was trying to pop me tonight, not Chris."

"Shit," the chief said.

Brett nodded.

"This second murder will hit the paper and trigger questions at Interpol and the FBI," the chief said. "They've got software that monitors all newspapers. My phone will be ringing in the morning. I'll drag my heels on reporting the specifics, but the meter is running on their taking this case over. You three go check the Saloon owner and guard that kid. He's our only witness and still a target. I'll take these crime scenes; I don't want my skills getting rusty in case I'm ever demoted back to detective. And I don't want anyone else shot tonight." He added, "Lieutenant?"

"Yes, sir?"

"I'll want to be filled in on why this guy is shooting at you."

"As soon as I know," Brett replied.

The three of us walked back to the Saloon, then Brett and I drove back to my house where we had stashed Chris with Pete Navarez. Joan drove her own car. While we were en route, Brett called the hospital and was told that Nancy had scrubbed in with the thoracic surgeon to remove the bullet from Jay's shoulder. The surgery was almost over. Jay was stable and he would be in recovery until 5 a.m. Brett said Bob was pacing outside the O.R. suite, but Nancy would be out soon to settle him down.

When we pulled into my driveway, it was a few minutes after midnight. As we got out of the Mustang, Joan pulled in behind us. Navarez heard the cars pull up, exited out the back door and came up on our flank at the side of the house, pointing a shotgun at us.

"Everything all right?" Brett asked.

"We've been playing chess. Chris is good," Pete said.

We all walked in the front door and found Chris sitting at the dining room table bent over a chessboard in the middle of a match.

"Chris, we'll have to finish this game later," Pete said. "I need to report to the watch commander. I'm sure he has things for me; I'm off-shift soon."

"Thanks, Pete. I can finish beating you later."

"Maybe. Remember that when things cool down, I'll take you out and show you the Indian Canyons. We'll meet some of my relatives," Pete reminded him.

"Cool."

"Glad you were available to help. Thanks," Brett said to Pete.

"Good job," Joan said.

"No problem. I'll call my wife's uncle about the Tribal Suburban. Say, you want me to go ferry the Doc's wife home if she's ready?"

"That would be great," I said, jumping at the chance to avoid talking with Nancy any sooner than I had to.

"You okay?" Brett asked Chris as Pete went out the door.

"Could use a drink to calm my nerves," Chris said.

Brett and Joan waved off alcohol; I got them two tonic waters. I went to the liquor cupboard and pulled out my best single-malt scotch, a cask-strength Lagavulin brought back from London by one of my patients. I poured two doubles, neat, and delivered one to Chris. Two sips of the cask-strength Islay scotch and I could feel the warm familiar numbness ease the fear in my body and warm the chill in my backbone. When the scotch wore off, I didn't want to see Jason's eyes.

"Here's to finding a new name for the Chris Parks Band." I offered the first toast hoping to cheer myself up.

"Here's to Jay. Takes more than one round to finish him," Brett offered the second.

"Here's to Doctor Reynolds. She saved Jay's life." Chris offered the third toast.

"Here's to Jason White. He wanted to be a cop." Joan offered the somber toast.

I sat in silence for a minute quietly enjoying the ancient ritual of scotch and survival, listening to sounds of my house, and trying to get Jason's body bag out of my mind. No one spoke for several minutes.

GUN PLAY

"Doc, what makes this guy kill for money? Why does he do what he does?" Chris was the first to break the single-malt silence.

"He took the easiest way for himself," I told him. " Nobody bothered to test him to see if he had a conscience, or if he knew the difference between right and wrong. Or they tested him too late, booted him out and didn't follow up. Nobody followed him to see how he did in civilian life. Being a soldier was probably the only family he had and the only skills he possessed. I'm just guessing, though."

"Is he crazy?" Chris asked me.

"Probably not yet but he could get there. All alone, making his own rules, is the place where crazy could start."

Twenty-five minutes after Navarez left, he was back with Nancy. He walked her to the door and then took off, hopefully to complete his voluntary extra shift.

Nancy walked in and surveyed Brett, Joan, Chris, and me sitting in the living room. She saw the bottle of Lagavulin, walked straight to the hutch, grabbed a glass, and poured herself a double without speaking a word. I could feel the heat of her anger from where I was sitting.

She turned toward us. "Me too. I need one of these. Dave Peters did the surgery. We called him at home from the medic unit, bypassed the ER protocol and got Jay into surgery immediately. Great surgeon, he was happy to let me scrub in. He completely stopped the bleeding, removed the bullet and I sutured up. The lung was spared. The whole procedure took less than an hour. Jay needed two units of blood; his pressure came back quickly. He's tough as nails. Bob's hanging in there, too. He's calmed down considerably."

"When will Jay wake up?" Brett was visibly relieved.

She was holding something back. It was in her eyes.

"Around two or three a.m. I expect he'll have a sore throat and will feel like the wind got knocked out of him."

"He s-saved Brett's life and mine," Chris said, slurring from the scotch.

"It's not your fault," I said.

"Yeah, why did Jay do what he did?"

"You know, Brett is more qualified to answer that question than me," I said. Brett had the most experience dodging bullets — the rest of us were catching up fast.

"Jay didn't get shot for you or me," Brett explained.

"Whattaya mean?" Chris asked.

"Jay got shot for himself, not for us," Brett went on.

"I don't get it." Chris said.

"Jay said he'd protect you," Brett said. "What he did for us was an extension of that. There are two kinds of people in the world: ones like Jay who would rather be dead than not keep their word, and the rest. It's not about you; it's about what kind of person Jay wants to be for himself."

"Wow, that's deep," Chris said.

"Dr. Brett," Joan said.

"Is Jay going to be all right?" I had to know.

"There's nerve damage. He's probably going to loose some sensation, some strength, and maybe some movement in his left arm. Time will tell."

Silence.

More silence.

"I hate violence." Chris spoke quietly as much to himself as to us.

"Don't we all?" Brett asked.

"Violence is never okay. And it seems to me men are always responsible for it," Nancy spoke, her anger bubbling to the surface.

"I've seen too many women killers to agree with that," Joan cautioned.

"Sometimes violence is necessary," Brett said.

"When?" Nancy protested angrily.

Nancy and Brett were beginning an argument they'd had many times in the past; they always ended up agreeing to disagree.

Joan shut up fast.

"No, I mean... my father hit my mother." Chris interrupted.

Silence.

"We know," Brett said, putting his arm around Chris's shoulder.

"How? Oh, the hypnosis. It must have worked." Chris wasn't as groggy from the scotch as I had thought.

"We're your friends," I said.

"I know that. It's just that I had to leave home as soon as I got through high school to get away from him."

"College for me," Brett said.

"Say what? You mean?" Chris asked, slowly realizing he and Brett shared more than a home.

Joan's sharp little inhale was quite audible.

"Yeah, my folks broke up the day I graduated from college," Brett said. "Before that he used to hit her."

"You mean both of us..." Chris didn't complete his sentence.

Five minutes of silence later, Chris headed to the guestroom, and Nancy brought Brett blankets and a pillow for the couch. Brett brought me his backup weapon, a Sig Sauer .40, from the Mustang's trunk.

Joan followed Nancy down the hall to the guestroom.

Brett reminded her, "Be sure to sleep with your weapon."

Joan looked at Brett with a soft, tired smile.

When the ladies were out of hearing range, I said, "I'm not sure her weapon is what she wanted to sleep with."

"Well, I'll need a clearer message, and a different set of circumstances," he said.

Nancy walked back to the living room before heading upstairs. "Brett, I almost forgot. Jay had a message that I was supposed to pass on to you. He gave it to me during the ambulance ride."

"What?" Brett asked.

"Now. Now, you owe him."

Brett nodded.

Nancy and I walked upstairs to our master suite. In the bathroom for an eternity, she came out seething with anger at the violence, and the one who had brought it home to her.

"I am totally pissed. You have a madman stalking you and our friends," she finally exploded.

"I know," I said. No point in not owning up.

"Brett owes Jay and ...." she said shaking.

"I owe you," I said.

She got in bed, and I walked out on the small deck off our bedroom. I made sure that I wasn't backlit and let my eyes adjust to the darkness. I noticed movement at the edge of the backyard near the same little-man cacti that Joan had hidden behind. Brett was sitting on a deck chair covered by a blanket. He looked up and nodded — his doing-the-only-thing-I-know-how-to-do nod.

When I came back inside, I expected to find Nancy asleep. Instead, she was awake and she was naked. She pointed at my pillow.

"You owe me, you pay," she said huskily, smelling like plumeria.

Thirty minutes later, underneath her, on my back, I had paid my debt — currency exchanged more than acceptable.

TIGER KILL

By the time Bocca walked up Tahquitz Canyon Way to Muriels, he was ready six times over for anything.

Logistics, that's all they drilled into you in Ranger Training. Always be ready. Rangers lead the way. Can't be over- prepared. Redundant planning and implementation. Gung-ho shit. Strak stuff.

He had decided to pop the lieutenant, get it over with, and go have a scotch. The lieutenant wouldn't expect him to hit them twice so soon. Bocca had staked out the doc's office that afternoon and followed him to the Saloon where he read the sign about the kid's band playing tonight. He even had time to grab some supper while the band played. He ate at a nearby place specializing in fresh fish; the scallops were generously portioned and excellent. He was a chowhound.

He'd planned three separate escape routes out of the downtown area, and had two cars parked two miles apart. He'd scouted three caches in the area behind the Palm Springs Desert Museum where the trail named after the museum branched into the North and South Lykken Trail. When he came across the sign on the Museum Trail where it crossed a private road, he stopped, drank some water, read the sign and looked down on the O'Connell Golf Course.

"Stay on the trail, Respect private property." Sure. Just like the government and the people he worked for did. Everything was private until a bigger fish wanted it.

If they used dogs, Bocca was ready with a silencer. He knew that only a few helicopters could operate that close to a mountain, especially at night. If they fooled him with an elite pilot and were light years ahead with infrared, he had reflecting blankets to hide under. There was no way they could spot him. They had no idea who they were dealing with. Period. If they were as prepared as most police departments, maybe, after he was long gone, they would have a clue how really good he was. The almost infinite capacity of a single man had been drilled into him during Ranger training.

He walked up the fire escape at the rear of the building and checked his watch. 9:30 p.m. He took out the Glock .40, leaving the silencer off. Without the silencer, the trajectory of the round would be truer and less likely to drop over distance. He had a clear view of the front door of the Saloon.

GUN PLAY

Waiting. Really good at waiting. Waiting twenty years. Waiting twenty minutes. Too bad for the lieutenant. Too bad for him. He's getting what he earned.

9:56 p.m. They'll be coming out any minute. Doors open. People coming out en masse. 10:06 p.m., ten minutes for the damn crowd to exit and disperse.

Targets.

Two cops out first. They're scanning, but not far or high enough to see him. Now the doc's wife, the kid and some other guy who looks like a pro. Big guy, six feet plus, two hundred pounds. Now the shrink's out. Put the weapon on the lieutenant. Wait. They're standing around in a little huddle. Big guy's standing next to the kid. They're all grouped in a tight circle. Could do three of them before they react. Be slaughter. Thumb the laser on. Put it on the lieutenant's chest.

Squeeze off the round.

Shit! Big guy spotted the laser. Pushed the lieutenant down. Had to be a pro to react that fast to the laser. Took the round in the left shoulder. He's down. Lieutenant's gonna return fire. Shit. Blew an opportunity. They'll be ready next time.

At the last second, Bocca noticed something. The lieutenant fell on top of the kid to shield him. The kid was that important to the lieutenant. Noticing that could prove profitable. After he screwed the silencer back on, he stowed the weapon in the pack. If he needed to use the gun again, he didn't want sound to pinpoint his location, and trajectory wouldn't be an issue.

Move. Down the fire escape. Cop's coming fast. Damn fast. Hit Palm Canyon running. Move. Head for the museum.

His nervous system settled down by the time he arrived at the end of Tahquitz Canyon Way. It took him a little over four minutes to cover the distance on foot. All he had to do now was cut through the Desert Museum parking lot, and he'd be home free. He needed to collect himself. He'd missed again, twice in the last few days. He was losing his touch. That happened before but it always came back.

What the hell? What's this?

Who's the uniform? God damn rent-a-cop. What's he want? You've got to be fucking kidding. Rent-a-cop ordering him to halt. Wants to know what he's doing there. Ordering him to take off the backpack. Guard's nervous. Drawing a big nickel-plated thirty-eight. Wants to search his backpack.

Take the pack off.

Now. Clear the weapon.

Pop the guard. Pop him in the chest. Pop him in the throat in case he's wearing a vest.

Michael Thompkins

Then Bocca was on the trail behind the Palm Desert Museum, and under the protective umbrella of the mountain. He couldn't make out the museum rooftop as he climbed but he could see the flashing red lights of the police units, and he knew instinctively that they would use a dog to follow his trail to the museum parking lot. The dead rent-a-cop would slow them down. The more he thought about it, the guard actually served him.

He climbed five hundred feet in a quarter mile then stopped to observe the intersection of the museum parking lot with the trail. Now, whether or not the cops kept coming, sent dogs or gave it up, he could watch them completely unobserved from his high post. From the parking lot, all they would be able to see would be the faint black shape of the mountain.

He knew that the lieutenant should scrub the pursuit right here and would take heat from his men because of his decision. He also knew that this was the last time he would catch them completely unaware. Next time they would be ready for him. Opportunity lost.

Invisible now. Back in control. Missed twice. It happens around tactically trained pros. Professional baseball players only hit one out of four pitches on average. If they're really good, they hit one in three.

Third one's the charm.

VERSACE PAJAMAS

The morning after Jay's surgery, we all rode out to visit him in the hospital. Desert Regional is located at the intersection of Tacheva and Indian Canyon, a mile from our house. Everyone was quiet and self-contained on the short drive — permanent damage to Jay's arm was possible.

When we arrived, the nearly empty hospital parking lot reflected my mood. Hospitals are strange, lonely places on Saturday mornings. Skeleton nursing and housekeeping staffs add to the emptiness; visitors and doctors are scarce. Looking into Jason White's dead eyes last night and worrying about Jay's arm had left me raw. Sex was an honest attempt at self-medication on both Nancy's and my part, but it hadn't lifted my mood.

As we walked through the front door of the hospital, the car jockeys were beginning to set up the hospital valet parking.

"Only in Palm Springs," I said, under my breath.

"What happens to your valet parked car if you end up hospitalized or worse?" Brett asked.

"Maybe it's a charitable donation after sixty days," Joan suggested.

My humor was returning. "You guys remember the drive-in Daiquiri stands in New Orleans?"

"Sure," Brett replied. "In Palm Springs, we got drive-in, drop-off diagnosis."

We walked through admitting and Nancy picked up a house phone to locate Jay's room. Desert Regional had two post-op floors in addition to the ICU. It turned out that Jay hadn't required intensive care so he went directly to one of the post-op floors. When we arrived at his room, he was propped up in bed wearing red silk Versace pajamas and the same ring he wore last night at the Saloon. Somehow, Bob had managed to get the nurses to allow them. Jay's fashion statement cheered me up. Jay was looking pretty drug-induced drowsy. Bob was sitting on the bed with him, looking pretty tired too. Jay's left upper arm and shoulder were bandaged and fixed in position with a sling.

He wasn't formally Nancy's patient, but she'd assisted at his surgery last night, so she picked up his chart from its rack on the foot of his bed and read the nursing notes. Then she scanned the readings on his vital signs record on the wall before she gave him a careful hug.

"How am I doing, Doc?" Jay asked in a hoarse voice.

"Just about as well as humanly possible. You had Dr. Peters, the best chest surgeon in the area. Has he been to see you yet?" Nancy asked with more than one question in her voice.

"Don't worry. He told me there's damage to the nerves in my arm and that he can't predict how complete my recovery will be. I might lose some feeling, some movement and some strength."

On the way to the ER last night, Nancy had made a call to the best on-staff surgeon, trading on a personal favor. She always had more IOUs to collect than to pay out at any given time.

"You saved my life. Thank you," Jay whispered a little hoarsely.

"You saved Brett's life," Chris said to Jay. "First me, then Brett, and now you. Man, am I tired of us being shot at. I'm going to have bad dreams with red dots in them forever."

Brett hung back. How do you thank someone for taking a bullet for you?

Jay solved it for him. "Lieutenant, you may have to help me pour whiskey sometimes."

Brett looked at Jay as if to say *"I can't ever repay you,"* but instead said, "I'm not wiping your ass."

That was all he said.

Jay tried to laugh and winced in pain.

I looked out the third floor window toward Mt. San Jacinto and south down Indian Canyon Drive, trying to make out the rooftop from where the shooter had tried to kill Brett and hit Jay. I couldn't see the rooftop, but I could see the trail leading up from the Desert Museum parking lot. It was a mile away. Brett looked across the room at me, and I knew he was thinking the same thing. Do better next time or somebody else will be dead.

Joan asked Jay how he had reacted so quickly in pushing Brett out of the line of fire.

"I'm used to scanning the parking lot for people who've had too much to drink, pulling their keys, and calling them a cab. It's part of my job," Jay replied. "The rest was just blind luck, I guess. As I was scanning, I caught the red laser dot on his chest out of the corner of my eye, reacted, and the rest is all about Nancy saving me."

"Thank you for saving Jay's life," Bob said to Nancy.

"My pleasure," Nancy said. " It's what I'm trained for. Besides, Palm Springs can't afford to lose the Mint Juleps that your partner makes."

Maybe Nancy was getting her humor back; she was way ahead of me.

"You can come in anytime day or night, alone or with company, and the drinks are always on the house for you, Doctor," Jay said.

"Is that what they call southern hospitality?" Nancy asked.

"Yes, and deep gratitude to you," Bob replied in perfect New Orleans drawl.

Seven of us were crowded into Jay's room, and we'd already drawn some disapproving glances from the nursing staff. So far, they had withheld comment because Dr. Nancy was in the room. We were pushing our luck, though. Brett solved the dilemma by calling a breakfast meeting in the cafeteria for Joan, him, and me.

"Chris, why don't you come back to the Saloon with me and we can handle the new contract with the rest of the band over lunch?" Bob suggested. "You can practice at the Saloon this afternoon and be ready to play tonight. If you need anything from home, I can drive you out there."

"I don't want any of this getting in the way of our plans," Jay added. "We can't let this bastard scare us."

"Thanks," Chris said. "I want to work on some of my songs this afternoon so we'll be ready for next Thursday night's opening. Man, I need to get my mind off the damn red laser too. I am so tired of this."

"You don't mind protecting him?" Brett asked Bob.

"I'm hoping the shooter tries something," Bob said, patting his fanny pack.

"Don't," Joan protested. "Why don't we assign a uniform to them?"

"Done. We'll put uniforms with you all day," Brett ordered.

"I can live with that," Bob said. "We'll be fine, I promise."

Brett picked up the house phone and ordered officers to meet Bob and Chris at the hospital entrance. He reminded them that Bob was carrying. I was nervous that we wouldn't personally have Chris under guard, but we needed to continue the investigation and work out a plan to greet our shooter next time he visited. Like the chief said, we needed to be ready next time. We walked out the door, waved goodbye to everyone, and left Nancy to finish rounding on her other patients.

We made our way to the cafeteria. Brett and I were starved as usual and ordered full breakfasts. I ordered bacon, eggs, and hash browns, Brett had a Denver omelet, and Joan ordered fruit salad, yogurt, and granola.

"Are we are still assuming that he'll try to hit Chris and Brett next at Brett's house at night?" Joan asked, chewing on a mouthful of granola.

"Exactly," I said, while savoring the bacon — fried crisp just the way I liked it.

"He'll try. This time we'll be ready." Brett held his index finger and thumb like a gun.

"How long you figure it will take for our shooter to figure out where you live?" Joan asked.

"I figure he already knows. He had to have connections to find out I was a Ranger. His connections could be whoever hired him or someone who specializes in selling intelligence to criminals. Lots of ways to get my address besides following Doc," Brett suggested.

"He's been having a field day following me so far. Some ex-Intel officer I am. I thought police officer's addresses were kept hidden." I was surprised at the availability of this information.

"They used to be, in the good old conservative days, before the liberals came along," Brett said.

"Don't start on me. You're the one taking Chris in," I replied.

"Doc's got a point," Joan said. "It's not good for your hard-ass conservative image."

"Just because I'm sometimes conservative doesn't mean I'm a fascist or I can't help people," Brett said with feigned indignation.

"Me too. Just because I'm sometimes liberal, doesn't mean I'm a communist or I can't carry a gun," I said.

"Ah, the culture war. You two will have to start a new party," Joan quipped.

"We're working on it," Brett said.

"Something else we need to work on first…" I said.

"Catching this guy," Joan said, focusing on the job at hand.

"I want this bastard. He tried to kill me and my friends." Brett changed the subject with an uncharacteristically warm-blooded tone. He didn't usually take it personally.

"He'll keep coming until we nail him," Joan said.

"Okay, then let's go rattle some cages," Brett said. "I want to go out to the Imperial Valley Golf Association. We need to understand what that note means — what Imperial's relationship with Global is. It's our only clue. I know it's Saturday but we have a warrant and who knows what we'll find. Imperial has been notified that we're coming soon, but not specifically when. Then we'll go to my place, hook up with Matt Davis, my SWAT trainee, and plan a surprise for our shooter. Tonight. Shooter's not going to give up the cover of darkness."

Our plans for the day in place, we stood up to bus our dishes and leave.

"Jay and Bob are sure stand-up guys. They just kept moving forward after Jay was shot. That takes guts," Joan said.

"Takes more courage just to be who they are," I said.

"They're stand-up *gays*," Brett said.

K-MART COUTURE

We drove out Interstate 10 past Indio, against the fringes of Joshua Tree National Park, and into the southeast corner of the Coachella valley. The original Interstate, Highway 111, meanders through the valley cities. But the folks who built the new Interstate 10 used the old railroad tracks as a straight edge, kept the rails on their right, lined up their sights on the Salton Sea, and came straight on through.

We turned off Interstate and into the gravel parking lot of the Imperial Valley Golf Association. Its business was selling golf course equipment and supplies, including natural gas and electricity, to all of the major golf courses in the valley.

"This place looks completely innocent. It's hard to think about crime here. It smells like grass, fertilizer, and gasoline. I don't see any big power lines, either," I said.

"You can't judge a book by its cover," Joan warned.

"Crime's everywhere," Brett said.

"Optimists," I said.

"Let's go see for ourselves." Joan led us in the direction of the main office.

The parking lot was filled with pea gravel with patches of grass poking through. Joan stepped on a little soft spot and lost her footing.

"Whoa!" She exclaimed on her way to the ground.

Brett, who was walking near her, quickly caught her fall — she was in his arms.

"Got you." Brett exclaimed, looking surprised at his sudden fortune.

Joan totally relaxed for a few seconds in Brett's arms, smiled, and then laughed out loud. Brett pressed her back upright effortlessly from a foot off the ground. She brushed herself off symbolically, although she never even touched the gravel.

"That's another reason I gave up marathons," she said. "I can't even walk straight."

The Imperial Valley operation was a one-story house; it looked to be one of the first built in the valley. We walked through the front door into a small reception area no bigger than a hotel closet. Everything was run down and coated with a fine dust. Microscopic plumes of white powder cascaded down from the plaster ceiling clumsily patched many times. The air smelled of ancient sheet rock.

"If cleanliness is next to Godliness," Joan said.

"Then God has certainly never been here," Brett finished it.

We stood and waited, avoiding the furniture. A door to an inner office was closed direct.

A young woman spoke to us as opened the door and stepped into the already packed reception area.

"Well, I barely heard you folks come in. What can I do to help you? I must have left the door unlocked. It's Saturday; I'm sorry to say we're closed."

"Miss, we need to talk with you. We want to examine your records." Joan held out her detective shield.

"Well, I'm Susan."

"Susan, I'm Detective Fleming, this is Doctor Reynolds, and my partner is Lieutenant Wade," Joan said.

Dressed in a cheap pastel shift that looked comfortable in the heat, Susan wore pink athletic shoes with matching laces. Her ankle socks were matching pink. Her dress was the kind of smock called a housedress in the fifties, bringing back memories of Ozzie and Harriet — she was coutured by Kmart.

Definitely flustered by the badge, she continued, "Mr. Forester has been in Phoenix this week, at his other company. I got your call yesterday. I contacted Mr. Forester and he said that he wanted to get back first before you examined anything. Our records are confidential and…"

"We would need a court order. We have it," Joan said, pulling the document from her black linen jacket.

"Yes, but shouldn't we wait for him to come back from Phoenix?" she asked.

We were in the cookie jar, and weren't leaving until we tasted the sweet stuff.

Joan was eager to pry open the lid. "Susan, I'm certain Mr. Forester would want you to cooperate with the police, so we'll just find the records we need and be on our way. I'm sure that the mayor and the chief of police will call Mr. Forester when he returns and thank him for his cooperation. How many people work here?" Joan just kept on talking, allowing little room for Susan to think about consequences.

"We have three salesmen, three receiving/distributing agents, and me." Susan seemed to enjoy talking so much that we might just chat our way into her cooperation.

"Who's in charge of electricity sales to the golf courses and how does that work?" Joan asked.

"Well, Global does that for us," Susan explained. "They send us copies of all transactions but they pretty much handle everything for our clients. We just provide the customers and Global does the rest." Susan seemed happy to share her knowledge of the company ins and outs.

"We'll need to see the records for all those transactions and have access to your computer records," Joan added.

"Oh, they're not in the computer yet. Global just sends us hard copies of the transactions and we're hoping to get them into our system soon. We need a bigger server."

"So they're kept separately?" Joan asked, barely repressing her glee.

"We keep them back there in a room that used to be a closet, until we can add them to our system." Susan pointed to the side door.

With Brett smiling and Joan one notch beneath beaming, we continued for the goodies.

"Can you set us up with a work area, a table, some chairs, and retrieve those records for us?" Joan asked.

"Maybe I should try to call Mr. Forester, and just let him know?" Susan asked.

"Why don't we get started and then you can call him. That way there's no chance the judge, the mayor or the chief will get upset with any of us," Joan bluffed, forgetting to mention the president of the United States.

"Of course. You do have a court order," Susan said, grabbing a set of keys from her pink housedress, and opening up the side door.

Joan waved the court order ceremoniously in the air. "I sure wish you worked for the police department. We have such inefficient administrative help. Have you ever thought of applying for a job with the department?"

"Do you think I could?" Susan jumped at the offer.

"Just let me know," Joan said, smiling back at her, innocent as a burglar.

Joan did suck-up almost as well as I did. Psychologist Handbook, page 340: learn to suck-up to anyone.

Five minutes later, we were sitting knee-to-knee around a table in the small office that served Imperial as a conference room. Boxes of transaction records and log sheets from Global on the floor were stacked between our chairs and the wall.

Dust continued to drop.

"If they used asbestos, we're dead," Brett said.

"You two take the log sheets and separate out any that list PaloVerde/Imperial/Palm Springs with a February 13th date," Joan ordered.

"Yes ma'am," Brett replied.

"Got it," I said.

Joan promised Susan to mind the store while she drove down the road to the drive-through kiosk for her coffee break; she was grateful for that and Joan's job hints. I hoped she would remember that gratitude when Forester returned and discovered our visit.

Twenty minutes later, Joan took off her jacket, shook the white dust off it and announced, "I got the date."

A log sheet and a record of transaction sheet in her hand, she carefully scrutinized them. She took a small notebook out of her pocket and compared the log sheet, the transaction sheet, and her notes.

She looked up at us, met our curious eyes and announced, "Bingo!"

"What've you got?" Brett asked eagerly.

"What I have is another clue. The city of Palm Springs paid five times as much per kilowatt as Imperial Valley Golf for the same block of electricity. Remember the note I found in his golf bag: 'Global, Palo Verde; Imperial Valley/Palm Springs, 2/13, 2.22 p.m.' It took me awhile to figure out what it stood for. Late yesterday afternoon, I got a return fax from Arizona Public Service in Palo Verde, Arizona. I know what Global paid for that block of power even though their tape on that day is 'missing.' The bottom line is Global charged the city of Palm Springs five times what they charged Imperial Valley."

"Is that illegal?" Brett asked.

"Not illegal, but damned interesting," Joan said. "They charged Imperial Valley basically what they paid for the power from Palo Verde. Then they turned around and charged the city five times that amount. It's not illegal, but the city is sure going to be pissed off. Why is Global making such a large profit on the city and charging Imperial Valley so much less?"

"Couldn't Imperial and the city have long-term contracts in which Global delivers at a certain rate no matter what their cost? That's one explanation," I said, seeking a simple solution.

"That wouldn't explain such a big differential," Joan said. "Like I said before, I love this stuff; it's what I live for: a giant jigsaw puzzle. Right now I feel like I've laid out all the pieces and I'm arranging the pieces into different little piles based on where they go, but I'm a long way from assembly."

"Let's get a tech out here to copy all this stuff," she suggested. "Have the tech be real chatty with Susan about employment possibilities with the city. Better make it a woman; I'll instruct her to make notes on anything Susan volunteers."

"What are you going to do if Susan actually applies for a job with the department?" I asked.

"Help her, of course," Joan said.

"Liberals," Brett said.

"Look whose talking," Joan responded.

"I, for one," Brett said, changing the subject quickly, "would like to hear Conto's explanation of Martin Jonas's note now that we've discovered price differentials. I'd also like to hear her explanation of all the late- night cell phone calls between her and Bergman."

"You've been holding out?" Joan challenged.

"Just found out this morning. My request for data on Bergman and Conto's cell phones came back. The tech left me a voice mail but I didn't listen to it until this morning. Bergman and Conto have been a couple of Chatty Cathies every night," Brett added.

"Doc, you might just be right about Bergman and Conto boinking," Joan said.

"Boinking?" Brett asked teasing.

"You know what boinking means?" Joan asked, looking directly at Brett.

"Yes. Yes, I do."

BRETT'S GUN SHOP

Ten minutes later we pulled into Brett's driveway in Cathedral City. His house was a half-mile north of the intersection of Highway 111 and Cathedral Canyon Way. He'd recently purchased the three-bedroom brick-stucco bungalow at the end of a little cul-de-sac near Lawrence Welk's Desert Oasis. Cathedral Canyon Golf Course was across the road from his house and also butted up directly against Tahquitz Creek Golf Course where our first victim, Martin Jonas, had been shot.

"We must be, what, a mile and a half from the eighteenth at Tahquitz?" I asked.

"If we walked straight across Cathedral Canyon Golf Course due west from here, we'd end up in the arroyo where we found the shooter's weapon. Be a mile and a half," Brett said. "Let's go inside."

Brett steered us around the side of the house and through the patio directly into his kitchen, which smelled of grapefruits and lemons picked from his front yard.

"You guys want a beer?" he asked.

"One for me," Joan said.

"Me, too," I said. We took our Pacificos out onto the patio that faced due south into the Santa Rosa wilderness and the San Bernardino National Forest.

It was hot. The beer was cold.

Directly in front of us was a five hundred-yard wide-open area with the White River dry creek bed in the middle of it. The desiccated river's original source was five miles north of Palm Springs where both Highway 111 and Highway 10 started their descents into the valley. On the other side of the ravine was the light industrial area where Chris had been living. Except for an enormous crane parked in an equipment rental company yard, the whole area was flat as a pancake.

Brett went back inside to the kitchen to fix some sandwiches for lunch and left Joan and me on the patio. We were quiet, enjoying our beer and watching the bike riders and joggers passing by several hundred yards away on the trail at the opposite side of the ravine. It was almost noon and it must have been 85 degrees. A few trees lined the dry riverbed and provided welcome shade.

"Nancy was incredible with Jay last night," Joan said. "The way she just stopped the bleeding and kept him alive, assisted in his surgery, and still got up to do rounds on patients this morning makes her my new role model."

"She's pretty amazing. I feel like the coward in the family. I'm not sure that I have what it takes to do what you and Brett do. I went through the whole 'Nam thing gathering intelligence from soldiers who got shot at every day. The one time I did get shot at, I wasn't supposed to shoot back. I wasn't supposed to be there. They extracted me before I could shoot back. One thing I am sure of is that I can't look into Chris's eyes the way I looked into Jason's eyes. I can't let that happen."

"I've never been shot at either. It frightens me, too," Joan confessed. "I don't feel like I have any choice either, but not just because of Chris. Returning fire comes with being a cop. How can I be a cop if I doubt myself in that way? Sure the men accept me on the job, but not completely. They don't say it but I can feel it."

"What does being a woman have to do with it?"

"Male partners never really trust you until you prove you can return fire," she said.

"Really?" I asked

"They trust each other without proof but they need proof from women. Goes with being a woman cop."

"We got the same problem," I said.

"Yup," Joan said. "Do we have what it takes?"

"We can form a support group," I said.

"I'm glad you're in," she said. "There's a lot I can learn from you. What makes this shooter tick is over my head. Something else…"

"What's that?"

"After the last few nights, it's time for you to carry your own gun," she said.

On that cue, our sandwich chef and gun dealer, Brett delivered the sandwiches from the kitchen. He'd made sliced avocado and cheddar topped with tomatoes and lettuce; anything with avocado spelled California to me. It was a great sandwich, and he'd made fresh-squeezed lemonade to go with it.

"What were you two talking about while I slaved over lunch?" he asked.

"Joan thinks I need my own gun."

"I got one for you," Brett said.

"What about a permit?"

"Chief signed it. He has it," Brett said.

"Never any doubt you could arm me," I said.

We finished eating, put our plates on the kitchen counter, and followed him to the garage gun shop.

His 1800 square foot bungalow was a mixture of an Army and Navy store, and backpacking outfitter. Constantly living ready to deploy with his Special Forces Unit, gear bags were everywhere. His large two-car garage contained a pair of olive-drab gun safes that rivaled the size and security of those of a small arms dealer. I had visited his garage many times before to view his gun collection, but this time I wouldn't just be window-shopping. Joan was getting her first visit. She liked guns. Maybe it would rub off on Nancy.

"Joan's right, I'm right, and the chief agrees. You need to start carrying a handgun." Brett worked through the security system codes on the first gun safe.

"The newspapers will call you *'The Shooting Shrink'*," Joan said.

"The Shooting Shrink," Brett repeated. "Good PR for the department."

"Do I look like a 'shooting' anything?"

"You're going to take some heat from the left," Joan said.

"Not any more than Brett will take from the right for helping Chris."

"Offend the left and offend the right; we be getting close to the truth." Brett reminded us of our often-repeated political motto.

Brett and I had read up on centrist political philosophy, and had spent hours building a fantasy political platform that contained elements from the left and the right.

"You two are my heroes," Joan said, encouraging us on.

"We be centrists," he said.

"So that's what you meant by you two were 'working on it,'" Joan said.

"It's our favorite game," I said.

"After watching women," Brett corrected me.

"I don't know about that. I do crosswords and they can be tough. But I want in on this centrist thing," Joan said.

Brett and I looked at each other, gave Joan a long "sizing-up look," smiled and nodded her in to our politics.

"Moderates from both sides are welcome," I said. "Faith-based fanatics from both sides, tree huggers on the left and fundamentalists on the right — unwilling to apply evidence-based solutions to problems — are out."

Joan picked a gear bag off a peg and looked in it while Brett worked the electronics on the second safe. The garage reminded me of my grandparents' basement when I was a boy. My grandfather had been an English bobby in Ireland before

Michael Thompkins

moving to the United States in 1910. In his basement in South San Francisco he stored his treasures from that world, just like Brett stored treasures from his journeys. A walnut map cabinet with a marble inlay top big enough to lay out a full-size map sat in the center of Brett's garage.

Brett finished disarming the alarms, opened both safes, and the garage suddenly smelled sweetly of guns. The seductive aroma of Brett armory was a blend of gun oil, gunpowder, walnut stocks, and the best steel in the world.

"About seventy percent of my weapons are tactically useful. The rest of them are just souvenirs of armies I have advised for or against." Brett started pointing out weapons to Joan.

"You must have a couple hundred weapons here?" Joan asked.

"Three hundred and six," Brett replied.

"Isn't that a Chinese rifle?" Joan asked, her curiosity growing by the minute. "I saw a picture of that once in a gun magazine."

"That's a Sino-Soviet SKS. It's rare," Brett said, looking clearly impressed.

Joan knew about classic cars, was a good detective, and she understood a thing or two about guns. Could he find a more ideal woman? Christ, don't let this one get away.

"What makes it rare?" she asked.

"You really want to know?" Brett replied. He picked up the SKS, made sure the weapon was empty and handed it to Joan. She took the weapon and held it in both hands in the classic "port arms" position: rifle stock held by the left hand at the left shoulder, butt held by the right hand at the right hip. She must have learned it at the police academy.

"It's rare because they were made for a year and a half, 1956 and part of 1957, by Soviet armorers. They taught the Chinese how to make these rifles which are chambered in 7.62 mm x 39. For that year and a half, and here's what makes them rare, the Soviet armorers used Soviet steel. When the Ruskies went home in 1957, the Chinese continued making them with their own steel. It was a downgrade."

"How'd you get it?" she asked.

"Took it off a NVA Regular," he said.

Alive or dead, I thought. I didn't ask. It would be tacky.

"Now, for Doc, we have a nice pistol from my 'Spring Collection.' It's light, easy to conceal and absolutely reliable: a Glock Model 17 chambered in 9mm."

Brett reached into the safe, pulled a black automatic pistol from the shelf, once again cleared the weapon, and handed it to me.

I took the weapon from him and felt what I always felt with guns, a parallel sense of fear and excitement. "I like the feel of it. I'll need to take it out to the range and fire some rounds. It's so damn light."

"Part plastic, some steel," he said. He reached into the safe and pulled out a little leather clip-on holster for the Glock and handed it to me. "Here, see if this fits it."

I clipped the holster onto my belt, checked the Glock to make sure it was empty a second time, and holstered the weapon. Not being used to carrying a handgun, it felt like a living thing on my hip. I was conscious of a sensation I always had when handling any weapon.

"When you guys are carrying, do you ever feel like everything revolves around the weapon?"

"Yup. It's like working with a chain saw. All there is, is the chain. The minute you forget where the chain is, somebody gets hurt," Brett said. "It's time to learn how to load the magazine."

He reached into the safe and pulled out a box of 9mm cartridges. I handed him the Glock handle first. He released the magazine and carefully demonstrated how to load a round into the magazine and then how to load the next round down on top of the first.

"The trick is to use the heel of the cartridge, 'cause it is stronger and needs to go in first." He showed me how to compress the spring-loaded magazine, and add one round after another.

"When we take it to the range, we'll practice loading magazines for speed. Here's a fanny pack to carry the Glock in when you're not wearing a jacket." He tossed me a North Face fanny pack.

I used the heel of my left hand to seat the magazine, holstered it, and stowed it in my new pack. I was armed and maybe dangerous.

As we were finishing up my outfitting, a golf cart pulled up in Brett's driveway. Through the small garage windows, I recognized a Palm Springs cop dressed in off-duty clothes.

"Why the cart?" Brett asked him as he raised the door enough for our guest to enter.

"In case your shooter is already watching the house," the blond man replied.

"Smart move," Brett said.

"Where did you get the cart?" I was curious.

Michael Thompkins

"Golf course pro shop is always willing to help Palm Springs' finest," Officer Matt Davis answered me.

"You know Joan and Doc?" Brett introduced us.

"Yes, sir, we've run into each other. Pleased to meet you again, Joan. Hi, Doc," Matt said, smiling at us.

"Drop the sir; I don't see any brass around. This is a volunteer gig," Brett said.

Matt Davis was a three-year veteran of the department. He was in his twenties, almost two decades younger than Brett and me, and one younger than Joan. I had approved his psychological profile for the job, and I remembered being impressed by his professional attitude about police work. Matt told me at his psych eval that being a cop was a job to do well, not something to build an ego around. Matt was a younger, white version of Brett.

He was part of a loosely knit group of officers in the valley who were preparing to become Palm Spring's first SWAT team under Brett's tutelage and command. The chief was lobbying for funds so that he didn't have to rely on Riverside County SWAT.

"Okay, Doc and Joan are in on this. Any problem working with a woman or a shrink?" Brett asked Matt.

"No, sir. I'm here to learn." Matt couldn't give up the 'sir' easily. "I like working with women and I'm getting a degree in psychology at night. Maybe I'll learn something from Doc that helps in my classes."

"All right, let's get to work. Matt, you bring your stuff?" Brett asked.

Matt nodded and went to the back of the golf cart, lifted out his backpack, reached inside, and retrieved a pair of camouflaged binoculars.

Brett laid out the plan. "We check out the area, and figure how to net this guy. Matt and Joan, you guys sort out how to set up positions along the ravine. I'll check out possible approaches through the golf course. Tom, you float. Everyone try to figure out the shooter's most likely approach and the place that he'll set up to shoot from. It's a 1000-yard perimeter for everyone. Be back here in twenty minutes."

We tried our best to appear as casual as possible as we went to our assigned areas; that was no small task for a party of four. I spent the next fifteen minutes making a 360-degree sweep of Brett's house wearing a golf cap and sunglasses, hoping to appear inconspicuous.

I figured the shooter would enter our soon-to-be trap from the hills due south of the intersection of Highway 111 and Cathedral Canyon Way. The hills came right down to within a hundred yards of the highway and would provide an escape route at night in almost any direction. It would be just like his approach at my house as well as downtown at the Saloon. This guy likes to have one foot in the wilderness all the time.

Eighteen minutes had passed on my watch by the time I returned to the garage. I used the code Brett had given us to open the door, closed it behind me, sat down and waited. Outside it was really hot, and I was sweating. It was cool inside the garage, with the pleasant familiar smell of weapons and gear.

"We're going to need excellent communication gear, not department walkie-talkies," Brett was telling Matt as they returned to the garage a couple minutes behind me. "Half of the valley has police band radios and the frequencies to all our channels, including the tactical ones. I don't want our shooter listening to us."

"What you got in mind?" Matt asked as the door rolled down behind them.

"Check this stuff out." Brett went to the garage wall and pulled down a small equipment bag containing six handheld portable radio units. "Uncle Sam catches me using these and he'll reactivate my butt. They use a special-ops frequency and I'm counting on us not being heard over in the L.A. basin. The mountains should effectively limit the unit's range to fifty miles."

Joan was the last to return, noticed the radios and whistled in appreciation of the commo gear. They were ultra-light and came with earpieces.

"We're all going to jail if they catch us using those," Matt said, not really worried.

He took one from Brett, examined the unit carefully and said, "Damn cool stuff."

"Doc, what do you think about the shooter's approach?" Brett down to business.

"I think that our friend is going to come in exactly the same way he did downtown and at my house. He likes to operate as if this were wilderness and not an urban area; that's part of his mindset. He always has a leg in the wild and a plan to escape. He couldn't get away with this in L.A., but Palm Springs is perfect for what he's been doing. Here, we're surrounded on two sides by primitive area, and he's been eating us alive because of it. If he approaches from the other side of 111 and then into the dry riverbed, he has a shot at the house with built-in escape back across the highway. Then he has 180 degrees of wilderness to disappear into. I'm pretty sure that'll be his choice."

"And you're saying he'll do this because he did it before?" Matt asked. "He just won't drive up in a car and take a shot?"

"Past behavior's the most reliable predictor of future behavior," I said. "Psychologist Handbook, page 65. He's running a pattern now. Two nights this week, he came at us in the same way. I think it's likely that he'll try again tonight from up the ravine."

"That gives us two miles of entry points to the riverbed," Matt said. "He'll have a lot of room to maneuver in."

"Sorry, but I can't pinpoint it any closer than that," I said.

"Doc's right," Brett said. "That's the way I'd approach, set up and have a clear shot at the front of the house. He knows Chris plays at the Saloon and what time he should be done. He knows we're protecting Chris, and we can assume he's guessed Chris is staying with me."

"He'd never risk being spotted on the golf course at night," Joan said.

"Probably not. It's too open an area. I get his pattern now," Matt said. "This guy is very good; he plans every move he makes, and he most likely has equipment caches, cars and places to sleep. He must have been paid a bundle to hit that accountant. He can afford to hang out and run this thing like he's deployed for a month. One thing I don't get is why he's sticking around."

"There's something you should know," Brett said.

"What?" Matt asked.

"Tell him, Tom."

I filled Matt in on the shooter's apparent grudge against Brett and the Ranger coin he left behind as a message.

"A Ranger coin! We're in deep here. This guy's a Ranger," Matt said, letting out a whistle.

"He seems to need to compete with Brett," I said. "This whole thing has turned into a contest. He crossed the line and became emotionally involved with this contract, with Brett and maybe with the kid. The psychopathology of contract killers doesn't include most of the things he's done. Most contract killers would have just shot the accountant and left. He's got something weird to prove here. This guy's a sociopath and he's beginning to unravel."

"If you want to un-volunteer, now's the time, without prejudice." Brett knew we all had to be a team.

"This guy's a disgrace to the coin. His ass is mine," Matt said. "I'm ex-Ranger, myself."

"You're wrong about that," Brett said with priority rights over Matt.

"Why?" Matt asked.

"He belongs to me. He tried to kill my friends and me. I own this creep."

Joan noticed we were all sweating, unclipped her water bottle and passed it around. She had squeezed a lemon into it.

"Okay. We set up every night at 9," Brett said. "Matt and Joan, you're in the ravine along his most likely entrance. I'll cover the golf course just in case and back you up. Doc will be bringing Chris home from the Saloon at approximately 10 p.m. We want to put this guy between us and then take him down. Everybody, and I mean everybody, wears a vest. When the shooting starts, watch your lines of fire and your backdrop. Pistols, no rifles; rifle rounds carry too far. Your sight picture should not, repeat not, include a residence or each other. The rules of engagement are that you fire if he even points a weapon at you — odds of his surrender are zero."

"Roger that," Matt said.

"One more big thing," Brett added.

"What's that?" Matt asked.

"There's no way to do anything about it but the shooter is probably expecting this trap. He may anticipate our doing exactly what we're planning and still come mess with us," Brett said.

"It would be part of his makeup," I said. "He spots the trap and tries to figure out a way to come to our dance and show us up, which hasn't been hard to do so far."

"Nothing to be done about that," Matt said. "No way to be ready for everything. All that could be true and he can still screw up; no amount of investigation or planning is a substitute for the perp screwing up. He takes a position, and he eliminates some options."

"He steps inside our perimeter and it's possible he makes a mistake," Joan said.

"Chief says a police officer is supposed to anticipate all events," Brett said.

My fear was easy to read or maybe Matt was just testing the logic. "Will the shooter expect to see Doc with the kid?"

"He's going to expect to see me or Tom bring him home from the club, and I need to be out there backing you guys up," Brett said. " We'll meet here at 9 tonight and take up our positions."

Matt shook my hand. "I've never worked with a shrink before."

"I've never chased bad guys before," I said.

"You'll be fine." Matt had a reassuring smile on his face.

"I can't help but feel nervous about all of this," I said. No sense hiding.

"Ever been shot at?" Matt seemed genuinely interested.

"Once but I was extracted because I was an intelligence risk. Then there's the two nights this week, at my house and downtown."

Matt had every right to question me.

"'Nam?" He knew that Brett and I had gone to the same old guys' war, not Grenada or Iraq.

"Yeah," I said.

"I make that three times you been shot at, and you're still alive. A few more and you'll be a pro," Matt said.

"Thanks," I said.

Or I'll be dead, I thought.

We spent another fifteen minutes going over the positions we would all be in tonight and each night until the shooter showed. Joan and Matt would be positioned in the dry riverbed itself. Between the two of them, they couldn't miss the shooter's approach. Joan was on the house side and Matt on the opposite side. Brett would be stationed where he could see any approach from the golf course side of his house and could also turn to back up Joan and Matt. Joan could back him up. All three of them would be able to see Chris and me pull into the driveway. We'd all have radios.

Brett called it, "Okay, Matt, hit the road, and we'll see you tonight at 9. Short of pulling in a rifle squad, which this guy would spot from a mile away, this is the way any team would handle this situation."

Matt said his goodbyes. "One more thing," he said, with something on his mind.

"Sure," Brett said.

"This witness, the kid, what makes him worth all this? With all due respect, I know it is none of my business. I'm just curious." Matt looked at Brett, hoping he hadn't crossed any lines. He'd obviously heard Chris had been homeless and now lived with Brett. It was all over the department by now. I'm sure he had a million questions about Chris, Brett, Joan and me. He only asked this one.

"Chris's a hell of a musician. He's playing at the Saloon tonight," I spoke first.

"He wants to be the next John Lennon," Joan went second.

"I'd like to keep this one alive," Brett said.

"More than enough for me," Matt replied. Then looking pensive for a moment, grabbing all our attention, he asked, "Who's John Lennon?"

We all looked at him wondering if we were lost in the generations.

Matt laughed, "Just kidding, guys...just kidding."

SEX ABROAD

The afternoon was really warming up as the three of us returned to Brett's patio to wait for Nancy. Before we left the hospital this morning, Brett challenged us all to a run, followed by pizza. Three or four miles in this heat would be good for the soul. We just sat and no one said a damn thing. We looked out at the dry riverbed and kept our thoughts to ourselves.

Then I asked, "You think we're exposing ourselves to this guy by running on the bike trail?"

"He wouldn't risk exposing himself unless he could hit Chris and me. He also doesn't like daylight," Brett answered.

Chris was safely ensconced at the Saloon.

"I guess you're right," I said.

"Joan and I will bring our weapons with us. And there is no time like the present for you to start carrying your new Glock."

"Yessir," I said.

"Anybody home?" Nancy called out from the front of the house.

"We're on the patio," Joan called back.

"My, aren't you the three mellow musketeers," Nancy said. "Hi, everybody. Are we going for a run or what?" Nancy gave Brett, Joan, and finally me, a kiss. "Let me put on some shorts and I'm ready. Joan?"

"I'm with you, let's go get ready," Joan said.

The women took off to Brett's spare bedroom with their running gear. Brett and I headed to his room.

While we were changing, he brought up the subject of Joan. "Joan and I are spending a lot of time together as partners and we're all becoming a family. I'm lost about whether or not to start something more with her. Help me out here. When it comes to women, I feel like I'll always be on deployment."

"Follow the Force; let the Force guide you," I teased in my best Obi Wan imitation, stalling for time while I thought about what to say.

"I followed the Force all over the entire planet and look at me now. One failed marriage, who knows how many old girlfriends, and now complete confusion about Joan. What'd the force ever do for me?"

"Look, you remember telling me not to carry the Glock unless I could kill someone if I had to?" I asked him.

"Sure do. Glad you were paying attention."

"And I'm glad to deal with that fact. Let's call that the prime directive for guns: don't carry one unless you can shoot someone. Right?" I asked.

"Absolutely."

"So what's the prime directive for women?" I asked. "We figure that out, and you'll sort out Joan, and I'll solve my new job thing with Nancy."

"So tell me. You're the shrink. If I knew, I wouldn't have to ask."

The girls were yelling for us to hurry up.

"Later. We'll talk again," I said, heading for the door.

"Damn straight we will."

Brett and I chased them out the kitchen door and we all fell into an easy eight-minute pace down across the ravine and up onto the bike trail. In minutes, I was soaked with sweat.

"There're really two Palm Springs." I said.

"Two?" Joan asked, breathing effortlessly while talking.

"One's the oasis we live in. Two, there's desert and mountains. They're gorgeous. What a beautiful place to live. "

"Our shooter goes with number two," Brett reminded me

"Forgot about him," I said.

"We can't afford to forget about him again," Brett warned, breathing with less effort than Joan did.

"Speaking of the mountain, Chris wants me to take him up there. He's never been on the tram," Joan said.

"I'll come," Nancy said. I good hear the effort in her breath.

"We can all go," Joan said.

"Amazing ride," Nancy said. "Every time I go up, I'm surprised that we ever built it. I love it; it's the signature location in Palm Springs."

"When was it built?" Joan asked.

"1963. Before we got here. I've been up once and it's a scary ride," I said, sucking for air while I spoke.

Nancy and I stayed with Joan and Brett for three miles, and then we told them to take off. Nancy and I usually ran about an eight-minute pace, but Joan and Brett were capable of at least a six minute pace. Nancy and I turned around and began to jog the three miles back the bike trail at an easier pace. We figured they'd catch us on the way.

The sun was beginning its descent into the Indian Canyons to the southwest. This time of year it was dead dark by 6 p.m. I was alert for the shooter, and kept touching my fanny back to reassure myself; the Glock was fully loaded with a round in the pipe.

"I'm sorry," Nancy said to me. "I've been treating you poorly. You aren't responsible for this madman."

"I don't really blame you," I said. "Look, I didn't know what I was getting into. They say they need me but I wonder if I'm too old for this kind of work."

"What kind of work?" Nancy was sorry but she wasn't letting me off the hook.

"Work where I get shot at. You know damn well what I meant. You know this is causing trouble between us. I know that you don't approve of guns, and we've been shot at twice already this week."

She surprised me, stopped, and kissed me hard on the mouth. She pushed all of her wet-from-sweat soft parts into me.

"What's that for?"

"I treated you badly. I hate guns but I know if you are interested in working with Brett this way, I can't stop you. I can only hope you don't get hurt. You never complain when I go out in the middle of the night to the hospital. My job is dangerous too; I could get a needle stick or contract a communicable disease. You never complain about that. I will fall apart again about this but right now, this minute, I can deal with it. I'm just going to have to work it through. I'm not saying it'll be easy for me. I feel bad that I used you last night."

"Anytime," I said. "Is there a man alive that's really offended by being used sexually?"

"We could go in the bushes," she said.

We looked around and turned to see Brett and Joan closing in on us. We were a quarter mile from the house, and we walked in together the final distance.

"Who's faster?" Nancy teased.

"Don't know, we didn't test it," Joan replied. "He's pretty fast for his age."

"What do you mean 'for my age?' I'm not ancient, just mature. Not only do we black folk all look alike, we all wear our age well, too."

We sat around on the patio and cooled down from our run. Brett called Wally's Desert Turtle, a world-class Italian place that has been around since Sinatra and the Rat Pack. The original owner's son was running the restaurant now and was an

Michael Thompkins

avid skateboarder. He could often be seen skateboarding from the top of Tramway Road. The pizza arrived, Nancy made iced coffee and we dug in.

"Tomorrow, I want to surprise Ms. Conto. I want to show up at 5 a.m. at Global and see what we can find," Brett said.

"Mayor's going to love this. Running a raid on a Sunday," Joan said, skeptically.

"Needs to be done. If we wait too long, then stuff could disappear. I want to see what might be lying around when she doesn't expect us. We'll meet at Global at 5 a.m.," Brett said, matter-of-factly.

"5 in the morning?" I complained.

"I don't want anyone's finger on the delete buttons, and I want room to look around without being watched," Brett said.

"I'll have a tech meet us there," Joan said, warming to Brett's idea.

"How we going to get in if no one's there?" I wondered out loud.

"You'll see; I got friends. Trust me. I'll get the search warrant," Brett said.

"I'll stop on the way and bring coffee," I said. I didn't have clients so I could contribute to the raid.

Nancy and I started on the dishes. Brett gave Joan a ride home to pick up some things she wanted. He also wanted to check on Chris's security at the Saloon. Chris was going to stay there until I picked him up at 10 p.m. What little plan we had was in place; I hoped we netted the shooter tonight. Now I needed to give Nancy a ride home so I would have her car to get home later myself.

She wasn't quite ready to leave.

It didn't take long to get her running clothes off. She tasted like woman-sweat, pizza and iced coffee; she was delicious. Gunfire might have brought us grief but it also added a new gusto to our lovemaking. Second time I sweated out since breakfast.

According to Nancy, there are many kinds of sex — at home and abroad being two of them. Sex at home was good. Sex abroad added a little extra something.

We used the floor.

"Ah. Sex abroad," she moaned softly.

BOCCA'S PERCH

Bocca had located the lieutenant's home address the day before. He'd reconned the area this morning, and had left a little surprise in the ravine, well hidden under a dense thicket of chaparral. The rental equipment yard near the ravine had an enormous crane parked along the back of the lot, and he calculated that from the top of the crane he could view the entire area for a mile in each direction. It was the highest point in a completely flat area. A high, chain-link fence marked the back of the rental lot. Behind the yard were some small businesses, the Southern Cal equipment yard, the bike trail, the ravine, the dry riverbed, and then the lieutenant's house.

Bocca knew that they'd be expecting him; it was logical for Bocca to target the kid here and certainly they'd set a trap. Bocca knew that they'd guess this move, and he knew they'd figure the possibility he'd anticipate their trap. The whole thing was a game in a game.

It was already dark when he arrived at the rental yard around 8 p.m., scaled the fence and climbed the crane lift. He was in a perfect position when the three of them left the house at 9. Completely hidden from their view, using the optics he had brought, he observed them skillfully take their positions in the ravine— his perch provided total purview.

Surprise. Show the lieutenant that he was all over his pathetic little trap. Absolutely no chance in hell of them catching him in this candy-ass trap. Lieutenant's skills were getting rusty. He would never anticipate the crane. Cool to show him who was the better soldier.

Always anticipate your enemy's next move. Generals are made of this stuff. Stayed in the Rangers, could have earned a commission. Officer and a gentleman. Maybe. Black ops leader's more like it.

Shrink's probably in the house. Shrink drove up to the house shortly before the others came out. Lady cop's to the right in the ravine. New guy — haven't seen him before — positioned to the left. Lieutenant's behind the house somewhere out on the golf course; he's the back up.

If Bocca hadn't anticipated this trap, he would have come right down from the hills, and been caught in the ravine by now. They were pretty good, but his little

Michael Thompkins

surprise would prove that he was better. Then maybe he would drive over to Vegas and get some playtime. If the buyer needed something, he could reach Bocca on his cell.

No need to kill anyone tonight. Think. What's the best way to really hurt the lieutenant. Think. Just have some fun tonight. Embarrass the lieutenant. Harass his ass. Kill him and the kid later.

Push the button on the remote for the flash bang hidden under the chaparral. Take out the cell; punch in the numbers for the lieutenant's home phone. Love the touch of technology. Should have been a commo guy. Not enough action in commo. Smart enough though. Not enough blood. Ten-second delay timer...

Nine, Eight, Seven, Six....

TIGER TRAP

I dropped Nancy at home, set the alarm system – wishing I could have armed her — and handed her the panic remote. I returned to Brett's house at five minutes to nine. I pulled in behind the Mustang in the driveway. Joan, Brett, and Matt were sitting at the kitchen table, checking weapons and radios. Our newly assembled team was ready to go.

"Let's see your weapon." Brett was all business.

I took the Glock out of my fanny pack, ejected the magazine, cleared the weapon, and handed it to Brett.

He ran a dry bore-cleaning tool down the barrel, inserted the magazine, and handed it back to me.

"No oil?" I asked.

"Too much sand out there," he said. "Oil and sand don't mix. Clean weapons jam less, though. Until we get you out to the range, just remember three things if you use this. Point at the target, make the weapon an extension of your hand, and fire three rounds center mass."

"I need practice at the pistol range soon," I said. "What do you want me to do while you guys stake out the perimeter?"

"Leave to get Chris at 9:30," he said. "If we need you, we'll radio you. If you leave from here to pick up Chris, the shooter will think I asked you to pick up Chris because I'm involved in something."

"We'll stay hidden until Doc brings Chris home unless something goes down," Brett said. "I'll be able to see the front of the house from the golf course."

"How are we going to recognize this guy?" I asked.

"He'll look like a professional," he said.

"What does that look like?" I asked.

"Trouble," he said.

"If he walks into the net before Doc leaves to pick up Chris, do we take him?" Matt asked.

"Absolutely," Brett said.

We clipped the radios to our belts and tested the one-piece headsets.

"Let's do it," Brett said.

Michael Thompkins

Ten seconds later, I was alone in the kitchen.

My radio came alive five minutes later. "Everyone in position?" Brett checked locations.

"Ravine, east of the house," Matt called in.

"Ravine, west of the house." Joan's turn.

"North of the house," Brett radioed.

"House," I spoke into the mike.

I moved to Brett's patio with my back against the door, and the lights behind me turned off. I wanted to help if they trapped the shooter before I left to go pick up Chris at the Saloon, and I wanted to be hidden. The night was dark with no moon, and the air was fragrant with climbing jasmine and freshly cut grass from the golf course. My quick shower hadn't removed all of Nancy's perfume. I could still smell her. Only sounds were the psst psst psst's of golf course sprinklers and the coming-going dopplers of the cars passing on Cathedral Canyon.

Boom!

The ravine erupted in a single giant firework. The sound was deafening, the light blinding, and the smell of gunpowder overwhelming all other smells.

The radio on my belt came to life with Brett's warning, "Change your position. Flash-bang. Not taking fire. Repeat, no incoming fire. Anyone taking fire?"

"Negative," Joan said, steady.

"Negative," Matt said.

"None at base," I said.

The explosion appeared to cover a thirty-by-thirty foot square in the arroyo and ignited a small fire in the chaparral. I was considering calling the fire department when the telephone rang. I hurried inside for the portable phone, and walked back out on the patio, so I could monitor the fire while answering the phone.

"Yes," I said.

"Bang, you're all dead," the voice said.

"Who's this?" I damn well knew the answer. I thought about pushing the transmit button on the radio to allow Brett to hear. Negative. It might jam the frequency and leave them without communication.

"Doc? It has to be you, Doc. I can see the lieutenant, the woman, and some other guy. They must have left you in the house. After all, you're a non-combatant; they wanted to protect you. How are you doing Doc? I'm Bocca."

There it was. The shooter's name was John Bocca.

"Bocca, you're a firebug. We'll add arson to your list of crimes."

"Collateral damage, Doc. Couldn't be helped. Take a message to the lieutenant," Bocca said.

"Yeah?"

"You people don't stand a chance against me," he said.

The radio in my left hand came to life again.

"Where's the shooter? Anybody have a visual on him? Anyone take fire?" Brett asked.

"Negative," Joan transmitted first.

"Negative," Matt was second.

"Doc?" Bocca's voice in my ear. "Doc? Panic in the ranks, Doc?"

Wait a minute. Bocca said he could see Brett, Joan and Matt. How the hell could he possibly see them? Then it hit me; he had to be up high. He could be in the crane in the rental yard. He had to be in the crane because it's the only place that would put him high enough to see all of our positions.

I lifted the radio. As I pushed the off button on the telephone, killing my conversation with Bocca, I pressed the transmit button on the radio. "I think I know where the shooter is. He's in the crane in the rental yard."

"Copy that. I'm moving," Brett's voice sounded controlled.

"Copy that." Joan's voice had the same degree of composure.

"Fire's burning out on its own." Matt's voice pilot-to-tower controlled.

"I'm heading down Cathedral Canyon toward the rental yard. I'll get there first," I radioed.

Tossing the telephone on the patio, I drew my Glock and ran off the deck in the direction of the rental yard. It was going to be a quarter-mile sprint, following sex twice in twenty-four hours and a three-mile run. My back complained with a couple of stabbing pains, then let up. Sweating intensely by the time I hit Cathedral Canyon, I would have to work a little harder on conditioning for this job.

Brett would be minutes behind me. Matt and Joan had to come out through the dry riverbed. They'd be minutes behind Brett — muster the posse.

I covered 400 hundred yards on Cathedral Canyon, passed the Southern Cal equipment yard and climbed the fence into the rental yard. Forklifts, Bobcats and bucket lifts were parked in neat rows up to the giant crane, fifty yards away from me. The yard was dimly lit.

Carefully approaching the base of the crane with the Glock held out in front of me,

I looked up at the platform on top.

Michael Thompkins

Empty.

I heard the unique, almost musical sound of shoes scraping fence links. Then, "thunk."

I looked up to see something go over the fence a hundred yards away from me at my original entry point. I saw movement without a form. At a hundred yards in the dark, it could have been my imagination. It wasn't. The form that materialized was denser than the dark. It moved from the fence directly across the road, and darted into the western entrance of the bike trail. The trail followed the dry riverbed directly across from Brett's house, circumnavigated the rental yard, traversed Cathedral Canyon as a crosswalk, and then headed west parallel to the highway toward Palm Springs.

Go.

I needed to let Brett and the others know in what direction I was chasing Bocca.

"It's me," I radioed.

"I hear you, Doc. Where's your location?" Joan's voice was reassuring.

"I think I'm chasing the shooter. I'm in the rental yard near the bike trail. He's heading west down the bike trail toward Bankside. I'm right behind him. He's got to be heading for the aqueduct and into the hills."

I crossed Cathedral Canyon, and immediately made my first tactical error of the night. I dropped the radio. Bouncing on the bike trail, it skittered into bordering brush.

Choose: follow the form or recover the radio.

I didn't know what I was going to do if I caught up to Bocca, but I was after him anyway. If I wanted to build a backbone, I had better get to work on it. I wasn't getting any younger.

I turned a corner onto the bike trail as it began to skirt a trailer park and head for a light industrial area called Bankside. Only in California could the neighborhood bordering a dry aqueduct be called Bankside. It was the same area that Chris was living in when I visited his homeless encampment. I was coming from the opposite direction this time. I knew the trail in the next half a mile would pass within 200 yards of the viaduct. I had to catch up to him before he got to the aqueduct. I didn't know how long I could keep up this run. The little stabbing pains were back.

He left the bike trail, ran across a large parking lot empty of cars and into the aqueduct. Damn. So much for Plan A.

I followed the shadow under the highway where it was even darker in the aqueduct. There were no lights, and the amount of reflected light was negligible. The bad news was that the others might not be able to find and follow me. The good news was I had to slow the pace because I couldn't see well enough to run anymore.

The aqueduct passed under the highway and began to ascend into the pitch-dark hills – a fifty-yard wide rock-filled escape chute. My only points of reference were the two sides, vaguely visible twenty-five yards on either side of me. I prayed that the others would catch me before I overtook Bocca. My ankles were taking a pounding from rocks that I couldn't see well enough to avoid. To my right, I began to see the top edges of several large rock formations that formed the side of the aqueduct. Behind the rocks, a few stars twinkled. My night vision was improving. I was beginning to realize the futility of following Bocca. He was a skilled elite soldier who could easily kill me in this barren place and leave me for my friends to find.

What the hell did I think I was doing— hunting a tiger's shadow?

Then I made my second tactical error. I turned my ankle on a damn rock and dropped the Glock. As I bent down to pick it up, I heard one thing and saw another — one warmed and the other chilled me. Voices sounded from several hundred yards behind me in the aqueduct, and a red laser dot flickered on my chest.

The others are coming.

Laser-scoped tag. I'm it.

I looked up to my right and saw the source of the laser; a shadowy form sat on top of a rock outcropping fifty yards from me. I grasped for the Glock on the ground.

The shadow spoke, "Don't!"

I pulled my hands back to my body.

"Doc, is that you? What the hell are you doing? You trying to get yourself killed? It has to be you, right? You're the shrink. Who the hell else would follow me, drop his gun, and fall on his face? Shrinks don't shoot." His mocking laughter hurt more than the rocks.

Ten seconds painted by the laser seemed like the rest of my life.

"It's me," I confessed. Stall for time and the others might get here. Bocca also had to know they'd be here in minutes.

"One time a medic patched me up a bit," Bocca said. "It's not like I trust you guys or anything, but I'm going to pay that guy back and give you a pass this time.

Michael Thompkins

I need you to deliver a message from me to the lieutenant. Tell him that he has to pay for keeping me out of Special Forces; he took something from me and I'm here to collect. I'm not in any hurry to kill him anymore. Or the kid."

The laser left my chest and withdrew to the ridge. I silently thanked the unnamed medic for my life.

"Bocca?"

"I'm still here, Doc."

"Give this up. I'll help you if I can. Tell us who hired you."

"No thanks, Doc," he said, "You shrinks never quit, do you? Listen, stick to shrinking and leave the tactical stuff to real soldiers. You could be dead. You shouldn't be carrying a gun or even be here. One of me against four of you, and you still fucked up. You people suck."

Then, Bocca was gone.

It was so dark in the aqueduct that I could barely see my own hands. I could smell my own sweat, and the only thing I could hear besides crickets was my heart.

Then, I heard more voices.

"Doc? Is that you?" Joan said.

"I'm here."

Joan came right up to me, but I couldn't see Brett or Matt. They had taken perimeter positions.

"He's gone over that rock," I said, pointing to Bocca's last position.

Joan flashed a small penlight once, and Brett and Matt joined us. Joan pointed to the rock outcrop. Matt and Brett shook their heads, no, in unison.

"Too many directions, too dark, and too clear a shot at us," Brett said.

"I couldn't give you my location," I said. "I dropped the radio."

Brett unclipped my radio from his belt and handed it to me.

"How did you find it?" I asked.

"Heard it." Brett pushed the transmit button on his radio and I heard the garbled squawk from mine. "I told you this guy is the best I've ever seen."

"You weren't kidding," Matt said. "He anticipated what we would do and was waiting."

We walked the half-mile back to Brett's house in silence. The mood was mixed. We had matched wits with Bocca again and came up empty. This time it was a draw. Our planning had failed, but we had at least guessed his location and had him running. No one knew yet that Bocca had lasered and talked to me.

Should I keep it to myself?

Shame burned in my gut. I'd acted like a kid on a camping trip who gets excited about seeing a bear, and chases after it with a camera. At some point, the bear stops, and turns on the kid — not a game anymore.

"What did he say?" Brett busted me.

"When?" I said.

Brett looked hard at me and I knew I was made.

"How'd you know?" I asked him.

"You look like a teenager who got caught parking by the cops with his hand in his girlfriend's crotch. That's how."

"I never could hide shame," I said.

"That's not a character flaw. What'd he say?"

Joan and Matt were listening too carefully.

"I twisted my ankle, fell, dropped the Glock, and he lit me up," I said.

"What'd he say?" Brett repeated.

"He said that one time a medic helped him, so I was getting a free pass. He said that you kept him out of Special Forces and he was going to collect in due time. He said to leave the tactical stuff to real soldiers."

Just before we reached the house, Joan spoke up. "How did you know that he was hiding in the crane?"

"He called me on the phone. He said that it had to be me he was talking to, because he could see all three of you. The crane was the only location that would allow that. He said his name's Bocca."

"The chief was right," Joan said. "Our shooter is the Intepol assassin. Remember? His name's Bocca."

"Sure looks like it," I said.

"When did he call?" Joan asked me.

"Right after the explosion went off," I said.

"What else did he say?"

"'Bang, you're all dead. You must be the shrink 'cause I can see the other three.'"

"Smart bastard. Good work, Doc. You figured out where he was, and we had him running." Matt slapped me on the back. Not a word about screwing up.

Brett nodded his agreement.

"Somebody needs to pick Chris up," I said.

"I'll do it," Brett volunteered.

"Doc," Joan said.

Michael Thompkins

"Yes?"
"There won't be a free pass next time."
"You owe the medic," Matt said.
"What else did he say?" Brett asked as we walked through his front door.
"One of him against four of us — we still fucked up. We suck."

FIRE DRILL

Sunday morning's pre-dawn light found me sitting on the steps outside Global next to the three coffees I'd picked up on El Paseo. After my encounter with Bocca, I slept like the dead and set an alarm for 4 a.m. Nancy didn't even stir when I left.

The early morning air was sweet and cool, and I could smell coffee brewing from one of the espresso joints on El Paseo. Palm Desert was quiet, and I was nodding off for a catnap on the steps with my back propped against the wall, hoping the coffee wouldn't be cold by the time Brett and Joan arrived. I needed it.

The monstrous red fire engine sans siren roared into the Global parking lot with more flashing strobe lights than seem fitting for a machine that didn't fly. The engine pulled up in front of me, the sound stopped, and the lights continued flashing with an intensity that threatened seizure in a well person. Four fully geared firefighters dismounted.

They passed by me with a cursory nod. As they opened the front doors of the building, Brett and Joan pulled in behind the fire engine. They had ridden together. I wondered if that meant anything. I didn't ask.

"We're in," Brett said as he walked up.

"How'd you pull this off?" I asked in disbelief. Handing out their coffees, I took a sip of mine. It had cooled.

"Friend's a battalion chief; he needs buildings to practice on. He has all the keys and was more than happy to schedule an early morning drill."

"I'm not sure I should know any more, in case the chief quizzes me," I said.

"He already knows," Brett said.

"And what'd he say?" I asked.

"If it works and we turn something, he gets the credit," Brett said.

"And if we turn nothing?" Joan asked.

"Then we get the blame."

"Guys, I have something new," Joan said, changing the subject.

"What do you have?" Brett asked.

"The warrant at Bergman's accounting firm allowed us to look at the private financial records of all the partners," she said.

"And?" Brett looked even more curious.

"Bergman transferred $200,000 to a European account a month ago. He'd tried to conceal it, but one of the techs found it."

"Where in Europe?" I asked.

"They're still digging. They've traced it as far as a London bank," Joan said.

Brett whistled sharply. "Good work."

Joan beamed in her gray Nikes, tan nylon army shorts, and a powder blue polo shirt. Brett was khaki shorted and vested as usual. He wore his everyday work shoes, Merrill Jungle Mocs. I was in my tattered Sunday jeans, Asics, a tee shirt and my fanny-packed Glock.

"Aren't we getting a little ahead of ourselves?" I asked.

"The victim had a note in his golf bag that leads directly here," Brett said. "Conto is one of Martin Jonas' biggest clients, and she's overcharging the city for electricity. She may have some sort of business scam going with Bergman, and they might be having an affair. Bergman wired two hundred grand to Europe."

"Maybe it's the hit money," Joan said.

"I like Bergman for this," Brett continued. "He hires the hit man to get the boss out of the way of his deal with Conto. Face it. We have plenty of reason to look deeper at both of them. What more could we ask for?" He was probably repeating the same speech he used on the Chief late last night when he convinced him to get a warrant.

"A lot more evidence?" I asked. All the pieces of the puzzle didn't fit yet.

"Here's how we play it," Brett ordered, not slowed by my question. "Doc, you open with what we guess about Conto and Bergman having an affair. Joan, you go after her about the business scam. I'll hit her with our suspicions that she and Bergman are in on it together and Martin Jonas found out. I'll imply Bergman had his boss whacked; I won't mention the two hundred grand. I'm betting Conto created this scam, things got out of her control, and now suspects that Bergman had his boss killed."

"I can try and scare her with what we know about our hit man," I said. "He's in Palm Springs, a sociopath and cracking. She could start to feel she's in over her head with Bergman." I was warming to Brett's strategy, a simple variation of trying to get the bad guys to turn on each other. It often worked. Honor among crooks was a myth.

"Maybe we can get her to roll over on Bergman," Brett said.

"We'll be giving Conto some information she may not have," I warned.

"True. Can't be helped," Brett said. "It's still a good gamble. I have to try and justify to my buddy that he called out one of his engines at 5 a.m. I'd like to be able to tell him that it was worth doing. I also have to justify talking the chief into getting a warrant."

Joan and I nodded our agreement with Brett's strategy; it had much to gain and little to lose.

"What'd you do with Chris today?" I asked him.

"I assigned two uniforms to him," he said.

"How do we know Conto will show?" I asked.

"Battalion chief has to call her as part of the drill. Fire department regs. I'm betting she shows soon."

We walked up to the Global offices; all the internal doors were left unlocked as part of the drill. Joan went back to meet the tech and started him searching for data in the trading room.

Brett and I were useless now so we took our coffees, and sat in Conto's office. Joan joined us shortly, finishing her coffee while searching Conto's computer and downloading data. Without Joan's computer expertise, Brett and I wouldn't have gotten this far. She worked ten feet away from us while Brett and I passed five minutes quietly drinking our now cold coffees.

"Coffee got cold," Brett complained.

"You two were late," I said, raising my eyebrows and thinking about him and Joan arriving together.

"She left her car off at headquarters," he said, shaking his head, as if to say, "no, nothing happened."

Ms. Conto walked down the corridor toward us. She hadn't even taken the time to dress in office attire; she was wearing sweats and sneakers. Why had she been nervous enough to get out of bed, barely dress and react to a fire drill so quickly?

"Good morning Lieutenant, Doctor, Officer. What the hell's going on here? It's Sunday morning."

"Just what it looks like; we have a court order to seize your records," Brett said, pulling the document out of his vest and holding it up.

"How did you get in here?" Conto snapped. She stood in the middle of her office with her hands on her hips, looking very unattractive in her sweats. Anger's never becoming in workout gear.

"The fire department was running a drill in your building; we just helped ourselves," Brett said.

"Lieutenant, before I go home today, I will have your badge. I haven't worked hard to build my company to the success I enjoy to have it threatened by some poorly paid public employee."

It was never a good idea to threaten Brett.

Brett didn't respond. Simply looked at Conto — *take your best shot, lady.*

I wondered how much trouble she could cause him.

"You sure spend a lot of time at night talking to Mr. Bergman on the phone," I said, trying to take some of the heat off Brett. My accusation was the last thing she was expecting; it caught her off guard.

"I beg your pardon?" The color of her skin darkened several shades.

"You two have a little thing going on the side?" I asked.

"Doctor, you're way, way out of bounds," Conto hissed.

"Am I? All those late night cell-phone calls, they're strictly business?" I figured I was less at risk from her than Brett or Joan so I went for the jugular, and tried to run a screen for them.

"I don't think I like your tone, Doctor. What I do or do not discuss with my firm's accountant on the phone is confidential, and I don't care to discuss it with you."

"Ms. Conto, we know about you and Bergman," I said.

"Doctor, do you think that you can obtain some leverage over me by implying that Mr. Bergman and I are having an affair?" Her tone and tactics changed with her question.

"True, isn't it?" I asked.

"As a matter of fact, it's true," Conto said smugly. "But it isn't a love affair in the sense you are implying. Mr. Bergman and I have enjoyed each other's company on occasion, but we certainly are not having a love affair. We're simply sexual friends. Doctor, you should understand these matters better than most people. You're a psychologist, for Christ's sake. You're investigating nothing."

I had lost the first hand but there was something I could almost see about Conto, stuck in a part of my mind that I couldn't get to.

Joan handed Conto a copy of the golf bag note and moved to rescue me. "Okay, let's discuss something else," she said. "It's something we've talked about before. The note we found in Martin Jonas's golf bag, identifying a block of energy that Global purchased from Arizona Public at Palo Verde and then sold at two discrete prices. You traded at one price to the Imperial Valley Golf Association and to the city of Palm Springs at five times the price."

"Detective, it would take me most of the day to explain to you and your colleagues the complexities of market pricing. We have various contracts with companies and cities based on usage and demand. I am sure you're mistaken that this was the same block of power. Mr. Bergman has already explained to you that the tape from that day is missing."

Conto wanted to talk about herself and her business all day if we let her, but she didn't want to answer our specific questions about the business. Her tone became exasperated, not patronizing any more. She nodded at her computer. Joan slid her chair aside to allow Conto to type in some information.

"Then why would Jonas's notation identify them as the same block of power?" Joan pursued.

"I have absolutely no idea," Conto said. "The grid was probably at some level of emergency on the day of poor Martin's notation. Global buys power from independents in Nevada, some from Palo Verde, and some from up mid-Columbia, the major Northwest-pricing hub. These sources are priced 'at spot' from out-of-state, or local prices from in state. We're a market-maker, and you cannot possibly understand the complexity of our pricing. I believe that one of the traders was working under pressure, and simply made a mistake in recording the transaction. In an emergency like a brown-out, our traders are doing a tremendous volume of trade."

"Well, let me tell you what I don't understand, Ms. Conto. The city pays five times as much as Imperial Valley did for the same power," Joan repeated relentlessly. "I understand that electricity from outside the state costs you a lot more than electricity from California. But I believe that Martin Jonas's notation links these transactions to the same block from Palo Verde. We know what you charged Imperial Valley and what you charged the city for the same block. Why would you charge Imperial Valley pretty much what you paid and charge the city five times more?"

"I will try one more time to explain to you that we buy electricity from various sources. You will notice on that same day that we bought a block from E-Star, a Texas company, and we paid three times the amount we paid Palo Verde." Conto pointed to the computer screen. "I am confident that the power we sold the city was from E-Star, not Palo Verde. Martin was probably just trying to correct our transaction records. Most of that E-Star power was eventually sold back to them; the rest we sold to the city of Palm Springs. We do multiple transactions with E-Star on a daily basis, and I'm sure that you already noticed that in our records. Once we sell out-of-state electricity, how we deliver it is really our business anyway. Our commitment is to keep our customers from running out of power, not to sell to them at discount." She pronounced the word discount as if it were trash on the sidewalks of Palm Desert.

Joan kept hammering away. "Look, I have your records minus 'accidental' erasures, Imperial Valley's records, and the city's records. I'm sure I'll have more questions as I go through and compare them. Right now, I'm bothered that Jonas' notation places both the Imperial Valley transaction and the city's transaction at 2:39 p.m., and Arizona Public at Palo Verde also lists 2:39 p.m. on their records. Yet, you now claim the city's power from some E-Star block of power that was traded at another time."

"I've already told you, I think Martin was trying to correct the notation error," Conto said. "He knew we wouldn't overcharge the city of Palm Springs. He probably guessed that the electricity for Palm Springs was from a different block, from E-Star."

"One last question. Where are the records of the actual transmissions of the electricity that you broker? " Joan had a determined look on her face.

"Well, Detective, finally a new question. You'll have to go all the way to Folsom to get your answer. The California Independent Service Operator, the ISO, is located in Folsom near Sacramento. We file scheduling requests with the ISO and they're responsible for scheduling the transmission of power on all utility lines in the state regardless of ownership. I'm not familiar with their record-keeping process. For all I know, they may not even keep records; they've only been operational for six months."

Brett and I looked at each other. *Right*. Maybe we knew squat about electricity, but we both knew government agencies kept plenty of paperwork.

Brett moved in with his setup. "Ms. Conto, I know of no other way to say this, so I will just get to the point. The killer who was hired to silence Martin Jonas is a very dangerous man. He has killed Mr. Jonas and a security guard who worked at your company. In fact, when we visited here before, he was the guard who let us in. The killer is incredibly talented and resourceful. So let's just be hypothetical for a moment here. Let's just say you're running some kind of a scam here, Martin Jonas stumbled across it, and things got out of hand."

"Lieutenant, are you accusing me of doing something illegal? Do I hear you correctly? Are you accusing me of fraud and somehow being involved in Martin's death?"

"I'm not accusing you of anything," Brett said. "But if a person were involved in something like that, now would be a good time to come forward. It'd be a good time to talk to us about what they knew. Fraud is one thing: murder is entirely another."

Conto took off her glasses and wiped her face with her hand. She was sweating; she had worn the right outfit. She adjusted her position in her chair several times, failed to adjust her composure, and kept her eyes on the door.

My turn again. "I've had a telephone conversation with this killer and I'm convinced he's a homicidal sociopath. This contract has gone from being business to something personal for him. He's a loose cannon. His agenda is getting out of his control and not just tied to the original contract. Anyone involved with this man is putting his or her own life at risk."

"This interview is over," Conto said. She was going to cut and run.

"We'll finish up here as quickly as we can," Joan said.

"Just so you know, I will be calling the mayor," she said.

"Let him know the price differential between the city and Imperial Valley on 2/23." Joan laced it with sarcasm.

"Good day. I'll be calling my attorney, the chief, the mayor, and the governor," Conto said angrily and left the room quickly.

Joan finished downloading the data from Conto's computer while we waited; she left the tech to continue his work in the trading room. We retreated from Conto's office, down the escalator, across the indoor atrium, and stepped out into the Palm Desert morning.

"Joan, you're on the electrical scam," Brett ordered. "Figure out what Conto and Bergman are up to. Dig through everything we've seized from Bergman's and Conto's offices. Doc, you help Joan. Me, I'm going to keep Chris alive, and do some other training stuff the chief assigned me. It's wait-and-see time. I want Conto and Bergman to stew in their own juices for a while. We'll plan to meet at my house tomorrow for dinner and debrief at 5. Tell Nancy."

As we were standing next to the Mustang and talking, Peter Bergman drove up and parked his green Jaguar several spots down from us. He got out of his vehicle and looked up to see all three of us looking his way. I wondered what got him up at this hour.

"Morning, Mr. Bergman," Joan said. "You're up pretty early."

"Ms. Conto called me to come over and help her deal with your completely unwarranted visit at this ungodly hour." Bergman was a rumpled Armani this par-

Michael Thompkins

ticular morning, wearing a disheveled shirt and wrinkled slacks. "I have to go up and see if I can help right now."

"Did she really have to call you?" Joan asked, smiling.

Bergman ignored Joan's innuendo. "Ms. Conto is trying to run a successful business, and untimely intrusions like this cost time and money."

Brett made a toy gun with his finger and thumb and pointed at Bergman. He didn't shoot, just pointed as if to say, "it could cost a lot more than that."

"Good day. You people are harassing Ms. Conto and now me," Bergman said, practically running away from us. As he reached the bottom of the steps, the front door opened and Conto started to walk out. She looked at Bergman then noticed us. She quickly retreated inside the building.

"Hard to tell who's whose bitch," Brett said.

"I knew she and Bergman were boinking," I said.

"They aren't boinking," Joan said, smiling.

"Yes?" I asked.

"They're having a 'sexual friendship.'"

SHRINK TOO

Even with so many people out and about at this early hour, Bocca knew he could have followed this team in a tour bus. They would never have noticed him. He'd followed the shrink from home earlier and watched him sit on the steps of Global. The fire department showed up, then the lieutenant and the woman cop — they were all on his radar. It was smart, the way the lieutenant used the fire department to get into Global. The engines had arrived with lights but no sirens.

When the flash bang went off the night before, Bocca had watched them all scramble to change their positions. The night-vision optics he used were the best money could buy. Bocca wondered how had they known where he'd been hiding?

Weird, it had to have been the shrink, though there was no way the shrink could have seen him at the top of the crane. Had it been just a lucky guess or some kind of sixth sense?

Bocca had seen guys with that kind of ability in combat; they were uncanny and to be respected. Animals sometimes demonstrated the same uncanny sense of things. Bocca admired that.

Later, when Bocca had lit up the shrink from the rock outcropping, he had wished he'd had time to question him. With the rest of them closing so fast, however, there hadn't been time. When they had shown up, he had watched them from further up the hill. The lieutenant had known better than to chase him up the mountain. There were ways to run somebody up a hill, but it took two teams. They only had one last night, just like at the museum.

Now, in the early morning light using the optics he had in the car, he watched them through his tinted windows as they came out of Global. They were another loose end, and there were too many loose ends. The buyer had been urgently calling and emailing Bocca. He would have to meet with the buyer again soon.

Incoming. There's the goddam buyer.
Christ. Can't be in the same space as the buyer and the cops.
Risk evaluation? High.
Go. Go. Go.

Bocca started his car and pulled from the curb. The risk was too high for him when the buyer showed. He always weighed the risk against the gain. Somehow, on this contract, he had lost the scales. He would stick to the rules next time. Because of the nightmare, this time things had gotten personal.

Think. Contact the buyer. Then deal with the kid. He has to go. Kid's valuable to the lieutenant. Kid means something to him. Maybe there's a way to use the kid to trap the lieutenant. Kid's his weakness.

A little contest with the lieutenant would settle this once and for all. Show him he never should have voted to keep him out of Special Forces. Better man. They would all see it soon. Goddamn shrink's too good at figuring shit out. Make sure the shrink falls into the trap, too.

Bocca had had the nightmare again last night. He had been drinking to celebrate his success, to loosen up a bit. He fell asleep. This time the dream had more clarity. He saw both the lieutenant and the shrink. They both had been responsible for his rejection from Special Forces; it had been clear as a bell in the dream. The shrink was beside the colonel when they told him that he had not been selected. Then Bocca had walked out of the colonel's office and the first man he'd recognized was the goddamn lieutenant. The selection committee had just met and they were both involved. He should have known all along that the lieutenant and the shrink were both responsible.

Owe the shrink, too. Figured that out last night after letting him go. Dumb. Missed opportunity. Figures, 'cause they're still friends. They'll both pay now. Letting the shrink know will be fun. Jeez, thinking hurts, not to mention the scotch from last night. Need a plan. Need it soon.

The kid, the lieutenant, and the shrink. One, two, three. Pressure in the head will be better. Then back to London. Some serious down time. Time for a little female companionship. Travelling women only, nothing long term. Next job in Europe so there's no chance of losing it again. No chance of recognizing anyone from the nightmare. No chance of screwing up like this. Need to screw, not screw up. Need a woman.

Way to get them all. Just need some luck. Luck's overdue. Need a plan. Use the kid to guarantee a contest with the lieutenant. That's the plan. Show these people. Be the last thing they remember.

Pop 'em all.

TOO LATE TO BE ROCK STARS

Using the no-knock policy, I walked in Brett's front door at 5:10 Monday evening, smiling, as I smelled the garlic. I'd spent the morning seeing patients. In the afternoon I had driven over to department headquarters and helped Joan with the data from Bergman's accounting firm and Global. We'd made progress that culminated in Joan announcing that she needed to fly up to the California Independent Service Operator in Folsom near Sacramento.

When I arrived, Chris was practicing with the Martin on the deck.

"Hi, Doc. Sit and answer a question for me, will you?" he asked, without the street dialect.

"Sure, let me say hi to everyone first."

"Brett's tight," Chris warned.

"Jay?" I asked. Jay would come home from the hospital tomorrow if things stayed on schedule. The extent of permanent damage to his arm was still unknown.

Chris nodded.

When I walked in through the patio door, Joan was helping Brett slice garlic for bruschetta. She set out the olives and cheese. Nancy had arrived earlier and was sitting at the table, talking on the phone. She was instructing a patient to get herself to Labor and Delivery at the hospital. A pool of fluid on the patient's floor meant this patient needed labor evaluation. Brett and I were used to Nancy discussing various bodily functions on the phone, and learned to ignore the content — dinner and diagnosis don't mix.

"I know what Joan's been up to because I helped her," I said. "What about you? What've you been doing?"

"Training a couple of new officers and hoping I'd hear from Conto," Brett said. "No such luck. Whatever she knows, she's not in a hurry to share it. I slept outside last night under a bush, hoping our shooter would have another try. No luck there, either. Chris thought I was nuts."

I pitied the garlic cloves he was chopping with venom meant for Bocca. I could imagine some poor citizen freaking out as he came across Brett under a laurel armed to the gills.

"What about Joan going up to Folsom?" I asked.

"I got you a ride Friday to Folsom on a CHP helo," he said to Joan. "I'd like you to go earlier but this is a free ride. It's the weekly administrative run and the pilot is a buddy. Meet the pilot at 8 a.m. sharp at the airport. You know where the CHP hangar is?"

Joan nodded her head, "yes."

Nancy put the phone down, gave me a quick kiss and disappeared to change out of her work clothes. Joan tossed the bread into a basket and tagged along after Nancy, probably to share a bit of girl talk.

"Chris has something to ask me about. I'll be out back with him. No fair eating without us."

Brett looked hard at me. "You're the shrink. Have at it."

"So I have Dad's permission?"

"Go for it," he said. "I need all the help I can get. My roommate is twenty years younger than me." His edge was visible in the chopping and the stiffness of his shoulders.

"Look, Jay will live with this either way. He's strong."

"I know he will, but can I?" Brett asked. "I screwed up again and this time Jay got hurt."

"Shit happens. Isn't that what you'd say? If it doesn't kill you, it makes you stronger."

"I should listen to my own advice?" he asked.

"Only one person's fault."

He rotated the knife into a throwing position.

I nodded and retraced my steps to the patio where Chris was tuning his Martin. He kept it up softly while we talked.

"You pumped for Thursday night and your Palm Springs Saloon debut?"

"Pumped and nervous. For some reason, I've been worrying about my mother all day. When I took off from home, I told myself she was behind me. I wouldn't worry about her until I was ready to do something about it. But I couldn't sleep last night worrying about her. I feel like I abandoned her. Why now? Why is it hassling me now? I hate to impose on you. You guys have done enough already, but I can't ask Brett."

"Why not?" I asked.

"Man, he went through the same thing and now he's worried about Jay," he said.

"He's more qualified than me."

"You're a shrink; nobody's more qualified than you to talk about stuff. You're a head doctor."

"Psychology is over-rated."

"Jeez, Doc, gimme a break. I know Brett's more experienced with this. I just gotta build up my courage to talk to him and when he's not upset already."

"Then, the short answer to your question is that being shot at can drag up history."

"Cool, I get that. The red laser dot, right?" he asked.

"You said you were afraid that it wouldn't leave you alone, remember?"

"I remember," he said. "Now tell me what to do about it."

"Here's where I think real life is better than therapy."

"Whattayamean, Doc?"

"I mean that you ran away from home because you were looking for some things, right?"

"Yeah. Freedom from my father. The road. Space. Room to play my music, live in my own head not my father's, and enjoy women. That's just a few of the things I was looking for."

"You were also looking for a way to help your mother, right?"

"Absolutely. That's what kept me awake last night."

"Well, what to do about it, right? That's the question?"

"Yeah." He stopped tuning to listen.

"Get all the other stuff handled first: play your music, enjoy women, and live in your own skin. How to help your mother will come after that. Keep writing her. Brett will be a lot of help on this when you're ready to talk to him."

"Like handle myself first?" he asked.

"And the rest will come."

"You know something, Doc?"

"What?"

"You're working on this 'living in your own skin thing' too, aren't you? Like how your back bothers you?"

"Live in your own skin, complete with the scars. That's what Jay will have to do."

"Doc, sometimes people get so scarred they can't live in their skin, right?"

I looked at him. His father? Bocca? My entire career of scarred people. Some made it.

Some didn't. I just nodded.

"One more thing…" he said.

"Shoot."

"This whole thing is starting to block my writing music. Being bodyguarded all the time is getting in my way. I need time alone to think, write my music, and see Suze."

"No surprise here. I need lots of time to myself, too, and I'm past my creative prime."

Joan yelled. Time to eat.

"More later?"

"Rad. Thanks, Doc."

I walked in the door ahead of Chris. Nancy had left the portable phone on the table.

It rang. I looked at it. I picked it up. "Hi."

"Lieutenant?" the voice asked.

I was suddenly chilled. I made frantic motions at Brett and again watched him reflexively rotate his knife into a throwing position.

"Who's calling?"

"You must be the shrink. Didn't recognize your voice. Hi, Doc. This is Bocca. Listen; about last night, sorry about the fire. I hope it didn't frighten you. That kind of stuff happens with flash bangs. How'd you know where I was hiding?"

"We'll just add firebug to your list of crimes and pathology." I signaled Brett to trace the call.

Brett spoke softly, "Can't, Bocca knows how long he can talk before we can lock a trace."

I ignored Bocca's asking me how I knew where he was hiding. There was a different tone in the way he spoke to me. What was that about?

"Give the gun back to the lieutenant. It's not in you, Doc. You're a non-combatant. Seen it before. Good medics never make good soldiers. You're a shrink, not a shooter."

Bocca liked to talk and he definitely had his opinion of me.

"We'll see about the gun," I said. He struck too close to my bungling my first outing with the gun for me to say anything else.

"I figure Interpol is here already, but they're dumb. They'll have sent some rookie, figuring I've already left. They know my name because I wanted them to know that much. By now, they may have my military records and my prints. Hey, put this on speaker so I can talk to the lieutenant, too."

I pushed the speaker button on the wall receptacle. "Can you still hear me?"

"Sounds a little tinny, but it's good enough. Lieutenant, I was sure ahead of you last night, wasn't I? I had the perfect observation post, up high. How are you doing?"

"Not doing as good as the day I lock you up," Brett said.

"I can't figure out how the shrink knew where I was hiding," Bocca repeated.

"Yeah, Doc made your position. He can see right through you. You must be slipping." Brett had an edge I hoped would help.

"Whoa, Interpol has been trying for five years and they got jack. What makes you think you got better stuff than they do? This is just a small-town police department and you're just a small-town cop. Gotta admit whoever set that trap last night was pretty good at anticipating. I'll give you that. And the shrink just got lucky, I guess. Sorry about the rent-a-cop and the other guy. We sure have been having some fun, haven't we? Nothing personal, but the rent-a-cop was pathetic. He just took out that big nickel-plated .38 of his and tried to arrest me."

"Slipping up will get you killed. I hope I'm the reaper." Brett kept pushing back.

"Nice trap at your house. I'll give you that much. Tell you the truth, it took me awhile to spot you," Bocca said.

"More slippage," Brett said.

"True enough," Bocca said. "No where near the way you guys been screwing up. You seem like this is getting to you, Lieutenant. Like it's personal."

"The guy you shot was a friend," Brett said.

"Excellent. Personal for me, too. You figure out where we met before, Lieutenant? You, me, and the shrink?"

Bocca thought he had met me too.

"Tell you the truth, Bocca," Brett said. "You've never been significant enough for me to remember you. I'm betting that I helped keep your sorry incompetent ass out of Special Forces, though."

"Doc, please tell the lieutenant that there really isn't any difference between me and him. We're both hired guns. Tell him where we all met before."

Michael Thompkins

"I can't do that," I said. "I've never met you before the other night. And there will always be a difference between you and the lieutenant."

"Yeah, what?" Bocca asked.

"You killed two innocent men, wounded one, and tried to shoot the kid," I said.

"My hits are never innocent people. The rest was collateral damage. Happens all the time. Just ask the lieutenant."

"Bocca, everything you do is self-serving, designed to make up for being a loner since you were a kid and never fit in," I said. "Now you are imagining that we've met before. You're starting to lose it." Time to be the shrink that he clearly wanted me to be.

"There you go, Doc. Now you're doing it. You're just like all the shrinks I met in the military. They think they can take one look at you and decide who you are and what you're capable of."

"Being a shrink doesn't necessarily make me wrong," I said.

"Yeah, well, you shrinks can't help it. It's what you do. But the lieutenant is another matter; he should've known better than voting to block my selection."

Bocca visualized us both present when he was rejected from SF. Brett might have been there, but I certainly wasn't. Bocca was unraveling and I could use that against him.

"Bocca, could I've been more right about you?" Brett asked. "I don't remember you, but look at what you've turned into for Christsakes, a professional killer. It makes me sick to think of you in a uniform."

Nancy and Joan entered the kitchen. Bocca somehow sensed their arrival or heard them on the speakerphone pickup.

"It's the ladies. Nice action last night, ma'am, you're a good soldier for a woman."

"Not good enough. Count on me doing a better job next time," Joan said.

Nancy stopped dead in her tracks and tightened up.

"Feisty. I like that in a woman."

"Truth be told, I couldn't care less what you like in a woman." Joan's voice was ice-cold.

"Doc, keep trying to figure me out. Everybody needs a shrink. Fact is, I've had enough of you people. Who cares if the kid can make me? I need some play time. I'm going to end this deployment. I'm going to mosey on out of here. It's been fun. Certainly I've shown you who's the better soldier. I'll come back another time and settle up with you two. That way you'll never know. Always have to stay tense. Sort of like it's been for me after you kicked me out of SF."

The line went dead. The speaker buzzed the disconnect.

"Ugly man," Nancy said, finally finding her voice.

"Dangerous man," Joan added.

"Worse than dangerous. Crazy," Brett said.

"Not quite crazy. He knows where reality lies. More like wild without an ounce of empathy for another human being," I said.

Chris had been standing unnoticed in the doorway from the patio and overheard the end of our conversation with Bocca. He was holding his guitar and began playing a song:

"Where do bad folks go when they die? They don't go to heaven where angels fly.

They go down to the lake of fire and fry, Won't see them again till the Fourth of July"

When he was done playing the simple chorus a number of times, we remained silent for a moment.

"Do you think Bocca's really leaving?" Nancy was hopeful.

"I hope not," Brett said.

"Doc, what's his thing with Brett and now you?" Chris asked.

"Bocca claims he crossed paths with Brett and me in the Army and he blames us for his rejection from Special Forces. So we have to pay. It's possible Brett met him and it's possible that this guy is going psychotic and imagining Brett being there. He's starting to imagine I was there, too."

"How could they do that?" Chris asked.

"What?" I asked.

"Train someone to be an elite soldier without making sure he would know the difference between right and wrong?"

"Do governments always know the difference?" Brett asked.

"I get what you mean. That's what your music was about. Right?" Chris asked.

"I don't follow," I said.

"Sixties music. Like 'question authority.' 'You say you want a revolution,' 'Tear down the walls,'" Chris said.

"Dead on," I said.

"You and Brett never got over the sixties, did you?" Chris asked.

Michael Thompkins

Brett and I simultaneously shook our heads. *Not until the last 'Nam veteran was buried, and everyone knew better than to give a president permission to prosecute a war carte blanche and lie to the country.*

"So why do you guys go out of your way and do all this for me?" Chris asked.

Good question. Only a week since the first homicide and none of us, especially Chris, would ever be the same. Chris had a new home, Brett had a new partner, Nancy had a husband who carried a Glock, and I had a new job — just for openers.

"Do what?" Brett wasn't looking for gratitude. Not with Jay maybe crippled.

Joan, Nancy, and I weren't looking for thanks, either. We hadn't earned it as long as Bocca was still threatening.

"Take me off the street, protect me, invite this guy to come after you, too, and find me a job. You know what I mean," Chris said.

It was a good question.

Brett said it for all of us, "It's too late for any of us to be rock stars."

MINT JULEPS, GUNS AND SHADY BUSINESS

Nancy and I were sitting in the Saloon drinking mint juleps; mind you, just one a piece. It was 7 on Thursday evening and Chris's band's grand opening was in an hour. Nancy was wearing white silk deck shorts and a T-shirt logo'd with Bruce Brown's '60s surfing film, *The Endless Summer*. We could hear the band, sans a new name, practicing in the back, while we waited for Brett and Joan.

I was grateful to have a few days without Bocca's type of excitement. Things had quieted down since our Sunday morning visit with Conto and our conversation with Bocca the following evening at Brett's. Maybe Bocca left town, just like he said he would. I didn't believe it for a minute, but I didn't want to take Nancy's hopes away. She wanted a mint julep and I couldn't have refused or she would have guessed that I was still worried about Bocca. Nancy was willing to look at all the really hard things in the world, losing babies, death, except one — the use of necessary deadly force. It was like she was going to will the world a better place.

Conto was still not talking to the chief, the mayor, the governor or us; she had gone to ground; she was hiding out. Brett was waiting until we had the information we needed from Folsom to interview Bergman or Conto again. Also, he wanted to know the final destination of Bergman's $200,000 wire transfer before confronting him with it. He was hoping Conto would get really scared and call us. Sometimes silence can be as unnerving as accusation, Psychologist Handbook, page 211. On the other hand, she hadn't budged, and we were running out of time.

Joan had everything organized for tomorrow morning's helo ride to Folsom. She had been giving Brett and me constant updates, while Chris had been spending all his time practicing here at the Saloon under the watchful eyes of Bob and a uniform. Brett and Matt were sleeping in the bushes outside Brett's. I'd been see-

Michael Thompkins

ing patients. Novel idea for a shrink, seeing patients. I still needed some billable hours to buy mint juleps. I was hoping the mint juleps and the guns would balance each other out in Nancy's mind. Jay sat with us, his left arm glued to his shoulder.

"How's the shoulder?" Nancy dutifully checked up on the patient.

"If I stay on my pain meds, I manage just fine," he said without an ounce of self-pity. "A week of healing and I start rehab. See how much use my arm can get back." His right hand gestured flamboyantly as he spoke. One finger was adorned with a large diamond ring that looked like it was at least two carats.

"If I could bottle your attitude and sell it to shrinks, I could get rich," I said.

"Same here on patients. I wish all my patients had your attitude," Nancy said.

"When you're queer: sooner or later, you get over yourself. People hate us, make fun of us, ostracize us, and tell us we're going to rot in hell. But they always come to the entertainment we put on, ask us to decorate their houses, watch us on TV and buy the clothes we design. We give up being queer, the world's boring and ugly again. Besides, I could be the security guard — I could be dead. "

"Philosopher queen," I said.

He laughed, then squinted in pain.

"I can't laugh too hard, it hurts," he said.

"How is Chris working out?" I asked, changing the subject.

"He's hard working, talented, respectful and someday, he's going to be famous," he said.

"That's quite an endorsement," Nancy said.

"The band is so ready for their opening tonight," he said.

"I hear he's been practically living here for the last two days getting ready," I said.

"It's just fine with me. Brett drops him off in the morning and picks him up at night. The band did the warm-up every night this week, and the house was packed. Tonight is their baby."

Chris had definitely won over the Saloon crowd. Given the conflict in Chris's last home, it was no surprise that he made himself so welcome at Brett's home and the Saloon.

"Where are Brett and Joan?" he asked.

"On the way here," I said.

"I gotta go check on the liquor. Even a gimp can help. See you later. You need a refill, just whistle."

After Jay walked off, Nancy said, "Jay's a sweetheart."

Sure Jay was different. Scary for some, but interesting to me. I get up every morning and look in the mirror at a middle-aged WASP. Other WASP men, just like me, play the same games: winning at business, sex, church, and golf — losing at the game beyond the mirror. Jay — the other, the queer — might just teach me something about myself that I didn't already know.

"Now catch me up on the case," Nancy said. "We haven't talked much since Monday night."

"Where do I start?" I brought her up to speed and ended with our suspicions of Conto and Bergman.

"So you suspect fraud, murder, and 'sexual friendship'?" Nancy asked.

"Yes."

"Nothing wrong with 'sexual friendship,'" she said. "This maniac taking you and Brett so personally spooks me. I don't get his grudge, and I hope he's really gone. Continue."

"Well, I'm thinking maybe Brett was there when Bocca was turned down for Special Forces," I said. "I sure wasn't there, but he's starting to put me there in his head. He's confusing me with the shrink who was part of the selection process; it's symptom of his deteriorating state. Criminals like Bocca have to use a lot of their daily mental energy to maintain their feeling of superiority to others because it's what allows them to kill without empathy. However, it covers up a massive sense of inferiority."

"That's really good psychological detecting. I don't like it, but I can see how Brett and Joan need you on this case," Nancy admitted.

"I love that about you."

"What?" she asked, smiling.

"You hate this whole thing, you hate guns and still you won't blind yourself to Brett and Joan actually needing me. You are always willing to look at the hard things in spite of your feelings. I respect that about you."

"Thanks, but I still don't really like the changes in your job," she said. "I guess I always counted on you doing something safe. In the middle of the night when I was delivering newborns, I always knew you were home taking care of my babies."

"Can't there be room for both of us doing something that involves risk?" I asked. "Our babies are gone, and I'm going from clinical to tactical on this case. Some of what you do is dangerous. You said that already."

"The tactical part is really hard for me," she said. "Shooting and medicine are a little different. The day this madman shot at us at our house, my regular life collapsed. Now I feel like I'm in some new world. My mild mannered husband is carrying a handgun. You know how I feel about guns. I mean it's one thing for Brett because he came that way. Nothing changed with him." She let it all out with a deep sigh.

"Joan has certainly changed things with Brett."

"True enough, but I can deal with that change," she said.

"Then you're doing way better than Brett."

"I just want my old life back," she said.

"I know. Me too. But I feel like I'm only going to get it back by finishing this thing. You're right to feel lost. I'm not the same person I was last week. I'm carrying a Glock, I'm talking to a homicidal sociopath on the phone, and I start my days meeting with cops. I don't completely know how this happened to me but I didn't go looking for it. I probably could have seen this coming and dodged it, except for Chris. He changed everything for me."

"What do you mean, Chris changed everything?" she asked me.

"Now, I'm someone between Bocca and Chris," I said. "Christ, I didn't even know Chris before a week ago yesterday, but I will not allow Bocca to kill him like Jason."

I remembered the awful hour Brett and I spent at Jason's funeral. Me asking him why he wanted to tag-a-long with me. Him saying, "He was going to be a cop."

"Don't you mean like the Marines you left behind?" She challenged me and brought me back.

I had nothing to say to that one.

"On one level, I understand and I'm proud of you, but on another, I can't stand it." Nancy was staring into the remains of her mint julep, tears pooling in her eyes.

"You're a physician. It's natural for you to hate guns. And there's your roommate in med school; I understand. I just hate Chris getting killed more. It's the lesser of two evils. If Chris were our child, what would you want? Is this the part you warned me about, where you fall apart again?"

After awhile, Nancy wiped her eyes with the cocktail napkin. "I guess so."

"I know we didn't really talk about this before I became involved. When this guy is locked up we can talk about where this police psychologist thing goes from here. For now, I need to finish this. Bocca is starting to unravel. I'd like to believe that he was telling us the truth Monday night. I hope he's gone; Brett doesn't, but

I do. I'd be happy if he left. I'd be happy if he forgot all about Chris. But I don't believe it will happen. Bocca is tired, starting to fall apart, and he'll have to make his move soon. We'll be ready this time, I hope."

"One thing hasn't changed." Nancy smiled.

"Us." Even as I said it, I wasn't a hundred percent sure of it. We sat quietly for a bit, holding hands, until I noticed Brett and Joan walk in through the front door and over to us.

"Hi, guys. Sorry we're late. The city is full of people. Biggest crowd for Thursday night Street Fair in quite awhile." Joan looked anything but a cop in her designer jeans and sage green tee shirt. The black silk brocade vest she was wearing just barely concealed her pistol. Brett held out her chair as she sat down.

Brett noticed what we were drinking, and got a beer for himself. Joan passed.

"What have you two been talking about?" Joan asked.

"Mint juleps and shrinks with guns," I said.

"It sounds like a rock band," Brett said.

"Actually, it has been rocky but getting better," Nancy said. "I don't like it but I may have to learn to live with it. I live with lots of things I don't like."

"'Love Doc Cop, Hate the Gun.' It's a rock lyric, I'm telling you," Brett said, giving Nancy a squeeze on the arm.

"Okay, Joan, you've had your nose in the Global data for two days. What's up?" I asked.

"I'm certain Global's dirty," Joan said. "When I go up to the ISO in Folsom tomorrow morning, I think I can prove it."

"How?" Brett asked.

"I want to compare all the Global trading data with the actual transmission records at the ISO," Joan said.

"What's an ISO?" Nancy asked.

"Independent Service Operator," Joan replied. "They're responsible for scheduling and controlling the actual transmission of electricity on all the power lines in the state. Conto told us about it, remember?"

"How do you think Global is cheating the system?" I asked.

"I copied a ton of Global records," she said. "It will take some digging but they could be justifying the steep prices they charged the city compared to Imperial Valley by making it look like the need for electricity was higher than it really was," Joan said.

"So that could be a motive for Martin Jonas's murder?" I asked. "If he discovered that Global was jacking up prices for some of their customers, like the city, would that be a reason to kill him?"

"It could be," Joan replied.

"The city would be 'shocked' if they learned Global was jacking them up," Brett quipped.

"And Global wouldn't want to lose the opportunity to keep overcharging some customers," Nancy said.

"Has Global done anything illegal here?" I asked.

"If they have, I'll find it," Joan answered. "I want to find out how they worked their way around the interstate/intrastate thing. If they relabeled intrastate regulated power then we're talking 'go-to-jail' illegal."

"Slow down. Somebody needs to explain the interstate-intrastate thing to me," Nancy said.

"Electricity generated in the state is regulated by the state," Joan explained. "Spot power, or out of state generated electricity, is not regulated. Global can charge whatever they want for it."

"Would it be illegal to mix the apples and the oranges?" Nancy asked.

"Go-to-jail-for-a-long-time illegal," Joan repeated.

"So there are two ways to steal here, one's legal, the other's illegal?" I asked.

"You have to love it." Joan slid her chair back and stretched. She'd been sitting at a desk for too long. "Their books are probably cooked, and I'm sure they're not sharing all this jacked up profit with the IRS. Also, we still don't have a final destination on Bergman's $200,000 wire transfer."

"Joan, this is fantastic. You've come up with a possible motive," I said.

"Thanks," she said.

"Between the mint juleps, the guns, and now the shady business, I could use some fresh air," Nancy said. "We have an hour until the band plays. Let's go walk the Street Fair, see the crowd, and stretch our legs."

Everybody agreed. We walked back to the band room to let Chris know we were going to the Street Fair, but would be back well before the show. When we walked in the band room, the group was practicing a new song.

"He lives in a house up high,
He lives in a house up high.
Watch out for the bad guy, Watch out for the bad guy.
He wants to be, He wants to be,

He wants to be,
The next John Lennon."

Chris had combined the song about his dream with one he was trying to write about the next John Lennon.

"Two half-songs make one?" I asked him when he stopped playing.

"Why not? Like it?" Chris asked me.

"You bet I do," I said.

"We're going to walk the Street Fair for half an hour and be back for the show," Brett told Chris. Chris signaled his understanding with a nod. We found Bob before we left and made sure he would still watch Chris.

As we all walked outside into the parking lot, we ran into the chief. He'd come to hear Chris play; the opening night party was growing. Walking through the door to the parking lot, I had two simultaneous feelings, pleasure at seeing the chief and knowing he came to hear Chris's music, and some vague fear. I wrote the vague fear off to prior encounters with a laser-scoped sniper.

"Chief, you caught us taking a stroll to the Street Fair," I said. "Chris plays in an hour. Join us."

"Thank you. Don't mind if I do. Who's watching the kid?" the chief asked.

"Bob's watching him, and he knows how to call for help. There are two uniforms detouring cars for the fair, right outside the Saloon," Brett said. "I told them to stay in the area."

The chief shook everyone's hand, and fell in with our little caravan. We cut across the parking lot to an alley that would put us out on North Palm Canyon. I noticed Brett looking up at the rooftop where Bocca had positioned himself last Saturday night; he had no more faith in Bocca's promise to leave Palm Springs than I did.

We walked through the small alley next to the building the shooter had used the other night and came out on North Palm Canyon into the middle of the Street Fair. I stepped on Buddy Hackett's sidewalk star tile on the way. We left the alley and walked out in the middle of the crowd. Street Fair, carnival, county fair, French Village Market Day, and Mardi Gras all had the same effect on me; I wanted to eat everything I smelled and buy everything I saw.

It was just after sunset. The sun had given up until tomorrow and we creatures who hang out in the deserts, humans and others, had made it through another day. Cause to celebrate. The Street Fair was the human equivalent of all the desert creatures waking up from their afternoon stupor of hiding from the heat, and scurrying about in the cooler evening air looking for food, water and even entertainment. The afternoon sun takes activity to a standstill in desert animals and humans— Street Fair and the Saloon replaced the animals' evening hunt for food and visit to the creek for water.

As we all walked, Joan filled in the chief on how Conto and Bergman might be gaming the trading of electricity. Nancy and Brett were discussing the events of the last week and my new job. I hoped Brett was softening her up for me.

I bought a shave ice cone and started eating it. I picked passion fruit, and offered to buy one for everyone; no one took me up on it. For the next five minutes, I strolled, along happily eating my shave ice.

"I love this," I said, pointing to one end of North Palm Canyon and then the other.

"But you're not going to love whatever this is about. Incoming," Brett said.

Bob was running towards us looking pretty upset. "Shit, Lieutenant, Chris went for a walk without saying a word to me. I was in the bathroom. I screwed up. Man, I screwed up. I'm really sorry."

Everyone listened; riveted by Bob's report that Chris was presently unwatched and unprotected.

"Don't be too hard on yourself. He's just a kid," I said. My shave ice cone suddenly tasted sour.

We all started scanning the crowd, desperately looking for a glimpse of Chris. Brett started giving us detailed instruction of how to search for Chris. Joan had her roamer out and was ready to call for some uniforms to help us search.

As quickly as the crisis came, however, it went. Chris appeared ten feet from us with an inappropriately wide grin on his face.

"Hi, guys. I caught up to you." He was totally oblivious to the risk he had taken.

Brett took one look at Chris and uncorked, "What the hell do you think you're doing? I leave you alone for ten minutes, and you pull this shit. What the hell were you thinking?"

The looks that Nancy and Joan gave Brett shut him up quickly.

Brett measured out his next words more carefully. "Please don't ever do this again. It's not fair to us. We're trying to keep you alive."

"I just needed some space to think," Chris said, resistant, as if to say, "I need my space, man."

The chief, God bless him, put his arm around Chris and said, "Son, we all screw up."

Joan and Nancy continued to bestow Brett chilling looks for his loss of temper. Bob decided he would make good his escape, perhaps afraid that soon he too would fall under Nancy and Joan's disapproval.

"I gotta go back, Lieutenant," he said. "Again, I'm sorry. It was my fault."

Brett nodded to Bob, who walked away.

Chris and Brett stared at each other.

We all stood in a little circle. I just wanted to return to the moment when I was enjoying my shave ice cone and the Street Fair. My brain was burned out, and I just wanted a little peace and shave ice to cool it.

More incoming.

Conto and Bergman appeared twenty feet from us. She saw us and waved.

"Bitch and bastard." Brett really had grown to dislike them.

"No, bitch and bastard, 'sexual friends,'" I said.

"Hello, Chief," Conto said to the chief when she was close enough.

"Hello, Ms. Conto. My officers have just been telling me they're continuing the investigation at Global."

"Unfortunately. They're suffering under some misguided ideas about Martin Jonas's death. I can assure you that the doctor, the lieutenant, and the detective have continued to bother me; they've practically accused Peter and me of being involved in Martin's death. They also hold some other preposterous and completely uninformed notions about the way we do business. They invaded my offices on Monday morning and copied data. If they make any of their libel public, I will file a monumental lawsuit against each of them individually and the Palm Springs Police Department." Conto's voice was dripping with implied innocence.

"Slander," Brett said.

"What are you saying?" Conto was really angry now.

"We would be slandering you, not libeling you. Libel is written, but slander is spoken," Brett said.

"Chief, do I really have to stand here and be corrected by your lieutenant? His attitude as a public servant is completely disrespectful."

"I be nobody's servant, Missy," Brett said, using a touch of southern slave.

"Chief. Stop him. You know that's not what I meant," Conto said.

"Enough, Lieutenant," the chief said. "Ms. Conto, the lieutenant can be an absolute pain in the ass sometimes but he's also my best officer."

"A tough cross to carry. Imagine him as a friend," I said.

The chief gave me the "you-shut-up-too' look." So far, Bergman had been absolutely quiet.

He finally spoke, adding to Conto's complaints. "Ms. Conto has been extremely generous with her time with all of you, and yet you continue to treat both of us with disrespect and innuendo."

"Mr. Bergman, we're investigating serious crimes," the chief said. "Both your firm and Global are parked squarely in the middle of our investigation. I will not tolerate any disrespect on the part of my staff, and I will not tolerate any disrespect of their authority on your parts. Lieutenant Wade is in charge of this investigation, and he believes he has good reason to investigate both your firms."

Go Chief.

"Bergman, explain a wire transfer of $200,000 that you made to Europe last month." Brett had wanted to confront Bergman about this after we knew the precise endpoint of the transfer and after returning from Folsom. However, it was more important now to back up the chief's trust in him as an investigator. Show the chief we had something substantial.

Bergman held his breath for a moment, organized his thinking and opened his mouth to speak.

I held my breath too.

The red laser was back.

It danced on Bergman's forehead and blossomed into an evil red blotch.

We were all frozen in its red micro-light beam.

As Bergman fell, his eyes revealed his end. It's not possible to be shot to death with elegance — he was gone without grace.

People were screaming and running.

Brett had his gun out and was moving in the obvious direction of the shot. He hand-signaled Joan to protect Chris and motioned me to follow him. I drew my Glock, and followed him. The chief and Joan were leading Nancy, Conto and Chris in the opposite direction.

Conto looked strangely calm.

Brett suddenly reversed direction and went to the other side of North Palm and headed toward Tahquitz Way.

"Museum parking lot. Same route he took last time," Brett said.

The crowd was screaming and in full panic.

Sirens sounded.

Brett took command of the tactical situation. He unclipped his radio and broadcast on the department tactical frequency.

"Chief, Doc and I are heading to the museum parking lot. I hope to get there ahead of our shooter. No, repeat, no back up. I don't want him picking anyone off. Do you copy?" Brett spoke into the radio.

He got a "copy that" back and put the radio back on his hip. He managed to not drop his radio or his gun.

"Let's find cover at the back of the lot. If this guy shows up, and he has a weapon out, I'm going to shoot him and ask questions later."

"Is that legal?" I was working hard to keep up with Brett.

"No, but he's just too dangerous to try and arrest."

I'd never met anyone more dangerous than Brett until Bocca had arrived in town; I guess there is a first time for everything. I also knew that Brett wouldn't shoot him without warning him. We ran down Tahquitz, through the Desert Fashion Plaza, across Balfour and into the Museum parking lot.

We picked the backside of the museum parking lot on the same side as the trail entrance so we wouldn't be in each other's line of fire. Climbing a short distance, we got behind a couple of big boulders. At fifty feet of elevation gain over the parking lot and adjacent to McDonnell Golf Course, we had an unobstructed view over the museum, down onto Tahquitz and up to the backside of North Palm Canyon. Sirens in the distance. Nancy was with Joan and the chief so I didn't have to worry about her. Same for Chris.

"If he isn't here in five minutes, we missed him," I whispered.

"I'd like to bag him."

As we waited, I felt the vertical slope of the mountain behind me. A mile and a half, straight up. It was not a friendly place to wander at night.

We waited several minutes.

The incoming signal light on Brett's radio flashed and he took it out to answer the call. He listened and the look on his face suddenly made me feel lost on the mountain. He turned up the radio volume so I could hear both ends of the call as he walked the few feet toward me.

"He knocked me out! The bastard. It's dark. Too many people..." Joan's voice was weak. She sounded groggy and hurt.

Brett pushed the transmit button. "Are you okay?"

"I- I'm all right, just groggy."

"Where are you?" Brett asked.

Michael Thompkins

"In the alley next to the Saloon parking lot. Same one we w-walked over through." Joan sounded semi-conscious.

Any uniform monitoring the tactical frequency would respond to Joan's location. Her call for help would be rebroadcast on the regular frequency as an "officer down" call. Individual cops are transformed by this call into an army with a singular purpose — officer down, stand to, back-up.

"Doc and I are on our way," Brett said.

"I screwed up," Joan strained voice came from the small radio.

"We're coming," Brett assured her.

"The bastard's got Chris," she said.

BOCCA'S PLAN

Bocca put the final polish on his plan. After he shot Bergman, he would kidnap the kid. Snatching the kid was the only way to guarantee a contest with the lieutenant. It was the only way that he could get the lieutenant and the shrink to come to him on his terms at a location he chose. After he had the kid, he would dictate all the rules and could set the trap. He knew it would be suicide to just come at the lieutenant again.

After shooting Bergman from the office window, he picked up his gear, strode to the rear of the building that overlooked the Street Fair, walked down the rear steps, and started scouting for an opportunity to take the kid. By the time he looped around the building, he saw the lieutenant and the shrink running up Tahquitz Way in the direction of the museum parking lot. Their move was predictable; one more time he out-planned them. They didn't anticipate his doubling back towards the crowd, and assumed he'd use the same escape route as last time.

Gut rush when things go tactical. Make the right move, and win. Reputation grows. Make the wrong move, lose. Reputation's hurt. What other game has the same risk? The same rush? Nothing. Zip. Gambling? No way. Try gambling with your life.

After the lieutenant and the shrink passed, he walked against the panicked crowd out to North Palm Canyon. He passed in front of the shrink's office and around the corner. Although the human herd was in full stampede, it parted for him, realizing instinctively that he was more dangerous than the gunshot it was fleeing. The irony was not wasted on him.

When he turned at the shrink's office, he cruised the crowd on his way back to the car he had parked on Indian Canyon. Snatching the kid would require more than skill; he would need luck. The secret to luck was to be ready. Bocca had spent his whole professional life adhering to two underlying principles: be ready for absolutely anything, and be especially ready for luck.

Luck! The kid and the lady cop. Right there. Lady cop's carrying a Glock Nine next to her right thigh, and doing the best she can to be unobtrusive.

God, she's hot carrying the Glock.

Settle down. Capitalize on the luck.

Michael Thompkins

The cop and the kid were in the middle of two walls of people. One wall was pushing north, and the other pushing south on North Palm Canyon. Just like fans trying to leave a baseball game, they took a while to clear the stadium. Bocca slipped between the two walls and followed them.

Settle down. Follow them. Look for the opening. Accomplish the mission. May not get this good an opportunity again.

The location and timing were perfect. The lady cop and the kid had just parted company with the older cop and the shrink's wife. Her decision was Bocca's luck. He was closing on them. She decided to take a shortcut down the alley between Tahquitz and Indian Canyon; an unlighted alley that came out near the Saloon.

He knew the route made perfect tactical sense from her perspective; she was getting the kid out of the line of fire. She wasn't making a mistake. You simply can't protect a person from a pro. This was the perfect opportunity.

Bocca followed them into the alley. By the time they reached the halfway point in the alley, he positioned himself among a group of four old men who were within ten feet of her and the kid. Everyone in the alley slowed to a walk. The crowd was behind them on Tahquitz, and there were less than twenty people in the alley.

Unseen by the others, he tripped one of the old men. The old guy went down hard, crying out as he fell. Turning away from the cop, Bocca pretended to help the old man. She stopped, and came over to help the old man. She asked the guy if he was hurt as she walked towards him. She held the Glock by her right side and positioned the kid behind her.

Strike! Let go of the old man. Knock the Glock from her hand. She's quick but not quick enough. Stepping back. Blocking his first body blow. Sensing who he is. Second blow taking her down. Easier to attack than defend in the dark. She's staying down. Soft sounds as sweet as she looks. No shame, lady cop. Up against the best. Easy now. Don't need to kill her. One more kick and she's out. Old folks running away

Look at her.

Soft. She's so soft. Touch her.

Kid's moving!

The kid stepped toward Bocca. His message was in his move and his eyes — touch her again and I'll fight you.

Bocca stood up.

He led the kid by the arm down the alley toward the car parked on Indian Canyon. The kid could have tried to run away from him but didn't. He accepted capture.

Kid's behaving. Don't need the duct tape. Gotta give the kid credit. He's scared, but in control of himself. Tell him: run or alert anyone, everybody dies.

Kid nods his acceptance of the terms.

Ten minutes later, they reached the condo Bocca rented in the north end of town. They entered without encountering a soul. Most folks in the complex were still probably part of the frenzied Street Fair crowd. Again, his luck held up. He led the kid into the kitchen, sat him on the floor, and cuffed him to the refrigerator frame at floor level.

He found himself liking the kid. He told him when this thing was over, he'd leave him alive. Sure, the kid could identify him, but he wouldn't. If he left him alive, this kid would keep running from whatever he was running from. This kid was homeless like him. Sure there was his London base but even that could be abandoned in an instant. He wondered why was the kid homeless.

Bocca talked to the kid. The kid listened quietly. Sometimes he wished he had a way to share all he had learned living as an outlaw. Maybe he could convince this kid to learn his profession. Bocca knew about the Stockholm Syndrome: if you kept someone hostage long enough, you could get them to do anything for you. Maybe that was a way for him to have an apprentice. It wasn't really practical, though. How would he travel with the kid? Better to enjoy the kid's company a little while and then move along. Company would be good. He talked to the kid about the music he liked and the kid just listened for fifteen minutes.

Time. Move the kid to the garage. Cuff him to the eye-ring in the garage beside the mattress. Pain in the ass drilling that thing. Good to talk to the kid some more but need to think. Warn him again about noise and the consequences. Open a bottle of single malt. Need to think. Rest. Loosen up a bit. Think.

He had been surprised to get the additional contract on Bergman. The money was excellent. As long as the buyer and her people paid him well, he did what they told him to do. The buyer had balls for a woman; he blew Bergman away six inches from her face and she didn't even flinch. This would turn the heat up on her, though. He figured there was a good reason that she wanted the guy killed, but it wasn't his business. He knew that Bergman worked for the same accounting firm as the guy he'd shot at Tahquitz. Maybe too much heat was building on her, and she was just tidying up loose ends; he liked that kind of attention to detail in a person. She wanted him to hit Bergman, to clean up her loose ends. He had a few loose ends himself, but he'd take care of those soon.

Michael Thompkins

Shot itself was cool. Taking Bergman out. Target standing so near the lieutenant and the shrink was fantastic. Lieutenant was probably splattered. Hate blood and brain splatter. Bet the lieutenant hates it, too. Weird to be in a firefight, come close to getting your ass blown off, be upset by something like blood splatter. Occupational hazard.

Lieutenant took something from him. Take the kid from the lieutenant. Justice. Lieutenant fell on top of the kid last Saturday night to protect him. Anyone could see how valuable the kid was to the lieutenant. Why?

Now, the kid was leverage to get to the lieutenant without the cavalry coming to his rescue. Shrink would be a bonus. Maybe leave the shrink and the kid alive to tell the story.

He knew a good plastic surgeon and a new appearance was always possible. There were lots of ways to play this and they were all fun. Luck had been on his side, the mission had been really excellent, and it would all be over soon.

He would set up a meeting place. No way the lieutenant could predict the location. When he first arrived here in Palm Springs, he'd spent a week scouting locations. He had saved this particular one because the possibilities for escape were many and the terrain would eliminate most cops. He would take the kid there, call the lieutenant, and tell him to bring the shrink and no one else. He'd time it so it would be getting dark; the lieutenant wouldn't risk mobilizing backup to this meeting place, especially in the dark. The lieutenant knew what his men were trained for. None of them would be trained for this area. Bocca had picked the place because of this as well the elevation; he liked height. He decided he would do the meeting on Saturday at dusk after the crowds had thinned. Bocca's plan was in place.

Tie the kid and the shrink to the same tree. Challenge the lieutenant to "winner take all." No weapons, just hand to hand combat. No back-up possible. Settle it once and for all. Stop carrying this monkey. End it. Kill them all. Clean up loose ends.

Suck up sweet revenge.

Return to England.

He needed time to rest up, find a woman, and recover from his temporary loss of professional perspective. Maybe they'd make a movie about him someday — bigger and better than *Butch Cassidy and the Sundance Kid*. Bocca's reputation was everything to him. He was addicted to the movie. He had seen the movie at least a hundred times. His exploits as an outlaw already surpassed Butch and Sundance's adventures. He was wanted on many continents; the cinema outlaws had only been wanted on two.

Butch, you proud yet?

CAPTIVE AUDIENCE

We walked as fast as we could toward Joan's location. We knew that one of the uniforms would get to her first, but we still hustled. Running wasn't required; there was enough panic in the crowd already.

"It's not end-game yet," Brett said.

"What do you mean?"

"If Bocca wanted to kill Chris or Joan, they'd be dead," he said.

"I get it. Our tiger now has a plan. He wants all three of us so he snatched Chris to get us to come to him. He's really deteriorating; revenge is completely clouding his judgment."

Walking across Tahquitz Canyon Way, I noticed that the Street Fair had turned into a chaotic circus. Some of the original partygoers who had witnessed Bergman's shooting were fleeing in response; some had remained to gawk. I could see yellow crime-scene tape and techs. Some uniforms were helping restore order; we nodded at them as we strode by. This shooting would definitely make the papers and trigger the FBI and Interpol. Not only did Bocca have Chris, but time was definitely going to run out on us; the case would soon be out of our hands.

Bergman's body was being zipped into a body bag. Even Peter Bergman, Mr. Armani, didn't deserve a body bag.

"Bergman's gone," Brett said.

"Bergman was the consummate narcissist; he thought he was the center of the universe,"

"He was the center of something," Brett said.

"Yes?"

"He was the center of a target," Brett said.

"The bull's-eye."

"Bocca can shoot a one inch spot at fifty yards, easily," Brett said.

"He can sure shoot."

When we arrived at the alley, it was full of uniforms. Joan was sitting on the pavement halfway down the alley and a medic was evaluating her. The first uniform to reach her had called the EMTs. As we got closer, I could see that she looked a little dazed and shaky. The chief and Nancy arrived at the same time we did, from the opposite end of the alley.

"I want to examine her, please," Nancy asked the medic.

"Sure thing, Doctor Reynolds. Nothing so far except a possible concussion," the medic said.

Nancy spent several minutes quietly examining Joan with the help of the light reflected off the alley walls from flashlights. A group of four senior citizens stood at the end of the alley being questioned by a uniform; they looked dazed and confused.

"I screwed up and lost Chris." Joan finally looked at Brett.

"What happened?" Brett asked.

Even with little light, I could see that Brett's face was taut.

"He faked me out by pushing one of those old folks down and I walked right into his trap. By the time I sensed he was going to strike, it was too late. When I came to, Chris was gone. I don't think I was out more than a couple of minutes. I'm sorry, boss. I screwed up big-time."

"No way you could have seen that coming. Nothing you could have done differently," Brett said unconvincingly.

Nancy scowled at Brett and spoke to Joan. "I don't think you have a concussion, but we need to watch you tonight to make sure the blow to the back of your head has no lasting effect. I'll take a chance and not hospitalize you."

With Joan leaning against Nancy for stability, we all walked out of the alley. When we arrived at the Saloon, Jay met us at the front door. He took one look at us and escorted us to a booth in the bar. We all squeezed around the table.

"I heard about the shooting. The parking lot was full of people running from the Street Fair. It was a goddamn stampede. Who was it?" Jay asked.

"Peter Bergman, one of our suspects." Brett spoke first.

Then Jay noticed Chris was missing. "Where's Chris? He goes on stage in five minutes."

"I screwed up. I let the shooter take him from me," Joan replied. She was still leaning against Nancy, and her color was returning.

"Shit happens. This guy's starting to bug me," Brett said with a few less tension lines showing on his face.

"We all screwed up. It obviously wasn't Bergman who hired the shooter," I said.

"What about the $200,000?" Joan asked.

"Beats me," Brett said.

"Anybody else notice how calm Conto was when Bergman was blown away?" I asked.

"She didn't look frightened. I noticed that," Nancy said.

"I'm betting she and Bergman were in this together from the beginning," Joan said. "He helped her fudge the numbers for a cut. Then she re-contracted with the shooter to kill him. When she had Martin Jonas killed, Bergman's noose was already tied. We had it completely backwards. "

"Why did she do it?" I asked.

"Maybe she just was tired of their sexual friendship," Brett cracked.

"Maybe because he knew or guessed she hired the shooter," Joan said.

"She did it all right; I saw the look on her face," I said. "She knew it was going to happen."

"Excuse me. I'm going to have to cancel tonight's show and refund admission." Jay left us to tend to the immediate reality imposed by Chris's kidnapping. Bocca had ruined Chris's opening night.

The chief spoke for the first time since he showed up in the alley with Nancy. "This guy now has killed three people in my town; that's unacceptable. I'm already taking heat from the mayor, the city council and the chamber. Maybe, just maybe, I can keep this out off the front page of the morning papers. The mayor's brother is the publisher, but it will cost his honor. Soon after this shooting hits the papers, the Feds will send an apprehension team and Interpol won't want them to get all the publicity. They'll send in their own team and my town will be full of international and federal gunslingers. I'll lose control. You're still in command of this investigation but you have twenty-four to forty-eight hours. The meter is running out."

"Yes, sir, I understand," Brett said. "I'm certain Bocca will call us in the next day or two; he's not going to want to hold Chris forever. He'll set up a meet soon."

Since the moment Chris was kidnapped, Brett seemed to have total certainty that Bocca wouldn't just kill Chris. He would set a time and a place for a showdown.

"I'll get something on Conto in Folsom tomorrow. And we need to send techs to Bergman's home right now," Joan said.

"Why?" I asked.

"Because there might be something to tie them together," Joan said.

"Joan, I'm not sure that you're going any where tomorrow," Nancy warned.

"I'll be fine. Although I have mixed feelings" Joan said, trying to be every bit as tough as Brett.

"We'll see if you're fit to go in the morning," Nancy said.

"And the mixed feelings about Folsom..." Brett said.

"What if Bocca calls while I'm up there?" Joan asked.

"I don't know when he'll call but he won't set up the meet until dusk or later, sometime in the next few days." Brett said.

"I'll leave my cell phone number on my home answering system. We might as well make it easy for him. " Brett was thinking ahead tactically, as usual.

"Chief, what about Conto?" Brett asked.

"I noticed her reaction to Bergman being shot too," the chief said. "I told her she was not to leave town, and that she was a material witness. I implied that you would question her tomorrow."

"That's good, but I would like to have something solid on her before I question her again." Brett said.

"That's my job in Folsom," Joan said.

"We'll see about that," Nancy said.

"Lieutenant, it's still your show. There's nothing else I can do to support you." The chief turned to face me. "Doc, why didn't he just shoot the kid as well as Bergman? Why kidnap him? Why complicate his life? He'd have shown you and the lieutenant that he was invincible by shooting him and he wouldn't have taken as great a risk. He had a good shot at both of them. Why snatch the kid? Why take that risk?"

"It's all about Brett, me, and him now. He thinks we kept him out of Special Forces," I said.

"Did you?" The chief asked Brett.

"Damned if I did, damned if I didn't. Tell you the truth, I can't remember all the selection committees that I rostered up on."

"Doesn't matter. This guy is going to play it out for real or not," I said.

"One thing he wouldn't have if he shot the kid," Brett said.

"What's that?" the chief asked.

"Chris as an audience," Brett said.

"A captive audience," I added.

PURGATORY

After spending the night at our house, the next morning Joan was declared fit for duty by Nancy, and departed on time for Folsom. I spend the day seeing patients. Brett did paperwork. We both waited for the expected call from Bocca.

In the late afternoon Brett and I met at the airport fountain. We took seats on the concrete parapet surrounding the fountain, and waited for Joan and the chief. It was 5:00, and the sun was heading into the Indian Canyons. Evening was coming and, with it, increased worry for Chris. Joan's helo was due back from Folsom momentarily. The chief wanted a full report on our progress. Time was running out. We could see the CHP helo land and Joan, who Brett had informed of our meeting, walk across a 100 yards of airport tarmac toward us.

Dusk was falling. Airports are the best at night. I love them in the daytime, but at night the sense of being an adult who is free to go anywhere and do anything, as long as it's legal and harmless, just takes over. I was free to fly anywhere — could be paradise, could be purgatory. Waiting for Bocca's call felt like the latter.

The chief and Joan joined us at exactly the same moment. The chief pressed Joan right away, before they even sat down. "What did you learn in Folsom?"

"I haven't figured it all out, but Global is using its electrical scheduling transmission requests to the ISO to create the appearance of selling and delivering more electricity than it actually moves," Joan said. "I think Bergman and Conto were in on this together, and it cost Bergman his life."

"What do you need?" the chief asked.

"We need a court order to seize Conto's home computer. Maybe I can catch her with the real set of books," Joan said.

"I thought we had an order for that already," the chief said.

"We have an order for office records, but we are not supposed to interfere with their ability to do business," Joan continued on. "The order does not include her home. I suspect that she has three sets of books. One for the accountants to fool the IRS, one for the ISO to fool them, and one to keep track of what she's really doing. She has to know at all times what is really going on and what she fabricates — even thieves need to know the truth. I'm betting the real set is on her home computer.

She transmits daily to her home computer from the office. One of the techs found multiple daily links to Conto's home computer on the proxy server at Global."

"All right, I'll get her home added to the warrant," the chief said. "I sent techs to Bergman's home last night like you wanted. I like Conto for the Bergman hit, too."

"Yeah. Everyone saw the look on her face when Bergman was shot," Brett added. "I'd bet my shield she was expecting it."

"Conto can simply deny all of this," I said.

"And if we don't come up with something to connect her with the hits or prove she was criminally trading electricity, then her denial will stick," Brett said.

"She doesn't know that the shooter has Chris, and she would have had no reason to anticipate that," I said.

"Different agenda. The kidnapping is personal for Bocca, and has nothing to do with the Conto contract. He's lost control," Brett said.

"Right. So what does our shooter do next?" the chief asked.

"Like I said before, I know what he'll do next. I just don't know where and when," Brett said.

"Remind me," the chief said.

"There is only one reason that he snatched Chris: to challenge us," Brett said. "He'll use Chris to force us to meet him and settle this once and for all. He wants a showdown."

"When?" the chief asked.

"Tonight or tomorrow night," Brett answered.

"Do you want Riverside SWAT as backup?"

"No," Brett said. "He'll demand we come alone and if we don't, I'm certain he'll kill Chris. Each additional officer would increase the likelihood of Chris being shot. I don't want any needless deaths, especially Chris'. This guy is just too good; he actually is an 'army of one.'"

"A crazy one," the chief said.

"Chief, on my approach in the helo, I had a hunch about the top of the Aerial Tramway," Joan said. "Bocca told us he likes heights, and it's the highest point around here."

We were silent for a moment. All of our eyes focused on the red beacon at the top of Mt. San Jacinto.

"Joan, I want to you up there with your rifle tonight and tomorrow. I expect our shooter will set the meet up for dusk," Brett ordered.

"So he can get away easily if we show with a posse?" I asked.

"Exactly," Brett replied.

Brett's cell phone rang as if on cue.

The background was full of sounds from the fountain, jets taking off and landing, traffic on Tahquitz Canyon, and some city workers mowing in front of City Hall. Up close there was only the one sound: Brett's cell ringing. The air was full of the smell of chlorine from the fountain and cut grass.

Brett picked the cell off his belt and pressed the green button. "Lieutenant Wade."

We couldn't hear the voice on the other end of the exchange.

"I understand, you son of a bitch." Brett pushed the kill button and re-hooked the cell on his belt opposite his weapon.

"Lieutenant?" We all knew what the chief was asking.

"Bocca. He said three words and hung up," Brett said.

"Go on," the chief said.

"Tomorrow at dusk."

"Did he say where?" Joan asked.

"Just the three words."

"I'm betting on the top of the Tramway," Joan said.

"Me too. It's just a guess, though," I said.

"How did he know your cell phone number?" the chief asked.

"I left it on my answering machine at home. Figured he would want to talk to us sooner or later."

"Smart move," the chief said.

"This will save you tonight on the mountain," Brett said to Joan.

"I feel fine, but I could use a good night's sleep," she said.

The chief looked like he had something else to say.

"Chief?" I asked.

"Lieutenant, I'll call the judge and ensure the warrant extends to Conto's home. Get out there now and seize her home computer. You can run the meeting with the shooter anyway you want. I started with you three on this and I'll let my bet ride. The FBI's team is en route; they'll be here in a matter of hours. Last night's shooting triggered it. You are to run this on your own from now on and outside of regular channels. I don't know shit if you fail and …"

"The department will disown us." Brett finished it clearly having heard it many times before in other settings.

"Is that acceptable to all of you? I really can't ask you to do this," the chief said.

He got three affirmative nods in answer to his question.

"One more thing," the chief said.

"Yes?" we all spoke in unison.

"There's a State of Washington warrant out on your witness," he said.

"Say what?" Brett said.

"Assault warrant. He allegedly beat up his father," the Chief replied.

The three of us looked at each other.

Brett smiled.

Joan nodded her head as it to say, "all right Chris."

I hadn't seen the warrant coming.

"Lieutenant?" the chief asked.

"Yes sir," Brett replied.

"Make the warrant go away."

"That will take some IOUs," Brett said.

"You can go to Spokane later and straighten it out. Did you remember this guy, Bocca?" The chief changed the subject.

"Maybe when I see him, but I was on so many Special Forces Selection committees like the one he claims," Brett said.

"Just remember one thing," the chief added.

"About coming back from this sort of thing?" Brett asked.

"Yes." The chief had his eyes on Brett, but his words were meant for all three of us.

"And young lady," the chief shifted his gaze to Joan.

"Yes, Chief." Joan met his gaze.

"I have seen how hard you push yourself," the chief said. "You work too many hours; you need a life. I know you hold yourself responsible for the kid being kidnapped. I could see that last night in your eyes and the things you said."

"Yes." Joan's eyes met the chief's gaze, reluctantly confirming his assessment.

"Get over yourself. Do the job. I am not interested in perfect officers. For Christsakes, look at these two. They're far from perfect." The chief looked at Brett and Joan. He shook his head, stood up and left.

We looked the other way, and kept our mouths shut. That's never easy.

When the chief was far enough away, Brett and I repeated softly in unison, "Far from perfect?"

WHO'S THE BADDEST?

We kept to ourselves riding out to Palm Desert in the Mustang. Brett stuck a CD in the player, and we listened to more Smashing Pumpkins. Joan seemed lost in what the chief had said to her. She even volunteered to sit in the back.

We turned off the Highway and onto El Paseo when we received a phone call from the chief; our warrant now included Conto's house.

"Joan, explain the proxy servers at Global again. I'm still confused." Brett interrupted our private thoughts.

"Okay. Proxy servers function as a first line of protection between a computer network and the Internet," Joan said. "They keep a log of all incoming and outgoing data transmissions. The firewall, or the security software, resides in the proxy server."

"So if Conto is keeping the real set of books at her house, she would need to transmit data to her home daily." I was keeping up so far.

"Yeah, and as Conto does that," Joan continued, "she erases the data and any transmission logs on her computer at the Global offices. All the time she is unaware that the proxy server is keeping a record of the transmissions. Unfortunately for us, it's not the data itself, just the record of the transmission."

"But we need the data itself to prove that she's been jacking around with power prices," I said.

"Exactly," Joan said.

We were passing the Palm Desert Historical Society with its forty-year-old fire engine parked out in front. The old red pumper seemed small and inadequate for the task of extinguishing a fire. Traffic was light for 6 p.m. Five o'clock rush hour in the valley is pretty much confined to the highways.

Brett pulled up behind two cars at a red light controlling the intersection of El Paseo and Monterey. It was a long light at a now-quiet desert intersection. We would be turning right and heading up a gradual mile-long grade to the development where Conto lived. Most of the residential areas of Palm Desert were on a slope that began at Highway 111 and ascended a mile of distance and a couple of thousand feet in altitude toward the Santa Rosa Mountains.

Suddenly, vibrations hit us, then actual sounds of sirens and horns, followed by bright flashing lights. Fire engines — big-loud-bright-red-fighting-fire-get-the-hell-out-of-our-way—engines urgently approached us.

The lazy intersection woke up from its siesta. Our red light was locked by the strobe atop the Cove Cities Fire Department command car that slowed briefly, made sure the intersection was clear, then raced through—not really de-accelerating, just a split-second pause on the gas pedal to ensure the safety of Cove citizens.

"I got a bad feeling," Brett said.

We were still waiting; the train of fire department vehicles was still coming. It moved furiously fast through the intersection. An engine followed the command vehicle and was in turn followed by a fire truck. The caboose on the train was the EMT vehicle, the last to clear the intersection.

The intersection struggled to return to its siesta, but it would have to wait. Brett reached down, grabbed the police flasher on the console between us, and placed it through the open window onto the roof. He hit the siren, pulled onto the shoulder around the two cars in front of us, turned right on Monterey, and started up the hill. Uninvited, and without a ticket, we joined the train — the new caboose catching up.

Brett picked up the microphone, turned up the volume on the police radio and transmitted: "69 Whiskey."

69 Whiskey was his call sign in honor of the 1969 Woodstock Music Festival in upstate New York. Whiskey replaced Woodstock for the W that was the international call signal.

"69 Whiskey. Go," the dispatcher's voice said.

"I am following Cove Cities Fire up Monterey to a fire scene. Please notify Cove Command," Brett said.

"Copy, 69 Whiskey. Do you need assistance?" the dispatcher asked.

"Negative. Just notify them. And thanks," Brett said.

More than one cop owed his life to a radio dispatcher.

"Copy, 69 Whiskey. You be welcome," the dispatcher signed off.

GUN PLAY

The torque in the Shelby Mustang reminded me of the helo lifting off earlier today. We could have easily caught and overtaken the Fire Command vehicle, but maintained our tag-along-position.

The Mustang's engine, the fire trucks and engines, our siren, the fire sirens and klaxon horns together did not synergistically come close to the level of the rotor sound on a helo, but we lacked noise canceling headsets. My ears hurt.

The air was full of diesel exhaust and unspent fuel.

Deepening darkness. Spotty shadows expanding into blocks of blackness. Mercury switches activated by light-sensing photo-cells began to fire halogen streetlights.

We were moving up the grade at fifty miles an hour, not really knowing where the train was heading. About halfway up the hill, a plume of ugly black smoke resembling a signal fire rose straight up. I closed my eyes involuntarily and hoped, if it was a signal, it wasn't one about Chris.

The motor sounds from the fire trucks and fire engines pitched up louder each time they shifted to accommodate the grade; twice the command vehicle used its klaxon horn to wake up a driver who was failing to yield. We closed on the black smoke, and turned left off Monterey.

Lopez ran perpendicular to Monterey and the grade suddenly stopped. We came to a slight bend in Lopez and I lost sight of the command car. After we came around the bend, it was visible two hundred yards ahead. We pulled to a stop behind a Palm Desert Police unit. The entire train of fire vehicles pulled to the curb. Unlike train passengers, the firefighters hit the street running.

The house numbers still visible on the front door, Brett identified it as Conto's house. It was a conflagration. Firefighters were running hoses to get water on the fire as fast as possible. Two firemen were already entering the house, assisted by their Scott air-packs. I recognized Brett's friend from Monday morning when he ran a phony drill to get us inside the Global offices; he was the incident commander.

"Let's go talk to my buddy," Brett said.

We climbed out of the Mustang and walked past the line of fire equipment parked at the curb, carefully avoiding the water hoses. The air, full of smoke and superheated by the fire, smelled dangerous to breathe. Pumped water sizzled as it supersaturated the structure.

"Lieutenant Williams," Brett said to his buddy.

Michael Thompkins

"Lieutenant yourself. What the hell are you doing here?" Williams shook Brett's outstretched hand.

"Well, we were on our way here to search this house for evidence in an investigation. We fell in behind you at El Paseo and Monterey. You remember Doc and Detective Fleming?" Brett said.

Williams nodded to Joan and me. "I made you behind us before I got your relay. Same investigation as Monday morning at Global?" He had found out the name of the owner of the house en route and connected it to Monday morning's favor. No moss grew on Lieutenant Williams.

"Yeah. Don't be surprised when you discover that this is arson," Brett said.

"No surprise already; house is burning too fast. We won't save the structure. It was a gas explosion and then a fast burn. It'll be hard to prove its arson." Williams knew his business and was already ahead of us.

"Conto's a bad guy, and she most likely hired a badder guy to come out here and destroy evidence," Brett said.

"I'm glad we can help you chase crooks. It gets boring at the fire station, shining equipment, watching TV, playing hoops, cooking dinner, and sucking up to politicians."

"Hard life," Brett said.

"Lieutenant, we need you a minute," one of the firefighters called out.

"Excuse me. Gotta work." Williams moved quickly toward the fire.

"Bocca beat us here. Conto wanted a quick and dirty way to make sure there was no evidence here, so she had him burn down her own house," Brett said.

Joan looked puzzled by what Brett said; I was too. Something was wrong with Conto ordering the burn.

One of the windows on the side of the house exploded under the pressure of the hot gases inside. We flinched. Two firefighters, manning a hose, redirected their water cannon into the opening. A snake of red flame ran back into the house, retreating from the water that they instantly played on it. The noise of the glass breaking startled my thinking enough that I finally pieced some things together.

"No woman ordered this," I said.

"What?" Brett said.

"Women like order. And no woman I ever met would order personal stuff like her jewelry and clothes burned."

"Isn't that a little sexist?" Brett asked.

"Doc, you're right. And sexism is in the intent, not in the words." Joan said. "She could have ordered Bocca to come out here, fake a break-in and steal the computer with a few other valuables. Instead, he just torched the place. Why?"

"Good question," I said.

"Doc, you gotta be right. Forget about the sexism part," Brett said.

"This also explains last night," I added.

"How?" Brett asked.

"Conto was tying up two loose ends," I said. "That's why she chose to have Bergman killed last night. Bocca was leaving town soon; maybe he was supposed to stick around for only a week. Killing Bergman and getting rid of her home computer were all part of the same plan. Conto was creating order in her universe, tidying things up."

"Why did he torch the place?" Brett asked the same question Joan had.

"Yeah, Doc, why didn't he do what she asked?" Joan asked.

"He could have mistakenly thought he had a license to do what ever he wanted or...."

"Or what?" Brett asked.

"He just did whatever the hell he wanted anyway; Bocca in control again. Remember, he's a sociopath. They don't answer to anyone."

"That means Bocca thinks that she's no threat to his career," Brett said.

"Yeah," I said.

"Which one do you think it was? A mistake or control?" Joan asked.

"Don't know, doesn't make any difference," I said.

"This is going to frighten her," Joan said.

"Yes. Yes, it is," I said.

"Remember the way Conto talked about her relationship with Bergman?" Brett asked.

"Yes, like he was disposable; it's called pathological narcissism," I said.

"She's worse than Bocca, but we can't prove any of this," Joan said.

Brett's cell phone rang and he stepped out of hearing range to take the call. He was back in five minutes.

"We just got major lucky. The tech at Bergman's home found some mini-audio tapes hidden in his bookcase. He says they're telephone discussions between Bergman and Conto."

We had indeed got lucky for the first time in a week. We deserved it.

"Good break," Joan said.

"Wade!" Williams returned from helping his men. The fire was now under control; the smoke was gray-white as it mixed with moisture from the water cannon.

"What?" Brett asked.

"I got a question for you," Williams said.

"Shoot," Brett said.

"If this lady is a bad guy and she hired a badder guy to burn this house down?" Williams paused.

"Yes?" Brett asked.

"Then, who's the baddest?"

"We gonna find out soon," Brett said.

TELL-TALE TAPES

While driving in from Conto's house to police headquarters, we called in our order to California Pizza Kitchen. I ordered their walnut, goat cheese, and gorgonzola-pear pizza; Brett liked the meat-lover's special; and Joan shared some of each. We picked up the pizzas, drove to headquarters, found a quiet conference room, and waited for the tech to arrive with the tapes from Bergman's place. Nancy had a meeting at the hospital tonight so I was on my own for supper.

We had pretty much finished off the pizzas and a Greek salad when there was a knock on the door. A blond young man, barely out of adolescence, entered carrying a small box that he placed on the conference room table.

"Lieutenant, here are the tapes from the Bergman house. I brought you a micro-cassette player, too. I already copied them onto a digital player but be careful you don't touch the record button. They're probably going to be evidence. Right?"

"Right. We'll be careful. Thanks. Where did Bergman hide them?" Brett asked.

"In his shoes."

"You're kidding," Brett said.

"Nope. They were in a pair of black tux shoes," the tech spoke proudly of his find.

"Good work," Brett praised.

"Thanks, Lieutenant. Can I get a ride in the Mustang now?"

"Yeah, you earned it," Brett said.

"Can I drive it?"

"Don't push your luck," Brett said.

"Okay. Bring those back to me and I'll check them into evidence."

"Copy that," Brett said.

The young tech left. Brett emptied the box on the table and examined the contents. It contained a telephone handset, the micro-cassette player, and three tiny tapes. Brett pushed some buttons on the handset and revealed the hidden cassette player that recorded phone conversations.

"Switch this baby with your regular handset and you're in business," Brett said.

"So much for privacy," Joan said.

"Conto thought she was the only one capable of a double-cross," Brett said.

"That's the thing about narcissists like Bergman and Conto," I said. "They don't think about anyone except themselves. That makes it easy to ignore anybody else's feelings or needs, but it also makes it easy to underestimate other people and situations."

"Bergman underestimated Conto and it cost him his life. Conto underestimated Bergman and let's hope that it costs her," Joan said.

"We can only hope," I said.

"Well, let's get to it. There could be three hours of tape here." Joan displayed her usual eager attitude.

The conference room phone rang, and Joan walked over to the wall and picked it up. She stepped out into the hallway to take the call. A minute later she returned and said, "Conto is booked on a flight to Texas that leaves at 9:30, American 397. She has to check in by 8:30."

I looked at my watch. "It's 7:20 now. You had her watched?"

"Palm Desert Sheriffs had to notify her about her house burning, so I asked them to watch her for me," Brett answered. "A couple of uniforms get to play detective."

"How'd they find out that she was booked on the American flight?" I asked.

"Tip wasn't from the Palm Desert Sheriffs," Joan continued.

"Who was it from?" Brett asked.

"Pete Navarez," Joan replied.

"Indians?" Brett asked rhetorically.

"Nothing happens in Palm Springs that they don't know about," Joan said.

"They were here first. They're entitled," I said.

"She's running scared," Brett said.

"She must be," I said.

"Yeah, it supports your idea that Bocca was supposed to fake a break-in, but not burn her house down," Brett said.

"Bocca took control of the situation. It scared her," I said.

"What do we do about it? " Joan asked.

"Get lucky with these tapes," Brett replied.

Brett placed a cassette in the player, and pushed the play button. The recording was clear without static.

"Are you ever going to stop working for the day? I miss you and could use some company. I don't like drinking alone. It's no fun." It was Bergman's whining voice.

Then Conto's voice: "Peter, I warned you when we started that this was just recreational for me, and not to get too involved. If you're going to get needy, then I'm going to have to stop seeing you for a while."

I motioned Brett with my index finger to pause the tape. "There's Bergman's motive for taping their conversations, right there."

"What do you mean, Doc?" Joan asked me.

"Control is a strong motive," I said. "The weaker the personality, the stronger the need for control. Bergman is more involved with Conto than she'll allow. So he taped their conversations to maintain a sense of power. It was a way for Bergman to counter her control of their relationship."

"Like secretly videotaping sex with your girlfriend," Joan said.

"Exactly. I wouldn't be surprised to find some of those too," I said. "Bergman sounded desperate enough."

Brett thought for a minute, went to the wall phone, called the tech and ordered him back to Bergman's to collect all the videotapes he could find. He hung up the phone, sat back down, and said, "I should have thought of that one myself."

"OK, let's get back to work on these," Joan reminded. "Tick-tock," she added, looking at her watch.

Joan pushed the pause button off and we heard Bergman's voice at end of the same conversation confirm my assessment:

"You're such a hard little bitch. I'll figure out a way to get inside you."

"Peter, I'll be over when I'm done here at the office. Relax," Conto replied.

Joan pushed the pause button and said, "Nice little control freaks."

"Conto could never have imagined Bergman taping their conversations," Brett said.

"Just like Bergman wouldn't have imagined her ordering his death," Joan added.

We listened to thirty minutes of tapes before we hit pay dirt.

"Peter, if you can't hold up your end of this deal, then I'm going to have to take over. You might not like what my people will suggest." Conto's voice was threatening.

"What are they going to do? Have Martin killed?" Bergman's voice dripped with sarcasm.

There was no response from Conto's voice on the tape. It slowly dawned on Bergman that his sarcasm had been precipitous.

"Oh, my God! I don't want anything to do with that. Please! I'll get Martin to forget about the stupid transaction. I'll tell him that it's my client and leave me to solve the mistakes." Bergman voice was full of panic.

We listened to twenty minutes more of tape with boring hellos and goodbyes peppered with Bergman's whining. There was some fairly controlling sex talk and plans to meet in various places for dinner. There were also allusions to deals that Conto had done that day.

"Guys, there is nothing here so far to show that Bergman knew anything about the $200,000 being wired in his name," Joan said.

"That fits perfectly with Conto having him eliminated. With Bergman dead and the $200,000 wired in his name, it was a nice little frame," Brett said.

"If it wasn't for the look on her face when Bergman was shot, we wouldn't have searched Bergman's place," I said.

After another five minutes of their plans to meet in various places, we finally hit pay dirt

"Peter, I'm not putting up with Martin's crap anymore," she said. "Even if I fired your firm, I would have to worry about what Martin knows already about our trading; he's a goddamn little pain in the ass. The best way is for him to be out of the way; then it's business as usual." Conto's voice was as calm as if she had been shopping for a new car.

"You've already done, it haven't you?" Bergman's voice came fast.

"Done what, Peter?" Conto's voice was calm.

There were a few seconds of dead air where Bergman screwed up his courage to ask a very dangerous question — the answer to which directed his own death.

"You've ordered Martin's death, haven't you?" Bergman's voice was beyond panic.

"No, Peter, we've ordered Martin's death. You are as responsible for it as me. If you'd done your job right, I wouldn't have to step in and fix it for you."

"I don't like it." Bergman was sniveling.

"You don't have to like it," she said. "Now, just pretend you don't know anything. It won't be difficult; you don't know anything. The cops will suspect you but you are ignorant of the details and the motive will be unknown to them. The whole thing will remain a mystery. After awhile, they will probably think it was a case of mistaken identity or a shooting accident."

"Are you coming over tonight?" Bergman begged like a little boy.

Joan pushed the pause button, shook her head in disgust, looked at her watch, and asked, "That's probable cause right there, isn't it?"

"Not only is that probable cause, but it's enough evidence to convict her on conspiracy to commit," Brett said.

Joan looked at her watch again. "Shouldn't we keep her from boarding her flight?"

"Damn straight we should," Brett said.

We secured the tell-tale tapes, left police headquarters, rounded the corner onto Tahquitz, and walked across El Cielo to the fountain. The spray from the fountain was caught by a westerly breeze and covered the walkway. We tracked wet shoes across the rental car return lot and walked into the main terminal of the airport five minutes later. The main lobby was not crowded and the overhead speakers reminded us to not leave our baggage unattended. The lobby smelled like luggage and restrooms.

Brett checked Conto's flight number against the departure monitor. "Plane's at Gate 21, boarding in two minutes."

"She should be at the gate waiting to board," Joan said.

We walked out to Gate 21 on the large concourse. When we arrived, there were more than 200 people crowded into the gate waiting to board. We split up and started searching.

Two minutes later, I was standing near Conto. She was sitting by herself, and hadn't noticed me. I held my hand up so Joan and Brett would notice that I had located her. I waited for Joan or Brett to question Conto first. Conto saw me and walked up to me.

"Doctor Reynolds, what are you doing here?"

"Looking for you."

"Why?"

"I'm sure Lieutenant Wade and Detective Fleming will be glad to tell you why we're here," I said.

"My house burned down today. I need a vacation. I'm leaving for Dallas in five minutes."

Brett and Joan walked up to Conto and me. We were standing in front of a water fountain. Brett nodded to Conto and took a long slow drink out of the bubbler, waiting to speak. Conto gave Joan and me an exasperated look.

"I just asked Doctor Reynolds what he was doing here. Now, I'm asking you the same question. Are you following me?"

"Following you, found you," Brett taunted her.

"Lieutenant, would you please tell me why you're here?"

"We need you to come to police headquarters with us. We have some questions about your relationship with Peter Bergman, and your dealings with a man named John Bocca," Brett said.

"Well, Lieutenant, those questions will have to wait until I return from my trip to Texas. My plane boards momentarily; I intend to be on it." Conto stiffened.

"I'm sorry, but we need you to come with us voluntarily, which we prefer. If you insist, we can place you under arrest."

"Lieutenant, if you arrested me and it was later proved there wasn't sufficient evidence, then I could sue you all for false arrest. Correct?"

"If there were no probable cause, then you would be immediately released," Joan said.

"Doctor Reynolds, you'll be my witness," she threatened. "I won't go with these officers voluntarily. I want the opportunity to sue them, and have their badges."

"I'm not an attorney, Ms. Conto, and you're not my patient, but I don't recommend you take that approach. I suggest you come with us," I said.

"No," she said stubbornly.

Brett gave her thirty seconds to change her mind and then took charge.

"Ms. Conto, I'm placing you under arrest," he said. "You have the right to an attorney…"

"You have no right. I insist on calling my attorney."

"Don't worry. You'll get to make your call," Brett said.

"You want her in cuffs, sir?" Joan asked Brett, never once taking her eyes off Conto in the remote case she was armed or going to run. She wasn't. She believed that she could talk her way out of anything.

"Yeah, pat her down, finish reading her rights to her, and cuff her," Brett ordered.

"Lieutenant, please, you have no right to handcuff me like a common criminal."

"Ms. Conto, that's what arrest means. Cuffs and cells," Brett said.

Joan led Conto ahead of Brett and me out of the terminal and past the putting green. It was maintained by the same golf course where Martin Jonas was found dead. We crossed the rental car parking lot, retraced our steps past the fountain and across El Cielo, and finally to police headquarters.

Conto was freaking out in the handcuffs. Joan had to keep moving her along in the direction of headquarters. Squirming in the cuffs, Conto kept stopping and asking to have them removed as if they were the worst part of her circumstance.

"I think she's losing it; do we really need the cuffs? Isn't it better to have her calm for questioning?" I asked Brett.

He gave me the "bleeding heart liberal" look, then took them off her.

Her panic subsided.

"Wait until she sees a lockup," he said after Joan led her ahead of us again. "It depends on how good her attorney is in the short term, but eventually she going to be confined, with worse than cuffs."

"Control freaks and confinement are not a pleasant combination," I said. "I've seen it before. She'll probably need medication to go into a cell."

A jet taking off overhead reminded me of my earlier thoughts about airports at night. I had missed another destination besides paradise and purgatory — Conto's journey would end in her own claustrophobic hell.

CONTRACTS AND KILLINGS

We used the same ugly conference room in which we had listened to Bergman's tapes. Headquarters needed a fresh infusion of cash. The entire building itself was outgrown and crowded a long time ago. The furniture in the conference room was old, the paint was chipped, and everything had aged to the well-waxed paint-worn patina of all public buildings.

We were sitting around the table and no one had spoken. The open window brought the already familiar of vaporized jet fuel from overhead. Between the interrogation room décor and her experience in handcuffs, Conto looked like she was ready to collapse from the indignity of it all. Brett was right, wait 'til she got to a prison cell. She hadn't seen anything yet. She managed to complain, though. Good thing, because where Conto was eventually going, complaint would be all she had.

"Lieutenant, I believe I'm entitled to call my attorney," she said.

Brett set a telephone in front of her, and we all stepped into the hallway outside the interrogation room so she could make her call.

"Let the bitch cook in her own juices," Joan said.

Brett and I looked at each other and said, "Okay."

Giving her the silent treatment was the exact opposite of the therapeutic behavior I was used to. Shrink silence was empathetic; cop silence was unnerving to start and went mean from there. I felt like I was playing on a new team and I liked it. Too many hours shrinking heads all by myself made me appreciate that my new job had company that came with it. I'd been lonely sometimes stuck in my office suite all day; patients and police peers aren't the same.

The hallway ceiling was lined with fluorescent lights that hurt my eyes. A window at the far end of the hallway opened to the parking lot, where on-duty officers were coming and going to file reports and get back out on the street. They tested their sirens on departure with a staccato squeal. The lights and noise made me realize that it had been a long day. I had been up at dawn. My back ached. I could use some exercise, a drink, or both, and bed. Conto finished talking to her attorney and hung up the phone.

"Doc, follow our lead but feel free to chime in," Joan said to me.

"A little matter of the killings," Brett said as we walked back in the conference room and caught Conto off guard fixing her make-up. Her hands were not steady, and her lipstick line reflected it.

"What killings are you talking about?" she asked.

"The contract killings," Brett said.

"You hired Bocca to kill Martin Jonas, and then Bergman. Those are the contract killings. Detective Fleming can speak to the killings you were making on the electrical contracts."

"We know that you've been gaming the electrical trading market in the valley, jacking up prices on electricity to the extent that the city was charged exorbitantly on its contracts," Joan said. "You did indeed make a killing on those contracts. I've been to Folsom and I know how you did it. You submitted scheduling requests to receive large amounts of power that you never intended to complete."

"There is absolutely nothing illegal about that, Detective," Conto replied.

"I think I can prove you did phony trades with E Star and you swapped regulated power for spot power. Now that's go-to-jail illegal," Joan said.

"Detective, you 'think you can prove?' That's hardly sufficient evidence of anything. You're simply speculating."

Conto was pumping up again and getting hopeful that we had nothing on her except the trading scam, and that we couldn't even prove that. I had no idea how long it would take her attorney to get here, but that's how much of a window we had. Brett nodded to Joan and she left the room; no secret what she was fetching.

We wanted Conto to listen to some of the taped evidence we had of the conspiracy to kill Martin Jonas, and gamble she might talk and implicate Bocca or E Star before her attorney got there. The DA would probably prefer us to hold the evidence until she went to trial, and let her sweat it out for months in a cell — disclose only what was required. Unfortunately, we didn't have that option. If she knew anything about Chris's whereabouts, we needed that information. We had to gamble for Chris's safety.

"Ms. Conto, we may or may not get you on the trading scam but we *are* going to put you behind bars," Brett said.

"You have absolutely no evidence to support the allegation that I had anything to do with Martin's or Peter's death. You can't prove an iota of this fabrication," she said.

"Ms. Conto, people like you eventually screw up," Brett said with feigned weariness.

"We have plenty of evidence to support our allegations; in fact, we have you on tape planning the murder of Martin Jonas."

"What? That's preposterous," Conto said.

"Your 'sexual friend', Bergman, taped every one of your phone conversations," Brett said.

"How? I don't believe Peter would do something like that," Conto said, her face tight.

Joan set the recorder on the table, plugged it in and sat down. Her timing was dramatically impeccable. Brett nodded and she pushed the play button. It was cued correctly.

"Peter, I'm not putting up with Martin's crap anymore. Even if I fired your firm, I would have to worry about what he knows already about our trading. He's a goddamn little pain in the ass. The best way is for him to be out of the way; then it's business as usual." Conto's voice played just as audibly the second time.

"You've already done it, haven't you?" Bergman's voice was still clear as a bell.

"Done what, Peter?"

"You've ordered Martin's death."

"No, Peter, we've ordered Martin's death. You are as responsible for it as me. If you'd done your job right, I wouldn't have to step in and fix it for you."

Joan pushed the stop button, then the rewind, and then played the sequence all the way through again from the beginning. The third time I heard the tape, it was no less damning.

Conto was caught — crushed like her house after the fire.

Brett made his second move. "Ms. Conto. As you heard for yourself, we have sufficient evidence to convict you of conspiracy to commit the murder of Martin Jonas. We will eventually prove that you ordered Peter Bergman murdered. And you are responsible for other crimes. You have an opportunity to help us save the young man who your contract killer kidnapped, and to tell us all that has happened here. You're going to jail for a long time. How long is, to some extent, up to you. The district attorney may consider this a capital crime. At the very least, you will be living in an eight-by-eight-foot closet-sized cell for a long time. You look as if that is going to be hard on you. You have one chance to tell us all you know and hope that its helps in your defense."

Conto hands were fidgeting, her lower lip was quivering, and her breathing was rapid. She shifted sullenly like a teenage girl angry with her parents, and then went to a place outside herself to calm down, a dissociated narcissist place. I knew in that second that we had lost our gamble. Conto had never thought the rules applied to her and she wasn't going to start now — the self-centered corporate-thief-turned-killer in her took over.

"Lieutenant, you're treating me like I was a common criminal," Conto complained.

I looked at Brett and shook my head no; she's not going to crack.

The hallway was noisy with arriving attorneys, Conto's and the people's. It wasn't going to happen. Whatever Conto was convicted of wouldn't come from any more confession than we already had on the tapes. Neither Brett nor Joan revealed an iota of disappointment or irritation.

My turn. She pissed me off.

"Ms. Conto, you are a common criminal," I said. "You're an increasingly common one. The man you hired, Bocca, is the uncommon criminal. Tell you the truth, I prefer him to you. He knows exactly what he is and does. He makes no excuse for it and doesn't pretend to be civilized. He knows he's an outlaw and hides because of it. You, on the other hand, think you belong with the rest of us. You live among us and pretend to be socialized. But in fact, you are worse than Bocca because you've lost sight of what you are. You pretend we're all like you. You could fly off on vacation, conveniently forget what you did, and never know how irrevocably fucked-up you are."

"Doctor, you have no idea how hard it is to get where I am."

"No, that's the easy part. The world we live in makes it too easy for people like you because you turn a profit. You'll probably be able to make money on your memoirs."

As we opened the door, we were inundated with the legal suits. At the end of the corridor, another set of suits, Feds, were talking to the chief. This was it; we were about to be taken off the case officially. The Feds would take over and we would pretend to back off to fool them.

We would wait for Bocca's call.

The risk for Brett and Joan was enormous. They were putting their careers on the line for a kid they had known a week. Me, I would simply risk a job that I had just barely started.

Brett looked over at me. "What you said to Conto…'irrevocably fucked-up'?"

"Yeah, that's a clinical term."

THEY WOULD PAY, TODAY

Bocca's fee had been $200,000 United States Dollars for the first hit and the same for any additional. The buyer didn't even flinch at his prices; perhaps he should have gone $300,000. It was a matter of professional pride that he never raised a fee unless there was an obvious complication. So he was $400,000 plus $100,000 for expenses for one week's work — half a mil. He couldn't charge her for the security guard, but maybe he could figure a way to recover something on the expenses for doing him. Before he did Bergman and went out to her house, he verified that there was $500,000 transferred to his Swiss account. Once before he had charged $300,000 for a single hit but that was for a political type who had security all over him and justified the fee. Sure, the lieutenant was a pro, but that was just coincidental.

The buyer might be upset at him for torching her house. He could have faked a break-in, taken the computer and destroyed it. He just didn't want to risk the time and he was certainly proved right. Torching the buyer's home was quicker and foolproof. Insurance would cover all her losses and provided her with a perfect alibi. Who was going to believe that a woman would torch her own house? His obligation was to her and the people behind her. He did her a favor: she was scared and not choosing the best option. He chose it for her, and the real power behind her would appreciate it.

Week's up. Actually, was up on Wednesday. No problem with the extra time and money. Buyer knows nothing about the kid or settling with the cop and the shrink.

Immediately after torching the house, Bocca joined a line of three cars descending Monterey. As they approached downtown Palm Desert, the line slowed and pulled to the right. The fire trucks were passing in the opposite direction. He smiled to see the lieutenant's Mustang at the end of a caravan of fire vehicles. He couldn't see inside the car since they were going fifty in the opposite direction. They didn't spot him pulling over like a good citizen. All of the fire vehicles were by him in five seconds. He turned around and watched the Mustang climb to

Michael Thompkins

the plateau where they would inspect his handiwork. As he took his turn, reentering traffic like any careful driver would, he looked in the mirror and watched the Mustang disappear.

Cool. One for the scrapbook. Wait till the buyer finds out exactly how close the cops had come to recovering the computer stuff they wanted. No argument. She better bonus bigtime.

He headed back toward the condo. The kid was there and he could tell him about the whole operation. When he got back to the condo, he removed the gag and un-cuffed the kid from the eye-ring in the garage. They had until tomorrow afternoon to kill time. As long as he had eyes on the kid, he would spare him the cuffs. No way the kid would run from him. He got out the Balvenie single malt and began talking with the kid. He knew he would ultimately be doing the kid so he could, for once, debrief an entire mission to someone.

He told him about coming to town and renting two condos and two cars. He told him about spending time hiking all the trails that surrounded the city and hiding weapons, medicines, dried food, and water. Then he detailed the first hit after their encounter on the bike trail. The kid was a good listener, and he wondered if maybe the kid might actually like him. The kid even began asking him a few questions as his story moved along. He told him about the shot he made at the Tahquitz green, that only ten people in the world could make.

Bocca was getting tired; the scotch was taking hold. He told the kid he was sorry, but he had to cuff him so they could both sleep. First he took the kid in the kitchen and made them both bacon and eggs. The kid was really a good listener; he asked Bocca about his home. He told the kid about launching from England. Since the kid was a musician, he talked a little bit about his favorite pub, the music they had there, and the really old cemetery next door. The cemetery belonged to the Village Church. It contained tombstones dating from 1200 AD. He was careful not to give the kid a location, just in case.

Full of food and partially drunk, he cuffed the kid to the tank and taped his mouth. Then he sat on the living room couch and finished another double on the rocks. He fell asleep on the couch and woke up suddenly in the early morning hours.

Nightmare again. Doc's and Lieutenant's faces. Proof again of them screwing him at selection. They're responsible. Heart going too fast, head hurts. Watch says 4 a.m. Strange noise? Check the garage. Kid's sound asleep with his hand cuffed to the eye-ring. Check to

GUN PLAY

see if the kid's okay. Make sure the kid's okay and then kill him tomorrow. Doesn't make any sense.

Bocca knew he couldn't return to sleep so he left the condo to stretch his legs and his mind in the neighborhood. The condo was located in a residential area. He stayed off North Palm Canyon, which was four blocks to his west. He didn't want to run into cops. He was always edgy around cops, and they were naturally more suspicious at night.

He felt a funny little stab in his chest. He walked by a little business area, glanced in the window of a real estate office, and realized he could afford to buy any home he wanted in Palm Springs. Then he looked in the window of a travel agency and saw an agent's desk.

Woman's desk. Sweater on the chair in front of the desk. Entire wall to the right of her desk covered with pictures of family and friends. Over a hundred photos of people of all ages. Woman must be queen of something. Her kingdom was full of family and friends.

Bocca finally realized the sensation he was feeling in his chest. He hadn't felt it since he was kid; he felt lonely. If it weren't for the lieutenant and the doc, he could have had a life here in Palm Springs or any other town of his choosing. Not that he would have, but it would have been better to have a choice. They had taken that choice from him. They had ruined it for him — they would pay today.

CHOICE

My old friend the nightmare was back. I was lost somewhere between the dream and the loveseat where I had slept. This time, when my old friend visited, I had convinced the helo pilot to turn around and go back to help the Marines. As the helo landed in the middle of the firebase at the same point we had just taken off from, I woke up completely. I tried to will myself back into the dream but didn't succeed. A memory and a feeling lingered — .45 Colt in my hand and fear.

It was 5:45 a.m., just starting to get light. I rolled off the love seat and could hear Nancy already in the shower. She would have patients in the hospital so she had to be up and out to make her morning rounds. Physicians seem to develop two sets of corresponding tendencies: the ability to function when awakened by middle-of-the-night phone calls and a need to jealously guard their sleep. Not me. When I wake up in the middle of the night, it always takes me awhile to function. I shook off the dream, picked up the telephone, and called Brett, who picked up on the first ring. Like Nancy, he was up and ready to go.

"Anything from Bocca?" I asked.

"Not yet. But I know it'll be today like he said. Joan is coming over for coffee before she heads up the tram. Want to join us?"

"Sure. Talk about the plan?" I asked.

"What plan?"

"You don't have a plan?" I asked.

"No, you got one?"

"No," I said.

"Shit will happen."

"That's not a plan," I said curtly.

"You seem a little edgy. Nancy still pissed?"

"Yes, I slept on the love seat. Does that give you a clue?"

"She'll get over it. Eventually, she'll accept it. She accepts what I do. Why not just sleep in one of the kid's rooms?"

"Didn't want to run too far from her anger or leave her unprotected. She'll accept it when she's ready. She doesn't do anything until she's ready. Until then…" I said.

"How is the love seat?"

"Misnamed," I said.

"Keep the edge. You'll need it today." With that warning, Brett hung up.

I headed down to the kitchen. I knew Nancy wouldn't drink more than a cup but I made her a whole pot of coffee, anyway. Five minutes, later she joined me. It was Saturday, and she had to round on patients, and assist on a surgery. She was dressed in utility-green scrubs.

"Bocca will call today," I said. "This thing will be over soon."

"Let's hope that means you four will still be alive," Nancy said. "As far as I can tell, Brett is doing a piss-poor job of keeping the people I love the most out of trouble."

After I arrived home last night, I filled her in on the fire at Conto's house and her subsequent arrest. Her reaction to that news, following Chris's kidnapping the night before, had prompted a fight and my spending the night on the love seat. It was a foldout but I was too lazy to open it. The love seat aggravated my back. When I stood up, I got the little electric pulsing pains. Bocca had to be stopped soon; we had to get Chris back

"Brett's the boss and he should be handling this better," she added. "I'll give you that you have Conto in jail, but that maniac is still out there. First he killed Jonas, then the poor security guard, and now Bergman. And he has Chris. Brett and the chief should turn this over to the FBI to hunt him down. I think you three are way in over your heads and it ticks me off."

"And what do you think would happen to Chris if they did that?"

"I need to get to the hospital. Thank you for making me coffee. I really do want you to find whatever it is that men your age are looking for," she said. "I just can't live with the thought of you dead. I want this over and I want us out of it."

Men my age?

She poured herself a cup of coffee in her travel mug; our fight was going to run out of time.

"Look, I need to do this. I don't feel like I have a choice. Why can't you get that?" I was angry now.

"Tom, I'm not stupid," she said. "Stop playing victim. I can see that you want to do this. You do have a choice. You spend your professional life teaching people

Michael Thompkins

that they have choices and then you pull this 'I don't feel like I have a choice' crap on me.'"

Busted.

The coffee mug traveled with Nancy attached to it out the kitchen door into the driveway. I followed her into the driveway. Moving fights never turn out well.

As she was backing out, I shouted after her, "You're right. I need, want, and choose to help get Chris back."

I showed her.

PARITY

On the drive to Brett's house, I thought about Nancy's reaction. As much as I didn't enjoy it, she was certainly entitled to it. It had been building up. My involvement in the case had sprung up suddenly, and she had no time to prepare. This was the time in our lives, forties and free, that we should be going on trips to exotic places, not waiting to be shot at. One day I'm a boring psychologist; the next day I'm carrying a gun. She was right; I was choosing to do this. It just didn't feel like it to me. Being correctly psychoanalyzed by my wife was more than a little turn-about.

When I pulled up in Brett's driveway, the garage door was open. He and Joan were carefully scrutinizing a rifle.

"What you got?" I was hoping the response to my question would be a well-constructed and foolproof plan.

"My favorite rifle," she said. "It's a Sako Target Model 30 chambered in .300 Win-Mag with a 225 grain Spear's target round. This will stop anything on two or four legs, with the exception of elephants." She was looking down the open breech of the weapon.

"That's the rifle you'll use today? It's not department issue, is it?" I asked, still hopeful for a plan.

"Yeah, I'll be using it because I've been practicing with this rifle for ten years," she said. "I can pretty consistently do a fifty-cent piece grouping at a hundred yards without the scope. No, it's not regulation, but it's way down the list of what we might get in trouble for today." Joan pointed to the rifle's sights. "This is a Leupold 14x Mid-Range Tactical scope in a swing-away mount. With it, I can do the same group with less consistency at one-seventy-five."

"Speaking of getting in trouble, keeping all this from the Feds be numero uno," Brett said.

Joan sheathed the rifle. We all moved through the kitchen and out to the patio where Brett had coffee ready. The dry riverbed and the air around it were starting to warm. It had been in the forties last night here and below freezing at the top of the tram. The smell of coffee and the rifle hung in the air.

"Good coffee," Joan said.

"One hundred percent pure Kona Peaberry," Brett said. "I brought it back on my last trip to the Big Island over two years ago. It keeps forever in the freezer. I know I'm happiest with 7-11 Folgers, but I need to serve something special to you uptown types."

Coffee was a minor religion to cops and shrinks. The ceremony of finding it, making it and drinking it covered a host of good and bad silences.

"Why were you on the Big Island? Vacation?" Joan asked.

"No, I was competing in the Hawaii Ironman Triathalon. I met up with a couple of army buddies, and we spent the week in Kona and competed together." Brett smiled at the pleasant memory.

"Oh, man, I would totally kill to do that." Joan looked sheepish as she realized she might actually have to kill Bocca today.

"We can do it sometime if you want." Brett's eyes were steady on Joan's.

"How? How did you get a ticket the time you went?" Joan asked.

"Well that time I got a military pass," Brett replied. "I had run a few marathons in reasonable enough time that they knew I would at least finish. The guys that started the Ironman are retired military, so they were generous. But it's gotten way bigger. If we were going to register now, we'd have to offer to be security. Maybe they'd say yes, maybe no."

"Nancy and I could be your support people and hang with my old friend, Mahulani," I offered. No way I could run a marathon, much less the Hawaii Ironman.

"Who's Mahulani?" Joan asked.

"My old friend and the last kahuna priest on the Big Island."

"First, let's survive today." Brett said.

Future festive planning took a backseat to the needs of the day. I took a sip of the rich Kona. I glanced at my watch. It was 7:25 a.m. and our day was just beginning. I had spent the last two weeks rescheduling patients and today was no different. My two regular Saturday morning patients would have to wait until we got Chris back safely.

Sorry, your shrink may be shooting someone today.

"This is for you, Tom. It's our hole card." Brett handed me a Baby Glock Nine without a holster, same as my new gun, but smaller.

"Stick this in the pocket of the jacket you'll be wearing when we head up the tram," Brett said. "Bocca thinks you're a screw-up with weapons, and he's all about weapons. He will never, ever expect you to be carrying a holdout gun. Hopefully, if it gets to him disarming us, he'll expect any gun you'll be carrying to be in your fanny. He'll never find this one. If it comes down to it, shoot him right through the pocket. Don't even aim. Just point in the general direction and empty the magazine. Nine rounds in the magazine and one in the pipe, okay?"

My mind was racing as it wrapped around Brett's instructions. "I can do it, but I can't guarantee that I'll hit him."

"Don't have to hit him," he said. "If it comes down to it, you might just give Joan or me the edge we need," Brett said.

"Joan, you head up to Long Valley at the top of the tram, fill the park ranger in and tell him we'll need him to shut the tram down on my command. Tell him to keep his people away from anything that goes down. Dress warm and white for snow camouflage; there'll be snow on the ground. Take one of the radios we used the other night." Brett was all business now.

"What happens up there?" I asked.

"Joan's already up there, Bocca arrives with Chris, and Joan takes him out. We all go out to dinner." Brett suggested simple; we all knew better.

"Or?" I asked.

"Shit happens."

"Yes?" I asked.

"Joan can't get a shot off, and you and I show up." Brett painted a different scenario.

"And?" Joan asked.

"We find out what he wants from us," Brett said. "He snatched Chris, he has needs here."

"Then what?" I asked.

"That's the part we don't plan," Brett instructed. "Maybe Bocca surrenders or maybe you shoot him. You may have to use some muscles you've never used before. Joan, lock and load. If the shooter calls and the meeting is somewhere else, I'll radio you. Get your ass to where we are and make it up as you go along. Keep the uniforms out of this."

"Yes, sir."

That was it for summit preparations.

After Joan drove off, I said, "Get your ass to where we are?"

"Soldier-speak," Brett said.

"You notice her ass?" I raised my eyebrows and smiled.

"I notice it often."

"I hope Chris is holding up."

"He's a tough kid," Brett said. "His old man beat his mother. He still wants to be a rock star. He has a good attitude. He'll be fine."

"What are you going to do about the warrant on Chris?" I asked.

"I already talked to the Spokane chief this morning," he said.

"What did he say?"

"He's been trying to talk the dad into withdrawing the complaint. Good cop," he said.

"He knows about the dad hitting the mother?" I asked.

"Yup."

"And?"

"Mother won't press charges," he said.

"Is he sure the father will withdraw the warrant on Chris?" I asked.

"Chief said the dad would probably fold if he thought we were interested," he said.

"Might have to go to Spokane,"

"Be a nice ride up there. We could go through Oregon, and do a little fly-fishing," he said.

We spent the rest of the morning and part of the afternoon cleaning the weapons collection in the garage. I found the work relaxing. It got to be a warm afternoon and we drank a half-gallon of lemonade and ate most of a pound of Dublin cheddar, two baguettes, some salad, and several grapefruits from Brett's trees.

"Eat before you're hungry, drink before you're thirsty," Brett said.

"I hope Joan and Chris get to eat."

"Joan can take care of herself; I don't know about Chris. Be foolish for our shooter to hurt the bait, though," Brett said.

"I hope you're right. Hey, why did you end up giving this job to Joan?"

"I asked myself what you would do in the same situation. How you would deal with it if it were Nancy." Brett surprised me with his thinking.

"Nancy hates guns."

"Besides that. You know what I mean," Brett said.

"Yes, I do."

"I can't explain why, but I do know that it's the right thing. It just feels instinctively right," Brett said.

"You want to know why?"

"Yeah, sure," Brett said. "You're the shrink, we don't want to waste your two cents worth."

"Because sooner or later Joan needs to know that you trust her as an equal. If the romance thing happens before you two succeed as professional partners, then she'll still be left in the dark, not knowing if you trust her as an equal. The whole 'can women perform as well as men' thing needs to be worked through first. That way, it's all settled before you buy her a second drink. The prime directive about women is parity, give 'em parity."

"I can see that now. It would have saved me a lot of grief if I'd seen it sooner," Brett acknowledged. "I guess I just gotta learn some things the hard way."

"Joan feels personally responsible for losing Chris. She needs to know you trust her to help get him back. Then for once, she screws up, she accepts it, and she begins to get over herself."

"One thing I don't get." Brett smiled at me.

"Yes?"

"Parity. You mean parity, 'equal' or parity, 'with child'?" English major, he had to have his fun with connotations. He knew damn well which one I meant.

"You better get past the second date before you worry about kids," I said.

We finished up the late lunch and carried the leftovers into the kitchen. The change of location stimulated a change in my thoughts. "We're taking a hell of chance here, agreeing to meet this guy without bringing an army with us. All we've got is the Three Musketeers."

"No choice," Brett said. "Any uniforms or a tactical team and he'd smell it a mile away. Try to take Bocca anywhere near citizens, and the kill count goes up automatically. Bad enough he has Chris, but the number of hostages cannot exceed one or our chances plummet. I've seen too many large-scale tactical blunders."

"And Chris would be dead and our shooter would walk away."

"Don't have to like it," Brett started.

"Just got to do it," I finished.

"I want that son of a bitch."

It was time to get a little rest in preparation for the meeting with Bocca. Brett watched a ballgame and I napped on the back porch. The day was warm, and I hadn't slept well the night before. The lounge chair was much nicer than the love seat. I had long ago learned to nap between clients; it's one of the perks of psychology. I did my lower backstretches and spread myself out on the lounge chair. The fight with Nancy and the love seat tightened my back.

Michael Thompkins

I woke up to the phone ringing an hour later; Brett answered it on the speakerphone so I could hear. I knew who it was by stiffness in my back, the rumbling in my gut, and the pull in my bladder.

"Afternoon, Lieutenant. Long Valley at dusk. Bring the shrink. But I have a good perch and if I see a uniform, the reflection of a scope or sense a team op, the kid is dead. Then we'll have to wait to settle our game another day. Keep the Feds out of this; it's between us."

"Copy that, Bocca. But we have no game, and I'm not playing you." Brett's voice was clipped and controlled.

"We'll see. Meet you at the top." Bocca hung up.

Brett picked his radio off his belt and called Joan. "We have a go for your location. You have a green light for Bocca. Kill your radio. And ..." Brett paused, stumbled for the right words, letting dead air last for embarrassing moments.

"Yes?" Joan's voice was waiting.

"Stay alive," Brett said.

Brett called the chief on his cell, and filled him in.

"Got a hunch," I said, replaying his conversation with Joan in my head.

"I'm listening. You've been right about Joan, so far," Brett said.

"Good things are in store for you and Joan."

"That's not a hunch; that's a damn fortune cookie."

DOC, YOU OKAY?

When we arrived at the Valley Station, Matt was sitting in a department tactical Suburban at the upper end of the parking lot, drinking coffee and reading the newspaper with his boots up on the dashboard. Brett had not requested his presence but looked pleased nonetheless. As we pulled into the spot next to him, Matt rolled down his window.

"What are you doing here? How'd you know?" Brett asked.

"Lieutenant. Doc. Chief said you guys might need some backup. He told me to get my butt up here, wait, and do whatever I can to help you."

"Okay. I'll fill you in on the way up the tram. We can use your help," Brett grinned.

We walked from the vehicles across the steeply graded lot up to the Valley Station. At 2,643 feet above the valley floor, it was considerably cooler here than in the city. The Valley Station was built on an elevated platform with concrete ballast sunk into the ground. The entire station was built so that a flash flood coming down the steep canyon couldn't wash it out, and fifty mile-an-hour winds wouldn't blow it over. Chino and other nearby canyons fed a giant underground aquifer that was used to supply water to the entire Coachella Valley. The tramway was a man-made monster standing perilously within the most pristine canyon in California.

Counting the thirty-nine steps up to the door helped quiet my nerves. We walked though the waiting room and out to the loading gantry. There was a tramcar waiting for us in the dock. Brett badged the car operator; we boarded and quickly pulled out of the station.

"Jim, the head ranger, will meet us at the top. Any questions about the mountain, he's our man," Brett said.

"I think I've met him before. He's a good man," Matt agreed.

This was my second ride up the "Eighth Wonder of the World." I didn't have to buy a ticket this time. Brett starting filling Matt in on what little plan we had, and, as we climbed to the first tower, my thoughts drifted to the car, the eleven-minute ride up the mountain and my mounting acrophobia.

Michael Thompkins

The tramcars were elegant in their Swiss design. The good news was that the outside of our car rotated 360 degrees around the inner frame, allowing unrestricted views of the canyon climb and the valley vista below. The bad news for me was that this added to the free-fall sensation that occurred when we passed over the towers. The tramcar rode on two track cables and was pulled by a third tractor cable. A fourth cable, the safety cable, was suspended over all the others.

The whistle of the wind, the hum of the small motor turning the car, and our voices were the only sounds. Lubricating oil and my fear were the only smells.

Climbing into the first stationary tower, I willed the car to stay on the track.

Bumping, the top clamp of the car rode over the tower. I grabbed at the car-rail.

Gravity and the pull cable combined to quickly accelerate the car over tower one on tracks that actually sagged after the tower.

My core felt like it was ripped right out of me.

Matt noticed me wince and asked, "Doc, you okay?"

"Nothing a little solid ground won't cure," I said. "Heights bother me."

"Gotta take you jumping. That'll loosen your back up," he said and returned to tactical discussions with Brett.

Matt probably thought I shouldn't be here, questioned Brett's better judgment in bringing a shrink along, and wondered if I would get us all killed.

Everybody had a cure for my back, but this was the first time anyone offered parachuting as a remedy. I had two minds about my back. One was resigned to having a quirky back forever, and the other mind was hopeful that someday I could be free of the problem. I thought about Matt's offer while passing over towers three through five, holding my breath each time, and collecting my core afterwards.

I had tried everything else; I was even carrying a gun. Heal your back, carry a gun.

The walls of Chino Canyon were close enough to see plants that had more courage than I did. They were trying to grow at this elevation. The last tower and my last chance to find some courage on the ride, was coming up.

I let go of the handrail, supported myself and pretended I was going to jump out of an airplane. I leaned into the climb to the last tower and readied myself for the free fall after the tower. The tower passed over my head and the car accelerated on the cable. Somewhere deep down, a burning started in the muscles of my pelvis, one I hadn't felt before.

Brett smiled at me. He knew about the acrophobia.

"You doing okay?" he asked.

"Looking for some balls," I replied.

"I need you on this one," he said.

I nodded.

The tramcar climbed into Mountain Station, unlocked from the main cable, and began docking itself by gliding back and forth between big rubber bumpers on either side. Snow glistened on the rocks beneath the car. Water dripped onto the glass roof from somewhere overhead in a constant trickle, and turned the docking station into an ice-cold sauna. The thermometer outside the car registered 36 degrees.

"Doc and I are going to walk into Long Valley until we run into our shooter's trap," Brett said to Matt. "If Bocca had wanted to just shoot us, it would have happened at Street Fair on Thursday night. He has something more personal planned for us. I want you to stay with the ranger. When we call for the cavalry, remember what we planned."

"Wouldn't it be better for me to go out ahead of you, but on higher ground? Maybe I can shoot him," Matt said.

"Joan's already out there — maybe he's spotted her already, maybe he hasn't — I don't want to give him an excuse to advance his timetable," Brett said. "By the time we call you in, it's beyond his plan. If you see him with the hostage, take him down."

"Yes sir."

We stepped out of the tramcar and onto the landing gangway. Visitors were preparing to download as we walked through the waiting area. The altimeter on the wall read "8,516 Feet Above Sea Level." The park ranger was waiting for us. The operator shook hands with him, introduced us, and took off to help expedite the downloading of some containers. The warmth inside the station was reassuring.

Jim was a California park ranger and a sworn California peace officer. He had talked to the chief so he knew what was going down. He also knew Brett; park rangers shared police training with their fellow officers in the valley below.

"Man, it's damn cold up here," Brett said.

"Got to have cold to make snow," Jim said. "Snow is almost as big a tourist attraction as the tramway itself. Right now, we got four inches here in Long Valley and several feet at the summit. Play golf in the sun, sit by the pool in your bathing suit, gamble at the Indian casinos, enjoy sex with your sweetie, ride our tramway, and then walk in the snow — that's the Palm Springs Snowbird Special."

"Pleased to meet you, Doc. The chief gave me a heads up about you. First time I ever met a gun-toting shrink." Jim's voice was strong and deep, like it was coming from inside one of his trees.

First time for me, too, I thought.

"Please to meet you, too," I said.

"You talk to my partner?" Brett asked.

"Like she's going to get by my people carrying a big gun? Besides, your chief called to explain what was up." Jim's smile was the warmest thing I had seen so far on this mountain.

"I appreciate your not calling your bosses in Sacramento until tomorrow," Brett said.

Jim didn't want to deal with his bosses yet and we didn't want them talking to the Feds. His loyalty was local.

"Can't seem to get a line out some days. If I ever need backup, I'm a long way from Sacramento. Rather be friendly with local law enforcement than Sacramento any day of the week. They're a bunch of suits. My boss is okay, but the rest of them are career desk jockeys, and they don't know horse manure about law enforcement in the trenches. You guys want some hot coffee?"

"Sure," Brett said.

Jim led us up a level on large open wooden steps to a small conference room with windows that looked down on Long Valley, retrieved a giant thermos and poured three paper cups.

"Good stuff," I said. The hot coffee warmed.

"We serve Peets in the dining room," Jim said.

Brett stood at the window sipping his coffee. Long Valley was probably two hundred feet below us. He turned back to Jim. "Optics?"

Jim reached into a cabinet and pulled out an enormous pair of binoculars. Brett took them and scanned the valley below for a minute or two.

Brett scowled as he held the binoculars. " It's too foggy. Lights failing. Can't see shit."

"Knew that. You guys want my help? I know what your chief said to me, but I really know the territory, and I want to help out," Jim said.

"Sure, we could use it. You do know this place better than anyone. Any moonlight tonight? Will this fog cover lift?" Brett asked.

"Maybe. Part of the fog is snowmelt evaporation caused by the temperature differential. Soon as it gets cold enough the cover could, I repeat could, lift; it's almost a full moon tonight. It will be pitch dark in thirty minutes and the only tourists left here will be eating in the dining room, and going down afterward. We get a few back-country extreme types showing up occasionally for the last car down, but the valley should be clear of any tourists in the next half hour. Tell me what you want me to do."

"I want you to stay right here as our observation post," Brett said. "If I need you to evacuate anyone, I'll radio you and Matt. If things are going badly for us, come in as backup. I'll give you the best location I can when we get there. And above all, keep anyone from leaving this station. Our shooter is already out there. He was on the mountain when he called Doc and me an hour ago."

"I stayed away from the landing gangway until just a few minutes ago like the chief and your partner instructed. I probably could have made him, but he also could have made me. I logged some years as an ATF agent before this job, so I've done my share of undercover. I can usually smell the bad guys. But your guy has a kid. Without the hostage, I'd have offered to take him myself. The orders from you and the chief were quite clear, however."

"Thanks. I knew I could count on you. No more hostages," Brett said.

"I seen some of those go bad, too," Jim said.

"Your partner was carrying a real nice long gun. Sako .300 Win-Mag. She left the case with me. Can she shoot it?" Jim asked.

"I would trust her with my life," Brett said.

"You are. She was all dressed out in a white snow powder suit so she'll stay warm. Can you fill me in a little on the shooter and the hostage?" Jim had questions; we were working his turf now.

"The hostage is a twenty-one year old musician friend of ours named Chris, and he can put the shooter at a murder scene," I said. "Our shooter's name's John Bocca. He snatched the kid at Thursday's fair to get the lieutenant and me up here. He has a grudge against the lieutenant for keeping him out of Special Forces." I hadn't spoken until that moment; talking helped my nerves. Being inside the warm Mountain Station helped more.

Jim absorbed all of it and turned to Brett. "You helped keep him out of Special Forces?"

"I sure don't remember it, but I might've had something to do with the process. It was twenty years ago. Usually I try and forget that stuff. Maybe when I see him?" Brett's voice reflected the question.

Michael Thompkins

"Wasn't a long time ago for him," Jim added.

"I think reality and dreams are starting to mix in his head," I said. "He thinks I was there too, and I definitely wasn't."

"Creepy dude," Jim said. "You guys want some vests? I notice you aren't wearing any. I got a couple of extras if you want them. They're rated to stop up to a .45. I can get them in a couple of minutes."

"This guy would just shoot us in the head. He's the best I've ever seen," Brett said.

"He better not be better than five of us," Jim warned us.

"Thanks for your help, Jim. We'll buy you a drink when this is all over. What's your drink?" Brett asked.

"Single malt scotch. Lagavulin's my favorite."

"Sign me up," I said.

"Pricey stuff," Brett said.

"You guys do something for me?" Jim asked.

"Yes?" Brett and I asked together.

"Kick this guy Bocca the hell off my mountain."

TROJAN GLOCK

It was time.
"Light's beginning to fade," I said.
"EENT," Brett said.
"What?"
"End of Evening Nautical Twilight," he replied.

We nodded to Matt, walked down the stairs and out the back door. The rear deck took us onto a concrete walkway that wound its way down the side of the boulder-strewn hill for several hundred yards. Fifty-foot bonsai-pines tenuously eked out every precious bit of soil and water they could from the monstrous boulder garden. We passed a few tourists hurrying for the shelter of the Mountain Station as daylight failed.

Moisture. Frozen fog falling or snowflakes?

The ground fog was impenetrable, and visibility was fifty feet. A hundred yards down the walkway, the Mountain Station disappeared from sight. Between the fear of confronting Bocca, the cold, and now the fog, I felt disoriented. I smelled horses. The only other smell in the air was from the pines. Brett caught me sniffing.

"Jim's corral is about a thousand yards to the west of us near the ranger's quarters. He needs the horses for search and rescue," he explained.

"I feel like we're walking into a trap," I said.

Behind us the backup, ahead the unknown.

"We are. Scared?" Brett asked me.

"Totally. I can feel my heart and my back is on fire," I answered truthfully.

"Right answer. We always had barf bags in the planes when we deployed. Can't feel the bad stuff, can't feel the good stuff. Probably why they booted this guy out of Special Forces. Without feelings, he was dangerous to the rest of the team. What's his biggest weakness, Doctor? Besides no feelings?"

"Bocca has a monumental pseudo-ego, not a real ego with any strength to it, just a thin lining like the shell of an egg. Inside is a pathetic little kid who knows he's a misfit. He has to protect that thin shell all the time, so he's busy on the border of his ego all the time. If not, he loses it. A strong ego is a strong wall that can keep out the unconscious most of the time."

"If the shell cracks?" Brett asked.

"Bocca probably can't sleep well so he's tired and pumping all the time," I said. "He's putting his finger in the dike to keep from fragmenting, and he starts making mistakes. That's why he left the coin, got emotionally involved with his contract, and confused me with the shrink who blackballed him. The dream is starting to take over with him."

"Maybe there's a way to use that against him," he said.

"What do you mean?"

"Something about the way he talked to you on the phone," he said. "Don't know exactly what it is. He hates you the same way he hates me, but with you, there's something else. He calls you Doc, refers to you as the shrink, and absolutely cannot see you with a gun. There's some kind of power you have over him. I don't know what it is, but I can sense it. There's got to be a way to use it."

Then it hit me. I hadn't seen that Bocca had transference with shrinks that he extended to me. This happened with patients routinely enough so I shouldn't have missed it. Some part of him was vulnerable to me and suddenly I could see how to use it. I despised him so much for killing Jason, hurting Jay, and now kidnapping Chris, that I'd completely fallen asleep on it.

"There is a way to use it. I just didn't see it until now," I said.

"That's why we call it on-the-job training," Brett said.

We kept walking down from the small ridge that Mountain Station sat upon. We reached the beginning of Long Valley, a small rectangular valley perched between the top of the tramway and the San Jacinto summit. I'd seen it on the wall map at the Mountain Station. The map had shown trails leading off in several directions. We chose the one going right down the middle of the valley and plodded along in four inches of snow, waiting for a sign.

We saw deer tracks and a single black raven.

Mountain mahogany.

Absolute silence except the sound of our breathing and footsteps in the crusted snow.

Visibility had improved from fifty feet to fifty yards. We reached a group of poorly visible signs on a post that was set in the snow-covered ground; trails led in three directions.

"Backcountry, Long Valley, Outlook," I read them out loud.

"About a half mile to the left, everything falls away to the city below," he said. "Ranger quarters are to the right and straight ahead is the summit. Pretty little valley's right in front of us for a mile when you can see it. It's full of Sugar and Jeffry

Pine. In the daylight, with the right weather, you can land a helo in the middle of the valley; the department has rescued climbers from here. They get the victims off the summit over to here and then evacuate them."

"You can land here?" I asked.

"You can do it with a big helo, a good pilot, and the right conditions."

My sweat was cold; I adjusted my parka to try and keep the cold and damp out. My body had been at seventy-five degrees and now thirty degrees in the same afternoon, and it was protesting the difference. My back still screamed.

I looked up. "Star?"

"Good sign. Some visibility will help Joan. With this ground fog, she'll be lucky to see her hand through the rifle scope," Brett said.

A large pine appeared from the fog, standing in solitude with a Christmas tree-like peaceful beauty to it.

I took a breath and relaxed.

Suddenly the cold reentered my body and my momentary serenity was shattered. Chris and Joan were tied together in some fashion at the base of the tree.

It wasn't a Christmas tree; they weren't presents under it.

A Sig appeared in Brett's hand. He whispered, "You see them? Thirty yards straight ahead. Shit."

"He has them both tied to the tree. How the hell did he get Joan?" I could barely hear my own voice.

"I don't know, but it's his game now. Nothing to do except go to them," Brett ordered.

"Where the hell is Bocca?" I asked.

"Close," Brett said.

As we approached, Chris was clearly conscious but Joan was slumped against him at the base of the tree. Ten feet away from the tree, Bocca stepped silently from behind it, and leveled his pistol at Joan's head.

"Evening, Gentlemen. Welcome to my party. Lieutenant, drop the weapon. Now."

"If you've hurt her..." Brett's voice had an icy chill as he dropped his Nine.

"You'll what? Haven't you noticed that I'm in charge here? I decide everything. I decide who's selected for the team and who gets kicked off. I select, and you two get to live with my choices here for the rest of your lives. Just like I've had to live with your choices these past twenty years. Try that on for size; see if you have what it takes to live with that kind of getting screwed-over." Bocca spoke in an angry voice lacking any sap of human feeling.

Chris spoke in a trembling voice. "She's been unconscious for about a half hour since he went out and shot her. He carried her back here. I'm okay."

Chris and Joan were flexi-cuffed to a chain secured to the base of the tree; it would take a good knife to cut them free. If we lived that long. There was a large frozen red patch on the right shoulder of Joan's parka but we couldn't do anything for her until we had dealt with Bocca. I prayed she was just unconscious.

"She came here before I arrived with the kid. I watched everybody near the tram station until the ground fog came in. How'd she do it? How'd she know to be here? She fooled me." Bocca seemed unnerved.

Another tree appeared out of the fog ten yards behind the Christmas tree. The fog lifted a little bit.

"You'll have to ask Doc about that," Brett lied. "He had a hunch that you would call the meeting here. It was uncanny. It was almost like Doc could read minds. Never seen it before."

"That's impossible," Bocca protested.

With the snow turning to slush under my weight, I desperately spun thoughts through my brain. *Get an edge on Bocca.*

"Just a hunch," I said. "I know how minds like yours work." My voice didn't quite reflect the confidence I was trying to portray.

"If I spot anybody else, I'm just going to start shooting and ask questions later. I don't know how you figured out where I was going to call the meet." Bocca's eyes bored into me.

He was not an unattractive man except for his mouth. Lean, sinewy and bearded, he would be non-descript to a passerby until his mouth revealed his reptilian coldness and hardness.

"Lieutenant, the other weapon, now. On the ground, in front of you. Carefully."

Bocca's game, his rules.

Brett slowly pulled up his pant leg and un-holstered his hideout handgun and tossed it on the ground in front of Bocca.

"Show me."

"It's cold." Brett protested, but did as commanded. He stripped down to his shorts exposing areas that might have a concealed weapon. Brett's naked black body still reflected the little light left in the valley.

"All right, get your clothes back on. Pity the bitch isn't awake to admire your muscles," Bocca said.

Brett gave Bocca the hardest look I'd ever seen him muster.

"Another thing I don't get. Who the hell is this kid to you? Why go through all this for a street kid?" Bocca asked.

"You'd never understand," Brett said.

"Yeah? Try me," Bocca said.

"Kid wants to be the next John Lennon," Brett said.

"You're right, I don't understand," Bocca said. "You're the one who's crazy. Forget it."

"Now, you, Doc. I know the lieutenant insists on dressing you up tactical but we all know non-combatants aren't supposed to be armed. You're not like him; you're a shrink for Christ sake. Take the belly bag off and toss it." Bocca's face showed a measure of contempt for non-combatants and a measure of something else.

He saw me as a medic first. I tried to act the way he saw me, the non-combatant caught with a bogus weapon. I clumsily unclipped the belly pack that contained my Glock, and tossed it on the pile of weapons, all the while looking sheepish. It wasn't hard.

It was time for a bluff. I started to unzip my coat.

"Forget the strip, Doc. You're about as dangerous as the kid."

Trojan Glock inside the gates, sir.

"How'd you make her?" Brett's voice had a venomous edge.

"Wasn't her fault," Bocca said. "Walking in snow makes noise like a train on railroad tracks. If you put your head down close to the ground, you can hear a crunch. You know that; you're forgetting some of your training. You went to mountain school, didn't you?"

"Dumb. I forgot to tell her," Brett said.

"Yeah, well, we all make mistakes, Lieutenant."

I was ready to play the part I had auditioned for. It was a part that would be more than Bocca's expectations of me, and less than an Oscar-winning part. Our lives depended on it.

"What kind of symptoms are you having, Bocca?" I asked.

"What the hell are you talking about, Doc?"

"Presenting like you are, you've got to have some symptoms," I continued.

"What do you mean? 'Presenting like I am?'"

"'Presenting' is clinical talk. Patients present symptoms. You present a sociopathic personality disorder with homicidal behavior. Strong feelings of superiority dominate your consciousness most of the time, however, your personality is probably de-compensating underneath. The dream is ready to take over."

Then I started guessing.

"Possible cause: one or both parents rejected you as a child. Unwanted baby, unwanted child. Your parents probably didn't want you but couldn't not have you. You were an unwanted child, then an unwanted soldier. Now you are wanted, but for all the wrong reasons. Possible physical symptoms can include anxiety, depression, cardiac arrhythmia, chronic muscle tension, some trembling, insomnia, and nightmares, to list just a few."

"Sometimes I do have trouble sleeping since getting an unfair deal from you two." Bocca's answer shouldn't have surprised me; he saw me as a shrink.

Act like a shrink and the patients come — patient transference in Long Valley.

"Nightmares?" I asked.

"Nah," he said, unconvincingly.

"There are some good meds these days for sleeping. Stuff like Trazadone that doesn't over sedate you," I said soothingly.

"I get this done, and I'll sleep like a baby." Bocca spoke in a cocky fashion, but didn't discount the medication.

People are complicated. Sociopaths like Bocca are crazy complicated. It wouldn't have surprised me if he asked me for a prescription and then shot me.

"You know, if the dream takes over, you're gone," I said.

"Yeah," he said. "You said that."

Bocca motioned Brett to step away from the pile of weapons and then picked them up one at a time, tossing them into the darkness. The only weapons left were in Bocca's possession and my right jacket pocket. While he tossed the weapons, his eyes never left Brett.

More trees visible. Fog's backing off a little bit more.

"Over here, Doc." Bocca motioned me to a small tree near Chris and Joan's Christmas tree and cuffed my left leg to the base of the tree. He was too close to me to make a move. He would see me reach into my jacket pocket and react. I was not a match for him in that kind of a close fight.

Bocca hissed between his teeth. "Lieutenant, now its show time for you and me. I'll put this weapon away and give you a lesson in who should or shouldn't have been kept out of SF."

Joan made a gurgling sound, involuntarily clearing secretions from her airway.

"Make sure her airway is clear; we don't want her to choke," I instructed Chris.

He adjusted Joan's head and the gurgling subsided. Noise from Joan felt good; it meant she was still alive.

"The bleeding from her shoulder has stopped but she feels so cold. She's starting to come around. Look, I need you guys to know that I'm sorry I got you all into this. If he hadn't seen me on the bike trail, none of this would have happened," Chris blurted out.

Bocca laughed, "I just shot her in the shoulder. I didn't kill her. If I wanted to kill her, she'd be dead. She was fifty yards from here over in that clump of trees when I shot her. She was getting ready to put a scope on our approach. Like I said, I heard her; I couldn't see her. She didn't see me until I had her covered. Even then she wouldn't give up the rifle. In spite of her shoulder, she still tried to get a shot off at me. I had to kick the rifle away from her. She and the kid got stones. I'll give you that."

Bocca holstered his Glock.

He and Brett were standing in a circle of trampled slippery snow.

"More stones than you," Brett said, challenging him.

Then, they were out of the gate.

Bocca charged with a vicious jump kick to the chest. Brett was ready. He managed to step back slightly and deflected most of the impact of the kick, but still must have felt the blow. He countered by kicking Bocca's pivot foot out from under him, taking him down. Brett was on top of him like a cat. They both moved too fast for me to see an opening to shoot Bocca.

Don't hit Brett! Wait for an opening. Back burns.

Twenty feet away from the mortal combat, Chris startled me, "She's waking up."

Chris's involuntary cry was sufficient distraction for Brett that he lost control of Bocca who flipped Brett over his prone shoulders and into the shallow snow.

Joan shook her head groggily and spoke out loud for the first time since our arrival at the tree. "What happened?"

"Bocca shot you. Be still," Chris spoke gently.

I listened as Chris reassured Joan and cradled her with his free hand. I touched the Baby Glock through my jacket pocket. I couldn't think about using it until there was a safer distance between Brett and Bocca.

A tiny shaft of moonlight shone in my frozen field of vision. Some small mountain creature, startled by the life-and-death contest between humans, darted through it.

Fog fading. Furthest trees disappearing.

The advantage flipped back to Bocca, who held Brett in a headlock. Brett maneuvered free and rolled away. Both men eyed each other for the opening to disable. Bocca moved toward Brett and launched another sidekick at his torso. He missed, but the kick landed on Brett's shoulder, forcing him to stagger backwards. As Brett fell, he rolled to his feet and came back, hitting Bocca with a vicious karate punch to the chest. The punch launched Bocca into the snow. Stunned, he lay on his back.

With Bocca on his back, Brett went for the pile of weapons, hoping to acquire permanent control. Bocca recovered quickly and before Brett reached the pile, he was on him from behind. Both went down in the snow. Bocca snaked free, grabbed one of the handguns and brought the weapon to bear on Brett. Same split second, Brett kicked it out of his hand. The weapon landed ten feet away, and buried itself in the snow.

Bocca launched himself in the direction of the weapon, fumbled down on his knees, and felt blindly for the pistol. His hands lifted sprays of snow. He grunted hungrily, stood up without the weapon and scanned for it.

Brett cut him down from behind with a sweep that folded his knees out from under him. Bocca rolled out, stood up and attacked with a slicing kick. Brett absorbed the impact, grabbed Bocca's arm, bent to one knee and rolled Bocca over his shoulders, throwing him to the ground.

Joan's detached voice whispered from the periphery, "I feel dizzy."

Her blood pressure was probably down from the loss of blood; she needed medical attention immediately. Shock alone could kill her.

Bocca panted as he recovered. For a few seconds, he just stood there looking at each of us with unfocused eyes. He and Brett were both bloodied and exhausted. Brett looked over at Joan. For just an instant, he broke his concentration. Bocca seized the opportunity and caught Brett with a blow to his side; the impact spun Brett backwards. Unbalanced on an icy patch of snow, he lost his footing. I watched him fall and hit the back of his head on a rock. He stopped moving.

Second officer down.

The clearing was shrinking, and the fog moving back in. I lost sight of the closest trees.

"That settles it. I took him. Special Forces would have been better off with me than with your lieutenant. I knew I could take him; I knew I was the better man."

"You don't get it, do you?" Chris challenged, shaking his head.

"What don't I get, kid? What's a kid living on the street going to teach me?"

"That Brett is ten times better than you," Chris said. He brought a team here to rescue me. Playing on a team makes Brett what he is; no team would have you. You beat him by luck, not by skill."

Stunned. I grazed the Baby Glock to remind myself it was there.

Bocca was still standing too close to Brett for me to risk a shot.

"Kid, all that matters is winning," Bocca said. "It doesn't matter how you win. Uncle Sam taught me that and I learned. Believe me, I learned. I learned about assassination, dirty fighting, shooting first, and asking questions later. All this crap about honor doesn't make a difference. There are two kinds of people in the world: winners and losers. How you win doesn't matter. Honor is crap."

Bocca reached into his pocket, took out his Nine and placed the barrel against Brett's temple.

"Rules of combat. You win, you finish the enemy."

"Watch out for the bad guy," Chris sang with a voice with a resigned timbre to it.

It was a line from one of the new songs he had been working on. It was the voice with which he expected his next action could be his last. He disclosed the rock he had been hiding in his free hand, and threw it at Bocca. The rock struck Bocca in the face. Bocca stumbled, but easily regained his footing.

Bocca moved measurably away from Brett, creating an opening.

Ready!

He looked stunned, wiped some blood from his face, and aimed the pistol at Chris. "I guess you want to go first, kid. You got stones; I'll give you that."

Chris was willing to buy Brett a few extra moments of in exchange for his own life. The gift was payment in full for all that had occurred since we'd first met him on the street.

"I'll give all this; you guys keep coming at me," Bocca shouted. "Who the fuck do you people think you are? The Goddam Pinkertons?"

"Bocca, you know what's really sad?" I said.

"What's that, Doc?"

"You could have been a good soldier," I said.

"I am a good soldier. I'm the better soldier here. I'm better than the lieutenant. I'm better than all of you together."

"No. No, you're not a better soldier; you're not even a good soldier."

"What are you talking about, Doc? You've just seen what I can do."

"Good soldiers protect innocents. It's the first job of a soldier. You kill innocents for a living."

"Say what?" Bocca asked.

I answered him by pointing the Trojan Glock at him through my jacket pocket and pulling the trigger. I pulled the trigger until the slide locked open — the fog forbid seeing if the rounds found him.

Bocca stumbled and fell to one knee. He dropped his weapon in powder.

I hit him. Something in my back released.

"What?" The gunfire roused Brett out of his stupor, and he rolled on to his stomach.

Bocca looked at me with bewilderment and cried out in betrayal, "You're a medic!"

I stared back and nodded an acknowledgment of both my profession and my deceit.

Smoke? Fog? What? Fog doesn't smell. Can't see anything.

Trojan pocket smoldering.

"What happened?" Brett asked, not conscious yet, but coming around.

Bocca. Where's Bocca?

When I looked back to Bocca, there was only blood on the snow where he had knelt. The ground fog had again receded enough to see the red aircraft-warning beacon atop the tower at the summit of the mountain.

"Where is he?" I shouted to Chris.

"He just..." He couldn't finish. He was exhausted.

"Disappeared?"

Chris nodded.

Like the wounded wild animal he almost was, Bocca had fled. He was stunned to be shot by a medic. He could have picked up his weapon and fought. Perhaps it was animal instinct, simple shock, or Brett regaining consciousness that caused his nervous system to roll over. He decided to disappear.

Brett was clearheaded enough to push himself erect. He rapidly scanned for Bocca, saw the pool of blood in the snow, and registered that I had shot Bocca. With one hand he unclipped his radio, with the other he pulled a small slide knife out of his pocket, walked over, and sliced my plastic leg cuff. He carefully extracted my right hand from what was left of my parka pocket and loosened the vise grip I still had on the Baby Glock.

He lifted the radio to his lips and pushed the transmit button. "69 Whiskey."

"69 Whiskey. Copy," Matt answered from the Mountain Station.

"Our 10-4 is six hundred yards from the signs at the end of the walkway in front of a large evergreen. Location of suspect unknown. Shots fired. Officer down. Proceed with caution. Suspect fleeing area."

"Copy that. Who's down? Who fired the shots?" Matt asked.

"Joan's down. Lost some blood. Doc fired at the suspect. Move!"

I walked over and cut the cuffs off Joan and Chris. I had to saw through the wire at the center of the flexi-cuffs. I examined Joan's shoulder; the cold and snow had stopped the bleeding, but I was still worried about her.

We could hear help coming. Brett took a penlight out of his pocket and flashed it several times. There was a return flash of light. A minute later, they were on us.

Jim said as he walked up to us, "Matt is making a sweep of the perimeter."

"When he's done, we can regroup and decide what to do next," Brett said.

"Joan, how are you feeling?" Brett was on his knees cradling Joan's head.

"I'm real cold, dizzy, and my head hurts," Joan said. "I'm sorry I screwed up. I'd taken a position and he showed up with Chris in tow. I moved close enough to have a shot. He tied Chris to the tree, and then I lost him for a couple of minutes. The next thing I knew he had the drop on me. I don't understand how he made me because I was well hidden. I tried to take him anyway."

"That was my fault, not yours," Brett said. "I forgot to tell you that walking in the snow can be heard from a distance by listening close to the ground. Bocca heard you first. We need to evacuate you. Matt, have the EMTs meet you at the base station. You're carrying Joan out; take Chris with you. Then get back here and help us find this guy. He's shot, holed up somewhere, or dead. There's no way he would head toward the Mountain Station; he knows I've got back-up there."

"The EMTs and the doctor are already at the Mountain Station." Jim's words brought tremendous relief.

"A doctor?" I asked.

"Your wife," Matt said.

Joan's chances were improving considerably. Brett smiled at me.

"Bocca told me some of his plans. He's hidden all kinds of gear in the mountains. I just remembered!" Chris said.

"Shit," Matt muttered.

"Go," Brett directed.

Matt handed his rifle to Brett and effortlessly picked Joan up from her slumped position in the snow; she grunted with pain. Chris fell in with them and they were gone back up the trail toward the Mountain Station. As they walked away, they disappeared into the darkness. It would be a half-mile in the dark and the cold, carrying a barely conscious cop. Matt looked like it was no more effort than walking to the mall.

Watching them leave, no words were spoken. We had survived our latest encounter with Bocca. Had Bocca?

The burning sensation in my back turned to comfortable diffuse warmth. I felt closer to the ground and denser.

"Our perimeter is clear. The tracks in the snow go due east out of here," Jim said, returning from recon. "Ready to start searching for this guy, Lieutenant?"

"Yeah, let's get started and Matt can catch up." Brett seemed to have his strength back.

"How many lives does a cat have?" Jim asked rhetorically.

"This guy has at least nine." I answered. I looked at Brett and said, "Bocca just … fucking disappeared."

He nodded, understanding.

We were only three. We had reinforcements on the way but we couldn't afford to wait and let Bocca escape. He could double-back on us, and shoot us. To sit or to search; we chose to search. The visibility was now excellent in the moonlight and my thoughts were clearer. They were of Joan and Nancy. One more time, Nancy had been there for us.

We walked silently at a turtle pace, acutely aware of the sound of footsteps on snow. We had to pick our path carefully over fallen timber and branches. I began to see the outline of some rock formations ahead. I walked blindly into a sign that read "Desert Trail to Outlook Trail."

We spaced ourselves twenty yards apart so as not to present too easy a target for Bocca. Considering what he could do with an impossible target, we didn't want to make it simple for him. I had Joan's rifle and extra magazines; Brett took point.

It was clear that Jim had gone on patrols before; he was ready. He was holding the biggest handgun I had ever seen. We walked for ten minutes.

"Over here," Brett motioned.

Jim and I moved over to find Brett's rifle pointing to a patch of blood in the snow.

"It's not heavy bleeding, but it's consistent. If Bocca doesn't rest and stem the bleeding, that alone will kill him." Jim said.

We heard a soft whistle from the direction we had come and all of our weapons came to bear on the penlight flash.

"It's Matt," Brett whispered.

Matt had made the trip to the Mountain Station and back to us, carrying Joan, in the same ten minutes we had used to reach the end of the Desert View Trail.

"The doctor took over and they were putting in a drip line when I left," Matt reported. "Joan didn't look too good. The kid's fine. Chief wanted to know if we needed more

help."

"What did you tell him?" Brett said.

"You'll call for help when and if you need it," Matt replied.

"You said that to the chief?" Brett asked.

"Pretty much. I added a few sirs. He trusts your judgment," Matt said.

"My judgment has Joan in the hospital," Brett said.

"It wasn't your judgment. It was the shooter, sir."

We continued the search for fifteen minutes, found no traces of Bocca and kept coming back to the end of the Desert View Trail.

The area was called Outlook. It looked down on the city below and dropped off precipitously to a staggeringly steep canyon all the way to the desert 8,500 feet below our perch. It was a breathtaking view in the moonlight. The canyon falling away below my feet was steep enough to be used as an Olympic downhill slalom course with no landing zone.

"Where could he disappear to up here?" I asked.

" I don't know, but let's keep looking. Watch your footing. Fall here and land on North Palm Canyon," Brett said.

"Over here," Jim called out.

We hustled over.

"More blood. Not as much as last time. He's managed to stop most of his bleeding," Brett said.

Michael Thompkins

Jim pointed to some small dark patches in the snow that left a clear trail over the side of the cliff we were standing on. Jim stood and shook his head in disbelief. He kept looking at the patches and then alternately down the mountain.

"He's headed down the mountain," Jim said.

"Say what?" Brett asked.

"He's headed down the mountain," Jim said. "Very few people know about this trail. It's called the 'Cactus to Clouds' Trail. It goes straight down to the city with one switch back after another for eight miles. First mile is in six inches of snow right now. He'll never make it; it's not humanly possible. He'll fall, bleed, or freeze to death. Eight thousand feet down eight miles of tricky trail, it could be a steeper grade than Mt. McKinley. We don't publish or permit this trail; it's too dangerous. No one in his right mind would attempt it under these conditions in the dark. But the snow says he's going down that way. This guy must think he's a mountain goat or the Demon."

"The Demon?" Brett asked.

"The Tahquitz Demon," Jim said. "Indian legend. Summit's supposed to be the home of an ancient demon that created bolts of lightning, slid down the mountain, snatched maidens, and frightened animals. That kind of stuff."

We all took it in. It fit Bocca like a glove.

"Something you need to know," I said to Brett.

"What's that?" he asked.

"When you were out cold, Chris was dumb enough to try to knock Bocca out with a rock. Bocca was getting ready to shoot him first," I said.

"What?"

"You heard me the first time. Chris tried to take him out with a rock. Thing is, he almost knocked him out. Bocca stumbled and then I..."

"You gave him the medicine he needed: tincture of lead," Brett said.

"'Cactus to Clouds Trail used to have another name...'" Jim interrupted us.

"What's the other name?" Brett asked.

"The Outlaw Trail," Jim said.

TIGER TRIAGE

Bocca was out of the clearing and on the Desert View Trail. He knew it would take them at least ten minutes to get their act together to follow him. Ten-minute head start and he knew where he was going; he was going straight down the mountain on the Outlaw Trail. He was dizzy from blood loss and cold.

Situation-report?

Evacuate.

Shoulder burns. Son-of-a-bitch shot me. Shot by a medic. Goddamn shrink. Never trust a shrink. Screwed up. Should've searched the shrink, too. Holdout gun. Shot by a holdout gun. Losing blood at a trickle. Venous, not arterial blood.

Hyperventilating.

Slow breathing. Slow bleeding.

Slow breathing. Slow bleeding

Wanted some excitement. Got it. They were shooting back.

Get to the cache.

Butch and Sundance would've liked the name. Outlaw Trail.

"Butch, if we gotta run, might as well be the Outlaw Trail."

"Sundance, we just lost one to the Pinkertons."

Nobody else can pull this escape off. One for the books. Dizzy. First sign of blood loss. Get to the cache.

Bocca knew that without the shoulder wound, he could get down off the mountain in six hours. 8,000 feet and eight miles. Now, it would take him eight hours. The shoulder could mean trouble to him and he knew it. The cold and the blood loss had begun to affect his heart.

He was going to need the morphine. The morphine would make the shoulder wound tolerable. The trick was to take enough but not knock himself out. His clothes were soaking wet from fighting the lieutenant. Hypothermia was his biggest risk until he reached the cache where he had stashed dry clothes.

In 'Nam he had learned to regulate his own physical energy from the VC. He tightened the drawstrings on the lower part of his vest, which was lined with space blanket and wind-stopper materials. He knew now that concentrating every ounce of energy he had into his kidneys and spine could insure his survival. The VC called it "riding the snake."

Bocca reached the lip of the Long Valley plateau and used several minutes to stop, sit, rest and slow his heart rate. Standing at the precipice, overlooking the lights of Palm Springs below, he was shaking. The initial part of the descent would be the most dangerous. The cache was located thousands of feet and four hours below him.

Just a few drips of blood now. They look black in the snow. Coagulating. Freezing. Bleeding stopping. Thirsty from the blood loss. Shoulder feels heavy. 100 grain round, third of an inch in diameter, feels like a hundred pounds of steel.

Gotta get to the cache. Lock and load. No fear. Stand to. One man can do anything. Army of one.

Bocca pushed himself off the edge of the cliff, and slid down the first slope without the aid of ropes or crampons— he disappeared into the darkness in a devil's slide — glissading away from the grave.

Hours later, with only the aid of moonlight, he reached the cache. He didn't traverse the mountain; he came straight down, skiing on his boots. Several times he stopped himself by running into rocks, taking hundreds of small abrasions from the rocks. When he reached the cache, he was mildly hypothermic and in desperate need of blood volume. He immediately stripped off his shirt and vest.

Can't stop the shaking. Hard to get this damn shirt off. Can't get the bag open. Use the knife. Eat the Clif bar. Don't puke it up. Open the heat pads and tape them to the IV bag. Pull the cap off catheter kit. Push it in. Warm rush.

Open the Quik-Clot , sprinkle it in the wound. Stuff feels like lye.

Burns.

Now, the morphine syringe. Stick it in. Can't push the plunger. Thumbs locked from the cold. Can't move it.

With the morphine syringe stuck in his shoulder and dangling off it like a porcupine quill, Bocca crawled over to a nearby boulder. He dragged the space blanket with him and held the drip bag above his torso. He set the drip bag down, gripped the syringe with his fingers, and used the rock to push the plunger on the syringe and inject the drug.

Morphine. Warm, sweet morphine.

Bocca taped the bag IV to his chest and put his clothes back on. The morphine slowed him considerably. The trick was to inject enough morphine to help but not enough to knock you out. He kept shaking his head to reject sleep. He drifted in and out huddled against the boulder — willing himself warm.

Bocca came to and realized that he had been asleep for thirty minutes. He could hear them on the trail above him, and was surprised that they hadn't waited until morning. Bocca was dangerously drowsy.

Move!

OUTLAW TRAIL

"Nobody can say we're in our right minds," Brett said.

"Be smarter to wait until morning," Jim said. "On the other hand, the fog is lifting and it can be done."

"We wait 'til morning and if Bocca isn't dead, he's gone. Can you get us down?" Brett asked.

"I'll need a few things," Jim said.

"Doc, you in?" Matt asked.

"Sure," I said. "This is getting better every minute." It wasn't really the way I felt but I was way past scared until this was over. When I shot Bocca, I felt as alone in my skin and as scared as I'd ever been in my life. Right now, I just felt an instinct to finish what I had started when I shot him.

"We have 8,000 feet and eight miles to descend," Jim said. He radioed the Mountain Station and asked one of his people to bring ropes and crampons.

"What are the odds of him surviving a night descent of the Outlaw Trail?" Matt asked.

"Slim to none. It's almost straight down eight thousand feet. It's in the teens on the upper part of the trail, and he isn't dressed for this kind of cold. He's lost some blood and he's wounded." Jim shook his head in disbelief at Bocca's choice of escape routes.

"Until I see his body, I won't believe he's dead. Remember Chris said that Bocca has supply stashes hidden all over this mountain," Brett said.

"We just don't know," I said.

"He's dead," Matt said, hopefully. With youth on his side, he could afford to be optimistic.

One of Jim's rangers showed up in ten minutes, dropped the gear in the snow in front of us, and shook his head in disbelief. "You're all crazy," he said.

"We know," we chorused.

Jim pulled fifty feet of climbing rope from a pack. We applied crampons over our boots, and put on the parkas that the ranger had brought.

GUN PLAY

Jim spoke while roping us up. "The lieutenant and I will take the lead and the rear; be prepared to arrest yourself if you stumble. A fall won't kill you, but it could break your leg."

We took the first slippery step over the lip, and began our descent of the trail with each other and the moon for company. We very gingerly picked our way down across a northeast-facing slope between boulders and an occasional scrub oak. Several times I lost my footing and was arrested by the others. After the first treacherous mile, we came out of six-inch deep powder. Our footing surer, we unroped, took off our crampons and continued our descent. At a mile and a half further down the mountain, we rested by a stand of oaks and a small creek. We'd been climbing down for four hours through the forested zone of the mountain. The air smelled sweetly of evergreens.

"I'm going to scout the perimeter, Lieutenant," Matt said, leaving to recon the pretty little creek.

"Careful," Brett instructed him. "You won't get a second chance with Bocca."

In response, Matt disengaged the safety on his rifle; the metal sound echoed smartly in the frigid air.

Jim was busy looking for tracks.

"Any signs of our man?" Brett asked him.

"Nope, guy's a freakin' Houdini," Jim said.

We passed a thermos of coffee around that Jim's ranger had included, and enjoyed the vast view of the Colorado Desert at night. Overhead, the moon was well into its arc from east of the interstate on its journey to the Indian Canyons; below, Palm Springs streetlights twinkled.

The radio coughed static. Brett put it to his ear and pushed the send button. "Chief?"

"Lieutenant. Is Doc there?" The chief asked.

"He's here," Brett said.

"No sign of Bocca's body, yet?"

"Not yet, sir."

"They tell me that you four are out of your minds," the chief said.

"Yes, sir," Brett replied.

"Nothing new," the chief said. "Let me talk to Doc."

"Sure."

I took the radio from Brett.

"Chief."

"Doc. First, let me make one thing clear."

"Sure," I replied.

"I always want to be on your wife's good side."

"Don't we all, chief," I said. Lately, everyone was doing better than me in that department.

"Detective Fleming is in recovery and she's going to be fine."

"Chief, that's really good to hear."

"Tell the lieutenant something for me."

"He can hear you, Chief," I said.

"Lieutenant, bring back Bocca's body."

"Yes, sir," Brett said.

I handed the radio back to Brett and we both smiled in relief at the news that Joan was out of danger.

"Nancy did it again," Brett said, smiling.

"I know," I said, enormously relieved.

"But it's time we give her a rest," he said.

"You got that right."

The relief I felt about Joan made me lightheaded. I sat down on a rock.

"Wounded and without ropes, this guy is unbelievable to have negotiated those last four thousand feet. He made it this far or we would have his body," Brett concluded.

"He was bleeding and he could have lost a lot of blood or gone hypothermic. How could he have survived?" I said.

"Lieutenant, check this out." Matt announced his return and was holding up a waterproof gear bag by its handle. His rifle slung, he held a syringe in his other hand.

"I found it under a rock outcropping. The contents were spread all over the place."

"How did you notice it was there?" I asked.

"Boot prints nearby. He didn't bother to sweep them," Matt said.

"What's in the dry bag?" Brett asked.

"Some food, water, Quik-Clot bandage wrappers, cover for an IV drip bag, " Matt listed the contents. "Bag was big enough to hold some clothes."

"Syringe?" Brett asked.

"Morphine," Matt replied.

"He made it this far, and was still alive when he left here," Brett said.

"Son of a bitch." I wasn't feeling as hopeful as moments before.

"Okay. Stand to. He's close. I can feel it. " Brett ordered us up on our feet and back down the trail. "The morphine will slow him down."

We moved out of the clearing and back on to the trail. I glanced at my watch. It was

1:00 a.m.

Two minutes later, Jim found fresh signs. "He's five minutes ahead of us."

Traversing one chaparral-covered ridge after another, we descended the next 2,000 feet in an hour at a trot. Creosote bush, cactus, and sage filled the frozen air with their acrid aromas.

"Lieutenant, I've never seen anything like this. How could this guy have survived? He's an animal," Matt whispered.

"He's got more lives than a cat," Brett replied softly.

"Will we ever be done with him? Where the hell is he?" I asked.

There were no answers to my questions.

Two minutes later, Jim held up his hand and gestured us to fan out from single file. We entered a flat little open area that looked like it might fall away into a sharp cliff into Tahquitz Canyon. The back of the open spot was lined with trees and I could sense the drop-off not see it. The open bowl naturally gathered ambient light and helped my eyes focus.

A single tree stood three feet in front of the tree line like it was inspecting ranks. Sitting on the ground with his back against the tree, Bocca sat unconscious. There was a pistol in his lap. Our four weapons simultaneously pointed at him — a firing squad if he made a bad move.

Brett walked to within twenty feet of Bocca and commanded, "Hands on the back of your neck. Now!"

Bocca opened his eyes. The smile on his face foreshadowed his next move, "Lieutenant, ain't gonna happen."

Bocca rolled into the tree line.

Brett's bullet hit the tree with a thunk.

The air was full of cordite.

In less time than it took me to inhale another breath, Bocca was behind the trees and we were all running after him.

We stopped and passed through the trees carefully.

The ground gave way to precipice.

We stood together and stared down the bald rock face of a hundred foot cliff that ran as far as we could see in the dark.

I grabbed a tree to secure myself.

"He must have jumped or fallen," Jim said.

We stood for several minutes peering into the abyss.

Brett said, "Son of a bitch." He was looking beyond me down the tree line.

"Whattaya mean?" I asked confused.

Brett pointed at the base of one of the trees behind me, "Look! A rope."

Wrapped around the base of the tree, the rope slithered at furious speed left to right around the base of the tree, making a whirring sound. The end of the rope arrived. The tail of the line exploded around the tree and sailed down the void.

I could not comprehend what my eyes showed me.

"What the hell was that? Where is he?" I was stunned.

"Bocca slid down on a hidden rope and then pulled it after him," Brett said. "It was wrapped around the tree. He went down on both ropes and then pulled on one."

"He really is a Houdini," Jim said.

Brett, enraged, emptied his weapon down into the blackness. The rounds ricocheted off the cliff walls.

Silence. Nothing sounded back.

"Jim?" Matt asked.

"It's not anywhere near long enough," Jim replied, referring to the rope we had used earlier to protect our descent.

"Dammit," Matt said.

"He was ready for us again," Brett said.

We lost him.

We retraced our steps to the trail. Dejection displayed on our faces, we continued down the trail knowing full well that Bocca had gained time and distance on us that we couldn't recover. Our only hope was that he would succumb to his injuries.

Hours later at first light, we pulled into the junction of the Lykken, the Museum, and the Outlaw Trail. Exhausted and hungry, we were a mile from the end of Ramon Road and looking straight into downtown Palm Springs. I could see the Desert Museum, my office, and the airport in the distance. We spread out and searched in three directions for ten minutes, found no signs of Bocca and returned to the trail junction. It had been a difficult and disappointing descent — frustration flushed our faces.

"Goddammit, this guy is something else," Matt said.

It was dawn and the sun was beginning to rise. The trail was wide enough to ride horses at this point; we were down from Long Valley safely. We pulled out the water bottles and took a break before finishing the last mile. Matt offered some trail mix. It was all we had to eat since yesterday.

We rested near a large rock and an old picnic table that some crew had dragged up here. Brett walked over to the table and picked up what I first thought was a small shiny rock. He tossed it in the air a few times. The object's surface reflected the late afternoon light in a unique way; it flashed silver. Brett started rolling it in his fingers and studied it carefully. He looked mesmerized by it, shaking his head in amazement.

"What you got there, Lieutenant?" Matt asked, watching Brett play with the object.

"A message."

"What message?" I asked.

Brett held the shiny object up for us to see. " It's a Limey coin; one pound British Sterling."

"Bocca's gone home to England," I said.

"Yup," Brett said.

He nodded, tossed the coin to me, and I examined it. On the front was a portrait of Queen Elizabeth II. I flipped it over.

"What's on the back?" Brett asked.

"A lion."

TWO PURPLE HEARTS

Tuesday night, two days after Brett found the British coin, we were all drinking Jay's Mint Juleps at the Saloon. It was the rescheduled opening for Chris's band, and they were still looking for a new name. The chief, Brett, Joan, Nancy, Chris, Jay, and I shared the best table in the room; Bob was outside the door getting ready to let the audience in. We were fifteen minutes from show time and the rest of Chris's band was backstage. Brett made sure the chief was invited tonight, and he seemed happy to be included.

The mood and the drinks were mixed. Everyone was still a little on edge, and justifiably so. Chris was off Bocca's list, as there were now four of us that could identify him. Bocca was still out there somewhere, but it wasn't about Chris anymore. I was the one who had shot Bocca. I was already instantly recoiling from anything small and red.

When the drinks arrived Brett proceeded to catch the edge of his glass with his elbow and send it plummeting to the floor. Jay quickly replaced the drink.

"Can I do anything right?" Brett asked rhetorically. All of his frustration with the last two weeks had fallen with the drink.

Joan immediately touched his hand. "Shit happened. You out-planned Bocca; we came out on top," she said.

Everyone nodded in agreement, but it didn't bring a smile to Brett's face.

The Feds, in company with an Interpol agent, had dragged the chief, Brett, and me to headquarters the morning after we came down off the mountain and, for the record, ripped us up for interfering in their investigation. The chief pretty much kept his mouth shut and, although the Feds didn't buy it for a second, went along with the ruse that we had acted independently of the department. They were powerless to do anything about it because the newspapers spared nothing in their glowing reports of Lieutenant Wade, Detective Fleming and "The Shooting Shrink."

The Feds, in reality, were happy to move onto the next item on their political agendas, and they didn't really object to the kidnapping going away. They would have been happy if we had nailed Bocca but "they were aware" that Brett and I were now ongoing "targets of opportunity." We had better "be cognizant of our situation." Where do they learn to talk like this? D.C.? After an hour of them, I realized how dead-on Brett had been not to entrust Chris's safe return to the Feds.

In the parking lot after the meeting, the agent-in-charge dropped D.C.-speak and pretty much offered Brett a job "anytime he was tired of Podunk Palm Springs." Then he told me, "You got balls for a shrink."

Later, I asked Brett if he had any interest in the offer.

"I need to stay here and train you to shoot straighter."

Joan's right shoulder was in a sling. Nancy had released her from the hospital this morning and she seemed to be recovering quickly. Her wound had been less severe than Jay's. They were bonding over their shoulder wounds, and we were going to hear about them forever.

"Joan, how's your shoulder feeling? I wish I had a big stuffed chair for you to sit in." Jay reached over with his good arm to touch Joan's hand.

"I'm doing fine," Joan said. "It hurts, but Nancy has me on some pretty good pain meds, so it's tolerable."

"My shoulder still aches in the middle of the night," Jay said.

"I promise that will go away soon," Nancy said. "It's just your body healing. I'm meeting you later this week for a follow-up visit, right?"

"I'll be there," Jay replied.

"And Joan, if you have any bleeding through those stitches, call me right away." Nancy gave quiet but stern directions. "I would have preferred you spend another night in the hospital."

"I hate hospitals," Joan said. "I'll pay attention to the stitches, though. I know I was lucky that the round passed through me without doing any serious damage. Thank you for taking such good care of me."

Brett had a surprise for Jay and Joan.

"We have a tradition in the military when someone gets shot." Brett took two of the real Purple Hearts that he had received during his career out of his pocket. He ceremoniously presented one to Jay and the other to Joan. They'd earned them. Everyone applauded.

Then the chief asked, "Chris, how are you doing?"

"Good. It's sure cool to be able to walk around without a bodyguard, sir."

This was the second time I'd heard Chris call anybody "sir."

"And, I guess I'm a little over-pumped about tonight," Chris said.

Brett reached out and put his hand on Chris's shoulder.

Michael Thompkins

I worried about Chris. I told Nancy earlier that I felt like we hadn't really helped Chris with what we had learned about his family. As much as she objected to my new job, she was still big enough to point out that this simply wasn't true. What Chris needed at his age was to deal with his past, as a by-product of moving on with his life, not as a full-time job. She reminded me that it's what we all sometimes needed, and that it had been one of my mottos for the last twenty years of my professional career. Psychologist Handbook, Chapter Ten: life first, then therapy.

Chapter Fifteen: listen to your wife.

"Joan, how are you doing?" the chief asked.

"Sir, I..." Joan started to say.

"If one more person calls me Sir, I'm going to leave."

Joan nodded and continued, "I know I goofed when I let Bocca take Chris from me on Thursday night. Also, I fell for the sounds-in-the-snow trick at the top of the tram, but I just don't have the energy to beat myself up about them right now. We all made it out alive, Bocca's gone, and we got Conto. I'm settling for that, for a change."

Brett looked at her appreciatively.

"The tiger's wounded and probably crawled back to his cave." I brought the conversation back to Bocca.

"The Feds and Interpol have a full-blown active fugitive watch out for Bocca. But with his skills, I'm afraid he's eluded us," the chief said.

"The coin tells us where he's probably going. He launches from Great Britain," Brett guessed. He extracted the coin from his vest without moving his other hand off Joan's. He tossed it on the table so that it spun and finally settled with the face of the Queen pointing up.

"Can I have that? I want to start a collection for all my cases," I said.

"Sure, no prints on it. Here, you can have the Ranger coin too," Brett said.

Nancy said, "Collection? All your cases?"

I shut up.

"When Bocca had me, he talked about his favorite pub in England," Chris said, changing the subject to my relief.

"What'd he tell you?" the chief asked.

"That it was near an old village church with a cemetery, and the gravestones dated from 1200 A.D."

"That would describe half the pubs in England," Brett said.

"Not much of a lead there. He's escaped," I said.

"Bocca's killed a cop in my town. It's not acceptable for him to walk away," the chief said.

"Jason White was a security guard, not one of your officers," Chris said, looking confused.

I wasn't confused; I guessed what was coming next. I knew the chief.

"He upheld the law in my town. Same difference. And Bocca also tried to kill two of my cops. Nobody tries to kill my cops." The chief looked at Brett, Joan and me in a way that said it all — the hunt for Bocca wasn't over.

"I hope that includes shrinks," Nancy said.

"Say what?" the chief asked.

"'Nobody tries to kill your cops or your shrinks," Nancy said.

"Yes, Doctor," the chief replied.

Then the chief took out the Charger tickets he had bet with Brett and paid off their wager.

"Thanks, Chief," Brett said.

"There are two tickets. You'll need a date," the chief said.

Joan actually blushed, and everyone smiled.

My thoughts shifted to the other bad guy, Conto.

"At least Global is out of business and Conto will stand trial for the killing of Martin Jonas," I said. Martin Jonas, unknowingly, was a feeder fish following the big-money-energy-trading Global whale — somehow he got eaten.

"Conto will go to trial in six months," Brett said. "Until then, she's out on a million dollars bail. Global has gone out of business; their trading will be done by the parent company, E-Star."

"Is any agency investigating the trading scam and E-Star?" I asked.

"Investigators have come down from Sacramento," Brett said. "They're examining records from the ISO in Folsom and the Energy Trading Exchange in L.A. But without the records on Conto's home computer, the trail may dry up."

"So Conto may pay for the murder, but prosecuting the whole electrical scam may just run out of juice?" I joked.

"That's often the case with white-collar crime," The chief said. "Expensive attorneys, lost evidence, and toothless laws make it difficult to prosecute. Truth is, this country loves robber barons. People don't really understand these crimes or care; corporate perps often skate. Often, we put the perp away on the violence attached to the crime or the IRS provides some justice."

"And E-Star?" I asked.

"I grew up in a small state up North. I've seen a few governors come and go, some to jail, but I've never seen a business go to jail, yet." the chief said.

"Was the whole Global investigation worth it?" Joan asked with resignation in her voice.

"Of all the things I've ever gone to war for, this one I'm certain was worth it," Brett said. "Conto goes to jail, Chris gets to open tonight, and we all came down off that mountain in better shape than Bocca. The tiger got away, sure. But he was one sorry wounded cat when he dragged his ass back to his den. We might not have won the war, but we did win some major skirmishes."

"Yes, you did," the chief said.

"How'd he do it?" Nancy asked.

"Do what?" Joan asked.

"Escape?"

"He probably dragged himself, shot up and drugged, to one of his cars and made it to one of the condos Chris told us about," Brett said. "He must have rested until night, taken more drugs for the pain and made it to some doc specializing in criminals. From there he put himself on a plane to anywhere. He probably picked the emptiest, least watched flight out of John Wayne or some smaller airport, maybe Vegas. He wouldn't pick LAX because international flights are watched more carefully. Then he probably made it out of the country from another airport."

"This is how you would've done it, Lieutenant?" the chief asked.

"Pretty much. I might even have had a corporate flight lined up and paid for in advance. Skip the whole commercial airline exposure," Brett said.

"Bocca set up his whole life to escape," I said. "He's an escape artist. Instead of spending any time living a normal life, he spent every moment he could preparing to escape every cage anyone could ever put him in. His escape is the product of his life, not something special. No normal person would ever spend that much time preparing."

"Does that mean that no one can ever catch him?" the chief asked.

"No, it'll be hard, but someday he'll underestimate somebody again. Sociopaths always do," I said.

"Like he underestimated you at the top of the tram?" Nancy asked.

"Exactly," I said.

"One more thing, Lieutenant?" the chief asked.

"Yes," Brett replied.

"Did you recognize Bocca from twenty years ago?"

"Hell, no," Brett said.

"Go figure. We still don't know if it ever happened," the chief said.

"Could find out. Probably will. Doesn't really matter," Brett said.

The chief just nodded.

The fact that Bocca was probably gone, and that Chris, Brett, Joan, and I had survived Long Valley had done wonders for Nancy and me. She was inspired by Joan and Brett, and placed her hand in my lap on top of mine. Make-up sex, another kind on Nancy's growing list, had been keeping us busy. The respite in our confusion about my police career was welcome, and we, hopefully, had time now to sort things out. A little breathing room always helped. For now, we were both alive and happy to have the time to work things through.

"You know the papers are calling you 'The Shooting Shrink.' Are you prepared to live up to your new reputation?" the chief asked.

"In time, maybe," I said, looking at Nancy.

"They covered the 'Shootout at the Top of the Tram,'" Joan said. "Front page spread on Monday: 'The Shooting Shrink Helps the Police Rescue Palm Spring's Newest Rock Star.'"

"It makes it look like a good idea the department hired you," the chief said.

"Yeah, the 'Shooting Shrink.' Totally cool, Doc," Chris exclaimed.

"Good press for your opening tonight." I tried to divert attention from me to Chris. Nancy and I weren't ready to deal with the 'Shooting Shrink' just yet.

Bob's opening the door saved us further discussion of my role with the cops. Over the next ten minutes, 300 people filled the room. The noise of their entrance made it impossible to continue our chatting. I swirled the remnants of my Julep, the part where the sugar settles to the bottom of the glass. Hopefully, Nancy and I would settle our disagreement about my gun, too.

Ten minutes later the room was filled to capacity, Chris had gone backstage, and Jay was getting ready to announce the show. Brett and Joan were holding hands now and as tired as she looked, I had never seen Joan seem more content. Brett noticed Suze, Chris's friend, in the crowd, jumped up and brought her over to our table. We did intros all around.

Brett looked over at me, happy with the hand he was holding, and said, "Bocca's a bastard. You shot him; you done good. You saved my life. Thanks."

"Me, too, Doc," Joan said.

Michael Thompkins

"You're welcome. Chris helped too," I said, remembering the rock in Chris's hand.

Never in a million years would I ever have imagined Brett thanking me for saving his life. I felt as if I had visited a strange new planet and was happy to return alive.

"I can't believe I emptied an entire clip at him and only winged him, though," I said.

"Doc, it's called a magazine, not a clip. How many times do I have to tell you?"

"You helped me too, you know," I said.

"How?"

"To use a muscle that I had never used before," I said.

"Now you know it's there," he said.

"My back feels better for knowing it."

My back had never felt better since 'Nam and I attributed it to using some new muscle and backbone.

Jay was about to leave us for the stage. He said, "When we're done tonight, everybody stick around for another Mint Julep, and I want us all to write our names on the ceiling. Joan, we'll lift you carefully so you can write yours. You too, Chief."

The crowd was quieting in anticipation of Jay getting up on the stage. He didn't disappoint them. The room was full of human energy being freely and honestly traded.

Jay lifted the microphone, "Ladies and gentlemen. This event was delayed from last Thursday night. I'm sure most of you know something about Chris being kidnapped. He's safely back with us now. Please put your hands together and welcome the Chris Park's Band to the Saloon stage."

The band came out, and picked up their instruments; they were ready.

Chris picked up the mike and said, "I wrote this song over the last two weeks. It's about a little adventure my friends and I had. I hope you like it."

"He lives in a house up high
He lives in a house up high
Watch out for the bad guy
Watch out for the bad guy.
He wants to be, He wants to be

He wants to be
The next John Lennon."

Then Chris surprised us with a new verse in a song that had room for many new verses.

"The bad guy took him alone
The bad guy took him alone
His friends brought him home
His friends brought him home.
He wants to be, He wants to be,
He wants to be
The next John Lennon."